INTO THE DEEP END

INTO THE DEEP END

A Novel By

LEESA FREEMAN

Published by Pimpernel Publishing
Bristol, Connecticut

ISBN: 978-0-9863986-0-5

Printed in the United States of America

For my Dad

My very own Uncle Wally,
My Gus McCrae,
and in the end, my Luke.

You asked me to write one for you,
and it turns out this was it, I just didn't know it then.

I miss you every day,
but love you more.

A Note About Spinal Cord Injuries

When I began this book, I knew next to nothing about Spinal Cord Injuries (SCIs), but I knew if I wanted to approach it with some semblance of intelligence, I was going to need to research the heck out of it. Especially after I realized that like most people unfamiliar with SCIs, I thought someone who was a "paraplegic" had no use of their legs at all. Or that a quadriplegic couldn't use their limbs.

Boy, was I wrong!

Depending on where the injury occurs, how it occurs, whether it is a complete or incomplete injury (is the spinal cord severed?), and a myriad of other matters affect how a person recovers use of their body.

I probably spent months reading every webpage and book I could get my hands on and watching every video I could find—from a "sex on wheels" talk given by Gary Karp, to the documentary *Murderball* about the athletes who play quad rugby (watch it, it's wild!), to hours upon hours of videos of men and women in rehab learning to reuse their bodies.

Anatomy of the Spine

Cervical Division	Nerves	Functions
C1		
C2		Breathing (C1-4) and head & neck movement (C2)
C3		Heart rate (C4-6)
C4		shoulder movement (C5)
C5		Wrist & elbow movement (C6-7)
C6		
C7		Hand & finger movement (C7-T1)
C8		

Thoracic Division
T1, T2, T3, T4, T5, T6, T7, T8, T9, T10, T11, T12

Sympathetic tone (T1-12) including temperature regulation and trunk stability (T2-12)

Ejaculation (T11-L2) and hip motion (L2)

Lumbar Division
L1, L2, L3, L4, L5

Knee extention (L3)

Foot motion (L4-S1) and knee flexion (L5)

Sacral Division
S1, S2, S3, S4, S5

Penile erection (S2-4) and bowel & bladder activity (S2-3)

If I was going to write this book, I felt it was important to honor all those who have had a SCI and to try my best to speak to their experience and share their journey. And while each individual has their own path to travel, I wanted Luke's to reflect that within his own story.

One of the things I discovered was that the majority of people (approx. 82%) who sustain a SCI are young men between the ages of 16-30.

Why?

Because young men are the ones who tend to engage in high-risk behavior.

Skateboarding, driving too fast, jumping off heights... you know, those crazy, wild, dare-devil things many guys do.

The thing that really stuck in my mind when I discovered that was how would a guy deal with that? Here he is, just at the start of his life—just beginning to figure how who he is, just beginning to explore his options, his future, his sexuality—and in a blink, all of that is gone.

Or perhaps *perceived* to be gone.

If you look at the diagram on the previous page, sexual function is rather low on the spine—south of T11 for ejaculation and erection is even lower, S2-4—which means most men with a SCI have a difficult time getting or keeping an erection.

I felt it was important to address that, not just the frustration and insecurity Luke feels, but the opposite side of that coin, that sexuality is an important part of every human's experience, and given communication and an open-minded, understanding partner, sexuality is still possible.

Finally, despite the technical and medical research I did, I wanted to make all that information accessible to readers—enough to educate, but not so much as to overwhelm. This isn't a textbook, nor is it meant to be; what it is, is the story of one man's journey of self-acceptance as he figures out who he is *now*, with enough medical information put in to make his story real.

While there are many great websites, if you would like more information about Spinal Cord Injuries and recovery, I highly recommend the following:

Project Walk at projectwalk.com

Christopher & Dana Reeve Foundation at christopherreeve.org

Gary Karp at lifeonwheels.org

and for peer support: apparelyzed.com and pushrim.com.

Hope you enjoy,

Leesa

Chapter 1

*B*efore didn't exist. Not for me. Not anymore.

Staring out the window and waiting for a car I didn't want to come, I exhaled smoke into the curtains and tried once again to make myself accept that idea: forget everything and everyone who came *before*, because no matter what anyone said—not Rosa, not LaVaugh—who I was before was gone.

Accepting that wasn't easy. Not when my room was still the same: trophies and medals lining my shelves, each with a tiny gold man in goggles and Speedo, toes curled around the starting block ready for the buzzer. My truck permanently parked in the garage, unable to take me anywhere because I couldn't drive anymore. Even Bethy's room was exactly the same as she left it; it even smelled like her all these months later. If I had the energy, I'd take everything—every trophy and medal, every photograph and bottle of Bethy's perfume—put it in my truck, and have Ty Campbell drive it off the nearest cliff. Not that there were any in Artesia.

I watched the car pull into the driveway, dropped the cigarette butt into the Budweiser can I'd been using for an ashtray, and moved away from the window, trying unsuccessfully to push away my anger. I didn't want to see her anymore than I wanted to go with her, but she'd given me little choice—calling up my parents and convincing them that this was a good idea.

For the first time in months, Dad had let his new, toothy smile slip as he explained in no uncertain terms that Adriana *was* coming, and I *was* going with her, whether I liked it or not. The entire time Mom sobbed into a damp ball of toilet paper, making me feel guilty and all of five years old.

"Luke," Dad called from the front door with the false enthusiasm he'd adopted. "Adriana's here."

It pissed me off, that enthusiasm, because what the hell was there to be so damned excited about? But what really made me angry was that he wouldn't *leave*. My whole life he'd been gone and now, *now* he refused to get back in the big rig he practically lived in and head off to Oklahoma City or Tucson or wherever the hell this week's haul took him. And with that stupid fake smile plastered on his mug, too.

Scrubbing a gloved hand across my forehead, I turned, ready to lay into her. I'd even rehearsed in my head a dozen times what I was going to say, settling on something along the lines of *I can't believe you did this.* But I couldn't look at her.

The last time I saw her, she was leaning on crutches and staring into the deep grave like it held her salvation. Then she looked lost and alone; now it was like looking into the very face of Hell and discovering a mirror of my own grief. I couldn't believe how much she had changed: how thin she'd gotten, how her once long, lustrous hair had lost all its chocolate shine and hung in chopped, wild locks. How the deep circles under her eyes accentuated how much weight she'd lost, making her appear skeletal.

"Luke's duffel is in his room," Dad said. "Lemme get it, and we'll get y'all loaded up."

"I can get it," I said, refusing to let him—anyone—take care of me, and scraped my knuckles as I went through the too-narrow doorway. Cursing under my breath, I situated the duffel and my backpack in my lap and returned to the living room, passing through the doorway without incident this time, avoiding Adriana's eyes.

"You got everything?" Mom asked. I just shrugged. I had no idea what she'd packed—I didn't care if I went naked; I didn't want to go at all. "All right then," she said, tears swimming in her eyes. "You'll call when you get there?"

I nodded. I owed her at least that much, and opened the door to go out to the car.

Hours later, the scent of pines invaded my nose. Once it would've excited me—leaving the desert behind always did—but not this time. Leaning my temple against the cool window, I feigned sleep, still caught between wondering how exactly I'd been talked into this, and why the hell anyone thought it'd be a good idea to put me in charge of a bunch of kids when I couldn't be trusted to shower and shave on a semi-regular basis.

I'd barely glanced at the bright brochures Mom and Dad produced, emblazoned with *Camp Caballero* on the front, "Where special kids find a special home." As if rubbing my nose in the fact that I, and the rest of those kids, weren't normal. We were *special*; a nice way of saying we were a bunch of cripples.

The car slowed, and Adriana made a right before turning down the music I'd insisted on blasting to make talking impossible.

"We're here."

I opened my eyes and took in the tall pines, split by a ribbon of black asphalt that led to a wide valley beneath a scrub-covered mountain. Dotted with A-frame cedar cabins, it could've been described as idyllic by anyone who gave a shit.

The car pulled into a parking spot beneath a long-timbered building, and

Adriana turned off the engine, letting in the scent of evergreens mixed with the gamy stench of horse manure. Better than the familiar perfume that insisted on filling my brain for the last three hours.

"Give me a second, and I'll introduce you to everyone," she said, resting her forehead on the steering wheel.

My twin sister, Bethany, found Adriana hiding out in the student center one day, escaping her first college roommate—a freak with the nickname Shadow and a penchant for tattoos and sex toys. Like all lost souls, Bethy tucked the girl under her wing to shelter and bring home. When I got her call that afternoon to help move Adriana's things across campus, I just figured this was like any other skinny kitten or baby bird she'd brought home at any point in our growing up. But when Adriana opened the door to her dorm room, well, I sent up a silent prayer of thanks that Bethany's Church of Lost Souls was alive and going strong.

Adriana was gorgeous, sexy, and unselfconscious in a white tank top that glowed against her Mediterranean skin.

Once upon a time I thought I was in love with her. Once I thought I'd move heaven and earth to be with her, but the moment she opened the door that afternoon to me and my roommate Rob Sanchez, she fell in love with my best friend.

"After you get it, do not help me," I said, unable to look at her. "Not in front of all these people."

"Luke, they don't care—"

"I care," I growled.

Without warning, her cool hand landed on my unshaven cheek, soft and comforting, and I pulled away like she'd electrocuted me. "Don't, Addy. Please don't."

"Just… give me a second," she repeated and got out of the car, taking the perfume that caught in my throat with her.

"Help me," I whispered to the empty car and closed my eyes, wishing for just a moment that I—

But nothing belonged after *I wish*. Or maybe everything belonged after those two words, and I couldn't settle on any of them.

I wish Bethy would come back.

I wish I could walk again.

I wish I could forget that night.

I wish… I wish they'd buried me, too. Next to her. Instead of her.

"Damn it," I muttered under my breath just as my door opened.

"Luke Stevenson, right?" a voice asked, and I turned to look up at its owner. Taller than Adriana, but not by much, gelled, spiky dark blonde hair, blue eyes behind black hipster glasses, he had one arm wrapped comfortably around Adriana's shoulders in the kind of easy embrace I longed for. "I'm Will Taylor;

we're gonna share cabin twenty-four."

I stared at his outstretched hand before shaking it just briefly enough that my dad wouldn't kick my ass for ignoring him completely.

"Gina's gonna be so excited y'all are finally here," he went on, looking at Adriana and seemingly ignoring my transfer out of the car.

My physical therapist at the rehab center, Rosa, made me practice this I don't even know how many times: from my chair to a bench, from my chair to a couch, from my chair in and out of her car on a sunny Spring day. I did it to humor her. It was easier to do what she wanted me to than to fight with her while she stubbornly dug in her heels and argued she wasn't just going to go away. If the only way to make her leave me the hell alone was to do what she wanted, then I'd get in and out of her car until my muscles ached.

"You and Adriana met at school?" Will asked the moment I heaved myself into my chair and started through the parking lot.

I grunted, figuring it was a rhetorical question.

"Now I gotta hate you." He laughed. "Spending every day with a girl as wonderful as she is. The rest of us mere mortals have to settle for a few weeks out of the year."

I tuned him out, following them into a large dining hall. It had the dusty smell of being closed up too long, combined with the moldy scent of the just-turned-on air-conditioner and people drenched in coconut sunscreen, deodorant, and sweat.

Nearly a hundred counselors, doctors, and volunteers, Dad told me days ago, reading the brochure in a misguided attempt to get me excited about this whole thing. " 'Inspired by their daughter Miranda, George and Tricia Wallace founded Camp Caballero in 1977'," he read, " 'because there wasn't a place in eastern New Mexico equipped to handle the medical or physical needs of a child with Spina Bifida. Each year specialists and volunteers come together to' "—and this was my favorite part—" 'inspire, encourage, and energize kids with unique challenges'."

In other words, a bunch of do-gooder able-bodied nut-jobs got together three weeks out of the year to put a few tally marks in the "good" side of their karmic scorecard as if it would save them from coming back in their next life as a toad. Or getting hit by a drunk driver on some country highway on a rainy, starless night. But I'm living proof it doesn't work that way.

Above the noise, a girl let out an ear-splitting squeal, and the crowd parted to release a cute blonde running at us full-tilt. "You found her," she screamed, slamming into Adriana so hard, if it wasn't for Will beside them, they might've landed in my lap. "We're gonna be cabin mates. Can you believe it? They put the four of us together!" At that, she turned, her eyes running the length of me, her full lips curved into a slow, sexy smile that once I would've thought meant something. "I'm Gina Howard," she said, offering a cool, slender hand, "and you're Luke."

I frowned before taking it. "How'd you know?"

Brilliant blue-green eyes smiled at me. "Uncle Wally put it in the welcome packet. There's always a bio of the newbies. You didn't get it?"

"I didn't read it," I said flatly, pulling my hand back to tuck under my arms. Whatever it said about me, I didn't want to know—anything that used to be true, no longer was, and what was true now was nobody's damn business.

"Y'all gather round," a man in his early sixties, dressed in Wranglers and a plaid button-down that strained to cover his large belly, shouted in a raspy bass, grabbing their attention like a dinner bell. He strode around the enormous circle of metal chairs in his worn Justin boots, shaking hands and passing out hugs like candy. This had to be the revered Uncle Wally, the co-founder of this place and the man Adriana once told me was like a grandfather to her.

Early on, when I still thought I might have a chance with her, I asked her about an old photograph in a silver frame on her desk. In it, she had an arm around a young boy in a wheelchair holding a long carrot for a spotted horse. His smile was cautious and hesitant, but hers, even with the mouthful of braces, stopped my heart in my chest. I don't remember what she said about this place or Uncle Wally that day, but I do remember how she looked talking about him—vibrant, animated, like I'd asked her about something so important words couldn't possibly express her thoughts. Then, I found it awe-inspiring. Now, I didn't want to have anything to do with it.

I parked myself between Adriana and Gina in the only open space in the giant circle of metal chairs and focused on the white linoleum squares beneath my feet, afraid if I met anyone's eyes they might take it upon themselves to start talking to me.

I ignored Uncle Wally's overly enthusiastic welcome speech and examined the other inhabitants of the circle, searching for similarities and coming up with nothing. They were basically split between men and women, young and old, all ethnicities, and—I assumed—all religions. No one thing seemed to unite them, *except* they all had their legs. As with the real world, I was the only one in a chair; as with the real world, I wondered whether that would make me invisible here, too.

Beside me, Adriana put a hand over mine, stilling my nervously drumming fingers and touching my emaciated thigh. "How much longer is he gonna talk?" I whispered, yanking my hand away and hating that she'd touched me there. I refused to even consider how it must feel to her.

"Not much. We'll play some games, eat some dinner, then later have a campfire."

"Games?"

"Sure. It's a fun way to get to know each other, and we'll play some of them with the kids."

Yeah, that sounded like *loads* of fun. "I need some air."

Outside, I started down the first asphalt path I found, not really caring where it led. It didn't matter as long as I got away from... that.

You didn't really give it a fair shake, Bethy whispered on the warm summer wind.

"I don't really want to," I murmured under my breath.

But it could be good for you.

"So could running a mile, but I don't see myself doing that any time soon either. Do you?"

"Luke," Adriana called, jogging to catch up with me. I looked up hoping she didn't just hear me talking to myself.

"You shouldn't have made me come," I spat.

She blinked. "I didn't kidnap you."

"No, you just went behind my back to my parents. And you know how they are now that..."

"Now that Bethany is gone," she finished.

"Don't you fucking say her name," I growled, glaring at her.

She took her lip between her teeth and closed her eyes. For just an instant, with the summer wind blowing her hair and standing in the brilliant sunshine, I almost let myself remember how much I cared about her. But rather than softening, it just made me angrier.

"Did you think that hanging out with a bunch of crippled kids would make me feel better about being crippled?"

"Don't use that word. It isn't—"

"*Nice?* God, Addy, none of this is nice. None of it. And if I wanna call myself a goddamn crip, by God I will. And don't stand there acting like you're all sympathetic and know what's going on, because you have no idea what it's been like!"

"Don't I? You think because you're sitting in that chair you're the only one who lost anything? You aren't."

"You look fine to me," I sneered.

"Fuck you, Luke," she shot back. "You're here whether you like it or not, because I'm not making that long-ass trip again until this whole thing is over. So either suck it up, figure out how to act around people again, and decide to have some fun, or don't. It's your choice, but either way your crippled ass is here for the next three weeks."

I stared at her. Based on the fire in her eyes and grim set of her mouth, I was stuck unless I wanted to go back inside and ask some other do-gooder to take me home. Defeated by the thought, I turned and went back to pushing myself down the path, ignoring her beside me.

"I was fifteen the first time I came here as a junior counselor," she said after a long time, her voice hanging on the wind. "I was the classic overachiever, on every committee at school, got straight A's, played tennis, ran track... God, thinking back on it, I must have been a real pain in the ass. I was certain I was gonna come in here and fix all these kids, perform miracles, and set the place ablaze with my brilliance."

Reluctantly drawn in, I glanced up at her. "What happened?"

She shrugged. "Uncle Wally took one look at me and assigned me to the barn, mucking out the stalls. I was pissed off and mortified. And really indignant. How could I fix these kids when I was knee deep in manure? I complained to everyone, certain Uncle Wally had no idea how foolish it was to waste *my* talents in the barn. Finally, Chuck, the horse master and a real, honest-to-God cowboy, took me aside one day and told me with my attitude I didn't have the right to work with the kids, and if it was up to him, he wouldn't let me anywhere near the horses either. It made me take a good long look at myself and why I was here, because they were right, I needed to change." She sighed and ran a hand through her hair. "Would you like to meet them?"

"The horses?"

"I'm not suggesting we saddle them up and go for a ride," she said, a slight smile on her face. "And if we go back now, we'll get roped into some game."

Neither option sounded particularly enjoyable.

"Horses," I said.

But as we neared the corral, I drank in the sight of ten powerful horses grazing beneath the mountain in the brilliant late-afternoon sun. Bethy would've loved this place. She was the animal person.

Beside me, Adriana whistled to a nearby tan horse, and it trotted to the fence, nuzzling an outstretched hand. "I'm sorry, I didn't bring you any treats. Next time, I promise," she said, rubbing the white spot between the horse's eyes. I marveled at her quiet confidence with the animal. It kind of terrified me. "Luke, this is Caramel."

"Uh, hi," I said, then laughed at my own nervousness. And for talking to the animal like she could understand me. She stuck her head through the fence rails, getting closer, and I carefully stroked the white spot between her eyes, imitating the gentleness of Adriana's hand a moment ago, surprised by the warmth and bristly softness of its coat.

"Horses are a lot like dogs," Adriana said, rubbing Caramel's neck. "They seem to intuitively know what people need."

I looked into Caramel's big brown eyes. "What do I need?" I whispered, then felt stupid for asking the horse, but when she snorted, I smiled. "Yeah, me neither... I'm not promising anything, Addy, but um... I'll try, okay?"

"Good," she nodded, meeting my eyes, "cause it's no fun mucking out those stalls."

"I think I'm safe. Crippled, remember?"

She smiled. "Uncle Wally doesn't care. He'll say you have two strong arms.

That, and a good pitchfork are all you need."

I cursed under my breath, sure she wasn't kidding and somehow pleased at the thought. "I'm sorry about Rob. I know I never told you that, but I am. Y'all were good together."

She turned back to the fence, propped one foot up on the railing, and ran her hand along the horse's neck like it might be the only thing that could keep her sane. "Thank you," she whispered. "Fucking drunk drivers, huh?"

"Yeah. Fuck them all."

Chapter 2

Morning came, and with it the butterflies of knowing a couple hundred kids were gonna show up with expectations I didn't know whether I could fulfill. Last night Uncle Wally gave Adriana a list of the eight kids in our family group. She seemed pleased; I just stared at the list, overwhelmed and sure that being afraid of a bunch of little kids was absolutely idiotic. Will had a similar list of the kids in our cabin, due to arrive soon, and I spent the morning fighting the urge to beg Adriana to take me home. It wasn't that I'd never been around children, it's just that coaching a team of swimmers at the Y twice a week was a hell of a lot different from being in charge of physically-challenged kids twenty-four/seven. What if something happened to one of them, had a seizure or something? Despite what Dad had read about the on-site doctors and nurses, just the idea that one of the kids might get hurt on my watch and I wouldn't be able to help them scared the shit out of me.

"You all right?" Adriana asked over her shoulder, pulling a red wheeled cooler of hamburgers across the blacktop to Uncle Wally's industrial-sized barbecue grill.

"Yeah, sure," I said, pausing to keep the box of buns in my lap from falling off.

With all the precision of a military operation, Uncle Wally and Tricia had the staff transforming the basketball pavilion behind the mess hall into a registration-landing zone. A good two dozen blue pop-up tents covered the court, each decorated with enough balloons that I half-expected the entire court to take off like Carl Fredricksen's house in *Up*.

"You've been quiet all morning." She put her cooler of patties under one of the six-foot folding tables Gina and Will set up as part of their assignment.

"Tired, I guess." It wasn't a total lie.

And anyway, looking around at all the people laughing, joking, and checking off tasks from Tricia's long list, how could I tell her last night I dreamed of swimming in blood and woke with screams ringing in my head? How could I tell her I sat under the stars chain-smoking and wishing like hell she'd come out of her side of the cabin, if for no other reason than I wouldn't feel so damn alone?

She paused, glancing around as if reading my thoughts, and tugged at her bottom lip before looking at me again at me, her eyes feverish and dry. "Luke, I…" she began, and then shook herself. "I'm gonna get the hot dogs, I'll be right back." She turned on her heel and strode away at a fast clip.

"Don't worry about it," Gina said, walking toward me. "It isn't you."

"No?" I asked, annoyed by how shaky my voice sounded in my ears.

"Anymore than what's going on with you has to do with her." I raised an eyebrow but said nothing, unwilling to go into it with a girl I didn't know. She just smiled, taking the hint, and sat on the table in front of me. "Where's your injury?"

"Excuse me?"

"I'm guessing south of the T6," she said with a slow smile, "but without doing a full physical exam, I can't make a complete diagnosis."

Was she flirting with me? I looked around, uncomfortable with the idea. Not because she wasn't beautiful; she was. Not because she wasn't sexy, dear God she was, but because I had no idea how to respond anymore. Take away what makes a guy a *guy*, and what the hell were you left with?

"My dad's a C8-T1," she went on. "Motorcycle accident when I was little, so I pretty much grew up with it. Anyway, I thought if you wanted someone to talk to about your spinal cord injury or… well, anything, I'm told I'm a very good listener."

"I'm an incomplete Thoracic 11," I said, no more surprised by hearing my own voice say the foreign words than if I'd just admitted to getting off looking up little girls' dresses.

She grinned. "Which probably means you have some use of your legs. Just how much remains to be seen."

I smiled, strangely relieved that she both understood and felt comfortable talking about it, laugh about it even. Unlike my parents and, well, everyone I'd talked to since getting out of rehab. Most people either refused to talk about it at all, or did so with such reluctance it was easier to stick to things like the weather. Even heated pro-life/pro-choice debates were preferable to the painfully uncomfortable discussions about why I was in a chair. Mom even acted like it was something I'd recently picked up—like some kids decide to try out the tuba—and she was just waiting for the phase to pass.

The one time she showed up at the rehab facility during my physical therapy and saw me awkwardly pedaling that damn recumbent bike, she about lost her mind in excitement. "I knew Jesus would heal you," she crowed.

I refused to see her during PT after that. It was too hard to deal with her overwhelming expectations and misguided optimism.

"Gina, would you want to hang out later? I'm not sure that I want to talk about this," I gestured at the chair, "but maybe we could just…"

"Get to know each other?" she supplied. "That would be great."

"Luke, would you get the ketchup?" Adriana called, lugging a big blue cooler.

"Yeah. Sorry," I shouted and turned back to Gina. "Talk later?"

"Absolutely," she promised, and hopped off the table.

"She seems cool," I said to Adriana.

"Gina's great," she said. "Kitchen?"

I nodded and went with her back in the direction she'd just come. "Addy, what are we supposed to do with these family groups?"

She stopped and smiled at me. "I swear they won't eat you if that's what you're worried about."

I laughed in spite of myself. "Who said I was worried?" She crossed her arms, raising an eyebrow, and I laughed again. "Fine, I'm a little…"

"Freaked out?"

"Concerned," I corrected. "What are we supposed to do with them? What if something happens? What if—"

She crouched in front of me. "We're just going to give them a place to make friends and talk about whatever they want to. And anyway, the campers who are coming today are cute, snuggly little kids who want more than anything just to be listened to and loved. You're good at that."

I looked into her brown eyes and wanted more than anything to believe her. "You're sure?"

"Yeah. And besides, it's the pre-teens you gotta look out for, but they won't be here 'til next week. By then you'll be an expert." She smiled and stood up. "Let's get the rest of this stuff set up. They'll be here soon, and I'm getting hungry."

~~~~~

I followed Adriana and the kids in our family group into Morgan Hall, wondering if it was possible to have low blood sugar issues—dizziness, light-headedness, sweating—even if I'd just eaten. I kinda doubted it.

Last night Adriana sat next to me on the deck our duplex cabin shared while I read the four pages about Spina Bifida she'd printed off Wikipedia. Handing them to me, she said she wanted me to at least have some idea of what I was getting into. Words popped off the page: limb weakness and paralysis; orthopedic abnormalities (i.e., club foot, hip dislocation, scoliosis); bladder and bowel control problems, including incontinence, urinary tract infections, and poor renal function; pressure sores and skin irritations.

In some ways it sounded an awful lot like Spinal Cord Injuries.

The words nearly broke my heart then, but now, looking at the children, I forgot the black and white jargon and took in the wide eyes and wider smiles on some, the anxious expressions of homesickness and uncertainty on others. And the thing was, even though they all shared the same birth defect, the range of how it showed itself was as different as the kids themselves.

Adriana smiled at our silent kids. "Welcome to Camp Caballero. I thought we'd go around and introduce ourselves. Share a little something about who you are and where you're from, okay?" Her enthusiasm was met with uncertain stares. "How about if I go first? My name is Adriana Toomey. I'm from Abilene, and one of my favorite things to do at camp is ride the horses." She turned to a tiny girl next to her and smiled.

"My name is Carrie," she said cautiously, her big blue eyes trained on the floor. "This is my first time at camp and, um… I want to go swimming in the pool."

"I'm Jared," said the next boy, looking at me, "and I think it's cool that you're in a chair like me."

"Thanks, Jared," I said, giving him a hesitant smile.

"Have you always been in a chair?"

I studied the boy, his short reddish-brown hair, his brown eyes enormous behind thick glasses, his wide grin, and took a breath. "Why don't we finish the introductions?"

Jared nodded, the grin on his face slipping slightly, but the moment the last child finished, he lit up again. "We're done," he reminded me. "Have you always been in a chair?"

I swallowed hard. "No. Have you?"

"Yep," he said almost cheerfully. "What happened to you?"

I looked at Adriana, unsure how to answer that, and hoped to God she could read the plea in my eyes. "Jared, that's a little personal, don't you think?" she asked gently.

The boy reddened. "I'm sorry, I just never met an adult in a chair before. I didn't mean to hurt your feelings."

I raked my fingers through my hair, feeling like a jerk. "You didn't, buddy. I'm just not used to talking about it."

Adriana took a breath. "It's normal to want to find out what you have in common with others when you first meet them, but how about we focus on other things for now? For instance, Carrie, you said you're looking forward to going swimming, right?" The girl nodded, smiling like she wasn't quite sure what she was getting pulled into. "Did you know that Luke is a fantastic swimmer?"

"He is?" She turned to me, her blonde pigtails swinging. I bit my lip, wondering where the hell Adriana was going with this.

"Oh, yeah, he's probably got a hundred trophies and medals. He was even training for the Olympic Trials."

"Addy…" I began.

"You're gonna kick ass," Jared exclaimed, his eyes wide and excited.

"Maybe once," I said, and cleared my throat. "And don't say ass."

Forcing air through my lungs, I focused on the distant mountain just beyond the large picture window like it held the key to my sanity. Shi'nali—my Navajo grandmother on my dad's side—used to take Bethany and me up in the mountains behind her house near Taos to teach us how we were connected to the trees, the animals, the land. Bethy, the more spiritual of the two of us, understood it better than I did, and God, she *loved* it up there. I used to tease her that she was Pocahontas in that Disney scene with the animals, singing in the forest until they all gathered around her. But me? I just wanted to wander amongst the pines: explore, get lost, find baby bears in the bushes, and get so filthy Shi'nali had no choice but to turn the hose on me before I was allowed back in her house. I'd give anything to be up there now, lost in my thoughts and rediscovering the perfect peace of remembering where I came from.

And that's what I hated most about this damn chair. For the rest of my life I was stuck with the knowledge of all the things I'd never do again. I'd never climb a mountain or run a mile. I'd never hold a girl in my arms and dance with her across the floor, half drunk on beer, the music, and her perfume.

I'd never have sex again.

That was probably the hardest to swallow, that even when I could get hard, which took a hell of a lot of concentration and even then it wasn't all that impressive, I couldn't *feel* it anymore. No matter how badly I wanted to.

For a while in rehab I tried like it was my job. But nothing. Nada. And according to this orderly, LaVaughn, late one night on the roof of the rehab center during a conversation I'd pay almost any about of money to have permanently deleted from my synapses, that sometimes that happened with SCIs. *Diminished sensation* he called it, exhaling smoke.

I called it the cherry on the goddamn sundae.

What killed me was I still thought about it, though. All the time. I *wanted* to get laid, but as with everything else, my body refused to cooperate. And rather than my brain getting the message and finding *other* things to think about, it was like I couldn't stop.

Christ, I needed a cigarette!

I checked my watch to see how much longer I'd have to stay here before I could escape and light up. I didn't want to do it around these kids, and my pride wouldn't let me do it around Adriana—God only knew what she'd say about it—but ever since burying Rob and Bethy, I was more or less determined to get myself addicted.

So far I was doing a pretty good job of it.

~~~~~

By the time our family group session was over, I was *done*. If I had to push myself back to Artesia, I'd do it—it was mostly downhill anyway—but I could not, *would not* stay here another day. I might've said I'd come to this place, but I sure hadn't agreed to have those kids look at me like I was some kind of... of hero.

"Luke?" Adriana called, pulling me from my thoughts, "you coming?"

I looked at the kids' faces and knew there was no way I could hang out with them a second longer. "You mind taking them down to the stable by yourself," I managed, "I need to go back to the cabin. I... forgot something."

She eyed me, seeing through the lie but smiled anyway. "Sure. See you at the barn?"

"Thanks," I muttered, ignoring grumbles from a few of the kids that I wasn't gonna go horseback riding with them, and pushed out the door toward my cabin.

Once I rounded a bend in the asphalt path, the dense trees and underbrush shielding me from view, I pulled a pack of Marlboros from the backpack slung over the back of my chair. Cupping my hands to protect the flame, I lit one. I can't even put into words why I started smoking in rehab—it wasn't something I ever *wanted* to do before. Hell, I knew it was a nasty, disgusting habit that would've screwed with everything from my breathing to my swim times, and no way was I gonna mess around with those when I was getting ready for the Trials. But now it didn't matter, and I started because it was kinda like *why not?*

LaVaughn used to sneak me out of my room and let me bum his cigarettes late at night while we stared at the stars in silence. In those liberating nocturnal escapes, I began to feel... not alive or hopeful—nothing could do that—but for those few minutes every night before I got into bed I felt *not dead*.

"It gets easier," a voice called behind me, and I turned to Uncle Wally clomping toward me in his cowboy boots, and carrying a couple large cardboard boxes.

I blew out a stream of smoke and inwardly sighed. Was it impossible to find ten minutes of solitude around here? "Does it?"

He nodded, shifting the boxes. "Everyone looks about like you do their first time, but they all come back."

I examined him. He didn't *look* like a head case, but to imply that my reasons for sitting here feeling like shit was somehow par for the course pissed me off. "Look, no offense or anything, but I really don't think I have a hell of a lot in common with your troop of self-righteous do-gooders up there," I said, waving my cigarette in the direction of the community buildings. "And whatever reasons *they* had for feeling sorry for themselves, have absolutely nothing to do with why I'm sitting here."

"I've gotta get these to my office," he said, his voice suddenly cold, "why don't you take a box and help me?"

I blinked at him, for a moment seeing the man Adriana must've seen when he assigned her to the stables that first time. This guy was a far cry from the man last night who was grinning broadly and hugging every person who neared him, laughing heartily. This Uncle Wally glared down at me, his faded blue eyes flashing with annoyance and something very close to anger. I put the Marlboro between my lips and reached for the box, full of Camp Caballero t-shirts it turned out.

"Don't drop ash in there," he warned. "I'm not going back to the printer cause some yahoo didn't have the good sense to put out his cigarette."

I swallowed a curse and ground out the cherry on the asphalt. Then, rather than flicking the thing into the nearby trees, shoved it back in the red and white pack. He probably would've made me go search for it if I didn't.

He nodded once and turned on his heel in the direction of his office, more or less forcing me to keep up with his pace. I used my chin to keep the box on my lap and did my best to stay with him; my ego wouldn't let this sixty-year-old man leave me behind.

"So, you're feeling sorry for yourself," he said, his tone completely changed from a moment ago.

I didn't like him using my words against me, or how they made me sound, but I wasn't gonna argue with him. "I don't know what Addy told you, but—"

"Adriana didn't tell me anything about you."

I glanced at him in disbelief.

"Donna Toomey, Adriana's mother, told me what happened. I called to send my condolences, and she's the one who told Tricia and me."

"Oh…"

"And it was my idea to see if you'd come this summer. I thought it'd be—"

"Yours?" I stopped so quickly I had to reach for the box before it slid off my lap. "I thought Addy wanted me to come."

He shook his head, looking off in the distance. "No, son. Adriana didn't want to come at all. From what Donna said it was a struggle to even get her to… But I shouldn't be sharing confidences. Adriana's like a daughter to Tricia and me, and it broke my heart to hear what happened to her. To you, too, son." He held my eyes for a beat before rubbing his forehead with a large hand and clearing his throat. "I know about the magic this mountain holds; I've seen it, and I thought it would be good for the two of you to have something positive to do. Plus, we have the facilities here to help you continue with your rehabilitation therapy. Without the damn insurance companies sticking their nose in it," he finished with a wicked grin.

"And all I have to do is sell my soul to the devil," I muttered, my head reeling.

"Sell your soul?" he repeated, starting up the ramp to his cabin, his boots clomping loudly on the wood.

"Addy told the kids I used to swim." Hearing the words out loud, though, I realized how stupid they sounded.

"And from what I understand, you were very good."

"The best," I said and laughed self-consciously at myself. "I mean…"

He smiled, the warmth emanating from his pale eyes seemed to wrap around me, and for just a moment I wondered if he'd hug me like he did everyone else yesterday. I looked away, feeling ridiculous and unsettled at the thought. "You worked hard to be good, you should be proud of that. Not many people have the desire or drive to do what you've done."

I ran a hand through my hair. "That was a different guy," I whispered, almost afraid to say the words.

"No Luke, that was you. And what I know for sure is that guy is still there, waiting for you to let him out."

Feeling way too close to unexpected tears, I put the box on his desk. "I promised Addy I'd visit them at the stables. If I don't go now, I'll probably miss them."

He nodded and walked me back to the door. "Thanks for the help."

"Yeah, sure… And sorry for what I said earlier," I told him.

"There's nothing to apologize for," he said, his eyes twinkling.

I smiled my thanks and started down the ramp, glad for the leather of my gloves as I kept gentle pressure on the rims.

Early on I refused to wear any, spouting some shit about they made me look "crippled," and got some pretty nasty blisters on my hands thanks to my stubbornness. Rosa showed up at rehab one day with these, gift wrapped in fancy paper and said they'd make me look just like Stash. It took me a moment to figure out she meant Slash, the guitarist from Guns 'N Roses, but slipping on the black leather half-finger gloves, I was so touched by her thoughtfulness, all I could do was issue a guttural thanks.

"Hey Luke," Uncle Wally called when I got to the bottom of the ramp, "hang on a minute."

He disappeared into the cabin and came back a moment later, jingling a set of silver keys.

"Give these to Adriana when you see her, will you?" he asked, handing me the aluminum keychain, inscribed with a wheelchair and flames that said *Hell on Wheels*.

"They're for Randi's van. I may need y'all to run into town occasionally," he said by way of explanation, then turned on his heel and strode back up the ramp. "See you at dinner," he shouted over his shoulder. I didn't know why, but I was sure he was laughing at some joke I didn't get.

A few minutes later when I handed Adriana the keys at the stables, she got a strange look on her face, and focused on our kids circling the corral, while Chuck the horse handler, and his junior counselors taught the kids the basics. "While the kids are at the pool, we should take the van out for awhile," she said.

~~~~~

Staring at the white Econovan twenty minutes later, the strange trepidation settling in my stomach made me slightly nauseous. "Well, the only thing it needs is some duct tape on the windows and we can start that kidnapping business we've always talked about," I said, ignoring the tremor in my voice.

"And maybe a bumper sticker that says *Jesus Saves*," she agreed, then went to the sliding door and unlocked it. "Come here, let me show you how this works."

Pushing a button just inside the door, a metal ramp lowered, and I saw the driver's seat was missing. The steering wheel had been jury-rigged with the kind of hand controls Daryl Johnson from Johnson Dodge offered to install on my truck after I got home from rehab. I had turned him down flat.

Conscious of her eyes on me, I toyed with the idea of just leaving. I couldn't even begin to say what about it terrified me—seizing control of my own freedom and destiny, learning a whole new way of driving that seemed a bit like giving up my old life, knowing how Rob and Bethy died—maybe some combination of the three, but sitting there with my entire body shaking and sweating, I really didn't want to do this.

"Luke?"

I closed my eyes and held up a hand, needing a minute.

"We don't have to do this right now if you don't want to. We could go swimming if you'd rather..."

"Swimming?"

"With the kids." She glanced at the far away pool full of bodies.

Those were my options? How about just offer to put me in front of a firing squad? *Bethy*, I pleaded silently, *please*...

Please what, though? Please get me through this? Please stop my heart from beating so damned fast? Please don't let me cry in front of her?

I pushed out a deep breath and made my way up the ramp, half wishing it was anyone other than Adriana watching me, and half certain she was the only person in the world I'd want here right now. If it couldn't be Bethy or Rob, then it had to be her.

"What do I do?" I asked after I installed myself where the driver's seat should've been.

"That lever on your left is the brake and gas. Push for the brake and pull down to accelerate." She blinked twice and looked at me. "I've never actually driven this before, but it seems straightforward enough."

"You've never done this?" I asked, incredulous.

"We'll figure it out together."

Stunned, I pulled my eyes away from hers and started the engine, hoping to God she didn't notice my trembling hands.

Keep us safe, I prayed, then put the transmission into drive and slowly pulled out of the parking spot. It was foreign, like using chopsticks for the first time when you've spent your whole life with a fork in your hand. Only in this case, I was hyperaware of the two-ton tomb that encased us.

And suddenly a green dumpster appeared in front of us. We rolled closer as I tried in vain to make my foot stomp on the brake, but it jerked helplessly, refusing to stop the van as the dumpster moved closer with increasing speed.

"Push the lever!" Adriana shouted, and placed her hand over mine, breaking the spell, and forcing the van to a stop. The van bumped the dumpster with a *bam!* that echoed in my heart.

"I'm sorry," I whispered throwing the van into park and shaking, I unhooked the harness to avoid looking at her.

But Adriana laughed. Not the strained, forced sound I heard last night during dinner or around the family group circle, but a *real* laugh. "Better than most," she said, through the bubbles of her laughter. "See that dent there?" She pointed to the crumpled green metal on the left side, somewhat obscured by black plastic garbage bags. "Freddy backed into it last summer. And Christine nearly took out that cluster of trees two years ago," she said, pointing to a sad copse of pines just beyond the passenger window. "You aren't part of the Caballero family until you've nearly wrecked Randi's van."

"You said you've never driven it."

Her eyes flashed. "I can barely drive *my* car, you really think I ought to attempt this mechanical contraption?"

"No," I said seriously, then grinned when she hit my arm lightly. "Put some music on, let's go for a drive."

While she searched for a decent radio station, I rolled down the windows and cautiously drove to the entrance gate. With the wind blowing through our hair and a George Strait song on the radio, I worked the post-cigarette piece of cinnamon gum, suddenly happy with the simple freedom of driving as we bisected the mountains and the million dollar red-tiled roofs nestled in the valley.

We'd driven through Ruidoso Downs before I glanced at my passenger. "Who's Randi?" I shouted over the roar of the wind.

"Miranda Wallace-Sutton. Uncle Wally and Tricia's youngest daughter. You'll meet her the last week of camp, I think. She has a son, so it'd be kinda hard to come for the whole time."

"She has a kid?"

"Jeffrey. He's eight, I think, and just the cutest towheaded boy I've ever seen. Take a right when we get to the Y up ahead."

The tourist traffic got increasingly heavier as we moved down Sudderth Drive, until we inched along, dodging pedestrians blatantly harboring death wishes. On either side of us, shops sold everything from rustic southwestern furniture to pottery and the prerequisite Kokopelli wall hangings. I concentrated on avoiding the ambling masses, but when I spotted a sign that said *Handmade Fudge,* made a hard left into the parking lot, pulling into the only spot left—the handicapped space.

I smiled at her quizzical expression and shrugged. "I want fudge."

Inside, I ordered a quarter-pound of dark chocolate fudge and quarter-pound of Dulce de Leche, aware that before I would've chatted up the cute girl behind the counter. Would've leaned against the glass and fixed my eyes on her, enjoying how she'd flirt back, or blush under my gaze. I even had this game with myself, trying to predict how she'd be in bed based on how—or even if—she responded. Would she be aggressive and up for anything, or would she just lie there, warm and supple?

It's not like I'm depraved or anything. I'd bet all the money in my bank account most guys have some version of the game; whether or not they'd admit to it is another matter entirely.

Before I might've walked out of here with her phone number in my back pocket, just to see if I was right. But now? Now I could barely see her over the glass display case. And anyway, even if I could convince her somehow to look past the chair, then what? It wasn't like I could rock her world anymore.

Handing her my money, I glanced over at Adriana, sitting at a little bistro table and smiling slightly at me. It was the same gentle, careful smile I'd seen on her all day—warm, but unsure, as if she was exercising atrophied muscles. Taking the white paper bag from the girl, I went to the table, aware my smile had that same unsure quality.

I ignored the thought and took out the dark chocolate fudge. "It looks good."

She nodded and took a tiny bite of the square I passed her. Watching her, I almost could've believed she was savoring the chocolaty flavor, letting it melt on her tongue, but something about that minuscule nibble bothered me. This was the same girl who once polished off half a large pizza all by herself and regularly fueled all night study sessions with giant bags of peanut M&Ms. But this was also the girl who'd lost so much weight, her collarbones jutted beneath her tank top.

"Can I ask you something?" I asked. "Why didn't you tell me yesterday that asking me to come wasn't your idea?"

She took another mouse-sized nibble, her eyes bouncing around the shop to keep from meeting mine. "It wasn't my idea to get out of bed at all, but Uncle Wally called about a month after I moved back into my old bedroom. Just like with everyone else, I refused to talk to him. I could only listen to so many *I'm sorrys* and *I'm here if you want to talk'* before I wanted to scream, you know?"

I nodded, knowing exactly what she meant.

"Uncle Wally was persistent, and after about the fifteenth message, I gave up and picked up the phone, ready to tell him something that began with *fuck off* and ended with hanging up on him. Instead, he asked if you might be interested in going to camp. 'Think about it, and I'll call back in a couple days,' he said quickly and hung up. Later I realized he didn't ask if I would be returning, he just assumed I would." She sighed and raised her eyes to mine. "Please don't take this the wrong way, but I didn't ever want to see you again," she said so softly I had to strain to hear her over the noise of the restaurant, and my heart sank in my chest. It was absurd since I felt the same way before I came, but hearing her actually say it hurt more than I was willing to admit. "It wasn't personal, anymore than the fact that I can't ever go back to the Permian Basin—there are too many memories."

"Yeah, nothing personal," I repeated, hating the hitch in my throat. "So why'd you ask?"

The pregnant silence stretched out, and she crossed her legs, letting her dangling foot bounce. "I can't remember what happened that night. My shrink said it's normal, but hell if I feel at all normal. I remember standing next to Rob's car, arguing with you over who would take shotgun and climbing in the backseat. I woke up in the hospital with pins in my leg." She ran a hand through wild hair and came away with a handful of brown strands. "I have problems sleeping, noise scares the shit out of me, and I can't eat. And not once have I cried. Not during the nightmare hours of that night, not at the funerals, and not in all the time since. I don't know how to even begin to think about the future and thinking about the past isn't an option, so I…I don't know."

Looking at her, I ached to make it all okay for her again, but I knew just how impossible that was. Maybe once I would've been foolish enough to believe there might be some way to fix what had gone so horribly wrong, but now… now I knew the light at the end of the tunnel didn't exist. The tunnel stayed pitch black, on and on, for all eternity.

"We should get back," I said, checking my watch and feeling powerless in the face of so much pain. "I promised Jill I'd stop by for PT before dinner."

"All right," she said, wrapping up the barely touched square of fudge in her napkin. "Thanks for this."

I nodded and pushed away from the table. "Thanks for teaching me how to drive."

Chapter 3

Here's the thing about physical therapy: it sucks.

With a spinal cord injury, all the messages that run from the brain down the spinal cord to tell the body what to do get short-circuited, so depending on where the injury occurs and how severe it is, that dictates how the body is affected. And it can affect everything—breathing, blood pressure, body temperature—it's all messed with.

As SCIs go, I guess I was pretty lucky. Sure, my internal thermostat was shot to hell, and if I got too cold, my muscles seized up painfully—I kept an old Artesia High sweatshirt in my backpack because even in the dead of summer, the cool early morning mountain air could wreak havoc with my body—but as an incomplete T11, I had full use of my arms, wrists, and hands, and to a certain degree, I could move my legs.

But you know how when a baby's first born he kinda flails around, learning how to use his body? His motor control isn't there and he's still learning how to move those strange, foreign appendages?

In some ways, it's the same after an injury. Or at least, it was for me. I'd look at these legs that *looked* like mine, but sure didn't *act* like mine. I'd tell them to move and they'd just lie there like dead weight, the message from my brain sidetracked somewhere in the middle of my back. PT was supposed to retrain my legs to work in conjunction with the messages my brain sent. Sounds simple enough, right?

Yeah, that's what I thought, too. But dear Jesus in heaven, it was honestly the hardest, most agonizing, painful work I'd ever done in my life. I'm no stranger to grueling workouts—you don't drag your ass out of bed before the sun without some measure of masochism—but this? This made previous swim team workouts seem easy, and my therapists made Coach Thomas seem like an out-and-out pansy! Rosa, for instance, was sweet enough about it and cheered me on with enough enthusiasm I sometimes thought if I let her down she'd be personally heartbroken about it, but there were times when I wasn't completely sure what the fuss was all about. Okay, so I could pedal a recumbent bike, but

I couldn't ride a real one. And while no one actually said so, I was fairly certain I'd never walk again. The one time I got up the nerve to ask anyone about it, Doctor Matthew just gave me an empty smile and said, "Your body's still healing, son."

I got the distinct impression he didn't want to break my heart or make me give up, and I couldn't decide if I appreciated that or hated him for it.

Jill, the therapist assigned to me at camp, leaned against a blue-padded table reading my chart, occasionally making little notes to herself or grunting at something she read. I just studied the large, timbered room, examining the torture devices installed around it: parallel bars at kid height, weight machines, a couple Chuck Norris Total Gyms... It wasn't as high-tech as the place I'd been released from, but it had the same scent of industrial cleaner and tears. I sighed, feeling at home.

"You've been keeping up with your stretches?" she asked, tucking a strand of silver-shot brown hair behind her ear.

I nodded, relieved that I wasn't the least bit attracted to her. Not that she wasn't pretty in her own way, but that had been one of my problems with Rosa. With her sexy body and perky magnetism, Rosa turned me on, but every time she leaned into me, her body against mine as she stretched out my muscles, it killed me that I didn't, *couldn't*, get it up. I'd get angry at her, simply because that was easier than getting angry at myself, and feel like a complete jackass in the face of her serene smile.

"Yeah," I lied. If I'd pulled out my ankle weights a half-dozen times since I'd been released from the rehab center, it'd be a damn miracle.

"You want to get better, you have to do the work," she said, leveling her gaze at me. "Do you?"

"Do I what?"

Her expression didn't change, but annoyance lurked behind her eyes. "Want to get better?"

"You're gonna make sure I can walk again?" I challenged, although part of me wasn't sure why other than I just felt like it.

"Look, you don't want to be here, I'll go lie by the pool and work on my tan, but either hop up on the table and let's get started, or get out. Your choice."

I stared at her for a moment, somehow sure the first of us to blink would lose. "Fine," I muttered, already exhausted. "Whatever."

She smiled in her victory, but for the next hour she worked me until my t-shirt clung to my torso and sweat stung my eyes. I wondered if she was this rough with the eight-year-olds who came in here, or if this was punishment for my obstinance earlier. Or maybe this was the kind of workouts she had planned for the duration of camp. I kind of hoped it was the latter. By focusing on my body, I wasn't focused on the kids this morning, or the way Adriana looked in the fudge shop, or even the way I felt when Uncle Wally fixed those warm, accepting eyes on me in his cabin today. As if he knew and understood exactly how lost I was.

Finally Jill smiled at me, looking just as crisp and cool as when I came in here and told me to go back to the cabin. "We've got twenty minutes before dinner, and you, my friend, are in desperate need of a shower."

~~~~~

By the time I'd showered, struggled into clean clothes, and made it to the dining hall, dinner was already well underway. I got a tray of meatloaf, mashed potatoes, corn, and two warm dinner rolls, and found an empty space in a far corner, vaguely aware of the irony that it was the first home-cooked meal I'd had in months. Mom, who was an exceptional cook, hadn't found the energy to turn on the stove since the night Bethy died, so we'd eaten a lot of Chinese take-out and cold cereal.

If it was up to me I would've stayed in the cabin, smoking and enjoying the silence before crawling in my bed, but I was also starving, and filling up on fudge until I got sick didn't have much appeal. Instead I hunched over my tray like a junkyard dog and tried to tune out the cacophony around me, the chaos of nearly three hundred campers and all those counselors laughing and talking, their metal utensils scraping and clattering across plastic plates. So different from the silent dinners with my parents, it felt like someone had opened up my brain and poured the sound in.

"I swear it gets easier," Gina said, placing her tray of half-eaten food next to me and sitting down.

I chewed a bite of meatloaf. "You're the second person today to tell me that."

"Then I'm the second person today to notice you look like ten miles of bad road."

I ignored her, concentrating on my dinner.

"Give it some time," she said, placing a hand on my arm, "I promise it will get better."

And just like that, I'd had it. I wanted to go home. I couldn't take this place, these *people*, any more. They were too friendly, too touchy, too overly empathetic, as if they had any idea what I was going through. Only Adriana did, and she as much as admitted she didn't want me here. "Gina, would you take me home?" I asked, pushing away my tray.

She regarded me for a long moment and took a sip of her iced tea. "I'm going to say to you the same thing I'd say to one of my homesick campers: it's perfectly normal for you to not want to be some place new and different, but I think if you give it a fair shake, you might find you really like it here. Have you given it a fair shake?"

"Damn it, I'm not eight," I responded, not liking how she looked at me—like I was.

I expected her to growl back, but instead she smiled like she was in on some secret that I wasn't privy to. "I promised Tricia I'd help out at the campfire tonight, but I'd be happy to drive you back after that."

"Fine." I pushed away from the table before remembering my manners. "And thanks."

That secret smile only got bigger as she stood up and picked up her tray. "No problem."

Within half an hour of Uncle Wally lighting that campfire, I knew with a sinking feeling that I wasn't going anywhere—definitely not that night and probably not until camp was over. And the more I thought about it, the more I realized what bothered me about Gina's knowing smile earlier—it was the same one Bethany used to wear when I was about to be duped and the only one who didn't realize it yet was me.

I stared into orange flames, listening to someone play "Edelweiss" on a guitar, trying to figure out just how seriously Gina had tricked me, when a soft voice said my name. From my family group, the girl held a long metal fork in one hand, a marshmallow in the other and a shy smile on her tiny face.

I glanced at the name tag around her neck. On the leather circle she'd carefully written *Carrie* and strung it with pink and purple plastic beads.

I wrote LUKE in giant, angry block letters on mine yesterday and tossed it across the table. Done. Last night I found it on my pillow, strung with blue beads—my favorite color—and wondered who'd finished it for me.

"I don't want to burn it," Carrie whispered, and just like that my heart melted.

"I happen to be an excellent marshmallow toaster. Even got a merit badge for it."

Enormous eyes blinked at me. "No you didn't." It was a question.

Suppressing a smile, I let out a deep sigh. "You don't believe me? Guess I'm just gonna have to prove it to you."

I moved closer to the fire, and after a moment's hesitation, she rolled up next to me and handed me the telescoping fork and marshmallow. "The trick," I said, "is to get it close enough to toast it, but not so close it catches fire."

"Yeah, I don't like that."

"Some people don't like that charcoal taste." Bethany didn't; I did and used to stick mine directly into the flames.

"I feel bad for it," she said softly, "it looks so scary on fire like that, like it hurts."

I stared at her, surprised, and on the wind I heard Bethy agree. "But you *eat* it; that doesn't hurt?" I asked, unsure who I was talking to.

Carrie shrugged. "You're supposed to eat it."

There was no arguing with that logic, so I turned my attention to the toasting, feeling her eyes on me.

"Do you have spina bifida like me? I know I'm not supposed to ask, and I know you got mad at Jared this morning, but—"

"I didn't get mad at Jared," I interrupted, chagrined, and made myself tell her the truth. "I don't have spina bifida. I was in an accident. I'm a paraplegic."

Her lips curled into a beatific smile, revealing three missing teeth—one she lost very recently. "Me, too. I'm a paraplegic, too."

For the first time I looked at her, really *looked* at her, and as insane as it was, I felt the earth start spinning beneath me. I heard kids singing "Jeremiah Was A Bullfrog" to the strumming of a guitar; I felt the warmth of the fire, the flames licking my face and neck; saw the sticky, chocolate-smeared faces of happy children. Children like Carrie.

Children like me.

"Luke!" she shouted, yanking me from my thoughts. "It's on fire!" The marshmallow was a goner, and I let it slide off the fork and into the flames. She frowned at me. "There's no merit badge, is there?"

"But there are more marshmallows," I said grinning at her, and caught Gina's eye. She glided toward us, a bag in her hand and that danged knowing smile on her lips.

"He burned the first one," Carrie said immediately, ratting me out.

"It's like pancakes, the first one never comes out right," Gina said, reaching into her bag. As she handed me a new one, she leaned into my ear. "You still want to go?"

"No, I—" I cleared my throat and made myself look at her. "I'll stay."

"Good, because I had no intention of taking home the hottest guy at camp."

I focused my attention back on the task at hand, determined to not ruin this one, when beside me Carrie pushed out a breath, miffed at me. "Gina told me you'd be good at this."

I laughed, understanding her admission more than she knew: we'd both been played.

Chapter 4

I couldn't figure out Gina and Will. Not that it was any of my business, but sitting with them on the dark deck of our A-frame cabin, the kids sleeping in their beds, what I saw intrigued me. Will sat on the long bench that ran the perimeter of the deck with Gina comfortably in his lap, her arms wrapped cozily around his neck while the fingers of one graceful hand twirled a lock of his hair. And sometimes, when she looked at him, her voice took on this soft purr that reminded me of sex and excitement and deep intimacy.

But.

But in a breath she'd fix those brilliant blue eyes on me, letting them roam the length of me with the kind of fire that reminded me of dark clubs and drunken parties, just before some nameless girl and I found a private corner. And lord knew I'd been willingly used more than once to make some chick's guy jealous—for kicks, for revenge, just for the strange of it—and more than once I kinda preferred it that way. I got mine and walked away, no strings attached. What they did afterwards was none of my business, but if they'd had a great thing going to begin with, she wouldn't've been in my bed.

Gina looking at me that way, though, was making me seriously uncomfortable. On Will's lap.

And was she some kind of chair chaser? LaVaughn once talked about them on the rehab roof. How he'd see these hot girls with flawless bodies and legs going all the way down to the floor come in to see her guy in a wheelchair. How she'd ride around in her guy's lap like he was a human rickshaw, giggling and wiggling on his cock in a way that didn't fool anyone. He said he wasn't sure if it made them feel a little naughty, or if it made them feel safe, or if it was because it made the girls feel better about themselves—they had to be a good person if they'd go out with a guy in a wheelchair, right?

At the time I blew out a long stream of smoke, staring up at the overcast sky, the clouds holding the city lights and making me wish I could see the stars. "Harmless Wheelchair Guy," I muttered, and LaVaughn nodded, the wooden beads of his cornrows punctuating the silence.

"…And you'll never guess what I heard about Dean," Will said to Adriana in a low whisper, then looked at me, "over in cabin 22A." As if then I'd know who the guy was. "He was a TA down at UT and got caught boffing one of his students. On the prof's desk!"

I tuned them out by fighting the urge to light up; it didn't help that the wind carried the pungent smell of someone else's cigarette. It was either light up, or go back inside and crawl in bed, but the prospect of staring up at the ceiling most of the night wanting desperately to not go to sleep had little appeal. Right now, though, neither did sitting here listening to gossip about people I didn't know and couldn't care less about.

Adriana curled into herself like the graceful spiral of a conch shell; wrapping her arms around her legs and resting her head on her knees, she pulled on her bottom lip. Looking at her, *déjà vu* pressed against me.

The scent of pines and laughter of other counselors on other decks all fell away, and I was in Bethy's dorm room, smelling pizza and one of their illicit vanilla candles—burning illegally for the purpose of combating the permeating pizza smell. On Adriana's bed, Rob played DJ, sorting through Bethy's bubble-gum country CDs and trying (again) to extol the virtues of an iPod. And Bethy was (again) extolling the virtues of her Luddite lifestyle. Wrapped around herself, Adriana caught my eye and smiled, her expression clearly pointing out the discrepancy between calling herself a Luddite and owning well over two hundred CDs.

It could've been one of hundreds of identical nights, sitting on my sister's bed while my best friend slid in a Jason Aldean CD, but it happened so often, it seemed almost impossible it would never happen again. The four of us, together.

In that moment I stopped caring what they'd think. If I didn't inhale copious amounts of smoke, their dirty looks weren't going to be my biggest problem. What was, was the fact that I couldn't catch my breath. What was, was the pounding of my heart in my chest, so hard and uneven it hurt. Fighting panic, I pulled out the pack and lit a cigarette with shaking hands.

"Are you okay?" Will asked, lifting Gina off him to cross the space between us.

"I'm fine," I whispered, exhaling.

He placed a cool hand on my forehead. "You're sweating, but I don't think you have a fever."

I waved him away, annoyed. "It's not dysreflexia; I'm fine. Swear to God, I'm not gonna stroke out on you. I just need a minute."

Gina caught his eye, and he went back to the bench, wrapping his arm around Adriana in that comfortable way he did yesterday, only this time she looked like she really needed it. Her eyes, round and bright, watched me with something that seemed less like disappointment, which I expected, and more like fear, which killed me. He leaned over and whispered something in her ear and when she nodded, they got up and walked away, Will asking us to excuse them.

Once they were gone, Gina reached over and took the cigarette from my hand. "Don't tell Will," she said with a wicked grin before inhaling. "He hates it when I smoke and refuses to kiss me when I do, but I'm not worried."

Unsure what that meant, I pulled out another cigarette and lit it.

"He grew up with my dad who *does* have dysreflexia, so he's seen my dad's nervous system go haywire," she said, turning in the direction Will and Adriana disappeared.

I grunted, letting her words float on the breeze.

We sat quietly, and smoking with Gina, staring up at the stars, I almost got that not dead sense I got up on LaVaughn's rooftop. She didn't say anything, didn't push for what suddenly turned me inside out, but silently smoked her cigarette, and when she was done, put it out under her shoe, picked up the butt, and placed a warm, gentle hand on my arm. "Thank you, Luke."

The way she wrapped her lips and tongue around my name stirred something inside me, just as the fire in her eyes did earlier, but where once I knew exactly how to respond, looking at her now left me lost and tongue-tied.

"I'm going to bed," she said, "are you staying?"

I glanced at the ramp Will and Addy disappeared down, reluctant to go, but uncertain about staying. "I don't know."

"It's hard for her, too," she said softly. "She doesn't understand what's going on with you, any more than she understands what's going on with her. And on top of it, she feels like she can't break. She thinks she has a role to play, and it's exhausting for her."

"She told you that?"

Gina shrugged. "More or less. Goodnight."

I watched her go inside, her feet gliding across the wooden planks, her hips swaying gracefully, and wondered again what the deal was with her and Will.

Not that it was any of my business.

~~~~~

In the days that followed, I hung out with Gina more. It was easier being around her, partly because I liked how she flirted shamelessly with me—not that I took it seriously, but the attention was nice—and partly because it was so damn hard to look at Adriana and not miss desperately the two people who weren't here.

As far as the Will thing went, turns out it was far more complicated than I figured. "It's not that I mind," she said during one of our late-night escapes, "I mean… I hate the way he told me, but that's not only water under the bridge, that bridge has been washed away."

"How'd he tell you?" I asked, trying to dribble a ball in the basketball pavilion and failing miserably.

She sighed, sitting a few feet away on the floor, her eyes a little misty with remembering. "You have to understand, I loved him. Maybe from the time I was eight years old, okay?"

I nodded, encouraging her to go on.

"When we were seventeen, I thought if I slept with him, he'd finally see me the way I always saw him. The moment it was over, he sighed and said, 'Well, that's it. I really am gay.' Can you imagine? There I am, sweaty and ecstatic and thinking surely he must love me now, and he tells me I don't have the right parts." She shrugged. "I've been in love with him for as long as I can remember. I always will be, but it changed after that. I know who he is, and maybe we'll never have the house and the picket fence and all that, but he's my best friend."

I closed my eyes, remembering a night long ago when I held Adriana in my arms, snug and warm in my bed. It was a mistake that night, my mistake, and one that I refused to consider or discuss with anyone, but seeing Gina's pain-filled eyes, I knew how she felt.

"But I don't want to talk about Will," she said, the mist cleared away as the pendulum swung back. "I want to know when you're gonna get back in the saddle again."

I concentrated on the sound of the ball hitting the concrete. "The saddle?"

She cocked an eyebrow. "How long has it been?"

"I don't want to talk about it," I finally told her. She may have understood a lot of things when it came to my injury in general and spinal cord injuries in specific, but no way did I want to discuss my impotence with her. Even thinking about it made me feel weak and broken. "Pick something else to ride me for," I said, and she shot me a wicked smile at the unintended innuendo, making me laugh. "That's off the table, too. I'm in no mood."

"Too bad." She grinned. "I am."

I rolled my eyes. "Are you always like this?"

"Like what? Sexy? Beautiful? Brilliant?"

"After something you can't have," I said. The ball hit a chair wheel and rolled directly to her. "Anyway, I'm off the table. For anyone."

Her lips pressed together, her hand absently spun that ball in the space between the wide V of her legs. "Luke, have you tried masturbating yet?"

"Jesus Christ!" I exclaimed, shocked.

"You need to. It'll help you understand—"

"That I'm a eunuch? I don't need to play with myself to—" I stopped suddenly and listened to my voice echo off the metal ceiling. "I'm sorry Gina, but I can't talk to you about this. And having a dad who's a quad doesn't mean you have any idea what you're talking about here."

"And not being in a wheelchair doesn't automatically mean I don't know what I'm talking about, either."

"Fair enough, but there's certain things I'm just not willing to go into with you, and my broken dick is one of them."

She picked up the ball and tossed it back to me. "I'm just suggesting you try it," she said, a tease in her voice. "If you want, we could start right now. I'll help."

I swallowed, taking in that wicked, sexy smile that did absolutely nothing to me. Good God I wanted it to, I wanted like hell to get so fucking hard it hurt, but I couldn't, and that right there was why I refused to masturbate anymore. What was the point if I knew it would simply end in disappointment and more frustration at my body and situation? I glanced at my watch. "It's late, we really ought to get to bed."

"Alone?" she asked, sounding disappointed.

"Gina…"

She stood up and walked to me. "Don't take me seriously. I only mean about half of what I say, and besides it's fun to play with you because you're—"

"Harmless Wheelchair Guy?" I supplied, trying not to sound bitter.

She smiled broadly. "You're far from harmless, and once you figure all that out," she said, eyeing my crotch, "you're gonna be a lot of fun. Too bad I won't be the one enjoying it."

"Go," I said firmly and put up the ball on my way out, letting her turn off the lights.

As we went back toward our conjoined cabin in silence, I couldn't think of anything to say to her. My brain was stuck on what she'd said and discussing that was out of the question.

"I grew up with twins," she said. "Mia and Maya, if you can believe that. It was the only thing they had in common, though."

I grunted, not wanting to talk about Bethy, either. God, was there anything I'd happily discuss anymore? Jack Kerouac, maybe. Beatles lyrics. The eating habits of *El Chupacabra*. Outside of that, no, not really.

"Mia and Maya's dad is a T9 from a skateboarding accident when he was fifteen."

I looked up at her, trying to make out her features in the dark.

"My point is, lots of men are capable of having fulfilling sex lives after spinal cord injuries. You've just got to be open to changing your definition of sex."

I didn't say so, but that might've been one of the stupidest things anyone had ever said to me. There was one definition of sex—I got that birds and bees talk back from Dad when I was sixteen, along with a box of condoms about six months too late—and the one thing I knew for sure was in order for it to work, you had to have a functional cock.

Up ahead, Adriana sat on our cabin's deck, staring up at the stars with the expression of barely hanging on. "Can't sleep?" Gina asked her, climbing the ramp.

"Nightmare." Adriana shrugged. "Where've y'all been?"

Gina sat next to her friend, wrapping an arm around her. "Luke's been showing me his skills on the basketball court. Good thing he's cute, huh?"

Addy rested her head on Gina's shoulder. "It kills me that I can't even remember how they died," she whispered. "Did they know? Did it hurt?" Her eyes fixed on mine. "Did he... did Rob say anything?"

Unable to take the pain that swam in them, I reached for my cigarettes and lit one. I couldn't tell her what happened that night, not because I didn't know, but because I couldn't possibly listen to my own voice say the words out loud. And honestly, she was lucky she couldn't remember. I couldn't forget. I prayed for the peace of amnesia and couldn't take that gift from her, no matter how she looked when she asked me to.

"Y'all do realize if the kids are the only ones who get some sleep tonight, we're gonna pay for it tomorrow, right?" Will said through a yawn, letting the screen door close silently behind him.

For a strange moment, I kind of envied him standing there comfortably in his boxers—I had on sweatpants, a long sleeve shirt, and the orange and white bulldogs sweatshirt of my old alma mater, and in the dead of July, too. Winter was gonna find me shivering in a parka.

He let out a long-suffering sigh and went to the girls. "Scoot," he commanded and planted himself between them, wrapping an arm around each pair of shoulders.

Ignoring their huddle, I brought the cigarette to my lips and inhaled, perversely thankful for the burning smoke filling my lungs. At least it was a kind of pain I could control.

"We should get to bed, sweetie," he said to Adriana. "The kids are gonna be up early."

After what seemed an eternity, she nodded and let him pull her up and into his arms.

"Sweet dreams," he whispered low in her ear, and she nodded again, her face buried in his neck.

"Night, Luke," she said, placing a gentle hand on my shoulder. "I'll see you in the morning."

I blew out a long stream of smoke and hesitantly covered her hand with mine, then watched her walk away with Gina. Just before she stepped inside her half of the cabin, she turned to me lifting one hand in a wave, her chin quivering with the tears her dry eyes wouldn't allow her to cry.

"You too, guy," Will said, giving me a warm smile, then going to our door to hold it for me. "There will be no sleeping through breakfast just cause you don't have the sense God gave you to not stay up all night."

~~~~~

By the time I settled into the family group circle the next morning, I desperately needed a Big Gulp of strong, black coffee but worked on my third Dr. Pepper since breakfast. Across the circle, Adriana looked about as miserable as I felt, but each time I tried to catch her eye, she'd focus on one of the kids.

I glanced at my watch. We still had twenty-three minutes before the kids were supposed to go down to the stables for horseback riding, but the idea of sitting there much longer depressed the hell out of me.

"What do y'all say we get out of here?" I suggested, then herded them outside where the brilliant sunshine and cool breeze immediately re-energized me.

"What're we doing?" Jared asked. Whatever it was, he was up for an adventure.

Adriana glanced at me, and when I shrugged, unsure what to do next, she grinned. "We're taking the long way to the stables, through Old Camp. But you have to promise me you won't mention it to Tricia. She won't like it."

"Why not?" Quentin whispered like she was lurking behind the nearest tree, spying on us.

"Some of the cabins are haunted," she said in a stage whisper, playing with them.

"We aren't scared," Jared said, his eyes wide in excitement tinged with fear. "Are we?"

"No," Noel claimed, and several kids shook their heads.

"All right then, follow me," Adriana said and started down a path that led past Morgan Hall and into dark pine trees.

"There aren't really ghosts, are there?" Carrie asked softly, falling in beside me.

"No, sweetheart."

She nodded. "But you won't let them get me if there are, right?"

Panic was written so clearly on her features, my heart seized with love for the girl. "We could go the other way if you want to."

She watched her friends retreat, weighing her options. "I want to go with them," she said with forced conviction. "Just don't leave me."

I smiled. "Never."

~~~~~

Old Camp was just that, old. And a little sad, as if it had lost its purpose without the kids around to give it life, but with layers of dead needles and overgrown bushes absorbing the laughter of the kids, it was peaceful under the tall pines. It also kind of reminded me of the camp Bethany and I went to as kids—tiny, one-room sleeping quarters; a screened-in art building, the rotting wood covered in peeling, once-bright painted handprints of kids who'd long ago grown up; a crumbling volleyball court, the torn net waiting for someone to come out and play. Adriana was right; it was haunted. Not by ghosts, but old memories of hot summer days and small children. Of watermelon afternoons and lightning bug nights.

"Luke," Carrie whispered, "look."

I followed her finger to the art building and spotted a fawn, watching us, frozen in fear. "Isn't she beautiful?"

"Yeah," I murmured.

"I want to draw her, is that okay?"

For some reason, she looked so much like Bethy right then, I had to remind myself to breathe. "Absolutely."

While she reached into her bag for her notebook and pencils, I closed my eyes and pictured my sister. Her long mahogany hair in a knot on her head, a half-dozen colored pencils sticking out at crazed angles, her luminescent fern-green eyes focused on the paper, chewing her bottom lip in concentration as her hand made bold, confident strokes. Sometimes I looked in the mirror and saw her in my features—we had the same green eyes from Mom, the same high Navajo cheekbones from Shi'nali, the same almost-too full lips of Dad's—and think it cruel to see her staring back at me.

"Luke?"

"Yeah?" I opened my eyes, surprised by how hoarse my voice sounded.

"I think we missed horseback riding."

I smiled. "Neither of us really wanted to go, anyway."

Carrie was afraid of heights, and even though I wasn't, I didn't trust the handicapped saddles. No matter how reassuring Chuck tried to be that they were perfectly safe, I had a mental image of falling and injuring my spine again. And this time maybe I'd get real lucky and lose the use of my arms, too.

Maybe I was afraid of heights, after all.

"What were you thinking about?" she asked. "Just now? You looked sad."

"My sister," I said softly. "You remind me a little of her. She was an artist, too."

Carrie studied me. "She died."

It wasn't a question but I nodded anyway. "Yeah."

"My cat died," she said after a moment, then flipped through her notebook until she came to a drawing of an orange tabby and handed it to me. "Her name was Ginger Rogers. Like the dancer?"

I smiled and gave the picture its due attention.

"My daddy said heaven has a special place for cats and dogs, but Lance McConnell who lives across the street, he's an ag... agnos..."

"Agnostic."

"Yeah, that. And he said dogs and cats don't go to heaven. But I don't believe that. Do you?"

I focused on her. "Do I believe cats go to heaven?"

"Yeah," she said, her eyes wide and ready to believe whatever I told her.

And the truth was, I had no idea, but wherever heaven was, Bethy wouldn't be happy there unless she was surrounded by animals of all kinds. "Yeah, I do."

She nodded once and grinned. "I'm gonna tell Lance McConnell you said that. You're way smarter than he is, anyway."

I laughed and handed her the tablet. "We should get down to the stables, they're gonna start wondering if a ghost got us."

Following the path, Carrie chatted about the deer, the cabins, the emptiness of Old Camp. I did my best to nod, grunt, and hold up my end of the conversation, but all I could think of was Bethany, somewhere in heaven, surrounded by animals. My own Pocahontas somewhere up there, singing off-key to the gathered wildlife.

Chapter 5

"You wanna get out of here for awhile?" Tricia asked when I took my tray to the garbage window after lunch. "The delivery company screwed up our order and isn't going to be here until Saturday."

With the images of Old Camp still floating in my mind, I tried not to look completely relieved at the idea of putting some space between me and this place, however briefly. "Sure."

She nodded, a grateful smile on her face. "Then follow me."

In the kitchen she had a detailed two-page list, written in her elegant hand.

"I thought you said it was just a few things."

"I suppose 'few' is relative," she said, touching her copper hair. "Take Adriana with you, you'll need some help."

But Adriana sat in the passenger seat, staring out the window, if not rigidly then warily, the miles to Roswell passing beneath the tires as uncomfortable silence filled the van. My hands nearly itched wanting to light up, my lungs ached for that deep burning sensation, and I desperately needed the slight numbing of nicotine. I couldn't handle her silence, but I had no idea what to do to fix it. And I wasn't about to fill someone else's van with the blue smoke of tobacco, poisoning Adriana in the process. Me, I'd happily contaminate, but no way could I hurt her like that. Rob would kill me.

I focused on a road I'd traveled enough times I could probably do it blind-folded—years of swim meets, football games, and a girl from Capitan I dated my junior year of high school had me driving out here more times than I could count.

Being surrounded by nothing but ecru sand and flat, lonely highway beneath a gray sky reminded me why I wanted to leave so damn bad. The omnipresent sand got into everything, and one of my earliest memories was of crunching down on the grains caught in my teeth. The ugly landscape beneath an oppressive sun that was the Hell the preacher yelled about when I was a kid. I swore I would leave it all behind, and somehow I found myself here again—stuck, afraid, and this time, completely alone.

Off to the south lightning flashed, and I glanced toward Artesia, picturing the rain falling on the house I grew up in. Falling on Bethy's stone and the brilliant red and yellow nasturtium I planted for her last Saturday.

By the time I pulled into a spot in front of Sam's Club, the sky was angry and bruised. "Hope it holds off until we get loaded up."

"Why won't you tell me?" Adriana asked, taking off her seatbelt and turning to look at me.

"Tell you?"

She took her bottom lip between two fingers, absently stroking her rose-shaded mouth; a gesture of thinking deeply, she used to do that during late-night study sessions while poring over her textbook. "You know what I mean."

"Addy, the sky's about to open up. Can we do this later?"

She closed her eyes and nodded, then reached for her purse, containing Tricia's list and Uncle Wally's Visa card, and hopped out of the van without another word.

Inside we methodically filled five carts. I took my time checking off each item: apples and bananas and bunches of green-globed grapes; enormous bags of frozen chicken breasts and cases of pre-formed hamburger patties; single-sized boxes of cereal for breakfast and single-slices of cheese for lunches. The food we picked up would later feed the children back at camp, and that made me feel good. Capable. Useful.

Adriana slowly thawed and declared a fragile truce, punctuated by rain falling on the metal roof. And each time a clap of thunder echoed throughout the warehouse, she froze. If the storm freaked her out this much inside the store with its bright lighting, windowless walls, and the noisy chatter of other patrons, how would it affect her in the van? How would it affect me?

But there was only so much screwing around we could do without admitting to each other that in all honesty, we were afraid of going out into the torrent.

By the time the coolers were filled, we were drenched—an excellent explanation for why I was trembling. *Damaged nervous system doesn't deal well with cold, remember?* I'd tell her if she asked.

From the expression on her face, though, looking out the windshield at the poor visibility and fairly significant ponding on the road, she wasn't gonna mention my trembling. She was dealing with her own.

"I don't think we're going anywhere for awhile. I don't feel comfortable driving one-handed in this," I said, making my voice sound light, but examining the sky with trepidation. "At least we won't starve,"

She unbuckled her seatbelt, dropped her soaking flip-flops on the floor, and curled up in her seat. "Yeah, no danger there. I just hope it's not raining this hard there. Some of those kids really don't like the thunder." As if she had conjured it, a clap exploded over our heads, making her jump.

"You don't seem to like it either."

"Loud noises." She laughed, although it sounded forced.

I nodded. "I have a thing with lights now, so I'm not really digging the lightning."

Curled up in her seat, she played with her bottom lip. "Luke," she said, her voice barely audible over the rain on the roof, "do you know what happened that night?"

I swallowed hard. "Yeah."

"Then you have to tell me. I have to know how they..." she ran a hand through her hair, letting droplets of water fall, her eyes saying the words she couldn't.

I closed my eyes, and for one moment I was there again, hearing Garth Brooks on Rob's radio and Bethy's pitifully out of tune voice singing about wild horses, a car lighting her up, then flipping over in slow motion, so many times...

"I can't," I whispered. "Please Addy, don't ask me to."

"No one else can."

"No one should. You're lucky you don't remember. If I had that kind of peace, I wouldn't give it up for anything."

"But it's not peace. It's guilt and foreboding. Every night I have these dreams, and I don't know if they're real or... Luke, please."

Lightning snaked across the sky, and she braced herself for the thunder that followed. I unharnessed my chair and pushed back from the steering wheel. "Come here, sit with me."

She shook her head, but another bolt lit the sky, and she launched out of the seat, burying her face in my neck as the thunder cracked again. When it ended, she pulled back and laughed, embarrassed. "I swear this is a new development."

I held her eyes. "I'm sorry I can't talk about it. It's not that I'm trying to be a jerk, I just... can't. I'm sorry."

She nodded and looked away. "My therapist said that when I was ready, I might remember. I just hoped you could—"

"Give you a jump start?"

"Something like that," she said, then grabbed me as the sky flashed again.

I shut my eyes, wishing for... *something*. Something so intense and pro-found, the words wouldn't come.

"I think I'm gonna talk to Uncle Wally about us driving," she said into my neck, her breath ticking my skin. "He's got a couple idiots sitting in a parking lot, too scared of the rain to drive. And at this rate, we're probably gonna miss dinner."

"Only a moron would drive in this deluge. Anyway, I kinda like that we can get away from the camp sometimes, just you and me." She rested her head on my shoulder, and I took a deep breath, smelling her shampoo and damp skin, just the two of us in a warm cocoon, the windows fogging from the steam inside the van.

Chapter 6

Saturday morning Will and I went around double-checking the cabin for wayward possessions for our boys to shove in their filthy duffels. Their moms would no doubt dump the lot of it into sudsy, near-boiling water before tossing anything that didn't come out clean enough. At least that's what my momma used to do, the entire time mumbling it was a good thing she had to get new stuff for school anyway.

Their little-boy laughter bounced off the timber ceiling and plaster walls in the surreal combination of homesickness mixed with the exhausted wish to linger just a little longer with new friends made over late-night whispers and the unique experience of living together for a week.

My duffel held dozens of little slips of paper—torn from camper notebooks, envelopes sent in the week's mail, and one or two napkins—each with phone numbers or addresses written in careful, tight script from kids who wanted to stay in touch. I gave them my phone number and told them to call me anytime.

Once again, I made a mental note to transfer them all to my cell—these connections seemed sacred, something I could not lose. They also made me feel oddly tenuous. Where would I be in two weeks?

Adriana was right about never going back to the Permian Basin, but not because it held too many memories. I couldn't go back because there was nothing for me to go back to. Since I couldn't swim, I had lost my scholarship. Oh, they were plenty apologetic about it, but rules were rules, and my ride was over.

"The meds cabinet empty?" Will asked, carrying a mop and blue bucket to one corner of the cabin.

"About. Cory has to finish his protein bar before I can give him his last dose," I said, raising my voice over the laughter and catching the boy's eye.

He made a big show of stuffing the rest of it in his mouth; his cheeks full, he chewed with his mouth open.

"Classy," I remarked, opening the bottle of Relafen to shake out a white capsule for the boy's osteoarthritis. "Now, please come take this and put the bottle in your bag. Your parents are gonna be here soon, and I don't want to be the one in trouble if you aren't ready to go."

Behind thick glasses his brown eyes rolled dramatically as he pushed across the concrete floor, still talking to Andrew, his best friend. All week the two boys had been inseparable, calling themselves the "Siams"—short for Siamese, I figured out a couple days into camp.

I watched him swallow the pill, then open his mouth and stick out his tongue to prove it was gone. Laughing, I handed him the bottle. "You got everything?"

He shook it like a maraca. "I do now."

"Excellent. If you and Andrew are all packed up, you can go hang out on the deck until your parents get here."

He let out a war whoop and sped back to his bed.

"And if you're done with those meds, you can find everything you need to shine up the bathroom in there," Will smirked, pointing at the closet.

I let out my own war whoop and went to get cleaning supplies, laughing.

~~~~~

With our cabin cleared out and sparkling an hour later, I stretched out on my bed, thinking a nap sounded awesome. Or a beer.

Will collapsed in my chair. "You mind?"

I opened one eye. "Nah, it's a good excuse for me to keep lying here. So, now what?"

He leaned back in the chair, balancing it on two wheels. "We could go into town. Go shopping. Grab a bite."

"Grab a beer…"

"I want to go dancing," Gina said, pushing open our cabin door. "What'dya think William, want to spin me around on the dance floor?"

"If I say no, you're just gonna pout all day, so… sure. I'd love to take you dancing."

"Isn't he just the sweetest thing," she said, crossing the floor to lean affectionately on him. "Luke? Are you in?"

For dancing? Once I would have said absolutely, donned my boots and Stetson, and danced with every girl in the place, but now?

She put one of Will's CD on and wiggled her hips as she danced across the floor to where he practiced wheelies in my chair—a novelty when you can get back out of it—and I sat back and watched them, feeling strangely removed. If Bethy were here, she'd join Gina on the makeshift dance floor, shaking her butt in that way that always had guys looking at her, and made me uncomfortable. And Rob? Rob would probably be going through Will's CDs, playing DJ and recommending new groups. Rodrigo y Gabriela or Little Joe, probably.

One time he even taught Adriana, Bethy, and me to salsa, showing us how to move our hips while dancing across the girls' dorm room floor. Adriana in my arms, Bethy in his—he swore the salsa was too sexy a dance for me to do with my sister. After about half an hour he had Bethy doing some pretty fantastic twirls and dips, and I gave up dancing with Adriana, using the handy excuse that there was no way I could compete with that. When the song was over he reached for Adriana's hand and twirled her around the tiny dance floor, and I leaned on my sweaty sister, trying to forget what Adriana felt like in my arms.

~~~~~

I felt invisible.

In the midst of hundreds of tourists—moms pushing strollers, dads with tired toddlers perched on their shoulders, ice cream dripping from cones onto baseball caps; groups of carefree teens playing cool, their pheromones thick as the perfume that clung to them; lovers hand-in-hand, fused together and tuning out the cacophony—I pushed my chair down broken sidewalks and searched for hidden ramps to follow my friends into overpriced boutiques or kitschy shops selling t-shirts and chili pepper wall hangings.

A year ago I wouldn't've taken thirty seconds to think about whether or not some store or restaurant was accessible, and now it was all I thought about while dodging pedestrians who refused to meet my eye.

I will say having Gina there helped. A lot. She was used to walking down the street with her dad and finding those shadowy ramps tucked behind the stairs as an afterthought. And Will—conjoined to her hip, his hand in her back pocket in a way that would have led any bystander to believe they were one of the couples clogging the thoroughfare—having grown up across the street from the Howard household was used to the side trips and ramp searches. For them it was second nature; I was still trying to get the hang of my new ride.

Thank God for the camp. A place where all the walkways were well maintained, all the doorways and hallways were wide enough, and not a step in sight, it was a crippled man's paradise.

"Oh, this is it, I think," Gina shouted, her long blonde hair swinging in a ponytail like a silky pale flag.

"You said that about the last three stores," Will said, then turned to me. "Who knew a bar of soap would have us racing all over town?"

"Homemade *lavender* soap. And you said you liked how it made your skin feel," she shot back, turning to head up the ramp to the store.

Beside me, Adriana let out a resolved sigh and started up the ramp, moving in slow motion. "You okay?" I asked, following her.

"Yeah, sure. I just have no reason to go into a shop like *that*," she said, then pulled her shoulders back and marched in like she was going to war.

And the moment I pushed through the narrow doorway and scraping my knuckles on the old, painted wood, I understood why—it was a lingerie store, full of barely-there G-strings, sexy bras, and see-through teddies guaranteed to turn a good night into a great one. I swallowed hard, faked a smile, and went past a mannequin display to where Gina held up a minuscule blue satin slip. "It's cute, isn't it?"

"Sure it is," Will said examining it. "But who you planning on wearing that for, honey?"

She smiled. "It's lost on *you*, but Luke likes it. Right, Luke?"

"I'd have to see it on," I teased, earning one of her broad, approving grins. For one gratified instant I was almost proud of myself, dumb as it was, flirting with Gina made me feel like I used to. Until Adriana turned on her heel, muttering something about soap.

Gina's smile fell as she watched her friend stomp away, then she turned to Will. "You don't need to be here sniffing soap with us. Why don't y'all go find something else to do?"

Watching Adriana pick up a bar of orange and white soap and inhale the scent, her chin trembling, I couldn't leave her like that. But Gina put a hand on my shoulder. "Give us some girl time," she said. "She'll be fine, she just needs a minute."

Will turned to me. "Where's that fudge place?"

"Up the street a block or so."

"Let's go get some. I think I owe you anyway, I ate most of the last batch you bought."

I followed him back outside and down the ramp I'd just climbed. "I don't like leaving her," I called after him. Without Gina by his side, he walked a lot faster, and my arms were aching from trying to keep up all day.

"I know, man," he said, consciously slowing down. "I wouldn't either, but Gina's right, whatever's going on, they don't need us. So how 'bout we gorge ourselves on chocolatey goodness until they do?" he asked, giving me an apologetic smile.

"Ah, what the hell," I said. At least it would give me the excuse to rest in the cool store and give my arms a break.

~~~~~

Hours later, after consuming vast amounts of cheap tacos, Gina took us to Mack's on Main, a dirty honky-tonk bar. I sat at a table creating a pile of shelled peanuts I wasn't going to eat and watching Will jitterbug with Gina. "You should be dancing," I shouted to Adriana over the music and lifted a beer bottle to my mouth.

She sat beside me stirring her coke with a black straw, a strange expression on her face. Sadness, yes. Grief, absolutely. But something else, something that I couldn't quite put my finger on.

"Probably," she shouted back, but didn't move.

"You don't have to keep me company, go dance." *Plenty of guys have asked you to*, I thought but couldn't say out loud.

"I know, I just..." she reached over and pushed all the peanut shells into a tighter pile, "I don't think I can."

I placed a hesitant hand over hers, glad for the leather of my glove between our skin. She kept her eyes trained on the pile of shells.

"It doesn't feel right to let some stranger put his hands on me. Even if it's just…" she raised her chin slightly, her eyes darting to the dance floor before focusing back on the table as if she could only handle the briefest of glances.

"How 'bout we get out of here? Go for a walk or something?" I said.

I followed her outside where the sudden lack of sound felt almost foreign, as if I'd been robbed of one of my senses. It was also a relief. I fell in next to Adriana letting her pick a direction and pace, not really caring where we were going.

"I don't know what I was thinking," she ran a hand through her hair, shaking her dark curls. "Agreeing to go to a bar where couples would be hanging on each other, listening to the same songs Rob and I used to dance to. I must've been out of my mind."

"Gina's very persuasive."

"Mm… that must be it. Promise me we don't have to do this again."

I looked up at her, thinking I'd promise anything she asked. "Didn't I hear something about a dance next week?"

"That's with the campers. It'll be different."

"Right…"

"Seriously," she said, her eyes brightening with the light they always got when talking about the kids. "They just want to shake their groove thang."

"Groove thang?"

"You know what I mean." She stopped and looked at me, bringing her fingers up to stroke her lip. "After my kids left this morning, I went to see Jill. Over at the Rehab Hut?"

"I know it well."

"Yeah… So, I asked her if I could help out in there."

"That would be good." It wasn't like Uncle Wally had us running out every day to pick stuff up, and most of the time when the rest of the counselors were busy helping out in arts and crafts, or music class, or peeling potatoes for dinner, we found ourselves drifting from building to building without a purpose or permanent assignment. "I'm sure the kids will enjoy having you cheer for them," I said, starting to pushing my chair again.

She fell into step next to me. "I don't mean for the kids. I want to go when you go."

"*Me?*" I stopped the wheels so fast, it took her a second to realize I wasn't still beside her. "Why?"

She shrugged. "I just feel like if I had something to do, some way to help, then maybe I wouldn't feel so guilty."

"Addy…" I began, not quite sure where to go with that.

"Jill said I had to ask you because… I don't want to make you uncomfortable. I really don't, I just… I just want to…"

"Help," I repeated, starting to push my chair again, not sure if I wanted to be her cause. After a moment, I glanced up at her. "Why do you feel guilty?"

"Bethany should be the one here with you," she said so softly I had to strain to hear her over the sound of a passing car. "She would know how to make this okay. Or I should have taken the front seat and then I'd be the one in the chair, and you'd still…" she let out a long, shuddering breath.

"Adriana, of course I miss Bethy. So much sometimes I can't breathe, but never once have I wished I could trade you for her. And maybe… maybe I took the front seat to save you. I'm okay with that."

As I said the words, I realized they were true. If the choice was between me being in the chair or her, I'd choose the front seat a thousand times over, even knowing the consequences.

"I'm not sure how I feel about you coming to PT, though," I admitted. "Can I think about it?"

She nodded, then placed a warm hand on my shoulder, and we moved slowly through the night, headed back to honky-tonk music pouring out of Mack's.

~~~~~

It took me days to decide whether I could handle Adriana being there. *Helping.*

It wasn't that I didn't trust her, I did. I just hoped to God that if I let her come it wouldn't be an enormous mistake. If Adriana were to drop to her knees and have a come-to-Jesus moment like Mom did that time she saw me on the recumbent bike—*I knew Jesus would heal you*—throwing her out wouldn't be an option, but neither would stomaching the misguided joy over something no one could promise.

So what clinched it?

Part of it was she didn't ask again after that one time in a dark parking lot outside a crappy bar. She went about her business and left me to my thoughts, watching me go off to PT, my duffel casually slung over the back of my chair, coming back sweaty and exhausted, and never once did she make me feel guilty that I hadn't given her an answer.

She just smiled and said, "Good workout?" It was the same thing she'd occasionally ask those early mornings when I'd pick up her and Bethany for breakfast—the two of them having just dragged their butts out of bed when I'd been up for hours already.

And then this morning, looking across the circle of our 'tween family group, I just knew.

They all knew each other, those kids, and unlike last week when getting them to talk was like pulling teeth, man, these kids couldn't stop talking. They had a year's worth of stories saved up, and it was a little like jumping onto a moving train. I loved it! I loved the energy. The camaraderie. The utter chaos of it all. And there, in the middle of it all, was Adriana.

"Okay, but tell the truth," she said to Zach this morning, leaning toward the boy and fixing her gaze on him, "do you want to hang out with those boys because you like them or because you want to be popular?"

He shrugged. "Who doesn't want to be popular?"

The circle buzzed with consent, making Adriana smile. "But there's a difference between popularity and having friends. Y'all are all friends, but does that mean you're all popular?"

"I am," Tim predictably shouted next to me, stretching his arms above his head.

"You think you are," Emily teased him.

"My point is," Adriana raised her voice before she lost control of the group, "you have to decide whether it's more important to choose to be friends with someone because you really like who they are as a person, or if you just don't want to be alone."

"Nobody wants to be alone," Zach pointed out.

According to his file, Zach was born to a sixteen-year-old girl; she took one look at his deformities and put him up for adoption. But placing a baby with spina bifida, potential paralysis, and years of surgeries ahead of him turned out to be a challenge greater than most were ready to agree to, and he bounced from foster home to foster home before finally getting adopted three years ago when he was nine years old. When Adriana told me that Sunday night, I wanted to hit something. Someone. I didn't even know the kid yet, but it killed me that this boy, this unknown boy, hadn't been given a chance. From the time he was a tiny baby, he'd essentially been written off.

"No, you're right, nobody wants to be alone," she said, "but I want you to surround yourself with people who encourage you. Honor you. Ask you to only be yourself because they see how magnificent you are, right now, right here, just as you are. Anything less than that is unworthy of you."

While Zach nodded, letting that sink in, something rose deep inside of me, something close to panic. Or hope... It expanded so rapidly as it ascended, that I had to pull my eyes away from Adriana and focus on the mountain past the picture window. Repeating her words in my mind, I swallowed repeatedly, trying to force down whatever pressed on my larynx, and knew I needed her at PT.

~~~~~

"When you stopped by the other day, I wouldn't give you any specifics on Luke's condition," Jill said to Adriana. The two of them sat in front of me on a blue padded table. "But now that he's here, I thought we could discuss some of those questions you had."

Adriana examined her hands in her lap. "I don't want to make you uncomfortable, Luke, but I don't know anything about spinal injuries, and I... I want to understand what's going on." She took her quivering lip between her fingers.

I fought the urge to take her hand in mine by turning to Jill. "Whatever she needs to know..."

Jill nodded and reached for the plastic spine beside her. "Let me walk you through how the spine functions, and then we'll tackle Luke's injury, okay?" She touched the top of the spine. "The first eight vertebrae are the cervical nerves. They affect the head and neck, diaphragm, delts, arms, and hands as we move down the spine. The thoracic nerves are the twelve here, at about the middle of the top curve and down to where the small of the back begins. The top six affect the chest muscles, the bottom six are for the abs, with me so far?"

Adriana smiled hesitantly. "As long as there's no pop quiz later."

"There won't be. Moving farther south, we have the five lumbar nerves that affect the legs, and finally the five sacral nerves for bladder, bowel, and sexual function. Luke has a posterior incomplete T11 injury," Jill went on, "which means the damage happened toward the back of the spinal cord. He has good muscle power, and pain and temperature sensation, but has a difficult time coordinating his limbs."

"I can pedal a recumbent bike," I told her, strangely proud of that accomplishment.

"The common misconception," Jill said, "is all spinal cord injuries are complete and permanent, as if an invisible line is drawn and everything above that line works, while everything below it is dead and always will be. That's not necessarily true. Each person, each injury and situation are different, and the job of a rehabilitation therapist is to help Luke understand how his body works now, while continuing to discover what his body may be capable of as he recovers."

"Which means what, exactly?" Adriana asked, picking up the plastic spine to play with.

Jill shrugged. "That's hard to say, but what I can tell you is Luke has an excellent chance for additional recovery, and the rule of thumb is as long as you're seeing some improvement and additional muscles are recovering function, your chances of seeing more improvement are better."

The spine made a rhythmic ticking sound as Adriana manipulated it, the vertebrae hitting each other as she considered all the information. "So he may be able to walk someday?" she finally asked.

I fixed my gaze on Jill's face, grateful to Adriana for voicing the one question I was too afraid to ask. Jill turned to me, a guarded expression clouding her features. "You might someday walk on your own, or you may need braces or a walker. Or you may need a chair for the rest of your life. I really don't know, but what I do know is as long as we sit around talking about getting better, without actually doing something about it, you'll never see results." She turned to Adriana. " And if you're gonna be here, I'm putting you to work."

"That's what I'm here for," Adriana responded, smiling.

On a foam mat on the floor, she walked Adriana through each exercise, each time showing her where to put her hands, how to position my legs, before moving out of the way so Adriana could do the exercises with me. At first the only thing filling my brain was the fact that a girl—*this* girl—held my calf in her warm hands. I couldn't even remember the last time someone I cared about had touched me—there was Rosa and Jill and occasionally LaVaughn, but he really didn't do anything for me—but it was all so clinical, professional.

But Adriana—with her big brown eyes so focused on my body, my skin nearly burned with her gaze, her sweaty, nervous hands holding a leg as she leaned into me to work the muscle, the air filled with the sound of her whisper-soft breathing—somehow it all felt so different. Not *wrong*, so much as intimate and maybe just a little bit dangerous; she was still Rob's girl, and I half-expected him to come busting through the doors and ask just what I thought I was doing with her.

I concentrated on the timber-beamed ceiling and aluminum lights above my head, already sweating from exertion.

"Hey," Jill called, touching my shoulder and pulling me from my thoughts, "we're headed to the Total Gym, wanna join us?"

I wiped sweat off my brow and sat up. "I don't suppose you'd be willing to start without me?"

"That's the thing about this *ménage à trois,* you're kinda the linchpin."

I shot her tired grin and hauled myself back up in my chair to follow them across the room.

"Have a seat," Jill said to Adriana, pointing to a stool set at the base of the Total Gym while I situated myself on the equipment. "Luke's going to work on his legs today. I thought about taking it easy on y'all and letting him do upper body, but then decided to just go ahead and throw you into the deep end."

"That's awfully sadistic of you," Adriana said wryly.

"I prefer evil genius. Now, what I need you to do is put your hands here," she positioned herself behind Adriana and placed her hands in the right place on my legs. "He's going to push against the foot plate and straighten out his legs. Luke, do a leg press."

I did.

"Good, now see how his legs are gonna want to bow? You need to keep them in this position so the proper muscles get the workout, okay?"

Adriana nodded slowly, watching as I returned to the starting position. When my knees were bent again, she met my eyes, and the warmth, the pride there was so real, I felt like I could do anything.

For the next hour Jill showed her the exercises I was supposed to do that day—tomorrow would be different, and the day after that would be another round of torture, just in a new form—but each rep was one more I couldn't do just two weeks ago. And every pound I lifted made me that much stronger, every inch forward got me farther from where I was. Sure, sometimes I felt like Sisyphus, pushing that boulder with all my might and never really getting anywhere, but I had to tell myself that all the agony, all the punishing pain was worth it. Gritting my teeth and pushing through pain so enormous, sometimes it was incomprehensible had to be for *something*, otherwise I might not be able to stand it.

"Excellent job," Jill said, checking her watch. "Why don't y'all get out of here since I've filled my torment quota for the day?"

"Ah, gee," I panted, reaching for a towel to mop my face, "I was just getting started."

She sent me a wicked grin and left us to finish some paperwork before dinner.

We headed back to our cabin in silence, except the birds twittering around us, and the farther we went, the thicker that silence became until I felt like I was pushing through it. "Hey, uh, thanks for going," I ventured, unable to take it any longer. "I wasn't sure how it would go, but it was kinda nice having you there."

"It was different than I expected," she said diplomatically, her eyes trained on the asphalt.

"Are you up for tomorrow or...?" I asked, giving her an out. I saw how her face paled each time she knew she was hurting me, and for a moment I almost wanted her to take the out. Not for me, but for her.

But she smiled, the one that lit her eyes. "You're going, I'm going," she said, and I let out a breath I didn't know I was holding.

Chapter 7

Hot water hit my tired muscles, washing away sweat and fatigue, and filling my lungs with warm steam. It felt so good, I closed my eyes and rested my head against the tile wall. Between the lack of sleep, bad dreams, and Jill's penchant for torture on a daily basis, and now the unlimited supply of water, if I were to take a nap in the shower, would that be completely insane?

"Mr. Luke? Are you in there?" Rog called through the glass block wall between us, making my eyes snap back open. No matter how many times I told the kid to just call me Luke, he kept tacking that "mister" on. But he did it to Will and everyone else, so whatever.

"What's up, Rog?" I asked, checking my wrist. I once used the Ironman watch to keep track of breaststrokes and butterflies; now I used it to keep track of kids. "Where are you supposed to be?"

"It's free time," he shouted over the water. "What are you doing?"

"Shaving," I grunted, reaching for the can of Barbasol in my plastic caddy. So much for that nap.

"You shave a lot, Mr. Luke." He sounded like he was getting comfortable on the other side of the glass block wall.

"Yep," I replied.

If I had thought about it, I would've brought the electric shaver I kept in the glove compartment of my truck, but since I refused to pack my own stuff—either through childish procrastination or some misguided belief that by not packing I would delay the inevitable indefinitely—it was no wonder the shaver was left behind, forgotten. And my skin was paying the price. Running a razor over it twice a day to combat the five o'clock shadow I had by early afternoon had me resembling the desert I grew up in. Maybe I would take Will up on that offer to try his super-fancy moisturizer.

"How come you aren't at the pool or the rec room?"

He was quiet for a moment. "Are you doing anything for the talent show tonight?"

"I don't have a talent," I admitted. Not since I was a freshman in high school, and Bethy somehow talked me into doing an act with her; basically she danced around me and occasionally I'd pick her up for some fancy lift she taught me in the backyard. A dip here, some flapper-looking move there, and it was over. Later my friends thanked me for showing them my sister's under-wear—which were really the bloomers she wore under her skirt—and after giving Terry McGee a bloody nose and receiving a month's grounding, I swore I'd never dance like that with her again. She claimed she understood, but I could tell I'd disappointed her. For the fight of course, but more so for refusing to dance when she asked.

I glanced at his obscured, wavy figure through the glass blocks. "Why?"

"I don't know… I was just thinking I might do something, but I'm not sure I should."

"How come?"

He was quiet, thinking, and I finished shaving. "It's not really cool…" Rog said. "The kids at school make fun of me because I juggle. They say it's for jesters and dorks."

"You juggle?" I asked, rinsing the leftover shaving cream from my face. "Shoot, if I could, I'd be up there with a big ol' grin on my face."

"Yeah?"

"Hel—Heck yeah! It's not doing something that makes you uncool, it's not doing it that's not cool."

"Mr. Luke," he said after a long moment, "do you know where I can find some tennis balls?"

I grinned. "Yep. In the Rehab Hut, tell Jill I said it was okay for you to get them. And then head over to the dining hall, it's almost time for dinner."

"Thanks, Mr. Luke," he called on his way out. And over the roar of the water I heard his reedy voice talk to someone out in the cabin. Will, I figured, because he was the only one out there when I got out of the shower.

~~~~~

Sometimes the difference between Camp Caballero and the one I grew up going to was so small, I could almost believe I was twelve again and with those kids long ago. The talent show acts were basically the same things: boys showing off to crack each other up, girls singing heartfelt ballads like they had any idea what the words meant, counselors pulling out all the stops to entertain the kids.

Uncle Wally and Dr. David played "Dueling Banjos," making me wish I had a musical bone in my body. Tricia told the story of Prinderella, her two sisty uglers, and micked wepstother. Apparently it was a camp favorite, and this morning during family group, Tim tried to explain its awesomeness to me. I thought the kid might be having a stroke. "She slopped her dripper," he kept saying, cracking himself up.

Gina danced barefoot in a shiny red bodysuit while Adriana clasped my hand, obviously thinking the same thing I was, that Gina looked a hell of a lot like Bethany up there. In some ways they were remarkably similar. Gina couldn't draw a stick figure to save her life—she proved that the other night when we played a massive game of group Pictionary, and even the slightest mention of sex turned Bethy three shades of crimson before she'd change the subject—but if my sister had known this camp existed, she would've been square in the middle of it, too, dancing on stage or cheering for these kids, just like Gina. And maybe that's why I was so drawn to her.

When she was done I squeezed Adriana's hand before letting go to clap. As Gina left the stage, Rog pushed himself up the ramp, Uncle Wally beside him.

"All right y'all," Uncle Wally said into the microphone, "this'll be the last act of the night. When Rog is done, y'all need to head back to your cabins for lights out…" Behind me a few kids booed, and I shot them a dirty look I didn't really mean. "Let's give Rog a big round of applause," he finished, placing a hand on the boy's shoulder before leaving the stage.

Rog took a deep breath and scanned the crowd, his eyes landing on mine; I winked at him, and he nodded at Benji in the corner to start a CD cued up on the sound system. Justin Timberlake poured out of the speakers, and all around me, kids started dancing to "Sexyback" in their seats as Rog picked up one of the neon tennis balls in his lap, tossing it easily in the air. A single ball going straight up and falling back down in his hand, over and over. I kept a smile plastered on my face, but the longer he tossed and caught that single ball, the more I began to wonder if he really knew how to juggle, cause *this* wasn't it.

"Add another!" someone yelled from the far side of the room, and Rog grinned.

"Should I?"

When another voice shouted yes, his smile got bigger, and he picked up another ball, tossing the two back and forth between his hands until someone else shouted at him to add another.

Uncle Wally stepped on stage, a couple cans of tennis balls under his arms, and each time a voice shouted at Rog, Uncle Wally tossed him another ball. Six, seven, eight balls blurred above Rog's head, sometimes bouncing off the floor, sometimes tossing one or two higher, higher, impossibly high above his head.

"Add another," a kid behind me shouted, and Uncle Wally tossed the last one he had, then held up his hands to show he was out.

"That's all they had in the Rehab Hut," Rog shouted over the music, sounding rather disappointed and leaving us to wonder just how many he could handle.

"He almost didn't do this," Adriana whispered in my ear, her warm breath tickling my lobe. I nodded, not taking my eyes from the kid. I didn't want to miss a single second of him up there; he was mesmerizing. "You did a good thing. Look how happy he is."

"I didn't do anything," I whispered back.

"It's not doing something that makes you uncool, it's *not* doing it that's not cool."

I stared at her, surprised.

"I stopped by to get Gina's CD from Will," she said and turned back to the stage to watch the rest of his act.

~~~~~

In the cabin, the boys wouldn't stop talking about Rog's act. Between mouthfuls of toothpaste, between tiny cups of medication, as they pulled off sweaty t-shirts in favor of pajamas, they acted like Rog was suddenly a rockstar. And the way he was grinning ear-to-ear and lit like candle, I kinda got the sense that for the first time he was truly proud of himself.

Eventually sleep stole over them one by one, and just before he fell asleep, Rog whispered from across the room, "Thank you, Mr. Luke."

I smiled to myself and listened to them sleep, the soft snores of exhaustion, repeating Adriana's words—my words—over and over in my mind.

Chapter 8

The next morning I woke before Will's alarm went off, and, feeling possessed, did something I swore I'd never do again: I slipped into the swim trunks in my duffel and went next door to wake Adriana. Her cabin was just as silent as mine, and I pushed across the concrete floor as if drawn to her. She was curled up on her side facing me, her dark hair wild from sleep, her jaw tight as if she didn't like what she was dreaming about.

With a hesitant hand, I traced her cheek, still not sure what I was doing. "Adriana," I whispered, moving my hand to her shoulder, a much more appropriate place to touch her, and gently shook her awake.

Her eyelids fluttered open. "Luke," she whispered, raising up on her elbow, "what's going on?"

I smiled, for a moment reliving all the times I'd seen her first thing in the morning, her crazy bed head and sweetish morning breath, the oversized tees she wore to bed, usually falling off one golden shoulder.

"Is everyone okay?" she asked, looking around anxiously.

"Everyone's fine, I just..." I swallowed. "Addy, would you go to the pool with me?"

"Give me a minute to change," she whispered, her eyes holding mine.

Outside the sky held the purple of early morning. A few last stars hung on, reluctant to relinquish their power to the day. I took slow, deep breaths, remembering why I loved this time of day more than any other—the world hushed and asleep, the potential of the day still a silent promise. I glanced at Adriana, walking beside me on the path in silence that I suspected had less to do with having just woken up, and more that she understood what we were doing even better than I did.

Past the chain-link enclosed pool, ethereal fog rose from the water. It was kept at a constant temperature by an electric heating system, donated by some big muckety-muck in Albuquerque, which I only knew because sitting poolside for nearly two weeks, you pick up a lot of gossip, and I overheard a couple counselors talking about it. I also had a pretty good sense of who was sleeping with whom, who wanted to be, and exactly why bed-hopping at camp was a *really* bad idea. There were no secrets here.

Adriana entered the security code to open the pool gate and smiled at me. "After you."

I didn't move. I hadn't been in a pool in months, and frankly, up until about half an hour ago, I had no intention of ever getting in one again. Yeah, some of it had to do with a recurring dream of saving Bethy from a pool of her own blood I'd had so many times, I wasn't completely certain if I dove in, the water would stay clear and clean. But it was more than that.

This had been my life. My salvation. My ticket out of Artesia and on to something better. I'd spent my life training and challenging myself to be the best. The very best, and honestly, I was afraid I would discover in that pool I was simply ordinary.

There was a pool at the rehab facility that Rosa pestered me to get in on a nearly daily basis; it was the only time her coaxing, cajoling, and wheedling met with a solid concrete wall. I wasn't ready. And the truth was, staring at that water, even now I didn't know if I was, but if I didn't, how could I go back to that cabin and look those kids in the eye and tell them they could do anything, *anything* they set their mind to if I couldn't do this?

How could I look myself in the eye if I didn't?

I pushed out a deep breath, sent up a silent *please* to Bethany, and went to the side of the pool before I could change my mind. And there, after shedding the Artesia Bulldogs sweatshirt, catapulted myself out of my chair and into the water.

It wasn't the same as before. I missed the perfect synchronization of my arms and legs working together, but my heart remembered what it was meant to do, my lungs reveled in their task, my legs working unevenly but trying anyway, my arms reaching, stretching—up through my sides, through my shoulders, and all the way to my fingertips—every part that could propel me forward pushing to reach the end of the pool. And when I got there, hanging onto the concrete side, I rested my head on my arms and listened to Bethy cheering my name so loudly, it reverberated off the clouds and the farthest reaches of heaven.

Adriana's eyes rested on me, and I turned to her, sitting in the pool lift, a strange, serene smile lighting up her face. Almost in slow motion she stood up, untied the orange sarong from around her waist, and draping it over my chair, dove gracefully into the water. I watched her body move underwater for a beat, before focusing on the sarong fluttering gently in the breeze, a bright flag against the black of my chair.

Above us, the sky had gone from purple to orange, the birds began calling to each other in the trees, and the mountain pulled itself to its full height, showing off.

That was the other thing I loved about getting up so early, that ordinary miracle of the world waking up again, or at least my little corner of it. Some mornings I'd miss it completely, too engrossed in challenging myself in the pool or another set of reps in the weight room, but some mornings I could almost see God's paintbrush.

Adriana surfaced and ran a hand over her face before smiling at me. Every detail of her was magnified, the water beading on her skin and matting her dark eyelashes, her lips wet and glistening. "Rob once told me when he was in the water, he found his purpose." Her eyes darkened for a moment as she studied the mountain before turning back to me. "In the water, he was free. Weightless. Who he was born to be. Seeing you now reminded me of that—this is your purpose, not hiding under the arbor watching someone else swim. You belong in the water."

"Thanks for coming," I said, wanting to fill the silence, but not knowing what else to say.

"I wouldn't have missed it for anything." She said, her eyes on me making me painfully aware my body no longer responded the way it used to.

And just like that, I had to get away from her. I needed to put some space between us; breathing her, feeling her eyes and smile on me, nearly had the power to kill me. Even if I *could* take this farther, even if it wouldn't somehow violate the guy code that seemed even more important now that Rob was gone, it still wouldn't mean a damn thing because she wouldn't want it to. And I couldn't follow through anyway.

"We should get back," I said, checking my watch and annoyed that my voice sounded entirely too hoarse. She blinked at me, clearly confused by my sudden one-eighty, but I had no intention of explaining. Instead, I cleared my throat and forced a smile. "I'm getting cold."

"Okay, but you're buying me a cup of coffee for dragging me out of bed before the sun even got up," she said smiling, and turned to swim back toward my chair and her towel.

"The coffee's free," I called and swam after her, pleased when she picked up her speed and raced me to the other end of the pool, a competitive fire lighting her eyes.

~~~~~

The boys moved in slow motion, having just woken up and immediately demanded to know *why* I got to go swimming when they didn't. I knew better than to tell them I was awake and they weren't, they'd all be up before the crack of dawn tomorrow if I did.

"Y'all better hurry, breakfast waits for no man," Will interjected, getting them back on track, then shot me a wink that said he both understood and approved of this morning's field trip.

Ten minutes later I sat in the shower, my body vibrating with a low hum that I used to take for granted.

"Am I meant to be everyone's alarm clock today?" Will shouted over the roar of the water. "I have it on good authority Tricia's pancakes are on the menu, and I'm not waiting for you."

I laughed. "I'll be out in two minutes."

Once I would've dried and dressed in under a minute, now it took ten times that, and that was with a fire lit under my butt, but it wasn't like I could do a whole hell of a lot about it. Dressed, I rounded the corner, went to my bed to hang my towel on a hook, and slipped my LUKE name tag around my neck—camp rules. Without it, I'd have to do laps around the dining hall while everyone chanted my name. That's the kind of thing you do *once!*

"Finally," Will said as I pushed the screen door open, "I was about to black out from low blood sugar."

"You could've left without me. I do know where the dining hall is," I told him.

"Ignore him," Gina said. "He's a total bear until he's had his morning coffee."

He pulled her into an affectionate hug. "I've always thought of myself as an otter."

Adriana watched them walk down the ramp, then fell into step beside me. "My girls wanted to know why we didn't take them swimming."

I smiled at her. "They weren't invited."

She rested a hand on my shoulder, walking beside me in companionable silence that left me concentrating on her hand, warm against the fabric of my shirt. I didn't want to do the math, but I had nine days left with her, and then…? I was going home, back to the nothing of Artesia, and she, well, I had no idea what her plans were other than to not go back to the Permian Basin.

I glanced up at her, her hair still damp from the shower—which I refused to think of her taking—stripping off her wet swimsuit, the warm water sluicing down soft, chilled skin, her back arched as she ran her hands through her hair…

"What?" she asked, a slight smile playing on her lips.

I blinked and turned back to the path, my ears hot. "Nothing. I was just wondering what you're doing after this…"

"Family groups, a bit of horseback riding, maybe some PT later on…" she teased.

"I meant after camp."

I felt her shrug. "I don't know. I don't want to think about it just yet." She pushed the button to open the door for the dining hall and smiled down at me. "Thank you for inviting me this morning."

I swallowed the lump that unexpectedly clotted my throat. "For some reason I needed you there."

She pushed a hand through her hair and started to open her mouth to say something, but one of the girls from her cabin ran over, interrupting her. "Adriana, Emily needs you."

Her eyes flashed with annoyance... or was that relief? "Can it wait a minute?"

The girl whispered something that made Adriana's expression change. "Would you excuse me? And if I'm not back in time for family groups, start without me."

"Is everything okay?"

Adriana lowered her mouth to my ear. "Nothing a box of tampons can't handle. See you soon," she whispered and traveled the path we'd just come down with a furiously blushing Emily.

~~~~~

The kids shifted in their seats, wanting to know why Adriana and Emily disappeared from breakfast this morning, and hell if I knew what to say. They weren't buying my they-just-need-to-take-care-of-something explanation and getting them to focus on anything else was like herding cats. "Let's go to the basketball pavilion," I suggested out of desperation. "Play a game or something. You want to?"

Tim grinned, always the first to agree to anything. "Yeah, man, floor volleyball! There's a net, right?"

I shrugged. I had no clue what floor volleyball was and couldn't begin to guess what they had in the supply closet, but it was better than sitting here. "I guess we'll find out."

Following his instructions, we hung the net we found about two feet off the ground and split into teams—the boys on one side of the net, me and the girls on the other—all of us sitting on the floor. "So basically the rules are the same as regular volleyball," he said, "except you scoot on your butt and you can't lift it off the floor. Okay?"

"That's it?" I asked, looking through the net at him.

"You want to make it harder?" he smirked.

I laughed and threw him the ball. "Nah, show us what you got."

With a big grin on his face, Tim tossed the ball in the air, then served it over the net, directly at Kathy, who easily spiked it back over the net at the boys. Brad slid six inches to his left and sent it right back at me, forcing me to scoot to my right to send it back to the other side. My fist connected with the ball, but at that odd angle, rather than sailing back, it bounced off the net.

"Crap," I muttered, making the kids laugh. This was harder than I thought.

"That's one," Tim whooped, and served the ball again.

A few minutes later, Adriana and Emily joined us on the pavilion floor; Emily, looking a little chagrined, took a seat next to me, while Adriana plopped her butt in the middle of the boys.

"Good?" I mouthed to Adriana through the net.

When Bethy got her first period, she and Mom took up shelter in her room for most of the day, whispering about God knew what all. At the time I had no idea what was going on, but she refused to meet my eye for days. Fed up with her odd behavior, I discovered her reading on her bed one afternoon and took a flying leap across the footboard, landing squarely beside her, determined to get my sister to quit acting so weird.

Lord, she lost her mind! Screamed at me to go away, and leave her alone. She was a woman now and didn't need me fooling around on her bed. I walked out of there, bewildered.

That night she snuck across the hall and climbed in my bed for the last time. "I'm sorry," she whispered, snuggling close to me like she did during a thunderstorm when we were little. The first storm after she died, I laid in my bed in the hospital, and remembered what it felt like all those times to whisper in the dark and breathe her sweet girl smell, all the while wishing I had known that would be the last time. I wouldn't've fallen asleep so quickly.

A strange expression slid across Adriana's face. "Yeah. Are you okay?" she mouthed back.

I forced a smile and nodded, and focused on Zach, who was about to serve the ball.

Chapter 9

The lights flashed pink and yellow, blue and green above the dance floor, crowded with sweaty bodies and their wheelchairs, walkers, and crutches, dancing with various levels of skill and commitment. I was only a little older than these kids when Ella—or was it Ellen?—taught me how to dance at summer camp. I might not remember her name, but I vividly remember her wrapping one arm casually around my neck and planting her feet on either side of my left leg, fitting the V of her crotch to my thigh, showing me how to move against her. We danced together in the darkness that night until we were drenched in sweat, then disappeared to a bench outside where she let me feel her up and kiss her until she was moaning, and I desperately wanted her to touch me and release the pain of deep need.

Watching the kids on the dance floor, it was almost impossible to imagine any of them disappearing for a little heavy petting, but I'd heard Uncle Wally say more than once that a pubescent kid in a wheelchair is the same as a pubescent kid out of one, one's just sitting down. And on that point I couldn't disagree. Hell, *I* wasn't any different. I still wanted to feel a girl's lips against mine, tangle my tongue with hers, run my hands down her body. The only difference was I didn't want anyone to touch me—there'd be no deep, needing pain.

"Dance with me," Gina shouted over the music, pulling me from my thoughts.

"I can't," I shouted back.

She raised an eyebrow like she could see my thoughts and didn't like the road they were leading me down. "You're sitting here watching these kids shake their asses, and you're gonna claim you *can't?* How about you be honest and say, 'Gina, I don't want to dance with you.'"

"Gina, I don't want to dance."

"Tough shit. Everyone dances, camp rules." She grinned wickedly and took my hand to pull me to her. "But I'll let you lead."

I knew that I've-got-a-secret glint in her eye. It was the same one she had just before Carrie asked me to help her at the campfire. I shook my head, suppressing a smile, and followed her to the dance floor. Just as she stopped, the song ended and a new, slow one poured out of the speakers. I froze. This wasn't what I had in mind at all, and seeing the people split into couples, I couldn't even fathom how to dance with Gina to this. But she smiled and took a seat in my lap, wrapping her arms around my neck.

"My daddy taught me how to slow dance," she said in my ear. "He's a great dancer."

Having her so close was like an assault on my senses. The heat of her body against mine, her subtle perfume filling my brain, a strand of blonde hair tickling my cheek—I hadn't been near a girl in so long, I almost didn't know how to handle it. "What, uh, what do I do?" I asked, hoping the music covered the hesitation in my voice.

Gina smiled. "What would you do before?"

"I-I'd move to the music."

"Then do that. Don't think about it, just do it."

I felt ridiculous, though. Pushing my rims wasn't dancing, it was... it was how I got where I wanted to go, and that was a far cry from holding Gina and spinning her across the dance floor.

All around us, kids leaned on each other and swayed. They at least looked like... okay, so they looked like they were at a junior high dance, but at least they *looked* like they were dancing. We just looked like a traffic jam.

"You're thinking about it," Gina said in my ear.

"I feel like an idiot."

"How did you dance before?"

I shrugged, embarrassed. "Like anyone else, I guess."

"Show me."

"Gina..."

"You'd lead?"

I rolled my eyes. "Yeah."

"Well, you're leading now. I'm going anywhere you want to go, right?"

I laughed self-consciously. "You're *sitting* on me."

She grinned and wiggled her butt. "Mmm... so I am. And before, would you go in a straight line?"

I began to see what she meant. "Hang on," I said, and as her arms tightened around my neck, I spun us in a circle—not terribly gracefully and we nearly slammed into a nearby couple, but Gina just tilted her head back and laughed.

"Try again," she said in my ear, and the second time I kept the turn a bit tighter, pulling out sooner to keep us on a straighter path. "There you go," she said, resting her forehead against my neck.

Like volleyball this morning, or swimming before that, it wasn't the same as before, but with Gina soft and warm against me, I almost didn't care. The music playing over the speakers, a girl in my arms—okay, so I was in hers, but whatever—while she let me lead her across the floor, was it really that much different?

When the song ended, she looked up at me. "You wanna go outside?"

Unbidden images of Ella flashed through my mind again, and I swallowed, knowing she wasn't asking for *that*, but for half a second, I wanted her to.

~~~~~

A breeze ruffled my hair, effectively clearing my mind.

It was just as well, I didn't need Gina's perfume cluttering up my thoughts and confusing the hell out of me. She sat on a bench, eye level, and smiled at me. "When my dad first came home from the hospital after his accident, for a while he was a different man. My parents nearly got divorced because of it."

"Because he couldn't do what he did before," I said, looking at the far away barn, lit by sodium lamps.

"No," she said, "because he forgot who he was before the accident. Your body isn't you, any more than your sense of humor is your body. Or your intelligence is your body. Or how much you love is dependent on whether you can walk."

I let my eyes drift back to her. I couldn't disagree with that, but I also couldn't yet hear my own voice agree with it either.

She leaned forward, placing her elbows on her knees. "I remember dancing with my dad before the accident," she said, smiling at the memory. "Putting my feet on his and letting him twirl me around the room. I was five, maybe, but I remember looking up at him and feeling safe, and I loved it. But you know what I loved more? When he took me to my first father-daughter dance after the accident. He didn't want to go, but he and Mom learned how to dance again in our kitchen. And that night? At the dance? I looked at him and knew he'd do anything for me."

"I know what you're saying," I told her, envisioning her dancing with her quadriplegic dad.

In my mind's eye, I saw her in a pink dress, her skinny arms wrapped around her father's neck like they were mine a few minutes ago, while her father nervously spun the two of them in his chair before God and everybody.

"I really do get it, it's just that when I think about what I can't do anymore, it's so overwhelming that I..." I ran my hand through my hair, unwilling to finish that thought out loud. Instead, I pulled the Marlboros out of my backpack and lit one, taking a deep, steeling drag.

Gina reached over and took the cigarette from my hand and placed it between her lips. "What can't you do?"

I looked away. Between the sensual shape her mouth made when she blew out the smoke and the first answer that popped into my head, no way was I gonna answer that.

"Oh, I see... You still haven't tried."

"Just when do you think I would have?" I asked her, the anger rising inside me so quickly, it was nearly blinding. "Late at night in my squeaky bed, surrounded by kids? In the shower before breakfast with Will yelling at me in his pre-caffeinated agitation? Or should I just whip it out right now to prove to you that it really is dead?"

I reached for my belt buckle and undid it, the metal and leather ringing like crisp bells against her stunned silence.

"Luke..."

"No. You want to see, let's see," I said and unbuttoned my fly.

Like a shot, her hand crossed the space between us, stilling mine. "Stop," she whispered, her eyes wide and sad. "I'm sorry. When you try, if you try, is up to you, and it really isn't any of my business. It's just that..."

"What?"

"You were right, a quad father doesn't make me an expert any more than going to summer camp three weeks out of the year makes me a spina bifida expert, I get that. But I saw what the accident did to my dad, and I don't want that for you. I really don't."

"I don't need you to save me," I said, reaching for my cigarette.

"I know, and I won't bring it up again. I swear. You wanna talk, I'm here. You don't, and I'm still here, okay?"

I studied her in the darkness, wishing I could fall for a girl like her. It'd be so easy, too. She was beautiful and funny and smart, but most importantly, she *got* it—what it meant to be in this chair. She understood, and it didn't scare her like it might some girls. Frankly, like it did me, and I was freaking *living* it. All I'd have to do is reach for her, pull her into my arms, and fall.

"Are we interrupting?" Will asked behind me, and I turned, surprised to see him and Adriana standing there awkwardly, while realizing my pants were still undone and wide open.

"No," Gina lied, "but I'm dying of thirst. Babe, would you get me a drink?"

Whatever he read in her expression, I don't know, but I had a pretty good idea—something along the lines of *we need another minute. And take Adriana with you.*

He sighed in a way that made me wonder if he was teasing or angry. "And you would've sat out here all night, thirsty and saying to yourself, 'I sure wish some knight in shining armor would come along with a Coke,' right? Come on, Adriana, you get to be a knight, too."

Adriana's eyes wide, she let Will fit his hand to the small of her back and lead her away as Gina yelled, "Thank you!"

The moment they were gone, I tucked my shirt back in, buttoned my pants, and fastened my belt. "Is Will mad?" I asked.

"That it looked like I was giving you a hand-job?"

"Did it?"

"Maybe." She shrugged. "Would that bother you?"

I turned to Suffolk Hall, watching silhouetted bodies flash blue, yellow, and red as they danced: arms in the air, torsos moving, wheelchairs spinning, freed by the music. Somehow I'd rather Will and Addy think they'd walked in on a hand-job in progress, than me about to pull out my dick to show Gina that the damn thing had turned into a foreign, useless appendage, as superfluous as my appendix. I could go my whole life without anyone knowing that, but really, why would anyone ever need to?

"No," I said, keeping my gaze on the building, "it wouldn't."

Chapter 10

I've never been able to put into words exactly what swimming does to me. Logically I know it isn't holy, and I'm fairly certain ministers don't go around blessing Olympic-sized swimming pools. They've got better things to do. Although Reverend Bates once did a blessing over all of us in Ty Campbell's pool during a back-to-school Youth Group party, but I'm pretty sure that doesn't count.

I don't remember the day I was baptized, but I do remember every time I needed to forget some problem at school, some girlfriend I couldn't deal with, and holy or not, the water always washed it away.

Backstroking across the length of the pool, I watched the sky lighten, sliding from cool, steely violet to the brilliant orange trumpet call heralding the sun, and heard ancient words whispered somewhere deep inside my soul:

In beauty, this day begins.
In beauty the day arrives.
I will protect myself with this corn pollen.
I will protect myself with this Eagle Feather.
I will protect myself with my prayers.
I will live a beautiful life.

When I was a kid, Shi'nali woke before sunrise to welcome the coming day, and from our creaky beds at her house, the ones Dad and Uncle Clay slept in as boys, we'd hear her outside our east-facing window, softly chanting the Sunrise Prayer. Back then I thought her words were a protective blanket she wove over and around all of us.

God, how Bethy loved that prayer. She'd pull me out of bed so we could say it too, but what I never told her was I liked hearing Shi'nali say it through the window. It was different hearing her words float in through the screen while I lay cozy and warm in my bed, drifting through the magical words on the wings of a dream, than standing in my pajama bottoms and robe, freezing next to Bethy and mumbling the words in a sleepy stupor.

I checked my watch. If I got out of the pool now, I'd have enough time to shower and not hear Will's Armageddon countdown, and I still wasn't sure if he was upset with me about that supposed hand-job snafu last night.

Swimming to the edge of the pool, I hoisted myself out using my arms. I refused to use that damn pool lift, even though I scraped my knee on the concrete yesterday afternoon. It was a pride thing, I fully admit, but I wasn't gonna use a mechanical lift if I could handle it myself, and a little skin was a tiny price to pay for hanging onto my self-esteem.

I got back to the cabin and showered and dressed in record time, choosing to use the sink to shave, rather than waste time utilizing one of the showers when one of the boys could be in it, when a shattering scream pierced the tiled wall.

"What was that, Mr. Luke?" Rog asked, his brown eyes wide in the mirror.

"I don't know," I told him, using a towel to hastily wipe off the shaving cream I'd just spread over my face.

He followed me through the cabin to the deck, where Gina was leading her girls outside, some of them only partially dressed. "Adriana could use your help," she said in a weird kind of forced calm.

Inside, Tori lay on the bathroom floor and covered in the blanket from Addy's bed, her lips and eyes swollen, and her breath sounded reedy and harsh.

"Anaphylactic shock. Wasp sting," Adriana said as she ran to the first aid kit, bringing back an epi-pen and dropping the casing like breadcrumbs. Sliding across the floor on her knees, she came to a stop near Tori's legs and flipped up the blanket, exposing a naked thigh, then with a lightning-fast jab, shoved the tip of the epi-pen into the girl's leg. Tori groaned, weakly lifting a hand to push Adriana away.

"I know, honey," Addy murmured, keeping her hand and the pen firmly in place, "eight... nine... ten. Get Will," she said to me, removing the pen to massage the place on her leg, "tell him he needs to take Tori to the infirmary."

I nodded and went back outside, aware that I hadn't done a damn thing to help.

By the time we gathered for our last family group meeting an hour later, the kids were visibly shaken, but then, maybe we all were. Adriana smiled at the group. "Crappy start to our last day together, huh?"

I caught a few hesitant smiles before she went on.

"I thought maybe we should talk about it."

The room was so silent, the rumble of the air conditioner in the window was deafening. Kids stared at the floor, kids examined their hands. For all their seeming maturity at times, they really were just children, not much older than the ones who had sat in this room last week, lamenting over how mean "normal" kids could be.

Adriana caught my eye, silently pleading with me to say something, anything. "I was scared," I admitted to them. "Seeing Will run her to the infirmary made me feel… helpless." Their eyes stayed trained on the floor. "I sat there thinking not too long ago, I would have been the guy coming to the rescue, but I can't do that so I've got to do other things to help."

"Such as?" Zach challenged.

I swallowed, thinking hard. "This," I raised my hand to gesture at the circle. "Talking to y'all has to be a way of helping, right?"

"But we're not helping Tori by just sitting here. Our *talking* isn't helping her. We're all helpless, just like you were this morning, because none of us can fix it."

Reading the challenge in that, but also the pain, I smiled at him. "All right, let's pretend we could go back to this morning. Close your eyes and pretend you are in the cabin, only this time you're alone, okay?" I pushed across the circle until I was in front of Zach. The boy shifted uncomfortably in his wheelchair and pushed out a sigh of disgust, but closed his eyes anyway. "Are you there?" He nodded. "You hear Tori scream, what's the first thing you do?"

Zach swallowed hard. "I go in there and… I put a blanket around her to keep her warm. And so no one can see her."

Tim snickered, and I shot him a withering look. "Then what do you do?"

"I would get the first aid kit to remove the stinger and give her a shot… The one for allergies?"

"An epinephrine shot."

"Yeah, and then I would… I would," his face clouded and he opened his eyes. "I can't run across the field. I can't save her."

"But you just did. You knew exactly what to do to help your friend, and you did it perfectly, just like Adriana did this morning."

~~~~~

"How'd you know what to say to Zach this morning?" Adriana asked later, holding my leg above her head. "And you really ought to be on the ground, you're legs are so long, I can barely reach to stretch you out properly."

I opened my eyes and smiled at her; our eyes locked for a moment, before she blushed and looked away, nearly dropping my leg. "You okay there?"

"Just heavy. Next time, the floor."

"You know you can touch more than just my ankle, right?"

She rolled her eyes and slid one hand down my thigh and the other to my calf, increasing the stretch. "Zach," she repeated.

I put my hands behind my head and examined the timber ceiling, ignoring the feel of her warm hands against my skin. "It's what I needed to hear, I guess."

She switched to the other leg. "But he seemed so combative."

I wouldn't necessarily call it combative, more like frustrated. I'd seen Zach watch Tori in that interested way a guy does, working up his courage to talk to her. He *liked* Tori, I'd put cash money on it, and seeing her like that and him unable to help, well, that was enough to make any guy damn argumentative.

"Put my ankle on your shoulder and lean into me. I think he's combative... Addy, that won't do anything." I laughed. "Get on the table if you need to, but you've got to stretch the muscle."

She frowned, realizing what I meant would basically get her on top of me. Sometimes I loved PT.

"Usually a guy has to buy me a drink before he gets that much action."

"You don't drink."

"So you see my point."

"Fine, hand me my phone," I said, reaching for my backpack, slung over the back of my chair. "I'll give Gina a call, she'll get up here with me."

"Oh, for Christ sake!" she grunted, climbing up on the table, and placing my calf on her shoulder, she leaned toward me, stretching out my hamstring.

"It's just vulnerability that causes the combativeness—"

"I'm not combative!" she sputtered.

I grinned. "*Zach*. But maybe we should come back to you after we're done with him. That child's been through so much, and God knows some of his foster parents probably weren't all that... I mean, a kid with spina bifida isn't exactly the poster child for the easily adoptable."

She switched to the other leg and leaned into me; I practically felt her wheels turning, considering that. "Let's get a really big house and adopt kids like Zach," she said after a long moment.

I knew she was just thinking out loud and meant it about as much as if she'd just proposed we go backpacking through Europe, living off the tips from street performing—her singing, me playing the tambourine, or some such thing. I knew she didn't mean it, but I could *see* it. The two of us raising three or four kids like Carrie or Zach or Tori in a big house.

"With a wrap-around porch and lots of rooms for all the kids. And a dog, like a shepherd or a retriever," I said, thinking out loud.

The words floated on the air like sun motes, brilliant and impossible. And though nothing about those words were real, they had the power to make her visibly collapse. She put my leg down and, like a ghost, disappeared, flying out of the room and scrambling my words in her wake. The slamming door behind her shouted a final *No!*

I sat up, wishing I could take my words back.

"Everything okay?" Jill asked, sticking her head out of her office.

"No," I said and cleared my throat. "I need to go."

Jill pursed her lips together and nodded, glancing at the door Adriana just ran through before going back to her office.

~~~~~

I found her at the corral, watching the horses graze in the afternoon sun. One foot propped up on the lower fence rail and her hands folded on the upper rail, she looked like she was praying for peace, or strength, or simply trying to hang onto her sanity. "I didn't mean we'd *actually* do it," I said, "it just seemed like a nice idea."

She pushed out a shaky breath and turned away from the horses. "It is a nice idea, but no matter how much I might want to, I won't plan a life with you. It's not fair to you, and it's not fair to me."

Her words stung as if she'd slapped me. "No, what you mean is, it's not fair to Rob," I said, then turned and headed back up the asphalt path.

Smoking a cigarette, I pushed blindly along the path and ended up back at my cabin, where I found Will blasting the Bee Gees and mopping the floor. "You don't want to wait 'til the kids leave tomorrow to do that?" I shouted over the music.

He grinned at me. "I have the time now. Tomorrow I'm gonna want to do other stuff."

Between the goofy disco and his goofy grin, I turned around to leave again; I didn't have the stomach for it. But before I got to the door, he turned down the music. "What happened?"

When I didn't respond, he put the mop back in the bucket and his bed squeaked under him.

"Tori's gonna be fine. She looks like hell, but Dr. David said it was a good thing y'all knew what to do."

"I didn't do anything," I muttered.

Will stretched out on his bed, and lacing his fingers beneath his head, he stared up at the ceiling. "You thought about what you're doing week after next?" he asked as if just making conversation.

I sighed. "No." And I didn't want to think about it, either.

"Gina and I have this real nice apartment in Lubbock. A couple miles from Tech, the rent is reasonable, the units are nice, and it has a heated pool."

I grunted. I couldn't care less where they lived.

"I called the manager; they've got an accessible unit available," he said. "If y'all want it."

"Y'all?" I repeated.

He sat up. "I don't know your Momma and Daddy, so I'm not gonna say anything against them, but I do know a grown-ass man doesn't need to be living with his parents. And as for Adriana, when she got out of her car two weeks ago, I nearly wept for the girl—she looked like she'd been drug through Hell and back."

I ran my hand through my hair and kept my mouth shut, waiting for him to get to the point.

"We want y'all to move there with us."

"Your timing couldn't be any worse if you wanted it to be, bro," I said, letting out a humorless laugh. "She as much as told me she doesn't want to have anything to do with me after next week, so, thanks, but no."

He followed me out to the deck and watched me light a cigarette, my second in less than half an hour. "You love her," he said after a long minute, and I couldn't tell if it was a question or a statement of fact. "I know it's none of my business, other than I've known that girl a long time and I love her like a sister. And God knows you got your shit, but she could do worse."

"Thanks," I said flatly, blowing out a long stream of smoke.

"I just mean—"

"Look Will, you're right, I do love her. She's all I have left, and I'm afraid if I lose her, I'll lose... *them*, too. But if what she needs is for me to walk away from her, then I'm gone."

"It's as simple as that?"

"There's nothing simple in any of this," I said, examining the trees like if I looked hard enough I might see an answer out there, "but that isn't really the point. I want her to be happy, that's all I've ever wanted for her. I can't make her happy."

Will leaned back on the railing and shook his head. "Then you're a better man than I am."

Chapter 11

The next morning after the kids went home, Gina and Will invited us to go into town with them. Adriana accepted; I couldn't. I wasn't ready to be with her and pretend I wasn't still hurt. And anyway, maybe it would be better for her to spend some time with her friends, forgetting.

Instead, under a cornflower sky, I wandered the empty camp with no destination in mind and ended up at the barn. Following the sound of someone whistling, I went inside and found Uncle Wally brushing Milky Way, a brown and white paint horse.

"Hey," he said over his shoulder, "shouldn't you be in town blowing off steam?"

"Probably," I responded, rubbing a brown spot between Milky Way's eyes the way Adriana showed me that first day. "I just needed to be alone…"

"And yet you're here with me," he teased, the corners of his eyes crinkling. "I was gonna take this old girl out for a ride. You wanna join?"

"I don't ride."

I felt like I'd admitted to popping the heads off kittens the way he looked at me. "You've never ridden a horse?"

"When I was a kid, but now…" I gestured at the chair, unwilling to say more. He turned on his heel and headed to a room to the right, returning a few minutes later with a saddle blanket and a larger version of the saddles I'd seen the kids riding the last two weeks.

"This is Randi's saddle," he said, situating it on a nearby bale of hay.

My eyes narrowed, and I ignored the pounding in my chest. "Oh, I don't—"

He turned again and walked to a phone over on the wall, dialed, and waited. "Hey Chuck, come on down to the barn, would you? Luke and I are gonna go riding." He laughed at something on the other end and hung up like it was all settled.

For a long moment I watched him saddle Caramel, debating on how to bow out gracefully even as he reached under the animal's belly to secure the leather belt, but nothing sounded right in the face of his happy whistling, and when Chuck showed up looking like John Wayne in every movie I'd ever seen him, well, I knew I was going riding. I might as well cowboy up.

Wearing one of Chuck's dusty John Deere caps against the sun, Uncle Wally and I rode along the trail in silence, except for the song he kept working on, an odd arrangement of what sounded like Dave Matthews "Ants Marching" merged with the Beatles "Love Me Do." Just when I'd start to figure out where he was in one song, he'd slide into some portion of the other.

I tuned him out and concentrated on the rhythm of Caramel beneath me, which was a damn sight better than freaking out each time the saddle creaked, certain it was gonna turn over and dump me on the ground. And after a while, I kinda got into it, crossing the field behind the barn, the brilliant sun shining down on us while a cooling breeze ruffled the trees and grass.

"You're thinkin' harder than grain growin' in a drought," Uncle Wally said, breaking my train of thought and making me laugh.

"I suppose I am."

"You wanna talk about it?"

I looked at him from under the green brim of the cap. "Nah, I just need to chew on it."

He picked up the Ants Love Me song for a few measures, regarding the mountain ahead of us with serious eyes. "I've always thought of this as God's country. I've seen prettier places, but there's something special in the peacefulness of this valley."

"I spent my summers with my grandparents in Taos," I said, pulling the peace into my lungs and letting it settle in my blood. "Other kids went to the skatepark or rode their bikes around the neighborhood. I got dragged all over the mountain, performing some half-cocked ceremony my sister cooked up with a dirty bird feather and some half-remembered words our grandmother taught us."

His blue eyes flashed with amusement. "What kind of ceremonies?"

I shrugged. "Bethy somehow got it in her head that she was a shaman or medicine woman or some such thing. She'd be up on that mountain repeating words that ninety percent of the time she had wrong, but she claimed it didn't matter because it was her *intention* that was important, not the actual words themselves."

"I think I'd have to agree with that," he said and started whistling again.

Studying the mountain, I could almost see two kids up there, a boy and a girl of about ten or eleven. One crashing through the fallen branches and undergrowth, loud and rambunctious, the other graceful as a deer. Opposite sides of the same coin, created simultaneously and fused together for all perpetuity. Or so I would have thought, if I'd taken the time to consider it. But until she was gone, I simply took it for granted that Bethany and I would always be together.

"You've been here two weeks, how you feeling about it, son?"

I took the cap off my head, scratched my scalp, and replaced the sweat-stained thing again, buying time before answering. "Would it be okay if I just stay here and not go home?" I finally asked. "Wherever that is."

"You don't know where home is?"

"Is that crazy?"

We nearly got to the turnaround in the path before he cleared his throat. "When Randi was born, I wasn't sure I could handle dealing with her disease. Back then the prognosis for kids with spina bifida wasn't good. Doctors told us she might not live through her first year, and if she did... it might be better if she didn't." He glanced at me. "I didn't want my daughter to die, but I didn't know how to deal with what we would have to put up with if she lived. I'm not proud of it, but I left. For nearly a year I hitchhiked around the US working odd jobs, and hiding from everyone I knew."

My eyes widened in shock, and I looked away, unsure how to respond.

"I was ashamed of myself for running, but I couldn't stay and deal with the pain of losing my little girl. Know what I mean?"

I nodded slowly. "But she didn't die."

"No, but for a year I didn't know if she had. I worked myself ragged, refusing to stop, refusing to breathe or think, because if I did, even for a second..."

"You would go insane," I said softly, knowing exactly how that felt. "When did you go back?"

"I called Tricia on Randi's first birthday from a pay phone in Topeka, certain she would tell me to go to hell, or they had a funeral with a tiny casket and I missed it, or most likely, hang up on me. But over the sounds of a birthday party in the background, she started crying and said two words: *come home.*"

I let his words sink in while examining the valley. Everything looked childish, brightly glowing in the mid-afternoon sun—the red barn in the distance, the green of the grass and trees, the brilliant blue sky—as if a kid had just opened a brand new box of Crayolas.

Somewhere a hawk called out, somewhere a woodpecker tap-tap-tapped a tree, somewhere cicadas buzzed insistently while the sun baked my back and a trickle of sweat escaped Chuck's cap and slid down my neck. The scent of warm pine and sweet horse flesh filled my nose, and on the buckskin horse, I finally relaxed, letting the valley whisper to me.

Uncle Wally let out a soft sigh of pleasure. "Every day you have to decide to keep moving forward, and some days you have to make yourself do it every single second, but eventually you will be able to look back and feel the distance between where you are and where you were."

~~~~~

By ten o'clock that night, Will and the girls still weren't back yet, and I was antsy. In the twenty-four hours since I left Addy leaning on the fence looking lost, we hadn't said two words to each other. My pride said I needed to wait for her to come talk to me; my heart said just suck it up and tell her... *something.*

One of the downsides to growing up in a house of women was I never saw my dad in the doghouse, trying to draw out my mom. Instead, he'd show up on Friday and we'd have two days of forced, happy perfection before he left again. It wasn't until we put Bethany in the ground that I heard Mom yell at him, and then it was like she'd broke the seal and couldn't stop.

I didn't want that for Adriana and me. And even if a week from today she dropped me off in Artesia and never saw me again, I did not want her to think back on these three weeks and remember pained silences and carefully guarded glances. I wanted her to remember the first time I drove again, scared as hell, but grateful she was the one beside me. That thunderstorm in Roswell when I held her tight. Swimming the other morning.

I'd changed so much in just two weeks, and while I could say some of that had to do with Carrie and Zach, Gina and Will, Uncle Wally... most of it had to do with her.

I took a long slug of the Magic Hat in my hand—Benji from cabin 5 and Louise, one of the nurses, ran into town earlier today to pick up what had to be twenty cases of beer—and decided to go to bed. I wasn't in any mood to watch these drunken fools flirt and make out tonight only to end up taking the long walk of shame back to their own beds in the morning.

And maybe the lights to our cabin would be blazing by the time I got over there.

They weren't.

Sighing, I flipped on the lights and stripped down to my boxers before going into the bathroom to brush my teeth. If it had occurred to me to grab it, I would've tossed my dog-eared copy of *Lonesome Dove* in my duffel.

I must've been fifteen the first time I took that cattle drive from Texas to Montana with Gus and Call, and had probably done it a hundred times since.

Rinsing my toothbrush under the water, I heard the cabin door slam. "Luke," Will shouted, "LUKE!"

"What?" I asked into my towel, drying my mouth as I left the bathroom.

He crossed the floor in long strides, his jaw flexing. "I swear we were only trying to help her, but she..." It took me about half a microsecond to understand what he meant, before shoving my towel at him to go next door.

Curled up on the floor in a tight ball, Adriana's hands were pressed to ears, her eyes screwed shut, but her mouth was wide open, releasing the heart-wrenching wail of deep mourning. Beside her, Gina held a wet washcloth as if she wasn't completely sure what to do with it in the face of so much grief.

"I'm sorry," she said when she saw me.

"Just go," I growled, launching myself across the floor to sit beside Adriana. "Addy, look at me," I said, ignoring the panic rising in my throat. I made my voice calm. "Come on, I'm right here. Look at me."

"Luke, you've got to get him out," she clawed at my chest; wherever she was, she wasn't here with me. "Please help him."

"Addy, you have to look at me."

"He's under the car! Rob is *under* the car."

I pulled her to me, wrapping my arms around her and letting her bury her face in my chest. With a thunderous *crack*, my chest fractured, and I was there again.

The rain was falling on Rob's car, his wipers valiantly working to keep the windshield clear. Garth was on the radio and Bethany's face lit by headlights when I turned to ask her, for the love of God, to please stop that caterwauling.

Bright lights illuminated her and suddenly the night was filled with sound. Rubber squealing on asphalt. Metal cleaving metal. Glass shattering. Voices screaming in terror.

Then…

Nothing.

I pulled Adriana closer, fighting gravity as it tossed us end over end, each rotation taking simultaneous seconds and an eternity until finally time slowed.

Stopped.

"That's why his casket was closed," Adriana said. "He was *obliterated*."

Like a wounded animal, a ragged howl tore from her throat and tears finally fell, wet and hot and originating from the deep aching in her splintered heart.

She sobbed, she screamed, and I hung on to her with all my strength, willing it to be enough. Willing the soft words I whispered in her ear to filter past the pain and somehow begin to heal her. And when she was finally empty, I pulled her even closer, hoping my closeness could somehow protect her from the images in her head.

"He's never coming back, is he?" she whispered, her voice hoarse and raw.

I wiped away tears from her face. "No, he isn't."

She looked at me with puffy, red eyes, a rivulet of mucus beneath her nose, searching for the courage to make that somehow okay. And the thing was, I knew I didn't have it—that courage. Not for me, not for her, and feeling like a coward, I looked away.

"Addy, could we get off the floor? This concrete is killing my back."

Trembling, she pulled away. "Where'd Gina go?"

"Next door, hiding, I think," I said, getting back into my chair. "I'll go get her."

"Don't. I don't want to be alone…" her voice cracked. "Please stay with me."

"Okay," I whispered, examining the spot we just vacated. "But I need to lie down a minute…" Thanks to sitting on the cold floor in my boxers, every muscle in my body was clenched as if I'd just spent the last half an hour naked in a snow drift, rather than a concrete floor in the middle of summer. I needed an electric blanket, a hot cup of cocoa, a steaming shower, but I went to the unmade mattress next to Adriana's, prepared to stretch on it and think of tropical beaches.

Except for the wet sound of her sniffles punctuating the air, she watched me in silence, and just as I put on the brakes, she cleared her throat. "Wait." She went to her duffel and pulled out an oversized black sweatshirt. "This should fit you... I pilfered it from my brother's drawer years ago."

"Thank you," I said, slipping it on

Then she went to her bed and pulled back the sheets, a hesitant, almost apologetic smile on her face. "The idea of you lying on that mattress is making my skin crawl. Lie here. It's cleaner, and I..."

"Thanks," I said again, and transferred to her bed. From between her sheets, I watched her take a tee and pair of plaid boxers from her bag—Rob's boxers, I noted.

"I'll be right back," she whispered and disappeared into the bathroom with the clothes and her toothbrush.

In moments she returned, leaving the light in there on, and switching off the overhead ones, then stopped next to me, wavering. "Do you mind?" she said, her voice thick. But before I opened my mouth, she slid in next to me.

I wrapped my arms around her, wishing I could somehow keep her from thinking about the images that had to be running through her mind right now. I couldn't think about that night without seeing Bethy's broken skull against the asphalt road, the rain running her and Rob's blood together, and the glass scattered around her like diamonds.

"I wanted to know what happened," she whispered. "I thought if I knew, I could understand or let go somehow, but now... Christ, how do I live with knowing how they died?"

I pushed a strand of hair away from her face. "Maybe you weren't ready to remember until now."

"I don't think I'm ready now."

"Yes, you are. And you don't have to go through this alone. You have Gina and Will and Uncle Wally. And me."

She bit her lip and buried her face in my chest, breathing slowly to keep her tears under control.

"Addy, look at me." When she did, I smiled. "Do you remember Halloween when we went to Stonehenge?"

She and Rob were Guinevere and Lancelot. Not terribly imaginative, but God she took my breath away that night!

Bethany and I dressed up as Superman and Lois Lane. She looked dashing in blue tights and padded muscles, but in a cheap Halloween wig, one of her skirts and bra—stuffed with half a drawer of socks—guys kept hitting on me at the Delta Sig party.

Somewhere around one in the morning, we ended up at the Stonehenge replica on Odessa's campus, and Rob and I scaled to the top of one monument, then stood up there daring Bethany and Adriana to join us.

"Bethany was so angry at you for ruining her favorite silk blouse," she said, sniffling. "That thing was so filthy, even the dry cleaners wouldn't take it."

I laughed softly. "The skirt didn't fare much better, but you try climbing a two-story rock in a miniskirt and stiletto heels."

"See, I know better, that's why I stayed firmly on the ground."

"And here I thought you were just scared."

She nudged me. "I wasn't scared, I didn't want to mess up that gorgeous costume."

"Rob had no problem with it."

"Not when you were up there calling him a wuss. You left him no choice."

"Says the girl who was firmly on the ground," I teased.

"Says the girl wearing a velvet and silk embroidered dress that weighed ten pounds and brushed the ground," she shot back.

Late into the night we laughed and told stories, like the time Bethy found a baby rabbit on her way to class one morning, its eye bleeding from an animal attack. She scooped the thing up, wrapped it in her hoodie and ran back to the dorm, calling Rob on his cell.

Adriana laughed. "Bethany kept saying to him, 'but you're *pre-med*, how can you not help her?' "

"He felt really bad about that, too. Kept putting Visine in its eye while telling her they ought to take it to a vet, but she didn't want to let it out of her sight."

"Until it was finally well enough to give to Professor Gladwell's daughter. That thing chewed holes in my favorite tops," she said without venom.

I pushed out a deep breath. "Addy, that's how we live with it. By remembering them for how they lived, not how they died."

She curled into me, lying still and close for a while. "Why did you always call her Bethy?"

I smiled in the darkness. "When we were little I couldn't say her name. Bethy just stuck."

"Hmm... then why don't you call me Adriana?"

Ah, the sixty-four thousand dollar question, but one that I couldn't answer. Not now, and God willing, not ever. I leaned over and kissed her forehead. "Good night, Addy. We'll talk more in the morning."

I listened to her breathing for long minutes, and just when I thought she was asleep, she looked up at me. "I'm sorry about yesterday," she whispered. "I didn't mean what I said, I just—"

"I know," I told her and pulled her even closer, letting the weight of her anchor me. And there, with her wrapped in my arms, I had the first real night's sleep since the accident. It almost seemed like a miracle.

~~~~~

It took me a long minute to remember where I was or even realize I was awake. Almost afraid to believe what I saw when I opened my eyes, I mentally inventoried the sensations: my hand in her hair; the soft, even whisper of her breath against my neck; her arm tossed across my chest, the other buried between my body and hers; our legs tangled beneath the sheets.

I took a deep breath, her warm scent invading my brain, clouding rather than clearing it.

A lifetime ago I woke and found her in my bed. It wasn't long after she and Rob started dating, but still early enough that I still called her Adriana and held onto some shred of hope that maybe I had a chance with her.

She showed up at our dorm room early one evening, her backpack slung over one shoulder for a study date. Biology, she told me without the slightest trace of irony. Rob still hadn't gotten in from waiting tables at the Olive Garden, and when I let her in, I filled my lungs with her as she walked past me. She dropped her bag on his bed and sat nervously, perhaps thinking the two of us had never been alone before. It's what I was thinking, anyway.

"Can I get you anything?" I asked, gesturing at our mini-fridge. There wasn't much in it; I'd have to run down to the vending machine if she said yes, wasting precious seconds with her, but my momma raised me right.

She shook her head and stood up, her eyes zeroed in on a photo I kept on my desk of Granpa, Shi'nali, Bethy, and me taken at their house. It was the last summer we spent with them before Granpa died.

"Your grandparents?" she asked, lifting the frame.

"My dad's parents."

Running a finger over the glass, she studied the faces. "Y'all kind of look like her. It's the eyes, I think. They're very wise."

"I always thought it was the high Navajo cheekbones," I joked.

She looked at me, a slight smile playing over her lips. "That, too."

In that moment I could've believed given time she might want me. But just as I opened my mouth to respond, Rob opened the door, lighting her eyes and stabbing my heart.

I left them and went drinking. A lot. And picked up this girl that I wouldn't exactly call a friend, but Cyndi and I were definitely *friendly*. Somewhere around two in the morning and in the middle of a raging thunderstorm, I slipped out of Cyndi's bed, still wasted, and went back to mine, dropping every stitch of drenched clothing between my door and bed.

I have no idea what Adriana was doing there, in *my* bed instead of Rob's, but I woke with her draped across me, very much like she was now. Only that time she wasn't dreaming contently, she was half-asleep and stroking a throbbing erection. Maybe I thought I was dreaming, maybe I thought she was Cyndi, maybe it was all the beer from the night before, but I pulled her to me, burying my face in her neck, needing her so badly, I didn't even care Rob was snoring in his bed mere feet away.

Except she whispered a single word that catapulted me out of my bed and changed everything between us: *Rob*. Like a choice made, like a door slamming shut, it echoed inside my brain for days, during which I spent a *lot* of time in Cyndi's room, screwing her with a single-minded desperation that left her sore and left me feeling worse because I couldn't forget what it felt like when Adriana touched me.

After that, when I finally found the courage to talk to her again, she was always Addy to me. It was just another way to keep her at arms' length.

She sighed in her sleep now, content, comfortable. Maybe she was right, maybe she did need to know what happened to Bethy and Rob. I pulled her closer and wrapped a strand of silky hair around my fingers, twirling it, and once again fighting the math. It was early Sunday morning and we had just six days left. Six days, and then…

Will was right about one thing, going back home would essentially be giving up. Moving in with Mom and getting a minimum wage job at the Sac'N'Sav like I was fifteen again would be the same as admitting defeat. This time I wouldn't be working to buy a truck, I'd be working to give me something to do to get out of the house. Ringing up groceries.

God, just put me on Prozac now.

I glanced at Adriana, tucked against me as if she were afraid to let go. Even the way her arm was thrown across my chest and her legs were knotted with mine, it was almost as if she needed as much contact as she could get, just to know she was safe.

Even though I protested coming to camp with a childish adamancy that now embarrassed me, after the last two weeks, God, I couldn't imagine her dropping me off at home next week and driving away and never seeing her again. I pushed out a deep breath and rested my chin on Adriana's head, breathing her shampoo.

What I needed was a plan, something to lay out in front of her so she could examine it from every angle, because I was afraid, deeply afraid, that if I just left it to her, she'd keep treading water. Will had given me the beginnings of one, though, and it was pretty good.

Adriana moaned softly, her eyes fluttering open, and when she looked up at me, the smile that reached her eyes was so serene, my heart nearly stopped in my chest.

"Hey," I said softly.

"Hi," she responded, then seemingly ran an inventory of her own, because the serenity drained from her, and she pulled away. Embarrassed.

"Where are you going?"

"We should get ready for breakfast," she said, her eyes bouncing around the room. "And I don't want to keep Gina from her cosmetics; that girl's rabid about her morning routine. In fact, you know she—"

"Gina can wait. What's up?"

"Nothing," she lied, shutting down. "I—"

I sat up and tossed the covers off my legs, preparing to transfer to my chair, annoyed. "Look, I get it. You've been closed off for so long it's hard to open up again, but I know when you're lying to me to stay locked up. I just would've thought that after last night, I might've gotten you back. The real you."

"But I..." she bit her lip, fighting tears. "God, I make the ugly cry look not so bad, and last night's was downright repulsive. Didn't I, aren't you—?"

I traced a line along her jaw, the velvet warmth of her skin nearly overwhelming. "So you nearly washed us away. It takes more than a few tears and a little snot to scare me away."

"That wasn't a *little* snot."

I smiled, wishing I could pull her back to me. Instead, I said the first thing that came to mind. "I know you said you wouldn't take that long-ass ride again, but what do you say we get out of here for a little while? Go see about getting hand controls put on my truck?"

She pulled on her bottom lip, hesitant. "You can't do that from here?"

I shrugged. "Yes, but let's go anyway."

"Yeah. Okay," she whispered, after a moment. "Just let me take a shower first."

~~~~~

Traffic was heavy, normal for a Sunday morning—Ruidoso was clearing out for Monday's workday. Back in her car, this time the music played at a decent level, a bag of Cheetos between us for breakfast, and in the back seat next to my chair, a small bag we borrowed from Gina with a change of clothes each and our toothbrushes. Beside me, Adriana concentrated on the road while worrying her bottom lip with a finger, a sure sign that she was lost in thought. I let her process whatever she was thinking about—no doubt what she remembered last night—and while part of me wanted her to talk to me about it, I figured if she wanted to, she would.

I watched the landscape fly past my window, and the farther she drove, the more I concentrated on fighting Bethany's voice calling me.

Just a few miles from the house, in the weeks between rehab and camp, I spent nearly every day out there. Every night I stuck two water bottles in the freezer, and every morning I pushed myself to her grave, my backpack loaded with the bottles, my iPod, sunscreen, and a spray bottle fan picked up on a trip to Six Flags when we were ten.

I didn't want to take Adriana out there. After last night it seemed wholly unfair to her, but the closer we got, the louder Bethy's voice shouted in my head until I wanted to press my hands to my ears to drown it out. Half a mile before the turn to my house, I turned down the music, cleared my throat, and asked her to take a right at the next intersection. "I need to see Bethy," I said, the words painful.

She kept her eyes fixed on the road, her body so still for a moment I wasn't sure she heard me, but she turned on her blinker and made the turn. "You'll have to give me directions," she said. "Last time I could barely remember my own name, much less the road my father took."

~~~~~

Under the baking sun I lay on the parched grass beneath her stone. A dove cooed in a nearby stunted tree. The wind blew hot and dry across our bodies. Adriana laced her fingers with mine as we watched wispy white clouds pass over a cerulean sky.

"I think I understand why you freaked out the other day during PT," I told her after what seemed an eternity. "I think part of you is angry at me for being alive when Rob isn't."

"Luke…"

I rose up on one elbow to look at her. "I saw you at his funeral, and if you thought for half a second they would have left you there, you would've been buried with him. Right?"

"No," she lied, but the truth of it was written all over her.

"It's okay, I get it. But Adriana, you know I'm here for you for as long as you need me, right?"

She sat up, pulling her hand away, and picked a handful of grass, sorting through it, examining each piece before letting it fly away in the hot breeze, while I studied the clouds above, waiting. Finally, she drew a shaky breath. "You said last night I had Gina and Will and you, and I do… now. But what happens next Sunday when I'm sitting back in my parent's house? I can't go forward, and I can't go back, which leaves me where?"

I chewed my lip, keeping my eyes on the clouds. "You start over in a new place."

"Alone," she said flatly.

"No… What if… what if we got an apartment. Jobs. Go somewhere new."

"Where?"

"Lubbock," I said, drawing the word out like it was a question.

She looked at me, her expression closed and giving absolutely nothing away. "And you're thinking we'll just pack up and go there to, what? Move in together?"

I sat up. "I can't imagine moving on either, I'm not even sure I know how. But I've felt more alive in the last two weeks with you than I have in *months*, and I—"

"It's the kids," she insisted, her voice shaky with panic. "They're the reason you feel this way."

"They're part of it," I admitted, "but if you think they're the only reason, we haven't been at the same camp. Addy, this isn't some fantasy idea of forever, I'm just asking for right now. You. Me. A little wheelchair accessible apartment... And Will said their complex has some nice ones—"

"You've talked to Will about this?"

I nodded. "The other night. After the corral."

She closed her eyes and tugged at her lip. "Let me think about it. I'm not saying no, I just need some time, okay?"

Chapter 12

Igrew up in a shrinking ranch-style house. When I was little it seemed large enough to hold all my dreams, but either my dreams got too big or the house got too small, because I had them stuffed in every corner, all the way to the rafters until there wasn't room to move. And now, staring at the white bricks with faded, peeling green trim, I had the distinct feeling I might not fit inside.

Adriana turned off the engine and reached for the handle, but I put one hand on her thigh, stilling her. "Thanks for being here. I'm still not sure how to do this. With them."

Her lips curled into a knowing smile, and she glanced at the large tree in the front yard. Dozens of once-bright birdhouses were nailed to it, each painted in a different theme—fish birdhouses and polka-dot ones, Victorian houses and monochromatic ones—some childish, others artistic and worthy of any store. "I wanted to ask you about those last time I was here, but it didn't seem like the right time."

"My favorite," I said, focusing on them, "is the one with the cat face. Bethy had some wickedly dark humor." At that moment a bird flew out, escaping the cat's gaping mouth.

"Bethany painted all these?"

"Built most of them, too. Had Dad teach her how when we were little. Mom hated that and insisted Bethy only work on them when Dad was home, so when he was on the road made for some *long* weeks."

She smiled, possibly imaging her friend with a jigsaw or paintbrush. It's what ran through my mind as a brown wren disappeared inside the yellow sunflower-shaped one.

"The wrong epitaph was put on Bethy's stone," I told her, the truth burning to escape since I first saw the granite. "It's not *bad*, it's just wrong."

"What should it've been?"

"'Keep me in your heart. I'll stay there forever.' It's A.A. Milne and…"

"And it's perfect," she whispered.

I wanted to touch her again, pull her close and bury my nose in her hair, breathing her perfume. My fingertips itched with desire to feel her skin, but at that moment, a roaring black Ram pulled in behind Adriana's car. The truck horn played the first few chords of "Dixie," announcing its arrival and shattering the moment.

Mom and Dad opened the green front door, and we got swept into a flurry of hugs. Ignoring the tightness in my chest, I focused on Adriana hugging my mom, hugging my dad, shaking hands with Daryl Johnson when my dad introduced them. "Daryl owns the Dodge dealership you passed on the way into town," Dad told her. "When Luke called this morning to say y'all were coming, Anna invited him to lunch after church."

I patted my lap, letting Pender, Bethany's awesome but unbelievably ugly dog, jump up. God only knew where she found him—covered in ticks and with an awful case of mange—she made me borrow Ty Campbell's truck and swore she'd keep quiet about my sneaking out and getting drunk on tequila shots the weekend before with Ty if I took them to the vet.

"She told me we'd be having brisket," Daryl said to Adriana, "it's her specialty, so I couldn't very well turn her down." He winked at Mom and turned to me. "I'm glad you finally decided to take me up on that offer to retrofit your truck."

"Why don't we go inside," Mom said in a tense voice, "we can discuss this over lunch." She turned on her scratched patent leather heel, linking her arm through Dad's elbow and went inside, Daryl close behind.

Adriana placed a hand on my shoulder. "She didn't sound too happy about this."

I shrugged, watching my mother. She looked different, less polished somehow. For as long as I could remember, Mom dyed her hair every sixth Saturday morning—Nice'N'Easy Natural Medium Auburn number 111—I know because when I bagged at the Sac'N'Sav, it was my job to buy it for her. But it didn't look like she'd coated her hair with that nasty-smelling red-brown crap since the funeral. And her always carefully applied makeup looked like it had been done with a shaky, heavy hand. Okay, so I don't know much about that stuff, but I know what my Momma looks like, and she just looked *wrong*. Mousy and depressed, rather than the stylish, sophisticated woman my buddies used to call a MILF. As she stepped inside the house, I couldn't decide which was worse.

~~~~~

"I've been using the Wells-Engberg CP-200 Right Angle Control," I dictated over lunch for Daryl who carefully wrote it all down in a small, grubby notebook he kept in a clean shirt pocket. "And a steering grip would be helpful."

Daryl nodded, reading what he had written down.

"Daryl and I have known each other since high school," Dad said to Adriana. "You're looking at two of the stars of the Artesia football team."

"Go Bulldogs!" Daryl said, lifting his beer bottle to his mouth before turning to me. "Your daddy is the only reason I wasn't cleaning my shotgun every time you stopped by the house to pick up Candice," he said, clapping a big hand on my shoulder.

"Old girlfriend?" Adriana asked, cutting off a piece of brisket.

I shifted in my chair. "We went out a few times," I said diplomatically, but Candice was the reason Dad took ten minutes out of a weekend to hand me a box of condoms and explain in no uncertain terms I was not to get a girl pregnant.

"A *few* times? This boy cleaned out our fridge two, three times a week all by himself."

"Better yours, than ours," Dad said with a laugh.

"I'm sorry, but I have to ask," Mom interrupted, "why are you doing this?"

"Doing what?" Dad asked.

She waved a hand at Daryl.

"So I can drive after I get home," I said, a forkful of beans hovering in front of my mouth.

"No, I meant, why are you doing this to the truck?"

"As opposed to?"

Mom dropped her eyes and smoothed out invisible wrinkles in the tablecloth. "I thought you could drive the minivan, and we'll trade in the truck."

"I'm not driving the minivan. *Your* minivan."

"But, honey, a truck isn't really conducive to your new… lifestyle."

"My lifestyle?" I asked, incredulous. "This is not a lifestyle, this is my *life*, and I'm not going to give up who I was just because I'm in a chair."

"Honey, I just thought it would be easier—"

"Easier?" I said, struggling not to shout. "You think it would be easier to drive around a beat-up piece of—"

"Son, I think what your momma is trying to say—" Dad interrupted.

"Oh, I know exactly what she is trying to say, and it's bullsh—"

"Luke, let's show her," Adriana said, putting her hand on my arm. "Let's go to the garage, and you can show her that it's no big deal transferring in and out of the truck."

The shock of her hand's warmth pulled my attention from my parents, and I met her eyes, reading the barely suppressed frustration in hers, just as I knew she could read it in mine. I pushed away from the table.

Whether or not I could physically get in and out of the truck wasn't a question in my mind; whether or not I ought to perform like a child, however, was beneath my dignity. I wasn't gonna give up my truck, and as I rolled down the ramp into the garage, that resolve grew even stronger.

Even with gray dust dulling her blue shine, she was beautiful, but more importantly, she was *mine*. When everything you've ever had was a cast-off or hand-me-down, that's a big deal. Not that I'm not grateful for all the sacrifices my parents made when we were growing up. I'm certain Dad would've preferred being at home than on the road five days out of the week, busting his ass to make it back in time to see Bethy cheer at a Friday night game. I know he would've rather watched my swim meets in person, instead of on the TV, Mom or Bethy's jerky camera work making him slightly nauseous.

And I know for a fact Mom wanted to stay home with us. I once heard her crying to Grandma O'Neal on the phone that this wasn't what she had in mind: a paycheck away from food stamps; buying clothes for her kids at the Goodwill and praying that none of the kids at school would realize that our clothes were once theirs; working thirty-five hours a week for a guy too cheap to give her those extra five hours and, therefore, health benefits, but constantly worried that we wouldn't make it home from school, or would burn the house down before she came home.

All she wanted was to bake cookies for her kids' after school snack and fried chicken for her husband's dinner.

I was twelve, and it broke my heart. Then and there I determined to not ask for another thing, and starting that summer, I mowed hundreds of lawns, raked thousands of leaves, babysat for the kids at church, bussed tables, and bagged groceries, anything anyone was willing to pay me for. Before I went off to college, I walked into Johnson Dodge with my checkbook shoved in my back pocket and bought the used truck outright.

Mom asking me to give it up was like asking me to erase all the dreams and sacrifices I made to purchase it myself.

I pushed the unlock button on the key fob, then positioned myself in the open truck door, using the steering wheel as leverage, lifted myself up to the seat, and reached back to my chair, popped it closed to flip behind the passenger seat. And sitting there, the urge to start the engine and ask Adriana to go for a ride was so strong, I had to bite my bottom lip to keep from saying anything.

Daryl cleared his throat and took his grimy notebook back out of his shirt pocket. "And you want this hand control mounted to the left of the steering wheel?"

~~~~~

That night in bed, my fingers stroked Pender's wiry fur, and I stared at my ceiling, orange from the street lamp outside, trying not to think of Adriana on the couch in the living room. Before she went to bed, Mom brought out two quilts and a blanket, apologizing that it wasn't terribly comfortable, but it was the only place to sleep. In the air hung the unspoken words that there was another bed, but even if Mom or Dad were ready for anyone to enter Bethany's room and take up residence there, from the look on Addy's face she'd rather stay in the living room.

But when I heard her soft tiptoe down the hall, I let the dog jump off the bed first and transferred to my chair. Bethy's room was exactly the same as the day we left for college with enormous orange, black, and white Homecoming mums hung on the walls next to shelves of cheerleading trophies and intricate birdhouses—significantly more beautiful than the ones outside.

Adriana stood at the white dresser, examining ticket stubs from *The Pirates of the Caribbean* and a high school production of *Fiddler on the Roof* shoved into the mirror's frame. We went to see them together, just the two of us—the first a birthday present to ourselves, the second we saw because her boyfriend at the time was Tevye. The dresser held two photographs, one of us at eight years old, each proudly holding fishing poles and matching small green and gold fish. The second was taken when we were sixteen at a swim meet. The blue water sparkled behind us, and Bethany leaned into my naked chest, my arm wrapped around her shoulders. Adriana held that one in her hands, staring at it like maybe if she looked at it long enough, she could will Bethy back into existence. Lord knew I had.

"No one's supposed to be in here," I whispered, causing her to jump and put down the frame with too much force.

"Sorry. I know I shouldn't be, but I... Sorry."

Embarrassed, she started for the door, but I met her in the middle, blocking the way. "I said no one was supposed to be in here, I didn't say no one ever came." I went to the dresser and picked up the picture she just put down. "I hated this haircut on her."

"It's cute. Not many girls can pull off a pixie cut and look that good," she said, defending her friend.

"That's why I hated it. As if I didn't have enough friends telling me how cute my sister was..." I ran a finger down the glass, touching Bethy's cheek. "This was taken at a Carlsbad meet sophomore year. Bethy was supposed to be at some cheerleading thing, and I'd never swum without her there, I didn't know if I could. She was my good luck charm, you know?"

Adriana nodded, taking a seat on the bed, and petting the dog's head when he jumped up next to her. "Yeah. And the loudest damn one, too. I used to walk out of those meets with my head ringing, loud as she was."

I laughed softly and put the picture back. "On that day, she skipped the cheerleading thing and got a friend to drive her to the meet. Caught so much trouble for that too, but she said she knew I needed her there, so where else would she be?"

Adriana smiled but said nothing, letting her eyes bounce around the room. After a long moment, she looked at me. "Would it sound crazy if I thought she was in here, and I came to check?"

I shook my head. I could still smell her in here, and sometimes, before I went to camp, I'd swear I could hear her CDs playing softly late at night. A few times I snuck down the hallway thinking maybe I'd find her, as if all this time she was in here and no one thought to look.

"It's not crazy," I said. My voice cracked at the admission, and I wiped at my eyes with a thumb and forefinger. "Hey, do you want to come back to my room? The bed is small, but it's more comfortable than the couch, and—"

"In your parents' house?" she asked with a surprised laugh.

Chagrined at her response, I turned back to the photograph. I just wanted to hold Adriana, bury my nose in her hair and let the warmth of her battle the cold ghosts. "I'm not suggesting anything more than sleeping."

"I know, but I would feel too weird," she said standing up to go back to the couch. "It seems disrespectful of your parents, but... thanks anyway."

"Right, well... Good night, Adriana."

"You, too," she whispered and disappeared down the hall, that traitor Pender on her heels.

~~~~~

Still in my pajama pants, I went to the kitchen the next morning where my parents sat at the table, drinking coffee in silence that weighed more than a wish to not wake the girl on their couch.

"Morning," I said, pouring myself a cup of coffee.

"Son," Dad replied over the top of his mug. He had on a pair of pressed jeans, the creases razor sharp, a blue shirt with gray pearl snaps, his favorite pair of boots, and on the table sat his tan Stetson. Dad was going to the warehouse to pick up another load. When he spent full days on the road, he claimed he didn't mind riding around in ratty old clothes, but going to the company headquarters meant dressing for success. Getting the cushy routes that allowed seeing his family every weekend rather than once every three weeks, meant impressing the big wigs with professionalism.

"You want some breakfast before I go to work?" Mom asked.

"Nah, I'll get it," I told her, joining them at the table.

Dad put down his mug, turning it between his hands, his eyes on the liquid swirling in the cup. "Your mom and I have been talking about when you get back. We're gonna take out a second mortgage to connect the bathroom and your room. Make it more accessible. Maybe the kitchen, too, if there's enough money. "

When Mom shifted uncomfortably in her seat, I ran his words through my mind again. "You want to turn Bethany's room into mine." It was the only way to connect the two, since mine was on the other side of the hall.

"It'll make it easier on you," he said with one of his wide grins that somehow managed to make my stomach turn over.

On the couch Adriana sighed in her sleep, soft and content, and I looked through the archway at her. "I'm not moving back here," I told them, my eyes lingering over her sleeping face. I didn't know if she'd agree to live with me, but I couldn't let them destroy Bethy's room. Not that it needed to stay a shrine to her, but I still needed to go in there sometimes and remember my sister. And I knew Mom did.

"Where're you gonna go? You can't go back to school without that scholarship, and..."

"Hoyt," Mom warned, straightening up to her full height and looking me in the eye for the first time in I don't even know how long. "What do you want to do, honey?"

I looked past her, once more focusing on the girl and dog on the couch, curled up together, Pender's wheezing snore filling the air. "I don't know, but I'll be taking Pender with me." I turned back to them, for a moment, letting the pain in their eyes actually past the wall I'd carefully erected since the night Bethany died.

Pushing out a deep breath, I searched for words while studying the kitchen that for as long as I could remember was exactly the same—clean but shabby, old but functional. And for as long as I could remember, Mom wanted to redo it, but often said with a resigned sigh, *maybe someday.* She was willing to do it for me, but not for herself.

"Two of the counselors live in a complex in Lubbock with accessible apartments, and I think I'm gonna see about moving up there."

"You'll have a roommate?" she asked.

"Maybe." I kept my voice neutral. "I'll know more by next Saturday."

Dad leaned back in his chair, balancing on the back two legs in the way that drove Mom crazy and scratched his head. I forced my mouth to stay shut; I wasn't sixteen anymore, and he didn't have a whole lot to say in what I did, but that didn't mean I had to be an asshole about it. "I just don't like the idea of you out there by yourself. Not now that..." He closed his eyes, for the first time in months letting that ridiculous goofy grin slip and showing his true grief. "I just thought we'd be doing something to help you. It's not like you have a whole lot of options when it comes to your... you know," he waved a hand at my chair and averted his eyes.

"Dad," I said, ignoring that, "I can't..."

My first reaction to coming back to town yesterday was going to see Bethany, and if I came back here, I was afraid I'd go right back to where I was before. I might just end up spending full days lying on her plot, picturing her down below in the sleek white coffin, rotting, and hating that she hadn't been cremated like she once told me she wanted to be. But I never told Mom and Dad, and their beliefs wouldn't have let them do anything but bury her. And so I had watched Dad and Uncle Clay, my cousins Adam and Joe, Ty Campbell from high school, and Granpa O'Neal support Bethy's box on their shoulders.

My own shoulder ached for the weight of her, and for the first time I understood exactly what crippled truly meant.

"If I come back here, I'll just end up lost again."

Mom's chin quivered, fighting tears as she reached for my hand. "Then you can't come back here. I couldn't stand it if you were lost, too."

Without warning, Dad's chair scraped across the linoleum so loudly, I glanced at Adriana to see if it woke her. It didn't, but Pender wiggled out from under her hand and came into the kitchen, yawning.

"I've got to get to work," Dad said and chastely kissed his wife. "I'll see you in a week, son." And with that, he disappeared through the garage door. A moment later we heard his sleeper cab roar to life.

Mom stood up and wiped her eyes. "I should get going, too." She straightened her somber navy blue skirt and oversized jacket that looked like it had come off a rack at the Goodwill—it probably had—and kissed my temple, lingering there for almost a moment too long. "Be safe, baby," she whispered in my ear and walked away, her heels clicking on the cheap tiles.

I stayed at the table, staring into my mug until the coffee grew cold, and Pender began whining at me for his breakfast. He was spoiled, really. Bethany got him started on this all-natural, organic, hormone-free dry dog food, combined in equal portions with *fois gras*—or may as well have been for all the fancy crap in it—warmed in the microwave. And while preparing the canine cuisine, I grumbled to Bethy that it really was ridiculous to spend this much time creating what amounted to a five-star meal for a dog known to eat his own shit, while promising Pender when we got that pad together, he'd be partaking in low-brow junk like any self-respecting bachelor.

He sat watching me with his bulgy brown eyes and breathing noisily with that squished snout. Although it was purely speculative, I maintained he was the product of an amorous dachshund getting busy with a pug.

He gulped down the food with all the manners of a coyote over a deer, then set in to licking the bowl, pushing it across the floor with a loud scraping sound. When Adriana moaned on the couch though, his head shot up at the sound, and he took three bounding leaps toward the living room before turning back to look at me, a hopeful grin on his face.

"You really are an attention whore, aren't you?" I whispered to him.

He sat down, patiently waiting, but his little butt wiggled in anticipation, giving him away. I checked my watch. It was nearly nine o'clock, and Adriana wanted to be on the road in fifteen minutes, which we were gonna miss, but glancing at her breathing heavily in deep sleep, she needed the rest.

"In a minute, after you help me make her breakfast," I told him and went to the fridge for eggs and milk.

Ten minutes and a phone call to Tricia later, I had a stack of French toast in the warm oven and a pretty decent burn on my forearm that I was trying to ignore. "All right, go wake her up, boy," I said over my shoulder and grinned when he took off for the couch. From the archway, I listened to her giggle as his wet tongue lapped her face, remembering a time when I used to send him in to wake my sister after early-morning workouts. It really was one of his best tricks.

"Pender, stop. Your breath stinks," she laughed, pushing his face gently away and sitting up.

The dog hopped down, proud of himself, and trotted to me, accepting my pat on his head. "Good boy," I said just loud enough for him to hear, then turned to her. "French toast and coffee are ready."

She glanced at the clock on the cable box. "We should be getting on the road, we're gonna be late as it is, and—"

"And I already called to let them know why we're running late. Tricia said it's fine, not to worry, and you hear one of Uncle Wally's speeches, you've heard them all."

She stood up and started folding my grandmother's quilt. "You called and told them we'd be late cause I was *sleeping?*"

I grinned. "I didn't want her to worry. You know how she is."

"But you told her I was sleeping. Like a lazy bum. Like… like…"

"Like Sleeping Beauty," I supplied. "Pender and I played Rock, Paper, Scissors to see which of us would get to wake the sleeping princess with a kiss."

She laughed. "I guess he won, huh?"

"Yeah, but that dog cheats. It's hard to tell his 'rock' from his 'paper' so I have to take him at his word. Now, are you hungry?"

Her smile lit her eyes. "I am."

Chapter 13

By the time we arrived at camp, the party was in full swing. Six-foot tables covered the basketball court, each decked out with white plastic tablecloths and green and white balloon bouquets twisting in the wind. Hidden speakers blasted country music while Uncle Wally manned the grill, filling the air with the meaty smell of smoke and burgers, doing battle with teen pheromones. Watching the new crop of campers, some of whom were old enough to have driven themselves to camp, shouting, laughing, hugging friends, I got the sense that in the span of just a few days, my purpose here had shifted. I wasn't here to roast marshmallows or pass out meds, this week my purpose would be completely different.

"Y'all are here," called a woman in an electric wheelchair, weaving drunkenly through the crowd thanks to the blonde boy in her lap working the controls. "This must be the famous Luke I've been hearing about."

"And you must be the famous Randi," I guessed, offering my hand.

She took it and introduced Jeffrey in her lap. Immediately he hopped off her and climbed up with me. "You can do wheelies in this thing, right? Mom won't let me ask the kids, but you aren't a kid, so you'll do wheelies with me, won't you? Tell her it's okay."

"Boy, we need to work on your shyness," I teased, ruffling Jeffrey's hair.

"But you're gonna tell her?"

I laughed, then leaned back, rocking us on two wheels. "Jeffrey can do wheelies."

"You've done it now," Randi said with false seriousness. "That boy's not gonna walk on his own two feet the rest of the week."

"Neither am I," I said, grinning.

"Y'all eat yet?" Jeffrey asked. "We were about to get burgers, wanna come? Please, Adriana, I want to tell you about second grade. And my new best friend, Jonas Butt. Can you believe that's his name?"

"That's not his name," Randi said, giving him sharp look.

"Okay, it's Butkovsky. But Mom, he *likes* it when I call him Jonas Butt."

Jeffrey hopped off me and grabbed Adriana's hand, pulling her toward Uncle

Wally's grill. "And we got this new puppy, but I had to leave him at home with Jonas Butt…"

"Quite the kid you have there," I said to Randi, the two of us following them.

She smiled. "You know how they say you'll get a kid like you were? Karma or retribution, I'm beginning to think it's true."

"Then I'm never having kids," I told her, laughing.

She helped Jeffrey fill a plate—potato salad and ranch-style beans, a burger and a hot dog, and a giant slice of Tricia's Dr. Pepper Chocolate cake—the entire time talking Addy's ear off. How he helped Grandma ice the cake. How Jonas Butt has a parrot that says *Hola, Jefe*, but that's because the guy they got it from was a police officer, and isn't it cool the parrot knew Jeffery's name? And how his new puppy, Obi Two, can already shake hands and speak.

"Obi Two?" I asked, placing my tray of food on a picnic table.

Jeffery's eyes fell for a minute. "Obi Wan died."

"I'm sorry, man."

He nodded solemnly, then brightened again. "He was daddy's dog, but he says Obi Two can be mine. He even sleeps in my bed. Except this week, he's sleeping in Jonas Butt's bed." Jeffrey grinned. "I told him Obi Two better not come home smelling like Butt."

"Jeffrey," Randi scolded, "that's rude."

"I know," the boy said with false remorse and covered his mouth to keep from laughing.

Randi turned to Adriana. "Remind me after lunch, I have y'all's family group list. And I was hoping you'd do me a favor," she said, turning to me.

I raised an eyebrow, waiting to hear what it was before I agreed.

"Water sports," Jeffrey said, his mouth full of potato salad.

"What about them?"

"Organize some. Whatever you think would be fun for an activity option."

"Water sports," I repeated, looking at Adriana.

"It could be fun," she said, betraying me.

"You have to volunteer to help me," I said, grinning.

"I volunteer, too," Jeffrey exclaimed, waving his fork and flinging chunks of potatoes in his excitement.

"They'll let you know," Randi said, reaching for a napkin to wipe a bit of salad off her shirt.

~~~~~

"You asked for my help, that means I get the whistle," Adriana said, taunting me the next afternoon.

"No, I merely suggested you volunteer. You know, out of the kindness of your heart."

The silver whistle flashed in the sunlight, twirling faster and faster on the black lanyard, winding around two fingers until it finally came to a rest against her hand for a microsecond before twirling back in the opposite direction. At her feet were dozens of sherbet-colored pool noodles and kickboards with tacky aloha-inspired prints that I spent the last half an hour hauling out of a dank, spider infested storage room she refused to enter but insisted on turning a hose to, the spray set to *stun*.

"Right, and out of the kindness of your heart, you should let me have the whistle. It's the gentlemanly thing to do."

"Gentlemanly?" I scoffed. "Lady, have you got your guys crossed. Now give me the damn thing, the kids are gonna be here, and I don't want them all confused thinking you're in charge."

Her eyes flashed with amusement, and she stopped the twirling, placing her hands on her saronged hips and letting the object swing against her leg. "But I *am* in charge. I guess you missed that part."

"Fine, your game, your rules." I threw my hands in the air and grinned. "So tell me, Ms. Toomey, what are we gonna do with these wet noodles?"

"I don't know, Mr. Stevenson," her eyes went over the pool toys before turning back to me, "but the sign of a good leader is listening to her subordinates."

I reached out and took the black cord, letting it slip through my fingers until I grasped the whistle on the end, pulling it, and her, to me. "This subordinate was thinking we could use them for races across the pool," I said, my voice husky and low.

"Oh, well that sounds good."

"There's a couple other games I know, but you know what I'd need first?"

She swallowed, her leonine eyes transfixed on mine. "What?"

"The whistle," I said, and pulled it from her loose fist. She laughed and lunged for it just as I slipped it around my neck, letting it rest against my skin. Her hands reached for it, and suddenly I had her in my lap, my hands around her wrists and pinned between my chest and hers, wrestling to keep the treasure.

I don't know which of us realized first what was going on, whether she was the one who went very still, or I was the one who noticed just how close she was, but the laughter stopped. And when her pink tongue darted out to lick her lips, I had an overwhelming urge to push her off me and leave the pool.

"I'm sorry," I murmured as she stood up. "I didn't mean..." but I didn't know how to finish that.

"I know," she said, not looking at me. "We should get this stuff out of the way. The kids are gonna be here in a minute, and I don't want anyone getting hurt."

I nodded and started picking up kickboards and noodles to place in an out-of-the-way corner of the arbor, but something about her words made me think she wasn't talking about someone tripping over them. Not solely.

~~~~~

After two hours in the pool, and God only knew how many laps across it—my ego refused to let some fifteen year old kid who didn't even shave yet beat me at my own sport—I was exhausted. By the time I got to the Rehab Hut, my arms were ready to fall off, and I took one look at Jill and told her in no uncertain terms that I wasn't capable of lifting weights.

"How about the standing frame, then?" she asked, crossing the floor to the gray contraption.

I shrugged. "Sure. Sounds good." Actually, just standing still for an hour sounded amazing, but I didn't feel it necessary to tell her that. Instead I pulled *Lonesome Dove* out of my backpack, transferred to the frame's seat, and after securing my knees and strapping myself in, cranked the lever until I was upright.

Standing on my own two feet was a strange, bittersweet experience every single time. It felt good; feeling the pressure of my body on my feet, my knees, my thighs. Seeing the world as I was meant to see it, from six feet up and looking down, rather than barely three and a half feet high with my tires fully inflated, looking up. And yet I often wondered if it wasn't some kind of false hope, planting seeds that maybe all it would take was a single step, and I'd be... *free.*

I placed the book on the tray in front of me and flipped it open to a random page. I'd read it often enough that starting at the beginning didn't seem necessary anymore and instead read it more like Granpa Stevenson read his Bible—letting the story tell me what it wanted to.

When I was a kid, I wished I could run away and join up with the Hat Creek Cattle Company, just like Newt. And just like Newt, I might not've known much about shooting or riding, but I would've worked hard and done anything Gus asked of me, looking up to him and the Captain. When I was a kid, this book got me through some lonely hours, wishing for my own father, who somehow seemed entirely too much like Captain Call, when all I really wanted was for him to take notice of me and let me ride with him. Unlike Newt, I never got my wish.

"Here you are," Will called from the doorway. "Adriana's back in the cabin standing under the shower, and I half-thought you'd be there, too."

I glanced at him. "You thought I'd be in the shower with her?"

He grinned, walking toward me. "That's not exactly what I meant, but now that you mention it..."

"What do you want, Will?" I asked, turning back to the book.

"It's weird seeing you standing up," he said after a moment. "You're taller than I thought you'd be."

When I didn't respond, he cleared his throat.

"Gina and I were wondering about the apartment."

"What about it?"

"Have you called the landlord yet?"

"No."

"You gonna?"

I pushed out a breath and closed the book. "I don't know."

I had just enough in my checking account to cover the security deposit and first month's rent, but on a purely practical level, I needed a roommate to help me cover the cost.

Without Adriana's consent to split the utilities and whatnot, I didn't see any way for me to realistically do it on my own. And anyway, I *wanted* to live with her. I wanted to wake up in the morning and see her first thing. I wanted hers to be the last voice I heard before going to sleep. And I... I wanted her down the hall to stave off my nightmares.

The funny thing was, as much as I hated the idea of coming to this place with her, letting her see me now, *after*, now that she had, I couldn't imagine not having her there every day to help remind me of who I was *before*. I needed someone to pick of a picture of Bethany and me and remember who that guy was. Who those people were when they were together.

I needed someone to look at me in a standing frame and not say *You're taller than I thought you'd be*, but to remember I was once this tall and wanted desperately to be again.

"She hasn't given you an answer," he said so softly, it made my breath hitch in my throat. "You want me to talk to her?"

"No," I said too quickly, and with a flash of lightning behind my eyelids, I realized just how angry I was at him and Gina. "Last time y'all talked to her, I found her a damn mess on the floor. I think y'all've done quite enough."

Will took a step backwards and studied the pattern in the linoleum. "We didn't mean... We just thought..." he looked up at me, his blue eyes wet with tears I didn't want to see. Not while I was locked in this contraption with no option but to stand here, awkward and really pissed off. "We thought we were helping."

"Helping," I repeated, my voice dangerous and low. And for one moment the urge to hit him was so strong, my fists ached with the need to connect with his jaw.

He must've seen it in my eyes because he took another self-preserving step backward. "Luke, I'm sorry. I'd never try to hurt her."

I stared at him, reluctantly absorbing his anguish, and swallowing my anger, let it drain out of me. As it did, an overwhelming sense of exhaustion replaced it, the fatigue pressing down on me.

"Call Ruby," he said, fishing his cell phone out of his pocket and checking it for bars. "Get things set up so that when she does agree, it'll be all taken care of."

"What if she doesn't?" I asked, forcing myself to say the words out loud.

He shrugged. "Then Gina and I know lots of people looking for a good roommate." He searched his contacts for the right number and handed me the phone.

After a heartbeat I reached for it. "Get my wallet out of my backpack, will you?" And I put the phone to my ear, waiting for someone to pick it up on the other end.

Chapter 14

Each day at camp, I felt more and more like I was in a rowboat with a small leak. At first the water in the bottom seemed minimal, manageable, as if I had plenty of time to get from the middle of the lake to the far away dock. But somewhere around mid-afternoon on Thursday, I looked down at the water sloshing around my ankles and realized I was never gonna make it. Fearful, I desperately wanted to bail water, but I knew it would only exhaust me, making it harder to swim to shore.

Randi had dozens of volunteers decorating the Suffolk Hall for Thursday night's dance. Unlike the dance of last week, this one had taken on prom-like proportions, including a vignette in the corner where later Uncle Wally would take pictures of dressed-up couples and friends. Gina told me late one night this dance was Randi's idea back when they started the camp. She never got asked to homecoming or prom because there was a misconception among her classmates that she couldn't dance. Or didn't want to. Or would feel too self-conscious. And she wanted at least one night a year to dance with her friends like any other teenage girl.

On the far wall beneath a red, white, and gold balloon arch, Gina, Adriana, and Will sat with a helium tank and dozens of flat, latex balloons, talking quietly while methodically working through the supply. For a moment I considered joining them, but something about the way they leaned toward each other, a circle of quiet intimacy in the corner, made me feel left out. As if by going over there, I would be intruding.

I took a breath and went in search of Randi, who was busy sorting through a giant box of white Christmas lights, checking to make sure each strand worked. "Need some help?" I asked.

She looked up and smiled, pushing the box toward me so I could reach them, too. "Absolutely. Why do working lights wear out sitting in the attic?"

"Mice," I said seriously.

"Mice?" she repeated, her face momentarily lit by the strand she plugged in.

"Sure. How else do you think they find their way in a dark attic? You don't keep flashlights up there do you?"

She laughed. "No."

"You should. It would save you from having to check hundreds of lights every year. And from the look of this box, y'all are serious about lighting up your house for the holidays."

"I'll be sure to tell Seamus," she said, keeping a straight face and glancing across the large room at her husband. "He abhors this job! Listen, I wanted to ask you about something, I'm told you're a competitive swimmer. Truth or rumor?"

"Both," I said, the humor of a moment ago slipping away. "I was a swimmer."

She unplugged one strand that worked and plugged in another that didn't. "I've seen you in the pool, there's no 'was' about it. You *are*."

I pulled a coil of lights from the box and stuck the metal prongs in the socket. "Randi, I don't know you very well, so please take what I'm about to say with a grain of salt, but whatever you thought you saw is bullshit." The lights flickered on, and I tossed them in the working pile. "I stopped calling myself a swimmer the moment I woke up in the hospital with my spine broken, so forgive me if I don't have the slightest inclination of discussing this further."

Undeterred, she looked at me, her face lit, although it was hard to tell whether that was from the lights in her lap or affection. "I really don't mean to piss you off, it's just that the whole point of this camp is to let kids know that physical limitations are no excuse for not achieving their dreams—"

"Not achieving my dreams?" My laugh had a hard edge to it. "Do you not get that I was on the very edge of achieving my dream? My times would've qualified me for the Olympic team, all I had to do was swim in the Trials. It's all I ever wanted, and now… now I'll be watching the damn thing on TV. Probably smashed."

"Or you could compete in the Paralympics."

I frowned, the image of racing some kid with Down Syndrome across the pool running through my mind. I closed my eyes, feeling like a total jackass, but somehow that seemed more like admitting my own defeat than never getting in the pool at all. I pulled another strand from the box, plugged it in, and tossed it in the not working pile, sure that the thoughts running through my mind would get me tossed out of here if I said them out loud.

She put another strand in the working pile and pushed away from the box. "I want you to come with me."

"What for?" I asked, putting my hand on another coil.

"Does it really matter?" she challenged, and headed to the door, whispering something to her father, who sent me one of his wide grins before going back to his task—hanging the Christmas lights Randi already sorted.

I sighed and followed her out the door. "Where are we going?"

"Dad's office. I want to show you something."

At her father's desk, she turned on his laptop, entered the password, and opened YouTube. "What's your favorite race?" she asked, grinning at me.

"The two hundred meter, individual medley," I told her, watching her type it into the search.

"I'm not sure what category you'd be in, so we'll try this one," she said, clicking on the one that said SM5, "but it might not be exactly right."

I nodded, and watched as the 2011 European Championships with its bright blue, crystal clear water came on the screen, the flags dangling high above the lanes. As the camera panned across the pool to focus on the swimmers shaking out their muscles, stretching, waving for the camera and their fans, I got a good look at these guys. They had that focused, adrenaline-infused look of preparing to go to battle. I had to smile, remembering how that felt. Of the seven racers, four were amputees and three looked as if they might've had spinal cord injuries. And these guys were *built*. I got the impression any one of them would give me a run for my money.

When the buzzer sounded, they launched themselves into the water for the butterfly, and I stared at the screen, transfixed and possibly not breathing the entire five minutes it took them to race across the pool. They were fast, focused, and just as serious at winning as I would've been. The thing that sunk in was forget the fact that they were "crippled," these dudes were world-class athletes, and Christ they were fast!

When it was over, Ricardo Ten from Spain won, although for a while there it was anyone's race, I let out the air I held in my lungs. "Fuck," I whispered, impressed, then looked at her. "Sorry."

"No, you're right. They're fucking amazing!" Randi grinned. "What do you say we get back; we got a dance to prepare for."

"One more first?" I asked, doing my best to imitate Jeffery's wheedling tone. "Please, Mom?"

She laughed. "One more, and then we're turning off the laptop."

I kissed her cheek before settling back in my chair to watch another race, practically smelling the chlorine in the air.

~~~~~

Suffolk Hall was transformed. Long after everyone else cleared out, the Wallace clan stayed to put the last touches on Randi's design. Now the place glowed with thousands of tiny twinkling white lights, covered with gauzy red and gold fabric hanging from the walls and dozens of flameless votives on tables around the room. Randi and her husband, Seamus, sat at a table handing out corsages to the girls and boutonnière to the guys. "I think y'all can handle these yourselves," she said, reaching for two matching white orchids for Addy and me.

I kept my eyes on her hands reaching for the flowers, mainly because I was having a hard time looking at Adriana in a light pink dress that glowed against her olive skin. When she came out of her side of the cabin, smoothing the skirt nervously, my mouth went dry.

"This is incredible," I said, accepting a corsage.

Randi smiled. "It's what I do. Parties, weddings, bat mitzvahs… But this is my pride and joy, this one night for the kids." She scanned the room again before handing my boutonnière to Adriana. "It's my way of giving them a magical night."

"It's beautiful," Adriana said, and took a step away from the table for the next group of people behind us. She wavered a moment, studying the flower in her hand, before going to a dark corner. "Did you ever go to prom?" she asked when I stopped next to her.

I grinned. "All four years."

"I never did," she said, pulling the pin from the single orchid in her hand and took a step closer.

"Why not?"

She shrugged and leaned in to pin the boutonnière to my shirt, while giving me a pretty excellent eyeful of cleavage. "I don't know. It wasn't my thing, I guess."

She was so close, I could either look at her breasts, or I could raise my eyes to look at her glossy bottom lip tucked between brilliant white teeth in concentration, the faint smattering of freckles across her nose and cheeks, her luminescent gold-brown eyes framed by the longest eyelashes I'd ever seen.

"Didn't you want to go with your friends?" I asked, conscious of how rough my voice sounded.

She took a step back and smiled, looking around at the people dancing before turning back to me. "I am."

I picked up the corsage in my lap and reached for her hand, and while keeping my eyes on hers, gently slid the flower up, slowly, to her wrist. Before I let go, I raised her hand to my lips and gently brushed her skin with a soft kiss. The shudder that ran through her pulled on something deep inside me. Something barely detectable, but a quake nevertheless, and I gripped the rims of my chair.

"Would you like to dance?" she asked, and when I nodded, she turned on her heel to the dance floor.

Following her, I felt my heart pound in rhythm to the bass of the speakers, smelled the perfume, cologne, and pheromones assaulting my nose in the pink and blue tinged darkness. I took a moment to look at the people around me, dancing with abandon. They didn't care what they looked like, whether they could do it well, what anyone else thought. These kids, these campers were here, in the middle of a dance floor, letting the music take over their body and turn it loose. I closed my eyes to let the music in, let it take over, let the rhythm of the drums move my chest and head, let the chords of the guitar move my arms, and when I opened my eyes again, I was singing the words at the top of my lungs, along with every person around me.

I was dancing, and I didn't care who saw.

~~~~~

An hour later we sat outside. My body was having a hard time adjusting to the combination of hot sweat and cool mountain air, and I shivered in my Artesia sweatshirt. "We can go back inside," Adriana said, watching me shake uncontrollably.

"I'm fine," I lied. "I've just got a short somewhere. It'll straighten itself out in a minute."

"Is there anything I can do?"

I shook my head. I hated sitting here freezing my ass off, but despite my tense, painfully clenched muscles, I was determined to ignore it. It was a beautiful, albeit cool, night, and I was sitting with a gorgeous girl. It'd take a hell of a lot more that just the breeze to make me leave.

"I told Rob about the apartment," she said before clearing her throat. "I mean, um…"

"I know what you mean." If anyone could understand, it'd be me. "And?"

She lowered her head, studying the flower on her wrist. "I know it was just my imagination, but he said…" Her eyes flashed up to mine, a slight smile playing over her lips. "He said I'd have to stay on you about keeping stuff clean."

I swallowed the excitement rising in my throat and made my voice light. "Anal retentive freak that he is, acting like he's the only one who ever picked up a toilet brush."

"Which explains why I'd have to hover-pee more times than not in y'all's dorm room," she teased.

"On the upside, now you'll never have to worry about the seat being up in the middle of the night if you live with me."

"There is that," she said, laughing.

Inside, the DJ played a Lady Antebellum song, and as the notes floated to us on the breeze, her laughter died away. I tried not to listen by studying my shaking legs.

Just a week after meeting her, I asked her to dance to this song in a country bar. She had on a black lacy top, short denim skirt, and heels that later she took off and carried when we wandered campus, but at the time they gave her enough height to rest her head on my shoulder as we slowly worked our way around the dance floor.

"Do you remember the first time we danced together?" she asked, turning to Suffolk Hall and listening closely. "I can't hear this song without thinking about that night."

I couldn't either, but it didn't seem wise to admit that. And yet, every single time I heard it, I felt her in my arms.

"I knew how you felt," she whispered, tracing the edge of a petal with a gentle finger. "But I'd already heard all about you, even before we met. You had a pretty serious reputation, you know?" she said and glanced up at me, a small smile on her face. "And anyway, you were Bethany's brother. I couldn't go to her crying when you broke my heart. I wasn't about to ask her to choose sides."

"Adriana, I wouldn't break your heart." My voice was hoarse with pain.

She tilted her head to one side, considering that. "No, you wouldn't. Now. But now, it's too late to consider that, isn't it?"

When I nodded, she went on.

"I want to move in with you, but I need you to understand that I can't open a door I shut a long time ago. I'm in this with you because of Bethany and Rob, and because you are the only person in the world I trust to understand and accept me as I am. Right now. With all my broken parts, but I need you to be my friend and nothing else. Okay?"

Somehow certain that's what she was talking so intensely to Gina and Will about while blowing up balloons this afternoon, I reached for my backpack and lit a cigarette. "I didn't mean to make you think… I'm sorry if I—"

She reached across the space between us to put a hand on my arm. "I know. But I felt like I needed to say something. I care about you too much to lose you, too."

Covering her hand with my free one, I closed my eyes and saw her and Rob together, the way she looked at him, the way he looked at her, as if she was this miracle created only for him and he was smart enough to not only see it, but thank God to have found it. Sometimes I'd see that look on his face and wish I could find that.

Maybe I should've wished he'd be able to keep it instead.

"Luke," she said, squeezing my arm, and I opened my eyes. "Before we do this, though," she paused and cleared her throat, "would you to go with me to my Uncle Marc's the weekend after next? He has a place on Lytle Lake. My whole family's coming for a reunion, although since they get together for every holiday, birthday, and ballet recital, it isn't a reunion like some family's. And they're loud, they're nosey, there's a whole bunch of them getting into everything, and I wouldn't blame you if you don't want to go. Rob said he's used to a big family and mine about steamrolled him, but I swear they won't eat you."

"Not alive, anyway. I hope," I said, alternating between trying to get a grip on the lingering pain in my heart over what she's said and the overwhelming relief over the thought that I didn't have to say goodbye to her the day after tomorrow.

"Well, yeah. If I'm going to move up there with you, I need them to meet you. I mean, it's not like we're—"

"Living in sin?"

"Well, yeah," she said again, blushing. "It's just that I need them to see that I'm… better. Not hiding under my covers or whatever. I need them to stop worrying about me, and I thought if you came with me, I'd be able to face them. If you don't want to go, Will said he would. Or Gina. But I want you to, because it's like you said, I'm still not sure how to do this with them."

"Addy, I get it," I told her, pulling her to me and sitting her in my lap. "I'll go."

With her in my arms, it was easier to release the last vestiges of pain and remember what I always knew—that she was Rob's girl. And in a lot of ways, she always would be. Anyway, it was better for us to keep that door closed, if for no other reason than the certainty that this, right here, wouldn't go up in smoke somewhere down the road.

Somehow that seemed like the last act of Bethy's Church of Lost Souls.

"I want Pender to live with us," I said, speaking into her hair. "He's Bethy's dog really, but I feel like if I can take care of him for her... We aren't really supposed to have pets, but I told them he's a working dog."

"They're gonna take one look at that mutt and know there's no way he possibly could be," she said, laughing softly.

"So? You really think they're gonna ask a guy in a wheelchair whether he's lying?"

"I doubt it."

Behind us, Randi and Seamus came out of the building; he held a sleeping Jeffrey in his arms. "How he fell asleep with that going on, I'll never know," Seamus said to us, a slight Irish brogue giving his voice a soft lilt. "Why don't you stay," he said to Randi. "I'll get the boy in bed."

"You sure?"

"Yep, this is your night. See you in a bit." He shifted Jeffrey so he could lean over to kiss his wife, then headed off for their cabin.

"That's a good man," she said, watching him walk away. "Y'all doing okay?"

"Yeah, we just needed some air," I told her.

Randi nodded once and turned to go back inside. "Y'all come get your pictures taken, Daddy's getting ready to put up his camera, and he said he hasn't gotten you yet."

Taking once last deep breath of Adriana's perfume, I pulled back to look at her. "Let's go get our picture taken," I said. "I want to remember this night."

She smiled. "The night I told you I'd live with you and that weird lookin' dog?"

"Pender's not weird lookin', he's handsome. And I want it to remember the night I danced with the most beautiful girl at the prom."

Chapter 15

I woke in the pre-dawn darkness, and moving silently amongst the slumbering boys, I was hyperaware it was for the last time. Only now they weren't little kids, wrestling with sheets in their sleep like they did each other when awake, as if even in unconsciousness their bodies simply couldn't relax. No, now, three weeks later, they were almost-men, snoring in that hard, unmoving way only a teenage boy can do.

Pulling on a pair of jeans and the boots I brought back with me last weekend, I slipped my name tag over my head out of habit before realizing I didn't need it, and placed it back on its hook with a deep ache in my stomach at the thought.

"Hey, Luke," Will whispered from his bunk, raising up on one elbow, "where ya going?"

"To the barn."

He rubbed his eyes. "You want some company?"

I smiled. "Nah, go back to sleep, I'll see you in a bit."

He grunted and rolled over, snoring again before I even got to the door.

In the barn, Uncle Wally already had Milky Way saddled and was methodically working on Caramel for me. It was funny, watching him happily whistling while he bent to adjust the saddle belt under Caramel's belly, I got the sense he was Gus and I was Newt, getting ready for a ride. Maybe into Mexico to steal back the cattle from thieves. Maybe it was just another morning on that long trip to Montana, but I'd spent my entire life preparing for this moment.

His face brightened when he saw me, and for the second time in as many minutes, my stomach clenched at the thought of leaving in just a few hours. "Mornin'," he drawled. "Tricia made us some coffee, if you want some."

"Yeah," I said, my voice rough with sleep and emotion, and I cleared it. "Yes, please."

He jerked his chin in the direction of the thermos tucked into a pouch on Milky Way's saddle. "It's black, but Chuck's got cream and sugar around here somewhere, if you prefer."

"Black's fine."

"Then let's get you on up here, and we'll go."

I wrapped the straps of a harness around my torso like he and Chuck showed me that first day I went riding, and once they were secure, Uncle Wally pushed a button on the winch that lifted me, dangling eight feet straight up in the air. I felt like a limp rag doll, precariously hanging from the steel cable, but he quickly moved Caramel directly under me, and holding her halter, pushed the button to lower me onto her saddle.

"Good?" he asked.

Removing the harness and putting my legs in the stirrups, I nodded. "Yup," I said, and while he got on Milky Way, I buckled the belt that attached to the saddle's seat back around my chest.

We left the barn just as the sun was beginning to lighten the horizon, and as he rode, Uncle Wally poured us each a cup of rich, black coffee from the thermos. Sipping it in silence, we let the horses cover the distance, content to let the steam curl in the early morning cool while the mountain before us slowly took on color. It was the kind of peaceful perfection that I could almost believe would last forever, Uncle Wally and me riding side by side, all the way up to Montana.

"I heard you were moving to Lubbock," he said softly, as if to keep from disturbing the tranquility around us.

"There really aren't any secrets around here," I said, smiling.

"Nope. I figure since there's no TV to watch *Days of our Lives,* people gotta make up their own drama. How you feeling about that?"

"Lubbock?" I shrugged. "I guess if I can't stay here, at least I'm taking a little bit of it with me."

"Told ya everyone comes back."

"Yeah," I said, chuckling. "I really didn't believe you at the time."

"I know. At the time I wouldn't've been surprised if you'd taken the keys to Randi's van and gone on home."

"Why'd you give them to me, then?" I asked, studying the deep creases around his blue eyes, the years of pain and laughter permanently etched into his features.

"Because if you were gonna leave, you were gonna find a way, and if you were gonna stay, you were gonna find a way. I wanted to give you the option, so you could make up your mind."

I turned to the mountain, digesting that. "It never even occurred to me to take it."

"Ain't nothing wrong with that," he said almost cheerfully, as if it wouldn't've bothered him one way or the other. Then he turned to me. "Can I give you a piece of advice, son? What you've lost can't be measured on any scale of justice. The people who have been taken from you, the future you'll never have, the person you were has been changed irrevocably, and don't think for a second that there's any amount of justification for any of it. But what I know is you are on a path only you can travel to create a life only you can build, and it is the moments in between that let you choose who you are going to become."

I forced down the lump in my throat, and it joined the unbelievable ache in my gut, turning into a pain so profound, I fought the urge to double over on Caramel and release it with shuddering, unyielding sobs. But if I started, I was afraid I'd never stop. And anyway, last time I was witness to that kind of unrelenting crying, Addy and I ended up in her bed.

I had no intention of spooning with Uncle Wally.

"I'm afraid…" I began hoarsely and cleared my throat, unable to finish that.

"I know, son," he said, reaching over to grasp my arm. "But you are taking with you everything you need. And when you forget, you just ask Will and Gina and Adriana to help you find it again. You got it?"

I nodded, reaching up to wipe my eyes with a thumb and forefinger. "You sure you don't want to ride on up to Montana?"

He chuckled. "We could, but that never turns out well, does it, Newt?"

For a long moment I stared at him, surprised he pegged me so succinctly, but he just grinned. "'Live through it, that's all we can do,'" he said, quoting Call, and with that, he wheeled his horse around. "Better get these old girls back. I promised Tricia we'd be back in time for breakfast, and that woman don't do well when I stand her up."

~~~~~

The blinding white sand raced past the windows; the heat shimmering in the distance made the cacti and scrubland waver and curl. I watched it fly by while listening to Adriana's nervous chatter that seemed to have little point other than to keep strained butterflies at bay. At least, that's how I took it, since her one-sided conversation had a stream-of-consciousness feel to it, jumping from topic to topic without any real participation from me except the occasional grunt or nod.

I took her hand and drew small circles on her palm with my thumb, hoping to soothe her. This morning watching the last campers drive away had an empty finality. That was rough, but saying goodbye to Randi, Uncle Wally, Tricia, and the other counselors nearly struck me dumb with grief.

But I couldn't keep my tears in check when Uncle Wally put his arms around my chest and pulled me up, into the bear hug I'd needed since that first time in his office.

The closer we got to Artesia though, the more her words tapered off, until when she pulled in next to Dad's sleeper cab and took her hand back to put the transmission into park, I realized the lack of sound for the last half hour had a kind of oppressive quality to it.

"We're back," she said, her voice flat with the same empty finality I felt deep inside.

The front door opened, and my parents spilled out of it like they'd been staring out the living room window, waiting for us.

Dad helped Adriana get my things out of the trunk, and in an instant we were sucked up in their whirlwind of energy and hugs. It was almost too much: too close, too loud, too hot, when all I wanted was a few more moments of peace with Adriana.

"Y'all come on in," Mom said, picking up a wiggly Pender to try and silence his excited bark that bounced off the canyon created by the sleeper cab and Adriana's car. "We've got mac and cheese in the oven, and Hoyt's gonna grill up some burgers for dinner."

Adriana took a small but noticeable step backwards. "That's sweet of you Anna, but I really need to get back on the road. As it is, I'll be racing the sun."

"Why don't you spend the night, sweetheart," Dad said, tossing my duffel over one shoulder, preparing to grab hers. "You look stone-tired."

"I'm fine, thanks," she said, staring at something off in the distance. "But I don't like driving at night, so I need to go." At that she turned on her heel and went back to the driver's side door.

"Will you call when you get there so we know you got home safe?" Mom called.

Adriana gave her a strained, vacant smile. "Yeah, I…" She pulled the door open, and stopped, resting her cheek on the roof of the car.

"Give us a moment, will you?" I asked, and watched my parents go back inside. When the front door closed, I went to her. "It's just a week," I said, taking her hand.

She laced her fingers with mine. "I know, but I don't know how to leave. I feel safer when I'm with you. I… remember how to breathe when I look at you."

I pulled her to me, letting her sit in my lap and making myself be strong for both of us. "It's just a week, and you're going to be so busy it'll fly by."

She snickered. "Yeah, right."

"Didn't you say you wanted to refinish a dresser for your new room?"

Nodding, she buried her face in my neck. "And the headboard and night-stand."

"See? You won't even have time to miss me," I said with a laugh and wrapped my arms tighter around her. "You're going to be fine." I willed it to be true.

"Yeah," she whispered, then raising her head, she lifted her chin, squared her shoulders, and stood up. "*We* are going to be fine." She turned and got in her car, and after rolling down the window, smiled bravely. "I'll miss you."

"I'll see you Friday," I told her and watched as she pulled out of the driveway and pointed her car toward her home.

~~~~~

The kitchen held the thick smell of baking cheese and raw hamburger meat, onions, and garlic. Dad washed his hands after dropping my duffel bag in the laundry room and stuck his hands back in the bowl of meat, saying something about bigger burgers for the rest of us. Mom said nothing, letting a sad expression pass over her as she glanced at the table, already set for four, and went to the laundry room to dump my stuff in hot, sudsy water.

"I'll get it, Mom," I said, following her into the small room.

"Don't be ridiculous."

She reached for the detergent on the wide shelf above the machines, the shelf I once caught hell for after clearing all the stuff from it to set up a ramp down the dryer for me and my skateboard. If I hadn't ended up with a broken arm and in need of nine staples that left a slight but noticeable scar on my forehead, Bethy never would've called Mom at work, and she never would've known, but the next time Dad was home, that shelf got permanently screwed to the wall.

"I'm perfectly capable of washing my own drawers," I said before catching the sadness etched into her features; she didn't want to do it because she thought I couldn't, but because she needed something, *someone* to take care of. "Let me at least help you," I said, "it's possible there's stuff in the pockets."

It killed me how her face brightened, and for a fleeting moment I wondered how Dad could leave her here alone, week after week. She put the bag on the dryer and pulled open the zipper, her face screwing up at the sweaty clothes, tossed lazily in the bag.

"Smells just like when you came home from camp as a little boy," she said, reaching inside to pull out a fistful of clothes. "Bethany's bag would come back just as neatly folded and fresh as the day y'all left, but I always wondered if you'd spent that time racing through swamps and mud bogs."

I smiled. "There aren't any swamps in Capitan."

"Then you can see where my confusion might come from."

Our eyes met, green on green, for a moment laughing and unwavering, and for an instant it was almost like *before*. And then hers dropped, roaming over my chair before turning back to the shorts in her hand, reaching inside to pull out the pockets. I did the same, turning t-shirts inside out, sticking safety pins through the toes of socks to keep them together, searching for the handful of notes stuck in pockets, although I was pretty sure I'd already put most of them in my camp notebook.

Caballero had a mailbox for campers to slip notes inside to have passed out at lunch, each marked *private* or *public*. Carrie sent me a public one that Uncle Wally read during lunch one day. In her careful, shaky hand, it read: *Your a grate counsoler but I don't want you burning my marshmalos any more. I am looking for a new chief.*

Gina sent a private one that was tucked somewhere in here that I didn't want Mom finding, although she wouldn't have understood it if she had. *Any time you want to try, let me know,* it said. *I'm up for anything.* When I got it, my ears got so red, Tim, sitting next to me, commented on it.

I refused to meet Gina's eyes for the rest of the day.

The next night, still trying to sort out how to deal with her innuendos, I pulled my dick out and let Adriana and Will think I'd be base enough to let her give me a hand-job not twenty yards from a bunch of kids.

"Who's Devon?" Mom asked, pulling me from my thoughts.

"One of the boys last week," I said, reaching for a pair of shorts that I thought might hold Gina's note. It didn't.

" 'I'm really glad you came to camp this year,' " she read from the note in her hand. " 'You're an awesome guy, and I hope next year I'm in your cabin.' " She gave me a watery smile. "That place was good for you."

"It's a good camp," I responded, turning a blue tee inside out.

"Yes, but that's not what I mean. You're different now." She rested her hip against the washing machine. "What they need is a summer camp for mothers who've buried their children."

I silently agreed, taking a safety pin from its tray to attach two matching socks by their toes. I also wished she'd at least start going to that support group at the hospital. She refused. But then, I refused too when I first got home. In my case, I didn't want to sit amongst a bunch of mourning strangers in my chair, the surviving, crippled twin.

"Try what?" she asked, and I looked up to see Gina's note in her hand.

"Basketball," I said too quickly, feeling my face get hot again. "Mom, have you tried that support group?"

She grunted, disgusted. "At the hospital? They're either pathetic widowers looking for someone to take care of them, or dour women who can't stop crying. It's depressing."

Yeah, but it's kind of supposed to be, I thought.

"The burgers'll be off in a minute," Dad said, leaning on the doorjamb.

"Thanks, honey," Mom said to him and dumped all the whites in hot water before going past me to the kitchen.

Running a hand over the stubble on my jaw, I tilted my face up to the ceiling and closed my eyes, suddenly, unbelievably tired.

Chapter 16

Following Will's directions through the serpentine apartment complex, past two-story brick-and-white-sided buildings and shadowy carports, I took in the place I'd put a deposit on, sight unseen. Thank you Jesus it wasn't a dump; I passed some a couple miles back that looked pretty sketchy.

Around the next bend I spotted Will's red Prius and pulled into a nearby spot, telling Pender to stay while I got into my chair. The whole time he whined to get down. He never was a good traveler, and four hours nervously roaming my truck left both of us frustrated and exhausted.

"All right, come here," I said, taking his leash from the pocket in the door, and attached it to his harness before letting him water the grass. When he was ready, I wrapped his leash around my wrist a few times and led him up the ramp and through the dark breezeway.

The moment I knocked on the black, glossy door, Pender plopped his butt on the Welcome mat and looked up at me expectantly, as if to tell me that after coming all this way, whatever was on the other side of that door better be good. I reached down and rubbed his ears just as Will, dressed in scrubs, opened the door. "Gina's gonna be so mad at you for getting here before she gets home," he scolded, then broke into a big grin. "And who's this handsome devil?"

"Pender," I told him. The dog immediately began wiggling in excitement, his head swiveling between Will, where he wanted to be, and me, waiting for permission to go. I chuckled and unhooked the leash. "Go on."

Will scooped him up, letting Pender lick his face and neck, the entire time talking to the dog in a voice at least a couple octaves above his normal range. "You didn't tell me we were getting a dog."

"Will, we're getting a dog," I said, laughing, and pushed past the two of them.

His and Gina's apartment was a shock of colors, as if they couldn't decide on a color, so they used them all. The walls were painted light yellow, except for the long one behind the sofa, which had horizontal stripes in bright green, orange, light blue, and dark red. The sofa was that same deep red, the chair to the left of it was lime green, the coffee table was glossy black, and the area rug beneath was a brown and white cow hide. "Wow, this is something..."

Will closed the door and turned around to see what I meant, then broke into a grin. "I can't stand white walls, but Gina wouldn't let me paint each one a different color. Said she didn't want to be living in the pride flag, so this was our compromise. You want anything to drink? Or I made some blueberry muffins before work, if you're interested."

Half an hour later we were out on the patio with two crumby plates and coffee mugs on the table. With Pender sitting contentedly in Will's lap, a fan circulating the summer air and keeping us cool, we considered going down to the leasing office to sign the paperwork, but despite the coffee in us, had yet to work up the energy.

"There's a big blue truck parked out front," Gina said, opening the sliding glass door, "with New Mexico plates and a *Swimmers do it in the water* bumper sticker, but I know it can't be Luke's because *someone* would've called me to tell me he was here."

"You were teaching, babe," Will said, standing up for a kiss. "You want a muffin?"

Gina leaned over to kiss my temple, then put down a pink duffel and pulled out a giant water bottle. "No, but would you get me a refill?" she asked, handing him the bottle and collapsing in the chair next to me, the fan sent a cloud of her perfume to me. "How was your drive?"

"Fine," I said, my eyes drawn to her. She wore a pink leotard, so pale she almost looked naked, and a sheer white skirt that shifted with every movement. "What, uh, what do you teach?"

She smiled, glancing down as if she'd forgotten. "Ballet this morning, and on Wednesdays and Fridays. Tuesdays and Thursdays, jazz. And Thursday nights I teach a belly dancing class at the rec center."

"Belly dancing?"

She raised an eyebrow, her smile wicked and wide. "Maybe sometime I'll show you."

"Show him what?" Will asked, opening the door to give Gina her water.

"One of my classes," she said simply, but winked at me.

"Oh, don't take him to watch those uncoordinated old ladies with their oversized jiggling bits and pajama pants." He turned to me. "Gave me nightmares for weeks."

"So do haunted houses, spiders, and chicks who roller derby," Gina pointed out, making me laugh.

Will rolled his eyes. "Are we gonna sit around here all afternoon, or are we gonna go get you an apartment?"

I pushed away from the table. "I suppose I should go sign a lease, I didn't come up here to be homeless."

"Y'all go on and get the keys while I change," Gina suggested, standing up, "then after we unload your truck, we can go get some dinner."

~~~~~

It took thirty minutes to sign all the paperwork Ruby Parry, the rotund leasing manager, had for me. I took the keys from her, saying we didn't need her to show us around the complex, and back out in the heat, we went to the building catty-corner from Will's. And then it hit me just how insane this was.

"What?" he asked, leaning against the brick next to my front door, watching me.

I shrugged. "I just moved somewhere new. No job, no plan... Alone. I'm not completely sure what I'm doing."

"You aren't alone." He took the key from me and unlocked the door.

Except for the utter white emptiness, it was identical to his with an L-shaped living room, dining room, and kitchen, with a fenced-in patio just past the sliding glass door.

"It'll be better once you get some stuff in here," he said, his voice echoing off the walls.

"Yeah..." I whispered.

"Tell you what, give me the keys to your truck, and I'll go get it and Gina, and we'll get you moved in. In the meantime, take a look around, figure out which room you want. I'll be back in a minute. 'Kay?"

After he disappeared with my keys jingling in his hand, I went to the kitchen. Other than the slightly wider doorway, it wasn't really "accessible." The cabinets were at standard height, making the upper shelves completely impossible to reach, the countertop was too high, and thanks to the kitchen's layout, if I wanted to pull a gallon of milk out of the fridge and put it on the counter, it'd involve a wheelie. Letting out a frustrated sigh, I went to the thermostat in the hallway to turn on the air-conditioner and discovered I couldn't see the switch on the top. Unsure if the a/c was to the left, or if that was the heater, I decided to leave it. Gina or Will could get it going.

At least the bedrooms were okay. And the toilet in the bathroom was at a comfortable height. And the tub was big enough to put a seat in.

"What do you think?" Gina asked, coming into the bathroom and taking a seat on the closed toilet lid.

I cleared my throat and made myself look at her. "It's a good thing I'm not much of a chef," I tried to joke.

"Tight, huh?"

"Yeah, but the only thing I ever really learned how to cook was breakfast, so..."

She smiled. "For the morning after? Well, at least you're a gentleman."

I ignored that and ran my hand through my hair. "What if I've talked Addy into moving her entire life up here for nothing?"

"She's scared, too," Gina said after a beat. "Asked if it might be better for Will to move in with you."

"She did?" Well, wasn't that just perfect?

Gina sat in my lap, wrapping her arms around my neck; her skin was warm against me. "I told her if I thought that's what she needed, I'd have Will pack his stuff before the sun set the day we got home, but it's not." She smiled, her blue eyes sparkling so brilliantly, my breath caught in my throat. "This is a good thing. For both of you. And besides, can you imagine Will leaving his rainbow room? He'd be heartbroken!"

I rested a cheek on her arm. "It is a little… loud."

"Watch out. He has plans to take you to the hardware store, too. He refuses to let y'all live with white walls."

~~~~~

Will backed up the truck to the patio, running over grass and a bush so he could stand in the bed of my truck and hand boxes down to Gina and me.

"I'm pretty sure you're not supposed to park here," Gina said, taking a cardboard box from him.

"And I'm pretty sure if anyone complains, we can just send the renter here out to talk to them," he responded, reaching for one of the drawers for my dresser to hand to me. "Besides, I'm not hauling this stuff farther than I have to just because some landscaping enthusiast is concerned about the well-being of a bush that was half-dead anyway."

I didn't have much; the truck was pathetically empty compared to the amount of space in the apartment, and it didn't take long to get unloaded; except for the six-drawer solid-wood dresser that Dad and I needed a hand-truck and a whole lot of cursing to haul up there. With everything else off and stashed in my room—the smaller one, there was no way Adriana would be able to fit all her clothes in that tiny closet—Gina, Will, and I stared at the dresser, stumped. They could barely shove it to the tailgate, much less get it down and carry into the bedroom.

"What if we got our desk chairs?" Will suggested, rubbing his jaw with one hand. "Maybe we could push that monster."

"Unless they're made of titanium and magic, I think you'd just break your chairs," I said.

"I'll be right back," Gina said, turning on her heel.

"Where ya going, babe?" Will asked.

She just grinned and walked back through the apartment, stopping by the side mirror of my truck to check her reflection, then strolled in the direction of their apartment, her hips swaying as she walked. Within minutes she was back, an enormous guy next to her—six-four, three hundred pounds of bulky muscle at the very least. Huge.

"Who is that?" I asked Will.

"Upstairs neighbor."

"Huh."

"Luke, this is Joe," Gina said as they approached, then giggled when he lifted her easily over the patio enclosure and placed her on the concrete next to Will. "He's going to move your dresser for you."

"Pleasure," Joe said, although I couldn't tell if he meant it was a pleasure meeting me, moving my dresser for Gina, or wrapping his enormous hands around her tiny waist and tossing her over the railing. Somehow that last one bothered me immensely.

He hopped up on the tailgate with more power than grace, and with a loud grunt that seemed completely unnecessary, shoved the dresser the couple feet toward the gate, making me glad for the bed liner. He hopped back down on the patio, and lifted it easily above his head. "Where to?"

"First bedroom," Gina practically cooed and followed him inside.

"Damn," Will said, clearly impressed.

"Whatever," I said. "I could've done that if you'd pushed my chair."

In my room, Gina had Joe position the dresser against the wall she and Will had already decided would be the best spot for it. The entire time they'd discussed my "optimal layout," Will went through all the clothes on my hangers, lining up the clothes by color, OCD freak that he is, and threw a few of them on the floor claiming they weren't "right for my coloring."

Now the three of them were happily moving my stuff around, Gina and Joe attaching the rails to my headboard, Will pulling sheets out of the box marked *sheets*, and I sat there, my eyes going over the twin bed that I'd had since I was five or six. Ancient then, it was picked up from some garage sale, and more or less screamed that I would not be getting any action in its narrow confines.

And then there were the boxes of castoffs Mom insisted Dad pull down from the attic for me: Shi'nali's old dishes, the ones with burnt orange and yellow flowers painted along the edges, three slightly warped pans and a harvest gold teapot, and a slew of mismatched plastic cups, old towels, and silverware. All of it ugly and beloved and made my stomach turn at the thought of them going through it, seeing just how little my family had. Just how little *I* had.

"Thank you," I said pointedly, the moment Joe and Gina got the mattress on the box spring. "I think we can handle it from here."

"It's really not a problem," he said, his eyes running over Gina. "I can stay."

"We wouldn't want to keep you from whatever you were doing."

"Yes, thank you for all your help, Joe," she said and went up on her toes to place a kiss on his cheek. "I'll walk you out."

As she passed me, she shot me a dirty look that I pretended to ignore. She also closed the door behind her, making it impossible to hear what she said to the giant, although I sure as hell did try. I wanted to know if that kiss might go farther, or if she might promise something in exchange for his manual labor, like her phone number. Or more. Or maybe he'd already had more—they didn't seem like they were *complete* strangers.

"Luke?"

"What?"

"I asked you to grab the other side of the sheet," Will said, snapping it. "Where are you?"

I shook my head and went to the far side of the bed. "I don't know."

He spread the fitted sheet, tucking the corners in on his side. "You know, there have been times when I've looked at her and prayed to God to make me straight. If I ever had a reason to be, it'd be her. But then you know what I figured?"

"Hmm?"

He smiled. "You can't pray away the gay."

"It doesn't bother you seeing her with a guy like that?" I asked, picking up the top sheet and unfolding it.

"A guy like that. A guy like you. Basically anyone who isn't me." He shrugged and pulled the top edge up to the headboard, letting me tuck the bottom in loosely—I couldn't stand having the sheet trap my feet anymore. "But I want her to be happy, so I've got to be okay with that."

I nodded, knowing what he meant. It was how I felt about Adriana.

"Y'all want to keep unpacking or go get something for dinner?" Gina asked, opening the door again.

"Dinner," Will said, spreading out my blue comforter. "Then we're stopping by Lowe's for paint chips. I've got big plans for that living room. Big."

Gina grinned at me and rolled her eyes. "Told you."

~~~~~

I spent my days job hunting and drinking entire pots of coffee while going through the want ads on Will's laptop. There wasn't much, unless I counted the ones for tow truck driver, roofer, or part-time fry cook at some local greasy spoon. The more promising ones included a receptionist job—but they wanted someone who could type eighty to a hundred words per minute, and I used to get Bethany to type my papers for me while I dictated and paced a hole in her carpet—and doing the laundry at a retirement center. It wasn't that I took issue with washing old people's sheets, after my surgeries more than one guy in the laundry room washed mine, and a retirement center would no doubt be a bit more open-minded than other places, but they were still old people's sheets.

I filled out a dozen job applications at the mall, figuring a job at the Gap or Old Navy couldn't be too hard, but the managers ran their beady eyes over me. "You ever done retail?" they'd ask.

"I used to stock shelves at the Sac'N'Sav back home."

"You did?"

"Before the accident," I'd say, annoyed that a balding forty-something guy in khakis or a ninety-pound girl with too much make-up and green streaks in her hair had the power to make me feel so damned small.

"Well, I'll put your application in my file and give you a call if anything comes up."

I didn't hold my breath anything would.

In the evenings Gina and Will dragged me to consignment shops and three different Goodwills, searching for furniture on my paltry budget. I argued that I'd rather have nothing than the crap-tastic couches and chairs we found, but Will assured me it'd all be fine by the time he was done with it. Apparently he had a plan that he wasn't willing to share, but he was more than willing to pull my wallet out, the whole time grinning like a little boy on Christmas morning. And Gina, when I asked her, gave me one of her dazzling smiles and said I should trust people more.

Anxious and increasingly agitated, I'd fall into the confines of my narrow bed and call Adriana. Somehow talking to her always made the empty apartment feel not-so-empty, even if I refused to put a voice to the fears inside my head: would she be happy here with me? Why did she want to live with Gina instead? Could I prove to her and myself that I could take care of us?

But instead of telling her how afraid I was that I'd made a mistake, I listened to her tell me what she'd done that day, her voice chipper, although I couldn't decide if she was excited or really, really scared.

By Thursday night, after another day of dead ends and managers who seemed to think I was incapable of doing the job a trained monkey could do, I'd had it. Done. Out of ideas and totally agreeing with all the kids last week that sat around our family group saying what a shitty deal the disabled got in an able-bodied world.

Last week I argued with them, blissed out in a Camp Caballero high, now I not only agreed whole-heartedly, but wanted the whole damn world in a wheelchair, just so they could appreciate what a pisser it was.

"You'll find something," Will shouted way too enthusiastically from his room where he was getting ready for a date.

I just shifted on the red couch and took another slug of beer. He had the same fanatical thrill in his voice I'd had last week, although it was hard to tell whether it was a latent high from camp or excitement over seeing Bradley. "What are y'all doing tonight?" I asked, not wanting to discuss my joblessness any longer.

He came out of his room, fixing the collar on his purple polo shirt. "We're making dinner at his place. A tofu stir-fry, he said, but he promised it would be good." He grinned. "Why'd I go and fall for a vegan?"

"Give him a hug for me, will ya? And that sweet M," Gina asked with a grin, coming out of her room ready to teach belly dancing. And holy hell did she look the part: a magenta bra, pink and orange skirt with gold coins jingling softly around her hips, and nestled in her belly button, a diamond glittered at me.

I took a long slug of beer and managed to pull my eyes from her. "Em?"

"Bradley has a hundred pound Great Dane. The Divine Miss M," he said with a flourish and laughed. "I was never so glad to work for Doctor O'Brien as the day Bradley walked in with that tiny puppy. Don't wait up," he said, kissed Gina, and walked out the door, whistling.

"You sure you want to do this?" Gina asked, slinging her dance bag over her shoulder and releasing the heavy blonde hair that caught under the strap. "I think there's probably a Rangers game on, and I'll be home in an hour."

For about half a second I considered staying here, finishing the beer I'd just opened, watching the game, but she turned, a half-turn, barely a movement at all. Her skirt swirled tantalizing around her, that diamond against milky skin mesmerizing, and I got in my chair, ready to go.

~~~~~

At a rec center across town, Gina led me to a large room with mirrors running the length of one wall. Her flip flops slapped the wooden floor as she went to the corner where a stereo sat housed in a glass cabinet. There, she slipped off her shoes and pulled supplies out of her bag: a couple CDs, dozens of brilliant scarves in bright jewel tones, and long, flat incense holders and a canister of sticks.

"You wanna light these for me?" she asked, holding out the canister.

I took them and the holders from her and placed them around the room, making them smoke with the lighter in my backpack, while Gina faced the mirror and stretched her muscles, warming up her body—ignorable until she rested one graceful hand on the horizontal barre in front of her, grabbed her left foot in her hand, and lifted it above her head. Her skirt fell in graceful waves to reveal a strong, muscular leg stretching straight up from her hip, all the way to the pointed toes above her head. Watching her, my breath stopped in my chest, and for one long moment I considered the possibilities of her body in my bed. Her eyes met mine in the mirror and a slow smile slid across her face as if she could read my mind.

I cleared my throat and purposely turned away, playing with the idea of going up the street for a cup of coffee while she taught her class. Somehow that seemed safer in the face of her limber body, belly dancing in the exotic, sandal-wood-scented room. Just as I started to ask her to excuse me, the door opened and the first of her students walked in—a couple of women in their early sixties, who welcomed me with such enthusiasm when Gina introduced me, it felt rude to leave.

The room filled with women of all ages, shapes, and sizes, dressed like they were on a Bollywood set, talking and laughing and sorting through the pile of scarves. Just as Gina asked them to line up, a little girl raced into the room, making a beeline for her teacher. Maybe seven years old, she was dressed in a turquoise Jasmine costume, complete with a matching tiara on her dark head.

"Madison," Gina exclaimed, bending to let the girl wrap little arms around her neck. "I've saved a spot beside me just for you." She glided across the hardwood floor on silent bare feet, pressed a button on the stereo, and in an instant rhythmic drums filled the space. "And Luke, I've got a spot here," she said, her eyes sparkling with amusement, "just for you."

"You want me to belly dance?" I asked, incredulous.

"Madison, what's the rule in my class?"

The child grinned at me. "Everyone tries, everyone dances." She was only a little girl—and dressed in a Jasmine costume for Chrissake—but the laughter in her eyes felt so much like a dare, I found myself pushing across the floor.

For belly dancing.

No wonder Will had nightmares!

Gina smiled at me in the mirror, then raised her eyes to look at the whole class. "Imagine there is a string connected to your sternum," she said over the drums. "Let the string pull your ribcage forward, then drop it back." She demonstrated for us, watching herself in the mirror and after a beat, the women around me copied her. "We're isolating the rib cage here, so remember to keep the lower abs tight to keep the hips from following."

She let that string pull her sternum a few more times, then reached over and nudged me for not letting the string pull mine.

Feeling clumsy, I did my best to follow along, keeping my shoulders in place, isolating my rib cage as I slid it to the left, the right, then around in a circle like she showed us. And just when I was starting to get it, she asked us to add our arms, circling our hands at the wrist while our elbows followed, stretching upwards. Something about the arm movements short-circuited the entire thing, even though watching her it looked simple enough. Gina stepped behind me and gently placed her hands on mine. "You're thinking too much. It's organic, simple, flowing. Just relax into it," she said, showing me how to move. "See what I mean?"

I met her eyes in the mirror and nodded.

"Great job," she said, going back to her spot. "We're gonna add the hips if you want to watch."

I gratefully joined the stereo in the corner, but couldn't keep my eyes off her. Her confidence, the way she moved, the way she kept a close eye on the others in the class, slowing down to help them on the things they were struggling with, just like she did with me, was so compelling I couldn't look away.

When the song ended, she told the dancers to pick up their scarves and hold them by the corners, letting the sheer fabric hang behind them like bright flags. A new track came on the stereo, filled with driving drums and plucked strings, rhythmic tambourines and jingling bells. Gina had them put everything together—the scarves waving around them, their chests moving in isolated circles in seeming opposition to their hips. Brilliant, and colorful, and watching Gina, exotic and mesmerizing.

Sensual.

Erotic.

A spell cast of sandalwood and percussion and the undulations of her body stopped time, making it eternal and fleeting, something I wanted to grasp and hold onto, making only mine. And when the music stopped for the last time, her scarf dropped from her hands and fluttered to the floor, and I became conscious of the fact that I was gripping my rims so tightly, my hands ached when I pried them loose.

She turned to me, expectant. "So? What'd you think?"

I swallowed hard, cleared my throat, and tried to think of something appropriate to say. When nothing came to mind, I settled on the wholly underwhelming, "That was good."

~~~~~

"*Good?*" Gina said an hour later, picking up a slice of pineapple and fresh jalapeño pizza from the box between us. "You disappointed those women, you know."

I took a sip of my coke, trying to wash down some of the heat from the peppers. They were her idea and while they didn't seem to have the slightest effect on her, I was sweating and trying to play it off as nothing. Or the result of the summer heat, but with the red sun kissing the horizon and a breeze blowing over us, that wasn't too believable either.

"What did you want me to tell them?"

"They were sexy. Or graceful… Something. Here they've got this hot guy to show off for, and all he says is 'it's good'? I expected more."

I raised an eyebrow. "You wanted me to tell a little girl in a Jasmine costume she's sexy?"

She smiled. "Okay, maybe not *sexy*, but even Will mustered up some applause. Before later telling me in no uncertain terms that I was never to subject him to that again."

"And how did you not know he's gay?" I asked, grinning.

Lightning fast, her fist shot across the space between us and socked my arm. "Don't be mean."

"Ow," I said, rubbing where she hit me. "You've got rings."

"Sorry…"

"Like brass knuckles."

"I said I was sorry. You want me to kiss it for you, you big baby?"

"Yeah, that'll make it all better," I quipped and started picking off jalapeños. "Where'd you learn to do that, anyway?"

"Belly dance?" She shrugged and shifted to look at me, tucking one long, bare leg under her and letting the other dangle off the edge of the tailgate. "I was a lot like Madison when I was little, taking any dance class my Mom would sign me up for."

"The guys must like it." I did.

"You and Will are the only two who've seen it." She took a bite of her pizza, and after a moment, hopped off the truck. In the middle of the empty cul-de-sac we commandeered and with the empty skeletons of unfinished houses all around her, she spun in pirouetting circles on her toes, like a top. The entire time she kept her eyes focused on me.

It was a trick of the light, I knew, the red-orange color of the sunset—the horizontal angle and long shadows—but somehow in those rotations, she became my sister. Gina, then Bethy, Gina, then Bethy; blonde hair morphing to dark brown, milky skin tanning to the light caramel of my own, bright blue eyes turning brilliant green.

"Why are we the only two?" I called to her, needing something to ground me back in reality.

She stopped spinning and shrugged. "I don't know. I wouldn't let a whole lot of people see me pole dancing, either."

My eyebrows shot up, and any confusion over exactly who I was looking at was gone; she was most definitely Gina. And anyway, no way would my sister wear a blue midriff top, no bra, that hugged the swell of her high, round breasts or short cut-offs that rode low enough to display her hip bones. Bethy was more of a baggy tee and jeans girl.

Laughing, she glided toward me. "I've never pole danced, but from the look on your face, maybe I should give it a try." She did a little shimmy with her hips, not unlike the belly dancing, but this time less sensual eroticism and more straight-up sex. The diamond in her belly button winked at me, the only thing that remained from changing in my truck while I picked up the pizza, studiously keeping my eyes on the man behind the counter making our pie rather than the girl getting naked in the cab.

Focusing on one of the unfinished houses, I forced all the images from my mind and examined the vertical studs, the beginning of rooms and spaces, empty and lonely and promising. I stared at it long enough that it began to make sense, until I saw not only studs and the rough plumbing, but drywall and mudded joints, wall-to-wall carpeting, windows and bricks and a front door. Only then could I pull my eyes away, once again in control.

"Luke?"

"Hmm?"

"I told you not to take me seriously," Gina said, hopping back up on the tailgate and popping a stray jalapeño from the pizza box in her mouth.

"I remember," I said, watching her chew the pepper that had me mopping sweat off my brow. "What I don't understand is why you wouldn't want to be."

"Taken seriously?" She let out a nervous laugh. "What the hell for?"

"Because… because you should be."

She didn't say anything, but stared at the horizon, popping jalapeños in her mouth like handfuls of popcorn. Finally she looked at me. "When are you leaving?"

"For Abilene tomorrow?" I shrugged. "I thought I'd go see if this retirement center would let me wash their dirty sheets first."

She frowned. "Why?"

"Washing old people's sheets is never more appealing as when you're facing destitution," I said, trying to pretend it didn't bother me that that's what I'd been reduced to—the urinated sheets of octogenarians. Why was I so bound and determined to not stay in Artesia? At least there I knew Mr. Roberts at the Sac'N'Sav would give me a job.

Gina reached over and laced her fingers with mine. "I might know someone who could use some help in his shop. If you want, I'll give him a call in the morning."

I lowered my head and studied our interlinked fingers, the way her paleness seemed to glow against my darker skin, even in the fading light. Her pale pink fingernail polish, in contrast to the electric blue on her toes, made me smile. "But I've already accepted so much help from you and Will," I said.

"Is that a bad thing?"

"No. I just don't understand why," I admitted, my thumb tracing small circles on her hand. "Y'all didn't even know me a month ago."

She wiggled closer and placed her head on my shoulder, and with the sweet scent of her filling my brain, I let the warmth of her become my reality. This moment, here, now, as the sun slipped behind the horizon and taking the light with it, leaving us alone in the soft, dusky purple night.

"Gina," I whispered, turning my head to look at her, her blonde hair spilling over my shoulder and faintly tickling my arm, her face in profile, and her eyes closed.

Slowly she lifted her head, her lids raised to reveal bright, feverish eyes, and so very close I wanted to bury my hands in her thick, heavy hair. I ached to place my lips on hers, I needed to feel her breasts against my chest, and for one moment I knew with every cell in my body that it was inevitable.

Except, then what?

I swallowed, moving away just enough to remember how to breathe again, but somehow it felt like I'd shifted miles away, not just a few inches.

"You don't mind calling about that job?"

She shook her head, but despite her smile, the light drained from her eyes. "No. And anyway, I'm selfish, I really don't want you coming home stinking of ammonia and bleach."

"What, uh, what kind of shop is it?"

"Printing. Graphics… Banners, brochures, menus. That kind of thing."

"Oh…" I swallowed and studied our conjoined hands again. "I'm sorry," I whispered, although I wasn't completely sure what I was apologizing for.

"Don't be," she said after what felt like an eternity. "If you want, I won't take you seriously either."

Nodding, I turned back to the horizon, almost dark now. Something in the way she said that reminded me too much of what Adriana said the night of the dance—that she knew I would break her heart. And the really hilarious part was the reason that I might've hurt Addy was the very reason I *couldn't* hurt Gina. Or anyone else. It's why I pulled away when I wanted to lean in. Why I pushed when I wanted to pull. Why I shut down when what I wanted more than anything was to open up and let her in.

"Luke?" she whispered, the fingers of one graceful hand touching my bicep and sending a shiver through my body. "You're shaking."

"Cold," I lied. "I have a coat in the cab. Do you mind getting it?"

She smiled and hopped down, returning a second later with the brown corduroy jacket Bethany gave me for our eighteenth birthday. Slipping my arms into its quilted sleeves, I could've sworn I smelled her perfume in its fabric—oranges and flowers woven into the seams.

Gina sat on the tailgate a couple feet away, studying me with a strange kind of intensity. "Adriana's told me about Rob. How they met; where he took her on their first date; the kids and dog and little hacienda they planned. But what she wouldn't tell me was what your sister was like."

"Oh?"

"Rob is hers to talk about, but Bethany is yours, and she didn't feel right telling me about her."

I reached for her hand, more to give me strength than anything. "She was a lot like you. Smart. Funny. Warm. You remind me of her sometimes."

She smiled. "Did she look like you?"

With my free hand I grabbed my chair, spun it around, and took the backpack off to pull out my wallet and a flashlight left in there from camp. Letting Gina hold the light, I opened it and pulled out a picture of us taken last Christmas when we were decorating the tree.

I stared at it for a long minute in the blue-tinged spotlight. On my shoulders, Bethy had the angel in one hand and the other grasping my forehead to keep her balance because she was laughing so hard at something I'd said.

"She was beautiful," Gina said softly, reverently.

Unable to speak, I nodded.

Taking the picture from my hand, she examined it. "This your mom?" she asked, pointing to the right side of the photo.

Leaning closer to her, I stared at it. For half a second I couldn't figure out who that happy woman in the middle of our living room was. "Yeah, but she doesn't look like that anymore."

"How does she look?"

"Broken," I whispered. It was the first word that came to mind. "You know that's what I miss most? Bethany's laugh. It was like bells on a crisp Sunday morning. Like joy unleashed, and when she laughed, I couldn't not laugh with her, it was…"

"Impossible," Gina finished for me, and I nodded. "What else do you miss?"

"The way her nose crinkled when she smiled. And the way her eyes darkened when she was angry at me." I smiled. "I never thought I'd miss that. And then there's all the things I'll never get—seeing her walk down the aisle, ecstatic and stunning in white. Watching her rock her babies to sleep. Her hair gray, her face wizened and wrinkled, surrounded by grandchildren. I don't know how to miss something I'll never have, but there's this ache in my chest that won't go away, and I don't know how to make it stop."

Her hand was cool on my cheek, wiping away tears I didn't know were falling. "I'm so sorry, Luke."

"I know," I said, releasing a deep, shuddering sigh from my chest and moving away, embarrassed that I was crying. But she reached for me, wrapping her arms around me, and burying my face in her neck, I gave into the drowning pain and let it wash over me in great, rolling waves. It pushed me under, held me down, and for the first time, I didn't fight it, but let the saline torment come and come and come as I held onto Gina.

Slowly the waves lost their crashing power and began to recede, letting in other sensations. Of strong arms around me, tight and unyielding and just as powerful. Of soft words in my ear, a rhythmic lullaby of tranquility. Of Gina's warmth wrapping around me, combating the cold pain deep inside me and melting the permafrost.

"She's still here, you know," Gina said, and when I pulled back to look at her, she placed her hand on my chest. "She's here. Inside you, and maybe that's not the same thing as being beside you, but she is here."

I wiped my eyes with the heels of my hands and tried to let that sink in, wanting more than anything to believe it to be true. "I'm sorry," I said again.

"Don't be." Her warm smile ignited something inside me. "I'm not."

I pulled her close and watched the stars come out, idly pulling at the slow burn inside me. Like a word forgotten, I wrestled with it, trying to figure out what that strange, familiar sensation could be. Finally, I gave up and relaxed into the calm that came from holding Gina in my arms.

Although a part of me wished I could've just kissed her.

Chapter 17

The next morning I found the print shop and pushed through the front door at a little before eleven o'clock. When Gina called, she didn't give me a whole lot of information. She was between classes and didn't have much time to talk, so entering Kerns Printing, I had no idea what I was getting into.

It was a wide space, packed with four-foot-high shelves, each with cubbies of bright paper organized by color in every shade of the rainbow, and almost as overwhelming as the sharp, pungent scent of ink in the air. Taking a breath, I went to the low counter and rang the silver bell. In a heartbeat, a tall, wiry kid with long black hair that clearly came out of a bottle and dressed in jeans and a ragged plaid shirt, rounded the corner. He pushed his hair out of his eyes and gave me a half-smile. "Help you?"

"I, uh, I'm looking for Kenny."

The kid turned his torso toward the doorway he'd just come though. "Dad!" he shouted, then went to the far end of the counter, and sat on it, letting his Converse sneakers whack the wood in a rhythm that was obviously meant to be annoying. Considering leaving, I watched the kid out of the corner of my eye as he tore a piece of heavy paper into tiny squares and let them fall to the floor.

"Sweep up every one of those, Alex," a voice said, and I turned to its owner, a man with a neat, gray-shot beard and light brown hair in his early-fifties, pushing a black chair identical to mine. Alex released a sound of deep disgust and jumped off the counter, letting his feet hit the linoleum with a *slap!* "The fruit of my loins," the man said with something that might've been anger—or amusement—and offered his hand, his fingers curled in a loose fist. "What can I do for you?"

"Gina Howard called you this morning," I said, wondering why she hadn't told me the man was in a chair.

"Luke," he said, smiling, his blue-green eyes crinkling at the corners. "She told me you just moved here and are looking for a job. You know anything about graphic design? Printing?"

I ran my hand through my hair, wanting a cigarette. "No, sir."

"Well, neither does my fruit," he said, nodding his head at Alex, who was pushing bits of paper into a dustpan, "and he's been working here all summer."

Alex rolled his eyes and shot us a look that said he'd rather be anywhere else.

"Come on in the back, and lemme give you a look around."

The back held a dozen large machines, basically souped-up Xerox machines, a couple of them humming and in the process of spitting out copies. The one in the corner was clattering, creating bound booklets. He showed me each one, his words washing over me senselessly, and by the time he was done, the only one I knew for sure what it did was the one that printed large banners. My brain had the foggy, heavy feel of caffeine withdrawal.

"So what do you think?" he asked, his eyes flashing.

I blinked and looked around the room; the first promising job offer I'd gotten and I was completely in over my head. "You got the part where I know absolutely nothing about any of this?" I asked with the distinct feeling of shooting myself in the foot.

"There's no way you'll be more useless than Alex," he said, and Alex grunted, either in confirmation or annoyance, I couldn't tell. "And anyway, he'll be starting school soon, so I won't have the pleasure of his company everyday. They're big shoes, but you look like you can fill 'em. Speaking of, Gina didn't say whether you're going to Tech."

"I haven't quite decided what I'm going to do."

He nodded just as the phone rang. When he turned to answer it, Alex crept closer. "How do you know Gina?" he asked.

"We met at camp."

"Three weeks ago." Narrowed eyes went over me, sharp and evaluating. "Gina told Dad you just moved into her apartment complex. Seems a little fast to me."

"This part of the interview?" I asked, smiling.

"Alex, it's Mom," Kenny said, holding out the receiver for his son. "She doesn't like him working here," he told me in a low voice when Alex got on the phone. "Thinks it's child labor or something to have a fourteen-year-old kid sitting here doing nothing, rather than sitting on his computer at home."

I studied the weave of my khaki shorts, refusing to comment either way, but by the time I was fourteen I had a paper route, a lawn mowing business, and nearly three thousand dollars in my savings account.

"So when can you start?" Kenny asked.

Surprised, I raised my eyes to his. "Monday morning?"

He nodded and offered his hand. "We'll see you then."

~~~~~

"How'd it go?" Gina asked, the moment I answered my cell, holding it to my ear with my shoulder to start my truck. Even with the windows cracked and parked in the shade, it had to be a hundred and thirty degrees in here.

I smiled and cranked up the a/c all the way. "You got a spy satellite trained on me?"

"Huh?"

"I left the shop thirty seconds ago. Either you're psychic or you're watching me," I said, laughing.

"Neither. I just got out of class, and thought I'd check in with you; did you get the job?"

"Yeah, I did. Thank you."

"I didn't do anything," she said, but I could hear her smiling. After a second she pushed out a breath. "You about to hit the road?"

"Yep. I dropped Pender by y'all's place on my way here. Thanks for watching him. I promised him no more road trips for awhile; he was pissed at me for days after the last one."

Her laugh made my smile grow bigger. "I think Will's taking him tomorrow for a doggie play date with the Divine Miss M, so you're really doing us a favor."

Last night Will got in at about two and found Gina and me on their couch watching an episode of *Breaking Bad* on Netflix. He was grinning so broadly it looked like his face had been split in half. "Can't stand in the way of true love," I said, trying to picture foot-high Pender playing with a Great Dane.

"Luke?" she said, my name like a sigh on her lips. "Be safe, and we'll see you when you get home."

"Bye, Gina," I said, aware that my voice had a similar quality, and before I could say anything else, hung up and pointed my truck south.

A few hours later, I worked my way around the perimeter of Abilene on highway 84, and the closer I got, the more nervous I got. I'd met Adriana's parents twice, once at Bethy's funeral and the other time at Rob's, and if I managed to say five words to them, I'd be surprised.

The funny thing was, I remember the quality of the light in the churches, I remember the scent of the flowers, I even remember how the organs sounded—haunting and pain-filled, as if someone was squeezing the music out of the valves of a heart—but I couldn't remember a thing about the people there.

So even though I'd met them twice, I couldn't for the life of me remember what they looked like. What Mr. Toomey's hand felt like when he shook mine. Whether Mrs. Toomey hugged me or merely ran her eyes over me, the only other survivor of the accident.

By the time I turned onto their street, I had to remind myself to breathe. The houses were large, two-story structures, set back from the street to give each enough room for a wide, circular driveway.

Pulling in behind a black jeep, I stared up at tan bricks and arched windows, looking down on me, judging me. And for a moment I wished Pender was here, to either give me the excuse to linger outside long enough to release the fear that nestled in my stomach like an egg, or to be another pauper in the face of all *this*.

"Cowboy up," I commanded, glancing in the rearview mirror.

So what if most dads *hated* me? I wasn't here to date Mr. Toomey's daughter, just shack up with her. With a little laugh I got out of the truck and made my way up the walkway to the front door. A brand new ramp placed over the steps made me smile; the smell of fresh paint somehow made me feel more welcome than if they'd hung a banner.

Mr. Toomey opened the door, tall, blonde, and wearing a smile that reminded me of the ones Adriana used to wear—full of humor and good-natured amusement.

"Welcome, Luke," he said, stepping aside for me to roll up the ramp and into the house. When I was inside, his grin got bigger. "It worked." He nodded at the ramp. "I had Eric roll up and down it a few times in my computer chair to test it out since my carpentry skills are pretty sub-par."

I laughed. "No, it's fine. Thank you."

Will could take a hint from this foyer; even though the walls were white, it was also welcoming. The tiles on the floor were a jigsaw of white, beige, and brown, laid out randomly. The L-shaped stair case had wrought iron railings and each step was the same dark wood as the floor in the dining room off to my right. Straight ahead was a wide doorway to what I assumed was the living room and off to the left was a set of double French doors.

Cinnamon, ginger, and nutmeg hung heavy in the air, along with the yeasty scent of baking bread.

"Luke's here," Mr. Toomey shouted up the stairs, and the muffled sounds of an acoustic guitar stopped. "We're so glad you could come down for the weekend. Although by mid-afternoon tomorrow, you may be seriously considering sneaking out." His eyes twinkled with amusement and he dropped his voice to a near-whisper. "And honestly, none of us would blame you."

"Don't pay any attention to him," Mrs. Toomey said, coming through the doorway ahead of me in a flour covered apron and wiping her hands on a towel. I was certain I was looking at Adriana in about thirty years, and good lord she was beautiful! "He's just crabby because I won't let him eat my apple pie filling out of the bowl."

"When you try the filling you'll understand," he retorted.

"Well, thank you for having me, Mrs. Toomey," I said, unsure what else to say.

"Call me Donna. And that's Peter," she said, wrapping an arm around me for a hug and filling my nose with that rich cinnamon smell. "You good with a knife?"

"I guess…"

"He just got here, Ma. At least give the guy a chance to shake the travel dirt off before you put him to work," Adriana's brother said, coming down the stairs, carrying the guitar I heard a moment ago.

I'd never met him, but Adriana used to have a picture on her desk taken at her sister's wedding. "That's my sister, Maria," she'd said, once after she caught me staring at it. Between Maria in a white gown, and Adriana, breathtaking in a simple burgundy bridesmaid's dress, stood her tuxedoed older brother. "And Eric. *My* twin," she said, grinning broadly.

"Can you blame Momma, though?" Adriana asked now, following him down the stairs. "Maria's not here yet, and all you and Daddy want to do is eat pie filling. Someone's gotta help."

"What about you?" Eric challenged.

"I've been elbow-deep in flour for the last two days making pie crust and bread dough," she said, giving his dark ponytail a tug.

"You see what I put up with?" he asked rolling his eyes, then held out his hand. "Nice to meet you finally."

I took his hand, but ran my eyes over Adriana next to him. Somewhere in the last month she'd changed. The sunken, skeletal appearance and the deep, bruise-like circles under her eyes were gone. Seeing her every day at camp, the change was so gradual I didn't even notice, but now it was hard to miss. She looked more like the girl who opened a dorm room door for me a year ago than the haunted ghost who showed up at my parent's house to pick me up for camp.

"Where's your stuff?" she asked, pulling me from my thoughts.

"In the truck. I, uh…"

"Wanted to make sure we were actually gonna let you stay?" Eric supplied. And while Adriana nudged him, I laughed, liking him.

"Well, y'all go get it," Peter said to his daughter. "Eric and I will help your momma in the kitchen."

"I just bet you will," Donna said, and the three of them disappeared, leaving us to stare at each other.

"You didn't bring Pender," she said, turning on her heel.

"He's not a good traveler." I told her, following her through the front door and back down the ramp. Fishing the key fob out of my pocket, I opened the door and reached for the lever to push the seat back out of the way for my duffel. "Your family seems nice," I finally said.

"We put you in the den. Momma and Daddy brought the guest bed down from upstairs, so it'll be comfortable, I think… There's a powder room on the first floor, but we'll have to figure out something for the shower. They're all upstairs."

I reached for her hand. "That's okay."

"Momma said we should renovate the downstairs, make it accessible, but Daddy told her she doesn't need an excuse to renovate, she'll just do it anyway."

I smiled since it seemed like that's what was expected of me, but a little voice inside my head pointed out that her mom was ready to renovate their whole downstairs for a guy that up until two minutes ago she'd barely met, but *my* parents couldn't make their home comfortable without taking a second mortgage out and going so deeply into debt they might never get out.

She opened her mouth to say something, but at that moment a Mustang started up the driveway. "Maria's here," she said, and took off in a run to the passenger side, leaving me to put my duffel in my lap, wondering what she was gonna say.

The rest of the afternoon was spent in the kitchen and adjoining den, Donna and her daughters chopping bags of onions, carrots, and celery to sauté in pancetta; Peter and Trent, Maria's husband, rolling out pie crust; and Eric, sitting on the bed they'd moved in there, playing his guitar. Donna gave me a paring knife to cut long S-shaped steam vents and a pastry brush to paint on an egg wash after Trent crimped the pie edges with a fork.

Over the rolling sound of the guitar, Maria talked about the dissertation she was working on: *Cognitive Factors in Semantic Conditioning,* followed by a long and jumbled explanation about the "frequency of reinforcement and repeated evaluation of stimuli on the conditioning of preferences."

I was glad I wasn't the only one who sifted through her convoluted description without understanding most of it. Finally Eric looked up from his guitar, his fingers expertly working the strings. "You're studying the effect of different rewards systems in educating kids."

"Essentially, yes," Maria said, pushing a strand of blonde hair out of her face.

"Then why the hell didn't you just say that?" he asked, grinning at his sister.

Trent told us about working at Dell—who knew software engineering could be significantly easier to understand than educational psychology?—and Eric talked about his internship at an architectural firm in Dallas.

Donna pulled a giant stockpot out of the pantry and placed it on the stove, dumping the sautéed vegetables in it, and reheated her frying pan to brown up ground chuck, veal, and pork, making my stomach growl. "What about you, Luke? What are your plans for Lubbock?" she asked.

I concentrated on sprinkling sugar over the egg wash, buying time to find the right response. "I got a job today at a print shop downtown, but other than that, I don't really know."

"What about school?" Adriana asked, her knife paused inches above the pile of oregano on a chopping board.

I shrugged and made my voice light. "Now that my fall-back plan has fallen through, I need a fall-back fall-back plan."

"What was your fall-back plan?" Trent asked in his thick Louisiana accent. With longish blonde curls and hazel eyes, he looked more like a surfer than a software geek.

"I was a petroleum engineering major, but I don't really see myself climbing all over oil rigs now, so…"

"But you could get a damn good education just working in the print shop," Peter said, smiling at me. "Learn how to use some of the design software to help clients create brochures and logos, advise them on promotional banners and merchandise… You could make a pretty good living that way."

"Yeah?"

"Sure. A lot of small businesses can't afford an ad agency, but need to compete in a global economy."

Cutting steam vents in another pie Trent handed me—the tenth in our assembly line—I considered that. Everything lately, it seemed, was about embracing the impossible.

"How many people are y'all expecting tomorrow?"

"A hundred?" Eric said, putting the guitar on the bed. "I don't know about y'all, but I'm starving. What do y'all say we order some take-out?" He got up and went to the buffet table behind me, pulled out a drawer crammed with take-out menus, and scattered them across the table, taking a seat next to me. "Barbecue, pizza, Mexican, sandwiches…" he said, like a barker at a carnival.

~~~~~

That night, lying in the bed in the den and staring at the ceiling, I felt oddly vulnerable amongst Adriana's family photos. It wasn't that her family wasn't kind, they were. They were gracious and warm and somewhere in the middle of it, I began to feel like I'd always been a part of their family, but for all the strange emptiness in the new apartment, at least there I was comfortable. And had a usable toilet and shower. Here I could only roll my legs into the tiny powder room, not close the door behind me, and kind of swing my ass onto the toilet using the pedestal sink as leverage. And that was after Addy, Maria, and Donna graciously cleared out of the den where we were playing Texas Hold 'Em. I had no idea what was gonna happen tomorrow when I needed a shower.

Bare feet shuffled down the hallway, across the tile floor, and for a second I thought it might be Adriana, coming to slip in the sheets with me.

It was Eric. With a towel tossed over his shoulder, ready for a swim, and he held a cell phone, the screen still glowing and lighting his strained face.

"Hey," I whispered, startling him.

"Oh, hey. I didn't mean to wake you."

"You didn't."

He stretched his neck, placing one ear on a shoulder, then switching to the other side. "You swim?" he asked, then laughed a little self-consciously. "I mean, you want to?"

I glanced outside. "Is it heated?"

He shook his head.

"Then I shouldn't."

Again Eric rolled his head backwards, letting it crack. "Come out anyway."

What the hell. It wasn't like I was gonna sleep, and I sat up and tossed the covers off my legs.

Outside, Eric turned on the pool light and watched me scoot out of my chair so I could dangle my feet in the water. "You mind holding onto this for me?" he asked, holding out his phone. "If it rings, pick it up. Okay?"

"Sure," I said, placed it beside me, and watched him go to the diving board to do an easy swan into the water, before swimming a couple of hard laps across the length of the pool.

The rhythmic splash nearly made my mouth water, I wanted to get in there so bad. It was nice, cool and inviting, but it would also set off a round of hypothermic shivering that I didn't want to get into or explain, so I shoved my hands in the pockets of my Bulldogs sweatshirt and laid back on the concrete.

The house towered above me, making me wonder if any of the windows were Adriana's. Was she sleeping peacefully somewhere above me? Did she still have nightmares of dark roads and loud noises?

I wanted to climb the stairs to slip into her room, her bed, like that night in the cabin when she slept so soundly in my arms, but the stairs weren't the reason I couldn't go up there, nor was not having the slightest idea which room was hers. I'd open every door to find her if I thought she wanted me to, but Gina's words came back to me on the night air: *She asked if it might be better for Will to move in with you.*

Eric pulled himself out of the water and sat on the edge of the pool a few feet away. "I'm getting a beer, you want one?" When I nodded, he got up, wrapped the towel around his waist, and went inside. Returning with two bottles, he sat next to me, dipping his feet in the water. "I met your sister once," he said. "She came to a gig in Dallas one weekend with Adriana. She was a cool girl."

I closed my eyes, remembering. A couple months after she moved in with my sister, they took a trip to Dallas to see Eric's band play at some club, and the one thing I distinctly remember about the Sunday when they came back was Bethy gushing over how hot Adriana's brother was on stage, playing his bass guitar in skin-tight leather pants, long brown hair, and dark guyliner. It would've been difficult to not see how uncomfortable it made Addy.

"Thanks," I said and took a long pull from the bottle.

"I can't imagine what you're going through. If anything ever happened to Adriana, I don't know how I'd..." he dropped his chin to his chest as if unsure how to finish that. "Anyway, I'm really sorry, man. I liked her a lot. Rob, too."

I watched the waves in the pool, glowing ethereally from the light under the diving board. "Addy brought him home for Christmas," I said to myself, then cleared my throat. "I'd forgotten you met him."

"Yeah..." He nodded then smiled. "*Addy*. I bet she hates you for that one. Course I used to call her Salami, and that's worse."

"Salami?"

He laughed. "It's what she smelled like. Used to sneak it out of Nonni's refrigerator and eat the whole thing, hiding behind the living room couch. Maria used to say that guys were gonna love her from all the practice." I raised an eyebrow, trying not to laugh, but he did. "Maria used to be a real bitch."

"Who's Nonni?"

"My grandmother on my mom's side. She passed about six years ago, but you'll meet just about everyone else tomorrow." He put his hand on my shoulder. "Good luck, and my condolences."

"That bad, huh?"

"You saw all the pies we made? The vat of sauce? Aunt Tina has a vat just like it in her fridge, and vast amounts of chocolate cake on her countertops. Same thing with Aunt Mia, and Uncle Marc…" He shrugged. "You ever been to a family reunion?"

"A couple times when I was a kid," I told him before taking a slug of beer. "At Uncle Harold and Aunt Jo's place, up in Oklahoma. Grammy O'Neal kept saying to Bethy and me, 'That's your cousin so-and-so, go play with him.' We found a good climbing tree and got as high as we could, ignoring the chaos down below."

He raised the bottle to his mouth. "You didn't like the crowds?"

"The pressure. She wanted us all to be buddies just because we were related. We probably would've been if she hadn't pushed so hard."

"Adriana used to get so mad that all the kids came and usurped her place," he said with a smile. "She was the baby the rest of the time, but then all these kids would show up, and Nonni would pay attention to them, too. It really burned her up."

"Bethy was the same way with Shi'nali when Uncle Clay's kids came to visit. Adam, Joe, and I would disappear somewhere up in the mountain, looking for bears or bobcats or whatever, and Bethy would sit around pouting because Shi'nali was messing with their baby sister."

"Sounds like Salami. So did y'all ever find one?"

I frowned, not following him.

"A bobcat or bear?"

"A family of skunks once. Adam wanted to keep one of the babies, even wrapped it up in his t-shirt and brought it home. Said we already stank, so why not keep it?"

Eric threw his head back and laughed. "Sounds like something I would've done. And Nonni would've tanned my hide for it, too," he said when he caught his breath again. "Why'd y'all call her that? Shi'nali?"

"It's Navajo for paternal grandmother."

"Huh. That's pretty cool." He leaned back and looked up at the sky. "I miss seeing the stars in Dallas. This probably isn't like what you're used to," he said, gesturing with his bottle, "but it's better than what we've got." Something about that we made his voice hitch and he picked up his phone to check it. "We should go in, Momma's probably got her alarm set for six."

"Okay," I said, but didn't move. "Who'd you think was going to call?"

He ran his hand through long, wet hair and wringing out the ends. "My girlfriend. You'll meet her tomorrow. She's at her parent's place tonight."

"She's from Abilene, too." It wasn't a question, but he nodded anyway. "Well, I'm looking forward to meeting another outsider," I said, smiling. "We'll sit on the sidelines and make disparaging remarks about your enormous family."

He laughed. "Long as you don't mind her taking pictures the whole time. Alison's kind of obsessed."

~~~~~

I felt like I'd just gotten back in bed when Donna started tiptoeing around the kitchen. I ignored her as long as I could, flipping on my side and burying my head under the covers. But when Maria joined her, whispering over coffee, then Peter, whose deep voice traveled as if he had an amplifier, I gave up and decided coffee wasn't such a bad idea after all. It was just as well because soon everyone was milling around the kitchen, scratching wild bed hair and yawning through their determination to be awake.

From there it seemed as if time sped up, Eric hauled my ass up the stairs for a shower, laughing as I rode piggyback. The women used up most of the hot water by the time I got in Donna and Peter's shower—the only one with a bench—but at least I was clean-shaven and ready to meet the rest of Adriana's family.

Sitting next to her in my truck, I followed Peter's SUV, loaded down with a vat of spaghetti sauce and ten apple pies. From the farthest corner of the seat, I felt Adriana watching me. "What?" I finally asked, feeling self-conscious.

"Nothing… I was just wondering when the last time that we went somewhere together was. In here."

I didn't know whether we ever had, Bethany was always with us. Or Rob. Even though his Geo was small and unreliable, it fit four semi-comfortably. And then it hit me. "That time you messed up your ankle."

"During that ice storm," she said, staring out the window.

Freezing rain had covered Odessa in two inches of slick ice, and the parking lots were filled with students skating in their tennis shoes like clumsy Apollo Ohnos. She slipped and twisted her ankle. Rob gingerly checked it out, his face a mask of calm, then took me aside to tell me I needed to take her to the emergency room. "I'm nearly certain it's broken, *Papi*," he said, his voice low, "and with my bald tires, she'll be safer with you."

She begged him to come with us, but he lifted her easily off the ground and walked sure-footed to my truck, whispering calming words meant only for her. Bethany, walking beside me and carrying Adriana's purse, gripped my hand tightly on the slippery ice and murmured something that later haunted me: "He would die for her."

Even now I could feel her foot resting on my thigh as I navigated the slick roads, telling her over and over that it would be fine, and when I carried her into the ER, I refused to put her down. Somehow I thought it's what Rob would do if he were there, and I needed to protect her the same way he would.

"That was the first time I knew I could trust you," she said to the windshield, and the words floated in the air the last mile or so, each of us lost in our own thoughts.

"Park wherever you want," she said as we came up on the wide field that served as parking lot for several dozen cars and a handful of RVs. "Uncle Marc said we could use the driveway if that's easier."

I got the sense that I was completely in over my head, despite the warnings Peter and Eric gave me. Up ahead, the cabin was so different from what I pictured, it nearly made my head swim. Somehow I thought it would be… I don't know, I guess I pictured Uncle Clay's two-bedroom bungalow on Possum Kingdom Lake. A little get-away for weekend fishing and just big enough for their family of five to not actually sleep on top of each other. Except they kind of did with the bunk beds.

What I didn't picture was a wide three-story log cabin with dozens of windows, a wrap-around porch, and topped off with a green patinated copper roof.

"The field is fine." Whistling under my breath, I turned to her. "Damn, this is what you call a place on the lake? What do you call the Sistine Chapel, a nice place to pray?"

She smiled. "I've brought enough guys out here to know I've got to downplay its enormity. Anyway, it's not *my* place, it's Uncle Marc and Aunt Bea's."

"And I'm just one in a string of ol' country boys you've subjected it to," I teased.

"I wouldn't say *string*," she said, opening her door to get out and come over to my side of the truck.

"Just make sure I don't embarrass myself by using the wrong fork or something," I said, transferring to my chair.

She laughed, leaning on the open door. "Sorry, I won't be much help there, either. The only time I've ever had more than two forks at a meal was at Maria's wedding reception, but I'll give you the same advice Eric gave me—start on the outside and work your way in."

I smiled and started pushing through the brown grass and parched dirt, chasing grasshoppers jumping out of the way.

As we approached a gaggle of kids, she had to raise her voice for me to hear her over their shouting as they played tag. "Okay, so there's swimming, bocce ball, inner tubing on the lake…"

Looking around at the yard filled with people—the old men playing what I could only assume was bocce and yelling at each other in Italian; the cluster of women sitting under a large tree and fanning themselves while watching the kids play; the game of sandpit volleyball underway, the shouts and insults as players dove for the ball—I suddenly understood how overwhelming this was. Watching the volleyball game for a moment, I half-wished I could join it, if only as a way to focus on something other than the chaos. Eric was playing in swim trunks, sweaty and sandy. So were Trent and Maria. And on the sidelines, a beautiful blonde held an expensive-looking camera to her eye, following the action.

"How about swimming?" I suggested, glancing at the lake down the hill.

"Right," Adriana said and led me past the porch where older men and women lounged on cushioned chairs, enjoying the whirring ceiling fans and watching their grandchildren playing volleyball or Frisbee or raucous games of tag.

Inside, she took me to a boys' bedroom where ten bunk beds made of rough-hewn logs added to the luxurious rusticness of the room. Along one wall were blue lockers. "Use any empty one you want to. The bathroom's just through that door," she said, pointing at the far end of the room, "and I'll meet you outside, okay?"

Dressed in my swim trunks a few minutes later, I went out to the living room. Just beyond an archway in the largest kitchen I'd ever seen, a dozen women and a couple men laughed and joked with each other in a combination of English and Italian. Standing around an island that might've been larger that my momma's entire kitchen, they were busy turning raw ingredients into the most mouth-watering dishes I'd ever smelled. Upstairs, just beyond a railing made of polished tree branches, four boys played pool beneath a long Coca-Cola billiard light.

I went to a bookcase that ran the length of one living room wall, crammed with thick tomes of James Joyce, Dostoevsky, and Dickens; photographs of family members grinning for the camera; and antique heirlooms, mixed with high-end knickknacks. A photograph of a woman in a white, floor length wedding dress captured my attention. Picking it up, I studied her sepia-toned face, gazing up at a man in a dress uniform, the rank on his collar was obscured by her bouquet. Looking at it, I got the sense that they had no idea the photographer was pointing his camera at them, they were too absorbed in each other.

"Told you there were a lot of us," Adriana said, surprising me. Dressed in a red bikini, she strolled toward me, making me light-headed. Silver metallic circles rested on each hip bone and between the cleavage of her breasts, white piping ran along her shoulders on top and disappeared between her legs below. Reminding myself we were just friends, *only* friends, I pointedly turned back to the photograph in my hands.

"Are these your grandparents?"

"On their wedding day. The first one in Italy, where they met. They had another one after they came to the States with Papaw's family. Supposedly they weren't too thrilled he married a Catholic."

Smiling, I put the picture frame back. "You ready?"

"Yep," she said, and I followed her back outside, past a couple boys play-ing with a remote-controlled helicopter and a group of giggling pre-pubescent girls, to a long deck floating on the rough water that made pushing my chair even harder on the uneven wooden planks. Someone in the water yelled what I could've sworn sounded like *poopstinks*, and the thirty-odd people in the roped off area between the dock and a floating platform cheered or groaned while moving to the opposite end of the swimming area. After a moment they were more or less organized on opposite sides again, tossing two soggy Nerf balls back and forth over the heads of Trent and another boy in the middle on kick-boards. When the boy caught the black ball, the girl who threw it left her end and swam to the kickboard in the middle.

"What are they playing?" I asked.

Adriana grinned. "Poopstinks. It's kind of like Monkey in the Middle, if you catch the black ball you switch out with the person who threw the ball."

Just then Trent caught the red ball and shouted, "Poopstinks!" at the top of his lungs. He and the other girl abandoned the kickboards and headed for opposite sides of the swimming area, two others grabbed the kickboards, and all the others repositioned themselves.

"How do you know who wins?"

She shrugged. "No one wins. Just play until you get tired, or it's time to eat."

"And it's *always* time to eat around here," Eric called, tossing me the red ball, and when I caught it, he yelled *Poopstinks* so loudly, a guy passing in a kayak turned to look at us.

The water churned as bodies swam across the no-man's-land. "I guess we gotta play now," I said, grinning at Adriana. And at the edge of the deck, I locked my wheels and dove in.

The water, warm and green, washed over me, compelling me, just as it always did, and I swam deep under the surface, headed for the rope on the far-thest end of the dock. The sensation of so many bodies treading water made the sensations against my skin more real as I pushed through the water, enjoying the strain of my arms, the uneven power of my legs kicking, the right one stron-ger, the left one struggling but valiantly working to propel my body as I reveled in the burn of my oxygen-deprived lungs. I forced my body through the water a few more feet before giving in to the nearly dizzying insistence and surfacing.

A half a second later Eric was beside me. "That's probably fifty meters."

I wiped my wet hand down my face and gauged the distance, panting hard. "It would've been farther if I could still kick." And gave up the cigarettes, those things were gonna kill me.

"I once saw him do seventy-five meters," Adriana said, coming up behind me. "It was a alpha-male thing between him and Rob, but it was pretty amazing."

I studied the algae-tinged Styrofoam on the platform a few feet away where Maria lay on a rubber mat between two other girls, their skin glistening in the sun, amused that Adriana knew I'd challenged Rob that afternoon just to show off. It was stupid then, and seemed even dumber now, not because neither of us couldn't do it—although that flip turn was always a killer when your lungs were already begging for air—but because I'd somehow gotten it into my head that if I could just beat him, then she'd see me differently. Or something. It was a total dick-swinging contest, but Rob didn't puff up his chest, determined to show-off for his girl. Instead, he flashed her one of his brilliant smiles and strolled over to the starting blocks, adjusting his goggles and swinging his arms like he did for any race. I should've known in that moment he was gonna beat me. Not because he wanted it more, but because he knew he didn't have to defend himself. Adriana wasn't his to steal.

"Adriana told you the rules?" Eric asked, cocking his chin toward the people tossing the footballs.

When I told him she did, he swam to the no-man's land in the middle, taking a little boy's place who'd been there long enough to look discouraged, and immediately caught the red ball and shouted at the top of his lungs.

I swam to the other end of the swimming area and stopped next to Addy. "Where'd y'all get this game?" I asked her.

"Eric made it up years ago," she said, beaming at her big brother on the other side, who now had a girl on his shoulders so she'd have a chance at catching the ball.

"Why didn't you suggest it in all those hours in the pool last week? I'd about had it with Marco Polo and sure could have used a break from endlessly racing everyone from one end to the other."

She smiled. "You had the whistle. And anyway, do you know how much those kids loved racing you? They're convinced you're a future Paralympian gold medalist. That gives them some serious bragging rights."

"I…" I began, but she caught the black Nerf ball, and when she threw it, a teen in the middle caught it, so she went to take his place on the kickboard.

Everyone, it seemed, took a turn in the middle on the kickboards, although some, like Trent, Eric, or the older players volunteered to relieve someone who'd been there long enough to get frustrated or annoyed. Others volunteered just for the relief of clinging to a kickboard, rather than constantly treading water.

A red and white ski boat and two matching blue jet skis came in and went out, just outside the roped area, churning up the lake, occasionally picking up waterlogged players to take with them. Others came to join, or left in favor of a volleyball game, sunscreen, or snacks, but the game went on. No winners, no losers, just cousins, siblings, aunts and uncles, most with golden Mediterranean-kissed skin and dark hair, playing in the water.

"Come here," Eric said, swimming to me and cutting into my thoughts, "there's someone I want to introduce you to." He turned, and I followed him to the platform ladder, where he put two hands on the rungs, preparing to pull himself up before looking back at me. "How are you gonna get up here?"

I laughed; the top of the platform was at least three feet above my head, and despite my general rejection of pool lifts, without one I had no idea. "Getting in was the easy part."

He just rolled his eyes and shook his head. "Hop on. Guess I'll be dragging your ass everywhere."

I laughed and grabbed his shoulders for him to pull us up the ladder.

Once he placed both feet on the swaying platform, he took me to a blue foam mat and kneeled, letting me slide off next to the blonde I saw taking pictures at the volleyball court earlier. Deep in conversation with Maria, it took her a moment to turn from Adriana's sister to us, and when she did, she fixed unusually blue eyes on Eric. It was as if the sun had come out after a storm.

"You know half the lake can hear y'all, right?" Maria asked as Eric sat behind the blonde, wrapping his arms around her and letting her rest her back against his chest. "People are staring."

Eric shrugged his shoulders. "Let 'em. We're having fun. Luke, I want to introduce you to Alison." He turned to the girl, his eyes drinking her in. "Babe, this is the guy I was telling you about."

Her full lips turned up in a warm smile. "Adriana's friend."

"The photographer," I said, shaking her hand. "Get anything good this morning?"

Her smile faltered for a second. "I don't know. I promised myself I'm not gonna look at them until Monday morning."

The girl on the other side of Maria raised up on her elbows, taking off her sunglasses. "Alison's working for Scott Mitchell."

"It's really just an internship," Alison said, her vibrant eyes focusing on the cabin across the lake. "I get coffee, haul around his equipment..." she shrugged. "It's no big deal."

"No big deal? He's *Scott Mitchell*," the girl said, her voice full of reverence. "You know he's shot more *Vogue* covers than any other photographer in the magazine's history? And Alison says it's no big deal."

When Alison didn't respond, the girl put her sunglasses back on and laid back on the mat.

"Joey's grown," Adriana said, climbing up the ladder to sit next to me on the mat. "And just when'd that kid get old enough to drive? He said he has Aunt Tina's old Plymouth now."

"Somehow Anita talked her into it," the girl said, flipping onto her stomach.

"Aunt Tina is my mom's sister, and Anita, her daughter, is Joey's mom," Adriana said to me and cocked her head toward the girl. "Theresa's Uncle Gene and Aunt Mia's granddaughter."

"Joey's my second cousin, once removed," Theresa said, managing to sound both worldly and bored.

"There gonna be a quiz later?" I asked, only vaguely following that.

"I'm still afraid there might be," Alison said, tracing a finger over the guitar tattoo on Eric's forearm, concentrating on the black lines. "But so far no one's handed me a number two pencil."

Wiping my hand across my brow, I feigned relief. With all the people in the water down below—not to mention the ones crowding the volleyball court, the men playing bocce ball, those in the shadows of the wrap-around porch, and God only knew how many were in the kitchen, but the racket coming from there earlier suggested a full-on mob—there was no way I'd ever remember all their names, much less how they were connected. And yet, there was something comforting in it. Only once had I experienced anything like this, and it wasn't at Uncle Harold and Aunt Jo's place.

Two months after I met Rob, he asked me to go back to El Paso with him to his sister's *Quinceañera*. To be honest, I wasn't sure I wanted to go, nearly five hours trapped in a rattling death-trap of a car with a guy I wasn't sure I even liked sounded like a pretty good definition of hell to me.

Meant to be my nemesis in the water when we first met, God, I was such a jackass to him! I hated to admit it, but I bought into the idea that Rob Sanchez stood between me and my Olympic dreams, and I was determined to send him home, crying to his mama. Of course Bethy—claiming not only was he my teammate, but my roommate, too—went and made friends with him. It pissed me off, and I went so far as to tell her to just sleep with the guy so we could move on with our damn lives.

It was the only time she ever slapped me, but I deserved it.

He and I were just beginning to be cool with each other when Gloria's birthday popped up, and somehow the guy got it in his head that what we needed was a little road trip bonding. His family wasn't as big as this, but seeing them together changed how I looked at him. They had less than Bethy and I did, which was saying something, but they had something even better—each other. And underlying all of it was a sense of belonging. Of knowing who you were and where you came from and that those people, no matter what, would always be there.

Laying back on the mat, I closed my eyes against the sun, letting it warm my skin, and absorbing the pandemonium around me. The boats and jet skis roaring on the lake, the shouts of Adriana's family occasionally drowning out the conversation on the platform, the scent of roasting meat on the air, the platform beneath me rocking gently, all of it lulled me into deep relaxation, and when Adriana reached for my hand, I laced my fingers with hers knowing there wasn't any place I'd rather be.

~~~~~

Later that night, with my stomach stuffed with enough pasta and meatballs and apple pie it was nearly uncomfortable, I held Adriana close as she sat in my lap while a bonfire roared in an enormous pit. A few feet away, Trent and Maria sat wrapped around each other in what Adriana called "newlywed splendor." Despite the smile on her face when she said it, there was a sadness in her voice that betrayed her. She refused to look at them, or Alison and Eric who sat on our other side, Alison on a hay bale, Eric on the ground, strumming his guitar while she ran graceful fingers through his long hair.

Watching the fire pop, listening to Eric's guitar blending with the sound of his uncle playing a violin and a cousin with a wooden recorder, and holding Adriana so close I felt the slow beat of her heart in her chest, I realized she was hanging on to me so tight as a way to fight the deep longing inside her.

"You okay?" I whispered in her ear.

She didn't move, didn't say anything, but then she buried her face in my neck and released a hitching breath. "He was supposed to be here. He promised he would be."

Burying one hand in her fire-warmed hair and pulling her even closer with the other, I closed my eyes. "Addy, I'm sorry," I said, knowing how inadequate it sounded, but not knowing what else to say.

"I know," she whispered and blew out a long breath. "Promise me something, promise me you'll always be here."

I pulled back to look at her, and gently placing my hands on either side of her face, stroked her cheek with my thumb. And in that moment I memorized everything: the heat of the fire on my skin; the sound of the music swirling around us; the way she fit against me, tiny and bird-like, but solid and strong; the way her eyes blazed when they met mine, as if drinking me in and memorizing me, too. "Adriana, I'm not going anywhere."

When she nodded, the relief was as palpable as the feel of her against me.

Chapter 18

The drive back to Lubbock seemed to take forever, and I kept glancing in my rearview mirror to make sure Addy's Honda hatchback was still back there. God love her, she was the most cautious driver I'd ever met, and the accident had only made her more so. Since leaving the Interstate after Sweetwater, she'd slow down through the towns and have a hard time picking up her speed again.

A less secure guy might think she was reluctant to leave her hometown. A less secure guy might think maybe we should've taken Eric and Alison up on their offer to come with us to move her stuff into the new place. Instead, I replayed the conversation Donna and I had this morning at the kitchen table in a dark, silent house over steaming cups of coffee.

"How're your parents doing?" she asked me with the kind of tenderness that only comes from living through something terrible and at the same time knowing what you lived through could have been so much worse.

"They…" I began, ready to tell her they were just fine, but I made the mistake of glancing at her and a truth I'd never even consciously considered fell out. "They're falling apart. Dad's always gone, not that he ever really knew how to stay, but now… Now he's using my hospital bills as an excuse. Mom told me that right after I left for camp, he volunteered for three-week hauls again. It was just a scheduling fluke that he happened to be home when I was, but he's leaving her there. Alone. And she is going crazy. I don't mean stir-crazy, but *insane*. She called me the other night to tell me she took flowers out to Bethany's place and met some of her neighbors." I studied the black coffee in my mug, searching for answers and finding none. At the time it seemed weird, but sitting with Donna in her cozy kitchen… "That's not normal, is it?"

"Sweetheart, there's nothing normal here. She buried her baby, her little girl, and as if that's not bad enough, she thought she was going to lose you, too. We didn't know if you were going to make it through those surgeries, and then when you did, we had no idea what kind of recovery you were going to have. Maybe she has the right to go a little insane."

"Maybe," I said. "I just… am I doing the right thing leaving her, too?"

"You can't fix her. Any more that you can fix your parent's marriage. That's up to them to figure out. Just like you have to figure out your own life for yourself. But Luke? You are a member of this family," she said, her gold-brown eyes like lasers, intense and honest. "Don't think for a moment that I don't see what you have done for my baby—"

"I didn't do anything," I said, embarrassed.

She smiled and covered my hand with her own. "You and she somehow figured out how to save each other from what happened that night. That means I get to adopt you if I want to, okay?" She turned toward the bed I abandoned when she came downstairs to make coffee. "And next time you come to visit, we'll have a proper guest room for you. With a toilet and shower."

"That's really not necessary," I began, but she gave me a warm smile and squeezed my hand. As far as she was concerned, the matter was closed.

Glancing in the mirror back at Adriana, I tried to imagine what she saw from her driver's seat: her parent's old dresser, headboard, and bedside table, pulled down from the attic and given a couple coats of glossy black paint; her mattress and box spring; boxes of linens and pots and pans, excess wedding gifts and donated by her cousin Laura. I imagined her back there—her car filled with Sara Bareilles, or Katy Perry if she wanted something a little wilder—nervous and excited and probably wondering what the hell she'd agreed to. It's what I was thinking anyway.

Resuming the cruise control, as much to not speed as to use my left hand to steer, I turned up Alan Jackson on my speakers and pretended that whatever happened next wasn't about to change my life irrevocably.

~~~~~

Two miles from the apartment and sitting at one of a dozen stoplights between the highway and home, I fished out my cell. I'd promised Gina I would let her know when we were nearly there, and by the time Addy and I opened the door to our place, she and Will were standing in the middle of our miraculously transformed living room.

"Come in," Will said, taking Adriana's hand. "Let me give you the two cent tour. Gina and I painted the hideous white walls, this gorgeous café au lait. All except this one," he pointed like Vanna, "Benjamin Moore calls it Pacific Ocean Blue, but I call it peacock blue. We set it off with a wasabi green slipcover for the couch and a café au lait cover for the armchair, and brought in dashes of red, blue, and that gorgeous green."

"Oh my God," Adriana said, taking a couple slow steps further into the room, wiping her eyes.

If Adriana was surprised to tears, I was shocked, sure there was no way this was the same living room I left just two days ago. The mismatched, haphazard Goodwill-chic look was gone.

"How'd y'all do this?" I asked, finally finding my voice.

He grinned. "You were there when we picked it all. Or most of it, anyway."

I shook my head, sure even though I'd handed over my wallet a half-dozen times to him, there was no way we'd bought any of this. Or at least when we had, it sure didn't look like this.

"He's amazing, isn't he?" Gina asked, grinning at Will.

"I'm David Bromstad in scrubs," he said with a laugh. "Let's get you unloaded, girl. Are we gonna need to get Joe?"

"Nah," I said, shaking my head. But I wouldn't've admitted to needing Steroid Joe if Addy had an entire suite of solid mahogany furniture in the bed of my truck.

Will raised an eyebrow, no doubt reading my mind, and let a slow smile slide across is face. "Then let's get this done. I've been moving stuff all weekend, and I need a beer."

Déjà vu hung thick in the air, and carrying another box of Adriana's things, it settled around me like dust motes. Once before I carted cardboard boxes for her, sure whatever came from that move would change the trajectory of my life. This move was no different; I might've even had the same box packed with the same t-shirts or picture frames or toiletries for all I knew. And yet, rather than Rob's iPod playing Tejano rock, Will's Disco filled the apartment. This time, it was Gina who provided the unrelenting enthusiasm to keep us motivated when collapsing on the couch with an icy beer sounded significantly better. And this time, rather than climbing three flights of stairs, carting as many boxes as I dared, claiming I could always handle another, I balanced one on my lap, using my chin to keep it in place.

"Next weekend we're throwing a party," Gina announced later, sliding a drawer in Adriana's dresser. Between the three of them, they were able to get it off the truck and placed it on the furniture slides Will picked up. He didn't want Steroid Joe sniffing around our girls any more than I did, it seemed. "Y'all don't have plans, do you?"

"With all the *other* people we know in town?" I asked, using a box cutter to slice through the tape on a box marked *Linens*. The clean scent of laundry detergent wafted out of the box, and I pushed aside white tissue paper to pull out a fluffy white bath towel. "Where do you want these?"

Adriana put the silver lamp in her hands on the dresser, grabbed the large wicker basket from the floor, and began taking the paper-wrapped items from it, gingerly placing them on the dresser next to the lamp. "In here," she said. Taking the towel from me, she showed me how to roll it up the way she wanted, then put it in the basket, standing up.

"It'll just be a few friends from school," Will said from the closet where he was busy organizing Adriana's wardrobe like he did mine. "We figured it wouldn't be fair to keep you all to ourselves. Even if we really want to." He held up a green dress. "This is fabulous, put it on."

"Now?"

"Come in here with me," he said and laughed. "Never thought I'd advocate *for* the closet." He took the dress off the hanger and looked inside. "Don't even need a bra, get in here and strip for me. I want to see it on you."

"He's just gonna pester you until you do as he asks," Gina said with a knowing grin.

"I won't even look at your tatas," he said. "Okay, I will, but it doesn't mean the same thing as for other guys. Right, Luke?"

I concentrated on rolling a towel.

Once the closet door closed, I kept working on those towels, but in my mind's eye saw her pull the brown tank top over her head, her white bra against golden skin and gently cupping her small, round breasts; saw her slowly unbutton her denim shorts; heard the teeth of her zipper slowly separate, exposing the elastic of her panties...

"Luke?" Gina asked, sitting on the bed next to the towel I gripped in my hands. "He likes boys. Boys with hairy chests. And a penis. I'm pretty sure Adriana has neither."

"I know that," I said, forcing my hands to let go of the towel and smoothing out the wrinkles.

"Then take a breath before that vein in your forehead explodes. The only thing Will's getting excited about in there is how the ruching on that dress is accentuating her tiny waist."

I studied her for a moment and released the air in my lungs. "Ruching?"

She grinned. "And that's how I know *you're* not gay."

"No," I said and returned to rolling up the towel. "We're just friends."

She took a towel and rolled it up neatly, sticking it in the basket. "You telling me or reminding yourself?"

From the closet door floated Will's voice, low and unintelligible, followed by Addy's nervous giggle. "It's better this way," I said as if convincing myself. "I can't lose her, too. She's all I have left of them, and I can't... *we* can't be anything else." I looked at Gina, sitting just a foot away. "Would it be weird if I told you I think of her even more as Rob's girl now that he's gone?"

"And that's why Will talking about seeing her tatas makes that vein throb?" she asked, running a finger along the offending vein. "I'm gonna tell you the same thing I told her: she doesn't have to move on right away or anytime soon, but she *does* have to move on. She can't spend her entire life in mourning, afraid to look forward and too scared to let go of the past."

"She's doing better," I said, defending her, but at the same time, feeling her arms around me, gripping me so tightly neither of us could breathe because Rob wasn't at a campfire as promised.

Gina smiled. "She is, but she needs to know it's okay to move on. She needs you to be okay with it, so she can be."

I closed my eyes and took a long breath, unsure if I could.

"You know, when Will came out, it took me a long time to learn how to let go of him enough to trust he would come back to me," she said, her eyes on the door. "But eventually I realized that letting go didn't mean I loved him any less, it meant I trusted him enough to not disappear. I know it's not the same with y'all, but maybe you and Adriana can figure out how to let go and not be afraid someone else will come between you. Because no one ever could."

~~~~~

We fell into an easy routine, Adriana and I. Every morning we'd get up around the same time. I made coffee while she showered, then, while she got ready for the job she found making deliveries for the florist around the corner, I'd shower as she shouted over its roar while doing her makeup. The first couple mornings I couldn't quite figure out why she'd want to do that—yelling at the naked dude in her shower about her plans for the day or the classes she was thinking of signing up for seemed like a step above actually coming in and sitting on the sink while I took a dump—but the moment I shut off the water, she'd leave and the stream-of-consciousness dialogue would stop until I came out of my room, dressed.

And then one morning it hit me, it was the same thing she did with Bethany each morning in their dorm room.

Each day Kenny taught me something new about my job, although my main task was monitoring the website for placed orders and answering the phones. Alex helped in fits and spurts, his energy the highest around mid-morning, during which he'd absolutely astound me with his creativity; despite what Kenny said about the kid not knowing anything about the business, he sure as hell showed me up every single day. But he also had about one brochure or logo design in him a day, and once that creative energy was used up, he spent the rest of the day texting his buddies or playing solitaire on the computer. Kenny would simply sigh, make a comment about school starting soon, and go back to showing me how to manipulate images in a menu for the new barbecue place up the road or a training manual for the factory across town. I had a notebook that I'd painstakingly record each mouse click or command, and after a couple days began to feel, if not proficient, then at least not completely incompetent.

By the time I got home each night, Adriana was already there and often making dinner with Will for the four of us while Gina sat on one of the bar stools she brought over one day, chatting them up and usually talking about this party they'd decided to throw.

~~~~~

Thursday night I sat on the couch reading *InDesign for Dummies* and making more notes in my notebook. Adriana sat on the other end, thumbing through the Red Raiders course catalogue and making little notes in the margins. The only sounds came from Pender, curled up in the tangle of our legs and snoring softly, and the occasional rustle of one of us turning a page. For the first time since she moved in, it was just the two of us, home alone at eight o'clock at night—Gina was teaching at the rec center and Will was at the vet's office taking care of a cat with renal failure—and something about their absence made me acutely aware of just how much they'd been around lately.

"What?" Adriana asked, looking up. When I frowned, she tilted her head to one side. "You were staring."

Was I?

"Just thinking, I guess," I said and ran a hand through my hair. "I have an appointment next week at Walk'N'Roll, and I'm hoping you'll go to with me."

"That the Chinese restaurant downtown?" she asked, going back to the catalog.

"Huh?"

"Wok'N'Roll... Isn't that the place we went the other night for dinner?"

I laughed. "It's where I'm gonna be doing PT. They called while I was at work today and have a slot open. It's basically the same stuff as before, but I thought if you wanted to go with me..."

She smiled. "Can we get Chinese after?"

"Absolutely," I told her, going back to the notebook in my hand, rereading what I'd just written about setting up bleed marks in a document. "Do you really want a bunch of people in here tomorrow night?"

She shifted, her bare foot sliding along my outer thigh until it rested between my hip and the couch cushion. "Not really," she finally admitted, speaking to the thick book in her lap. "But I don't want to hurt their feelings. Gina's so excited about it."

"Yeah..."

"But if I ask, sneak me out, okay?"

"Will says it's just a few friends," I reminded her but promised anyway.

Will's definition of "a few friends" and mine, I found out, were not the same. Granted, compared to some of the parties I'd been to on campus, this was a barely a soirée. Delta Sig used to throw some legendary keggers: wall-to-wall bodies gyrating against each other, the start of promises that would only last a night; the air heavy with beer and sex and sweat that would linger in the upholstery until the next party.

This would've been a quiet night, and yet, I was overwhelmed.

Sitting on the couch, watching Will and Gina's friends drinking beer and talking over the music, I wanted to move, to get out of there and pull calming tobacco deep into my lungs, but somewhere in the last half an hour, my chair had gone missing, and I was in no position to get up and find it.

"How ya doin'?" Gina asked, plopping on the sofa next to me, close enough that I could smell her perfume and the beer on her breath.

I let my eyes drift around the room. "Fine. Your friends seem nice," I said, looking past her to Adriana, leaning against the countertop in the kitchen and talking to a guy in tight jeans and a black Stetson.

Gina turned slightly. "Ryan. Psych major and a really nice guy. I hear you're doing a great job at the shop, really jumping into the flow."

Refocusing on her, I smiled, feeling my ears get warm. "Like Kenny said, I got big shoes to fill."

"Alex?" she asked with a laugh. "He's a good kid, he's just… young."

"How do you know them, anyway?"

"They're—"

"What'd you do with that case of Lone Star, babe?" Will asked from the kitchen, shouting over the music.

"It's in the freezer," she called back. "It was still warm when Bradley brought it an hour ago."

"I hope the Metzger's don't mind all the noise," I said, conscious of how loud it was in here. Our upstairs neighbor, they were a sweet old couple. They even brought us a pan of apfelstrudel two days after we moved in, the entire time she apologized that her eye sight was going, so she couldn't be certain of the recipe anymore. It was delicious.

"I talked to them yesterday," she said to me, then raised her voice again, watching Will. "They're all in there, but I had to take them out of the case to get them all in," she called.

"Then I better get them all out so they don't explode."

"They said they was going to see their daughter this weekend anyway," she said to me.

"Who?" I asked.

"The Metzgers. They have this beautiful grandbaby, showed me pictures of her. Kinda made my uterus hurt," she said, laughing.

"Seriously?"

She shrugged. "Sure. Not that I want one right *now*, but someday. Why, don't you?"

I played with a tassel on a throw pillow. "I don't know. I used to think maybe. Someday."

"I always have. My parents brought home my brother, and that was it. He was the cutest, sweetest baby, and even at six years old, I just *knew*. Course the way I carried him around, took care of him like he was mine, it's amazing he survived." She smiled, the memory lighting her up.

"Why's that?"

"You know how you can drag a doll around by the foot and it doesn't mind?"

I nodded.

"A real baby does."

I laughed, letting my eyes settle on her, once again stunned by her beauty and her proximity. Tonight a silky navy blue top shimmered against the swell of her breasts and enhanced the deep color of her eyes. A long tendril of hair had escaped the intricate knot at the nape of her graceful neck, making me want to touch it, wrap it around my fingers, tuck it behind her ear for her. As if reading my thoughts, she reached up, and with one slender finger, slid it behind her ear, where it dangled, tangling with her silver earring.

"Luke?" she asked, her mouth making my name a sensual entity.

"Hmm…?" I murmured, then shook myself, blinking.

Her laugh was musical, the kind that made guys want to say something funny just to hear it. "I asked if you want another beer."

I'd forgotten I even had a bottle in my hand and leaned over to place the empty container on the coffee table. "Not really. Do y'all know these people from Tech?"

"Some of them. Most of the people out on the patio are from school. Terry and Micah, in the corner," she said, pointing, "went to high school with Will and me. And Ryan and I have been dance partners for *years*."

I glanced at the guy who at that moment placed his Stetson on Addy's head. "He doesn't look gay," I said.

"He's not," she said with a low, throaty laugh. "And thank God, cause no offense to Will and his camp, but they've got enough hotties over there." I raised an eyebrow, not sure how to respond to that, but Gina visibly ran her eyes over the guy before turning back to me and lowering her voice. "You should see his body, the guy is *cut*."

Territorially, protectively, I studied the dude—his tall, muscular frame, nearly iridescent black hair, and pale blue eyes—resting one hand on the countertop, effectively trapping Adriana between it and his body, and her looking up at him with a soft, trusting expression. "But he's a…"

"*Ballerina?*" she supplied. "The two aren't mutually exclusive."

"I didn't mean," I began, but at that moment Adriana tilted her head back and laughed, a flirtatious peal dusted off to be tried out again, and I closed my eyes, all the times I heard that same laugh for Rob flooding back at me. Whatever Gina said about letting her go, no matter how much I wanted her to be happy, I wasn't ready to hear that laugh again. Not for someone who wasn't my best friend. "About that beer…"

"I'll be right back," Gina said, standing.

~~~~~

I knew the moment I heard that laugh. Or the first time he called and Addy disappeared to her bedroom for an hour. Or the evening they spent in our living room debating Nietzsche, Freud, and Piaget, while I lay on my bed listening to their voices blend in a kind of building symphony of his bass, her alto, and that soft, percussive laugh. And when I came home one night a couple of weeks later and found Gina holding a curling iron to tiny pieces of chocolate-colored hair, the two of them giggling over the sounds of the radio playing in Addy's room, I decided I had to be okay with Ryan. At least as okay as I could be with her going out with a ballerina.

"Hey," Gina said, meeting my eyes in the bathroom mirror, "how was work?"

Pinching the bridge of my nose, I tried to keep the headache that had been playing around the edges of my brain all day at bay for a little longer. The chemicals we used at the shop could bring on some pretty powerful migraines, and I took the last of the Aleve I kept in my backpack around lunchtime. Kenny told me I'd get used to it, but I was still waiting for that to be true. "When'd this become a beauty salon?"

"Since I got a wild hair and took a pair of scissors to my head a few months ago," Adriana said. "I'm tired of looking like hell."

"I thought of it more as weed-wacker chic," Gina said with a smile before wrapping another strand of hair around the barrel of the hot iron and filling the tiny space with the renewed scent of burning hair. "In any case, it's time to let that look go." She winked at her friend in the mirror, then turned her eyes back to me. "Unless you're next, you're interrupting girl time."

"No, no," I said, running my hand protectively through my hair. Just because it had gotten long enough to curl didn't mean I needed to participate in their hairdressing. "I need to take something for my head anyway."

Half an hour later, I was lying on the couch, stroking Pender's wiry fur, studying the inside of my eyelids, and listening to the muffled sounds of two girls making each other laugh. They'd moved into Adriana's room and with her door closed, I couldn't hear what was so funny, but between the medicine and the happy sound of them making me smile, that headache was receding quickly.

Pender raised his head and released a hoarse bark half a second before someone knocked on the door. "Will you get it?" I asked him, cracking an eyelid. When he didn't move, I closed my eyes again, and figuring it was Will anyway, shouted, "Come in!"

"You'll let just anyone in here, huh?" Ryan said, opening the door.

"Apparently," I muttered.

"Did I wake you?"

"Nah." I nudged Pender, who grunted and moved off my chest, and sat up. "What's up, man?"

He sat in the armchair, his assigned seat it seemed since that's where he *always* sat, but at least he wasn't curling up on my sofa with my roommate. "I'm taking Adriana to a jazz bar. You know if she's ready?"

I shrugged. "Hard to tell. She could be a while."

Pender hopped off the couch and went to the armchair for Ryan to pick him up. The attention whore didn't even have the decency to keep his traitorous ass on the sofa with me, but instead curled up on jean-clad dancer's legs and stared at me, clearly telling me I shouldn't've made him move.

Ryan concentrated on running his fingers through the fur on Pender's head. "You mind if I ask you something? What's the deal with you and Adriana?"

"The deal?"

"I know y'all are friends," he said, making me sound as innocuous as the dog on his lap, "but when I asked her about y'all, she wouldn't say much."

"I'm her sex slave," I said with a wicked smile.

His head snapped up so quick, he winced. Reaching up to rub his neck, he slowly smiled. "Oh, you were joking."

I just raised an eyebrow and repressed the urge to say something along the lines of *no shit.*

"Joking about what?" Adriana asked, coming into the living room and stealing my breath from my chest. Transfixed, I stared at her in the emerald dress she tried on for Will. It set off the golden tones of her skin, the gold flecks in her eyes, and held her body perfectly.

"Nothing," Ryan said, the first of us to recover. "Are you ready?"

She took a hesitant step toward him, then another, picking up speed and running her hands nervously on the skirt. At the door she stopped and turned to me. Locking her eyes with mine, a wan smile clouding her features. I didn't want her going out with this humorless ballerina any more than I wanted to hook my junk up to a car battery, but I felt Gina over my shoulder, silently telling me to let go.

Adriana needed courage. And permission. She needed to know not that *I* was okay with her going to a jazz bar with some dude who didn't even have the wherewithal to bring her a bouquet of flowers or compliment her—was he nearsighted or something?—but she needed to know Rob was okay with it.

Ignoring the pain in my heart, I smiled at her, winked, and made my voice sound absolutely normal. "Have fun."

She nodded and let Ryan open the door for her, and when he fitted his hand to the small of her back, I made my lungs keep breathing.

"I swear to God," I growled at Gina when the door closed, "if he hurts her, I will kill him."

Crossing the floor, she sat behind me on the back of the couch. "Your head still hurt?" she asked, placing her hands on my temples and rubbing them in slow, even circles.

Letting my eyes close of their own accord and focusing all my attention on her fingers, I groaned.

"You're a good friend." She guided my head back to rest on her right leg.

"How come she couldn't just go out with me?" I asked, annoyed at the tremor in my voice.

"Have you asked?"

I opened my eyes to her gentle smile. "Well… no."

"Why not?"

"Gina…" I began, and lifted my head. She moved off the back of the couch and sat on the cushion, tucking her feet under her and studying me intently. I couldn't look at her.

"Why not?" she repeated.

"I don't know," I said, reaching for one of the throw pillows Will bought. It had beaded tassels hanging from each corner that served little purpose except that Pender liked to gnaw on them, and I was always playing with them.

"Yeah, you do."

Shrugging, I let the green and gold beads slip through my fingers as I counted each string. *Fifteen, sixteen, seventeen…*

Gina reached over and placed a warm hand over mine, stilling it and making me lose track. "I think what's really bothering you isn't that she's going out with a guy who may or may not mean anything to her, but that she's going out at all."

"What does that mean?" I asked, my voice cracking from the panic rising in my throat.

"There were plenty of beautiful girls at the party, and you stayed on this couch the whole night sullenly nursing a beer."

"Someone stole my chair."

"No, Luke, you sat here because you're too afraid of talking to someone. You fight, you push away, you hide because it's easier than putting yourself out there as you are now. You're too damn scared to try, so you don't."

I pulled my hands from her, my fist clenched, although I wasn't sure whether I was angry at her, or the truth of it. "You need to leave," I said, barely hanging onto my control.

But either her self-preservation was on the fritz, or she really didn't understand just how tightly I was hanging onto my self-control, because she leaned in even closer. And when she took a breath, she sucked all the oxygen out of the room.

"Has it occurred to you that your chair is an excuse for *you* to not go out with her? Or any girl for that matter."

"And just what do you think I'd do with some girl on a date?"

"Go to dinner, see a movie, what most people do on dates."

"Right, and at the end of the date, I… what? Take her in my arms? Lean in for a goodnight kiss? Except that I can't, can I? So how about you leave me the fuck alone." And since she wouldn't leave, I transferred back to my chair and went to my room, shutting the door with a punctuating *slam!* Only it wasn't loud enough to drown out her voice in my head, asking me to face something I had no intention of facing. Ever.

Going to my dresser, I pulled a CD from its rack and ejected the holder on my player, prepared to blast the entire building if that's what it took to keep the voices in my head at bay. But just as I was about to hit play, Gina knocked on my door.

"Luke?" she called, "can I come in?"

"No," I said, but she opened the door anyway and planted her butt on my bed.

"I'm gonna go home, take a long shower, and play beauty shop in my own bathroom. You have about an hour."

I frowned. "For what?"

Her smile was slow and seductive. "You're gonna pick me up, take me out. I don't expect flowers, but I do expect the full Luke Stevenson experience."

Residual anger battled with confused amusement, and I stifled a smile. "Which is?"

She shrugged and stood up. "I don't know, but I'm pretty sure you've been on enough first dates to know how to impress a girl."

~~~~~

When I was a kid, there was this fire-damaged house down the street that Bethany and I used to pass everyday on our way to school. I vaguely remember the flashing lights of firefighters, but for almost as long as I could remember, the windows were boarded over, graffiti covered the brick, and it was supposedly haunted by the ghost of the woman who died trying to save her baby from the fire.

As kids, we dared each other to run up and touch the house; when we were older, we dared each other to break in and explore. The first time I kissed a girl was in one of the bedrooms, and Ty Campbell claimed to have lost his virginity two years later there, although the credibility on that one was suspect since none of us could imagine staying in that house longer than a handful of minutes—not when it stank of smoke, decay, and misery.

I was seventeen when someone finally tore down that old house, and even though we watched it come down brick by brick, board by board, the moment it was gone, I almost couldn't imagine it ever existing.

Watching Gina walk across the parking lot to go back to her apartment, I lit a stale cigarette with nervous, sweaty hands and realized that like that house, I couldn't remember ever actually dating. I couldn't remember standing on someone's doorstep, knocking and waiting for her with my heart in my throat. I couldn't remember taking a girl's hand and praying mine wasn't too sweaty. I couldn't remember what we would've talked about, or where we would've gone, or what the hell I might've done to impress a girl.

Back then I didn't try if I was really honest, though. Back then asking a girl out never made me nervous because, well, I knew she'd say yes. And I didn't have to try to impress her because... ah fuck, because I was Luke Stevenson.

Now, though? I rolled the cigarette between my thumb and forefinger, playing with the idea of calling Gina and canceling. Or turning off the lights, locking the door, and slipping into bed with my headphones in my ears, drowning out the sound of my heart pounding in my chest and my brain calling me a pussy.

Gina would understand I wasn't ready. Sure, she'd be disappointed for standing her up, but she'd get over it.

But Adriana was out with that ballerina—the only girl, by the way, who *didn't* want me. She somehow found the courage to walk out of here, nervous and radiant, and try. And in a few hours that ballerina was gonna bring her back here and maybe stand on our doorstep with her. And maybe he'd fit his hand to the small of her back, feeling the green silk of her dress and warm velvet of her skin, looking down on her. And maybe she'd take her bottom lip between her teeth, looking up at him with conflict and trust in her eyes. He'd take a step closer, promising to take things slow and not hurt her, and when he placed his lips on hers… I had to be as far from here as I could when that happened. Leaning over, I ground out the cherry on the concrete, then took it inside to flush down the toilet just before getting in the shower.

Growing up, I got two pieces of advice on dating: my dad said to treat any girl I went out with with the same respect I'd treat my sister; and Kellan Campbell, Ty's older brother and a washed-up football star—although at the time I just thought of Kel as the coolest damn guy I'd ever met—said to always pop off a round first. "Last thing you want to do, gentlemen," he said, dousing himself in a thick cloud of Gaultier Cologne, "is to go in with a loaded gun."

Ty and I figured he was a genius, and at fifteen any excuse to jerk off, right?

But sitting on my plastic stool in the shower, with my dick lying limp and lazy against my thigh, it wasn't so much that I thought I'd get anywhere with Gina, but it almost seemed like a ritual I was supposed to fulfill. Like holding a rosary while saying ten Hail Mary's… or something.

I worked at it, willed it to wake up, willed it to feel something, my mind drifting to Gina. Gina belly dancing, her hips swaying and sultry as drums and guitar filled the sandlewood-scented air, the diamond in her belly button flashing. Gina's warm body against mine as the sun went down that night on my tailgate, her perfume and the silkiness of her air against my arm bombarding my brain. How she looked when she met my eyes, as if she wanted me to kiss her so badly, it was all that mattered to her.

Finally, I gave up and grabbed my shampoo.

Chapter 19

"**D**own, M," Bradley commanded the giant gray Great Dane whose hot breath and wet jowls were inches above my face. He grabbed her collar and pulled her paws off my shoulders, but not before a big drop of saliva fell off her tongue and landed on my cheek. "I'm sorry, she thinks she's a lap dog. Like Pender."

I wiped away the puddle with the back of my hand and shook my head. "No problem."

Will handed me a wet dishtowel. "Bradley doesn't help, though. *He* thinks Miss M is a lap dog."

Bradley said something about Will sitting in his lap now, and I turned away, not really wanting to think too much about Bradley and his lap. Don't get me wrong, I was glad he made Will happy and all, but looking up at the guy who Will occasionally referred to as his "big brown bear," there were certain things I just didn't want to know. Bradley was a good six inches taller than Will, built like a brick wall, and with the tiny dark curls escaping at the top of his shirt where the yellow tee met coffee skin, the designation fit. But the way Will said it, teasing and deeply intimate at the same time, embarrassed me. As if I was witnessing something I wasn't supposed to.

"Aren't firefighters supposed to have Dalmatians?" I asked, wiping my hands on the towel.

"Bradley runs against type in all kinds of ways," Gina said, walking into the living room in skin-tight jeans and a shimmery dark pink tank top that clung to her bare breasts and advertised her perky nipples. I figured that probably would've done it for me in the shower, especially if she'd been in there with me; just taken me in her hands, and...

"Damn, baby," Bradley said, whistling low under his breath, "I mighta picked the wrong roommate."

"Aren't you just the sweetest thing," she said, crossing the floor in the highest heels I'd ever seen. "You ready to go?"

I couldn't seem to find my voice and just nodded, well aware the old Luke Stevenson would've said... *something*, but if I had any idea what, then I probably wouldn't be sitting there mute.

Outside, I fell in beside her, a thousand thoughts running through my brain at a dizzying pace. Finally I glanced up at her and blurted the first coherent thing I could grab onto. "In those heels, you're probably as tall as I am. *Was.*"

She smiled and touched my chest, the electricity of her hand igniting the skin through the cotton tee. Immediately I focused on the parked cars around us, illuminated by pinkish street lamps just beginning to flicker on. And the rhythmic swing of my arms, pushing my rims in even synchronization. And the sound of traffic passing on the main road just beyond the apartment buildings ahead.

"Luke?" Gina said, withdrawing her hand and leaving my chest strangely cold. "Forget what I said, okay?"

Stopping, I looked up at her, confused.

"I didn't mean..." she pushed out a shuddering breath and studied a ribbon of asphalt snaking across the concrete. "It's not a first date, and I-I freaked you out, didn't I?"

"No," I lied, then made myself look at her. Made myself see not just the sexy woman standing there, pink and glowing in the last light of day, but the girl who taught me how to dance again. And who saw not my limitations, but my capabilities. And sometimes, when she looked at me, made me feel invincible. "You didn't freak me out, any more than anything else tonight has."

She started to run her hand through her hair before remembering it was caught in a thick braid that fell down her back. "Tell me something undatelike."

I thought for a minute, then smiled. "My face smells like dog chow and hot saliva."

Leaning down, she gave me an eyeful of deep cleavage. "That is pretty gross," she said, taking a deep whiff before laughing. "So, what do you want to do tonight?"

"I don't know," I said, turning away to begin pushing back to my truck. "Alex once told about this Holly Hop place. Supposed to be good for dates."

Gina placed her hand on my chest again and stopped. "Do you mind waiting here a minute? I have an idea, and I can't do it in these shoes." And when I nodded, she turned on her stilettos and walked back the direction we'd just come.

~~~~~

"What was par again?"

I looked at the score card in my hand. "Three. Which means you're working on a triple-bogey. And that's *if* you make it this time."

Shooting me a look over her shoulder, Gina adjusted her grip on the club in her hands and bent over, tossing the long rope of hair over her shoulder. When the purple ball rolled eight inches and fell in the hole, I put another tally next to her name. "Triple-bogey, baby," she crowed at the sky.

"I knew I should've put money on this thing," I said, laughing, and placed my red ball on the mat to line up my shot.

Gripping the shorter club in my hands, I focused on the curving path, the three consecutive humps that Gina had trouble with, and the unnaturally green Astroturf leading to the hole ten feet away. My swing had less power than I would've liked, I blamed it on the awkward angle and trying to maneuver around my knees, but at least when the ball fell in the hole, it was only one over par.

"You're gonna have to try harder," Gina teased, casually placing her club on her shoulder.

"Harder? That was a bogey."

"Right, which means I'm beating you by two strokes, and unless you want to lose to a girl, you're gonna have to work a little harder," she said walking away.

"It's the *lowest* strokes that wins," I called to her.

When she got to the second hole she dropped her ball, lined up her club, and turned to look at me. "Why in the world would you want *fewer* strokes?"

Watching her bent over the club, her hands gripping the shaft, and preparing to tap the ball, I honestly couldn't think of a reason why you would. "Highest strokes, then," I said, and damn if we didn't shut down the park.

Other couples played through, a birthday party of nine-year-olds came and left, and an elderly couple with their two grandchildren hung out with us for awhile until even they got bored of our antics, but no one laughed harder or had more fun.

When my ball finally fell in the eighteenth hole, the preppy college frat boy in the ticket booth took our clubs. "I thought I'd be out of here fifteen minutes ago," he said, barely covering his animosity. "My girlfriend's waiting for me."

Gina leaned on the counter. "You had to stay because of us?" she asked.

That annoyance drained from his eyes as he fixated on her cleavage. Whoever his girl was, she either had nothing on Gina, or he couldn't think past her breasts. In any case, he had to clear his throat before he could answer. "Yes, but, uh… she's used to it."

"Y'all been going out long?"

He glanced at me, obviously calculating just how big a threat I was. He must've decided I wasn't much of one because he leaned on the counter opposite her and ran a finger over the milky skin of her forearm. "Not really. Not long enough that if something better came along…" he let his voice trail off, but his eyes drifted to her breasts as a slow smile spread across his face.

"Good," Gina said, pushing away from the counter, "I won't feel guilty for keeping you then." As she walked away, she called over her shoulder to me, "Loser buys the ice cream."

The guy scowled at me, even angrier now that she'd played him like that, and as I followed her to my truck, twin thoughts ran through my head: one, that we better find another miniature golf place, because wheelchair or not, that kid was clearly mad enough to kick my ass given the chance; and two, under Gina's bizarro-world rules, I had no idea who was supposed to buy.

Chapter 20

"I must've moved this picture of the Kung Pao chicken three times," I said in frustration, "and I just can't seem to get it and all the text they want on this page."

Kenny turned away from his screen. "You want me to give it a shot?"

"Nah, I'm determined to do this myself. I'm just talking out loud, I guess."

He smiled and went back to the cookbook the Junior League turned in this morning. Watching him work always astonished me, although I had no idea why. With his red roller-ball mouse and knuckles, he'd fly through pages, creating, repositioning, fixing—in this case, a cookbook that was supposed to be done when they turned it in but wasn't—with a kind of speed and ease that I wondered if I'd ever have.

"How long have you been doing this?" I asked.

"Couple hours," he said, focusing on a picture of a cheesecake dripping with red cherries.

"No, I mean graphic design. The print shop. How long have you been doing this?" I clarified, lifting a hand to indicated everything around us.

He looked up and blinked as if coming out of a trance to see where exactly he was. It always amused me when he did that—surfaced. "I was about your age, I guess. Back then Meredith Kerns ran the shop himself, and I'd come in to get stuff printed for my classes. Mere's a good guy, he'll talk your ear off, and I found myself just stopping by to say hello and share a coke." He smiled, remembering. "One day he offered me a job."

"Just like that?"

"More or less. Why?"

I shrugged. "Curious, I guess."

"He needed help, and I needed money. Plus, it was a different business back then, and I had some drafting experience. Or as Mere put it, I knew my way around a T-square. He wanted to get away from straight printing and more into design. When I had my accident, though, for a while I didn't know how, or even if, I'd be able to keep working here. At that time software was still in its infancy, and with these," he raised his curled hands, "I couldn't do much. But Mere was determined to make it work. Maybe more so than I was."

My eyes drifted around the shop. It was probably exactly the same as it was then with its paneled wood and faded posters. "Why was he so determined?"

Kenny smiled. "Because he had no intention of letting his daughter and grandchildren starve."

"You married the boss's daughter?" I asked, grinning.

"And if you'd seen her the day I met her, the sunlight playing in her blonde hair, and a smile that lit up the entire place, you'd understand."

As if on cue, the bell over the door tinkled.

Maybe it was Kenny's story and the *déjà vu* of it, maybe it was the simple joy of looking up and seeing her unexpectedly on a Tuesday afternoon, or maybe it was her easy, warm smile, but my heart skipped a beat, and for a moment I forgot how to breathe.

"Hey, Sweetpea," Kenny said, pushing away from the computer desk. "What're you doing here?"

"I thought I'd bring y'all some lunch," Gina said, holding up a sack from Rosa's Cafe and leaning over to kiss him. "You hungry?"

"Starving," he said.

"Wait," I said, feeling slow. "Kenny's your *dad?*"

How had I not put that together until now? But looking at them, side-by-side, it was obvious. They had the same brilliant eyes and the same full lips. I'd stared at Gina's so many times in the last couple weeks wondering what it would be like to kiss her soft pink, rosebud mouth, I'd memorized its shape, but somehow it never occurred to me that I also looked at that same mouth every day at work. Not that I went around fantasizing about kissing my boss.

"That's what her birth certificate claims," he said, grinning. "Although now that you mention it, she's too pretty to be my daughter."

Gina smiled at me. "You really didn't know?"

"No, I..." But I was too bewildered to finish that. I didn't even know why, though. How many middle-aged quadriplegic men did I think she knew well enough to just up and call one night to get their friend a job the next day? And yet, I had this weird sense of the world colliding. The girl who I found myself thinking about more and more, her father was the one who wrote out my paycheck. Or to be more accurate, her father's accountant, but still... slippery slope.

"Oh, quit chewing on it and come eat," Kenny said, smiling at me.

Gina, thankfully, changed the subject, and soon they were talking about other things. Gina's classes at school: pedagogy and choreography; some of the other students in her classes he knew; the little things and big things that dads and daughters save up to tell each other. And watching them, I again wondered how it was that I never noticed just how very much alike they were. He had the same almost uncanny ability of examining something, and in a word, a sentence, nailing exactly what was going on. The difference was when he did it, perhaps because his pronouncements were always work-related, they never seemed to knock me off balance the way Gina's did.

Unsettled, I reached for my Dr. Pepper and finished it in one long swallow. "Y'all want another?" I asked, holding up the empty can.

Gina checked her watch and stood up, gathering her trash. "Actually, I've got a class in fifteen minutes."

"You go on. Luke and I'll clean up this mess. Thanks for lunch," Kenny said and opened his arms for a hug from his daughter.

"Bye, Daddy," she said, then came over to me. "I have it on good authority your roomie is going out with my dance partner if you'd like to catch a movie or something."

"Oh, uh, sure," I said, conscious of Kenny's eyes on me.

"Then I'll see you at home," she said, planting a kiss on my temple and hurrying out to get to class.

As the bell tinkled over the door, I threw away my trash and went back to that menu, trying not to wonder what he thought was going on between Gina and me. Trying not to wonder it myself.

~~~~~

I went out with Gina on the nights Ryan picked up Adriana. Each time Addy came out of her room, she was a little more confident, a little more self-assured, a little more like the girl I remembered from a dorm room long ago. She was figuring how to move on, she was learning how to not forget Rob, but how to be okay without him. How to think about a future again, and each time Ryan showed up on our doorstep, she lit up a little bit more. But even if it was nice seeing her happy, it was easier knowing that I had my own "date" to get ready for, even if Gina and I used that term so loosely, it became a joke.

Sometimes Pender and I would end up on her couch, watching *True Blood* on DVD with pizza and beer. She loved it and could waver endlessly between Eric and Alcide—she gave up on Bill sometime in season three. I, on the other hand, would down my beer and ignore the parade of breasts and sex, trapped in my own oscillating confusion of being aroused and unsure what to do with it.

Or we'd go to a dark theater, some flick on the big screen and trying to ignore the couples around us on *real* dates. She insisted on going Dutch, which kept it from feeling like a date, but also insisted on holding my hand as forty-foot high characters fell in love, killed the bad guy, or explored distant planets.

Or we talked for hours, snuggled under a couple of sleeping bags on some forgotten county road, far enough out of town the stars shone brilliantly above us while my speakers blasted Toby Keith or Alan Jackson. Until she confiscated my iPod and loaded it up with her music, claiming she couldn't keep listening to my shitkicker tunes *ad nauseum*.

What amazed me, though, was despite her alleged dislike of my music, she'd sing along to it. Softly. Under her breath. To every song I played, no matter how obscure. A couple times I even went out of my way to upload a few just to test her, and every single time she knew all the words. When I asked her about it she just grinned, said she was a musical savant, and went back to singing the old Waylon Jennings tune.

Occasionally I wondered why me, why she'd rather be with me on a fake date, than out on a real one with a guy who might…

But that's as far as I got with that. That's as far as I let myself go with it, because I… I didn't want to consider the answer, or ask and hear her give me one. I knew I was on borrowed time, waiting for her to find someone else, I was the In-Between Guy, the Until Guy, the Placeholder Guy, and I made myself be okay with that.

Besides, going out with Gina was easier than staying at home, wondering about Adriana and her ballerina, because, let's face it, that's a small step from creepy.

Then one afternoon at Walk'N'Roll while I crawled on my hands and knees across blue gymnastics mats, my back bowed painfully—but as Frank, my five-foot-nothing trainer liked to point out, you can't walk until you can crawl—Adriana asked if Gina and I might like to double date.

I looked at her, on her hands and knees, crawling with me. "I guess," I said over the sound of a bunch of guys at the other end of the gym playing quad rugby and insulting the hell out of each other.

"I thought it might be fun," she said. "And anyway, I want you to get to know Ryan. You'll like him, I think."

"Will I?" I asked, pausing to wipe the sweat from my forehead on my shoulder.

"He's a good guy, Luke. Different than Rob, but he's nice."

"Come on, Luke, this is your last lap," Frank called from the end of the mat, and I continued the slow, agonizing task of pulling one knee forward, followed by the other, inching my way across the floor.

"Gina said the same thing," I told her. "You mind getting my water?"

"You can have a drink when you get to the end of the mat," she said, sounding just like Frank and making me smile. "The thing is, I don't know if Ryan is a rebound thing, or someone I want to spend my life with, but I know I need you to like him."

"Why?"

She didn't say anything for a long time.

Long enough for me to get the remaining five feet to the end of the mat and my water bottle. Long enough for me to haul myself back up in my chair, drenched in sweat. Long enough for me to head to the locker room for a quick shower and clean clothes.

When I found her in her usual place—sitting on a leather chair in the glass and steel lobby overlooking a Zen-like courtyard—she had an open textbook on her lap, but her eyes were focused on a guy slowly working a walker along the curved concrete path outside, his forehead a complex configuration of concentrating lines while the woman next to him glowed so brightly with excitement I couldn't bare to look at her. Somehow it felt too intimate to see that much emotion written naked and vulnerable on her, but Addy wore the same expression of undisguised excitement, transfixed and hopeful, an everyday miracle.

"I look at him and wonder if that could be you. If maybe someday…" her voice cracked, and she reached up to wipe away a tear. "Sometimes I imagine you walking like the guys I see in here, using the parallel bars or a walker, and I think maybe it's just a matter of time."

"Maybe," I said.

I didn't like to go too far down that road because it seemed dangerous; like the standing frame, it was a matter of balancing Hope with Realism. I only had it in me to see the couple of feet in front of me. What was around the curve ahead was something to discover if I got there.

I watched the guy put one hesitant foot in front of the other. He paused to wipe sweat from his pale face, and when he grabbed the handle again, quickly as if uncertain how long he could hold himself upright with one hand, I noticed his knuckles were white from gripping the walker so tightly. Turning away, I watched Adriana watch him until finally she smiled, her eyes meeting mine, and suddenly I understood why she needed to do this double date thing. We were a package deal, and she needed me to like whoever she spent her life with.

Chapter 21

By the time I got home on the night of our double date, our apartment was awash in aroma that simultaneously reminded me of Donna's kitchen and made my stomach growl. "It smells amazing in here. What are you making?"

"A goddamn mess," Adriana said, pushing a brown curl away from her face with her wrist and leaving a smear of flour.

"Hi, Luke," Maria called from the countertop, her voice chipper and canned coming out of Adriana's cell. "Tell my sister dinner's going to be delicious and to chill out."

"Maria, the kitchen is a disaster, my raviolis are too big, and I burned some of the hazelnuts, so now the whole apartment smells bitter."

"Luke just said it smells great in there," she pointed out and even from a couple hundred miles away in Austin, I could hear her smile.

"He's used to eating pizza out of a box," Adriana said, dismissing the compliment.

"What can I do to help?" I asked, reaching for her hand.

"The ravioli are in the fridge?" Maria asked and when Addy nodded, wiping her eyes, I told her they were. "Then baby sister, go take a shower. Luke can straighten up the kitchen. And I'll walk him through the asparagus, okay?"

With a resigned sigh, Adriana went to the bathroom and shut the door behind her. "She's so nervous," Maria said quietly, "but it doesn't help that she picked one of Nonni's most difficult recipes. She really wants to impress this guy."

"Does she?" I asked, going to the sink to begin loading the dirty dishes in the dishwasher.

Maria's laugh was vibrant, even over the satellite waves. "I guess she didn't tell you, pumpkin ravioli is what Nonni made Granpa when they were dating. And what Momma made Daddy when they fell in love. And what I made Trent the night he proposed."

But surely she wasn't expecting... I stopped, a wet pot in my hand, water droplets sliding to my elbow. "It's only been a month or so," I said, putting the pot in the lower rack and wiping the water on my jeans.

"I'm not saying y'all need to start planning a wedding just because she called me up, begging for the recipe. I'm just telling you, Luke, this is a big deal for her."

She was quiet for a long minute, during which I finished putting the rest of the plates in, filled the utensil caddy, and started the machine.

"Watch out for her, will you?" she finally said. "I don't think she could stand getting hurt again."

"I will," I promised, wondering if that's what my objection over this guy was all about—not that I didn't like *him*, but that I wouldn't like anyone who potentially might hurt her. "Now about this asparagus," I said, reaching into the fridge to pull it out.

I got the asparagus salted, peppered, and drizzled with olive oil and balsamic vinegar, and had enough time to take a quick shower and put on a clean shirt and jeans—I hated wearing the smell of oil-based ink—before Gina opened our door. She came in like a fresh breeze on a sweltering day wearing a short gray skirt and a black silk top that clung and shifted and made my mouth water.

"How's Adriana doing?" she asked, resting a hand on my chest and placing a soft kiss on my temple.

"Fine. I think. I haven't seen her since she disappeared to get ready," I said, fighting the urge to pull her back to me and kiss her. And it sure wouldn't be on her temple.

"Gina?" Adriana came out of her room in a deep purple blouse that I knew belonged to Gina and a white skirt. "I can't decide which shoes to wear. Or jewelry. And I tried to do my hair like you did, but it's not working."

Gina gave me a bright smile. "Excuse me, girl emergency." And as she walked away, she ran her hand over my chest, sending a shiver through me.

The more I got to know her, the more I wanted to know, and lately I couldn't stop thinking about her. The things she said, the sound of her laugh, the way she looked at me, as if she could see deep inside my soul. But...

Every time I thought about her, I also made myself remember why I pulled away the one time I almost kissed her.

If I was honest, I *did* want her. God, I wanted so badly to touch her it sometimes hurt. I wanted to feel her lips against mine, her skin under my fingertips; I wanted to make her moan my name—call it out as if that was the only way to release the need inside her while she trembled and writhed beneath me. But no matter what Gina once said about changing my definition of sex, I couldn't look this gorgeous, amazing, sexy woman in the eyes and ask her to change hers. She deserved everything, and what I had to offer amounted to very little.

A knock at the door pulled me from my thoughts, and I went to open it for Ryan, who stood there holding a bottle of red wine in one hand and a bouquet of white roses and lavender in the other.

"Hey, man," I said, letting him in. "Those for me?"

He looked down at the flowers in his hand and let a hesitant smile slide across his face. "Oh, uh, no. They're for Adriana," he said as if it needed explanation.

"Just as well, I like tulips," I told him. "The girls'll be out in a minute. Something about shoes or hair. Or both."

He went to his usual spot and sat down, staring at the flowers, at the bottle of wine, at the pictures Adriana hung on the wall near the TV—some of her family, some of mine, and a few she found God only knew where of Bethany, Rob, her, and me taken at swim meets or various parties we'd gone to. After a minute he got up and went to take a closer look of the one taken at the Delta Sig Halloween party. In it, my Lois Lane wig was tangled and cockeyed after Bethy slapped it on my head rather haphazardly for the picture; I'd taken it off since too many of my drunk buddies had hit on me, and since I was well on my way to completely plowed, I didn't want to wake up the next morning and find the night had gone way off the rails. Beside me, Bethany was flexing for the camera, imitating a bodybuilder in her Superman muscles, but next to her were Rob and Adriana. Like Guinevere and Lancelot, were gazing at each other, the only two people in the room.

He stood there for what seemed like an eternity, staring at the two of them and barely breathing. I wanted to say something to him about Rob, about them, but I heard Gina in my head, *Rob is hers to talk about.* At the time, when she said that in the back of my truck, it seemed strange, as if she was taking my best friend, my teammate, my brother away, but what he meant to me was different than what he meant to Adriana.

And maybe someday that would change. Maybe thanks to this guy, standing in my living room, staring at a photo of two lovers.

"Great picture, isn't it?" Gina asked, standing behind me and wrapping her arms around my neck.

"I almost didn't put it up," Adriana said softly, her voice hitching.

"But I told her that shot of Luke alone was worth its price in gold."

Ryan turned and ran his eyes over my roommate, and for just an instant I could've sworn he looked just like Lancelot in the picture. "Hi," he said, going to her and placing a kiss on her lips, "you look *amazing.*"

She smoothed her skirt nervously. "Thank you. And if I can finish making dinner without ruining Gina's blouse, it'll be a miracle."

"Would you like some help?" he asked, and I watched them go to the kitchen together before turning to Gina.

"You're the reason that picture's up there?" I asked her.

She smiled and took a seat in my lap, draping one arm over my shoulder and filling my brain with her perfume. "It's too good to keep in a drawer, and somehow I get the sense that that's exactly how y'all were together."

"You can't go by *that*, I was drunk," I said, laughing.

Giving me a look that said she was pretty sure that was a semi-regular occurrence, she shifted toward the kitchen. "Can we do anything to help?"

"You don't cook, Gina," Ryan said, chopping sage.

"No, but I open a mean bottle of wine."

I followed her to the kitchen, where she opened the bottle Ryan brought and poured some for each of us in mismatched plastic cups.

"I thought about getting some real wine glasses, but Luke only drinks beer," Adriana said from the stove, turning on the flame under a giant pot of water for the ravioli. "It seemed like kind of a waste to get them for just one night."

"Maybe it shouldn't be for just one night, then," Ryan said, winking at her. When she blushed and turned to the cream sauce in the saucepan, he looked at me. "Beer only, huh?"

I took a sip of the Pinot in my cup. "It's not that I don't like wine, I just like beer more. And anyway, wine makes me thirsty."

"Would you rather have a beer?" Adriana asked.

"Nah, this is fine for now," I said, taking another sip and trying to find the berries or currants or whatever wine people always talk about when drinking wine. To me it just tasted like wine. "Besides, if I'm gonna be hanging out with your family, I figure I'm gonna need to learn to like it."

"They're big wine drinkers?" Ryan asked, scraping the sage into a bowl for Adriana.

"Big?" I repeated with a laugh. "How many cases would you say we went through at Uncle Marc's? Seven? Eight?"

"I don't know, but you get a bunch of Italians together, you better have plenty of wine," she said.

"Kinda like my family and meat," Gina said. "Roasted animal as far as the eye can see."

"Which makes it damn hard as a vegetarian when you go to Gina's house," Ryan said.

"How long have y'all known each other?" Adriana asked after a minute.

He looked at Gina. "Ten years?"

She took a sip of her wine. "Something like that. We met doing *The Nutcracker*."

"The Spanish Dance," he said with a laugh. "You know all my friends had a crush on you after that?"

She grinned. "So did mine. Including Will, I later found out."

"And you didn't know he was gay?"

I laughed, Gina gave him a dirty look, and Adriana pulled the asparagus out of the oven to give them a turn before putting them back in. And that's pretty much how dinner went: Gina and Ryan doing a lot of the heavy lifting, Adriana keeping busy to work out her nervous energy until she relaxed, and I switched to beer after that first cup of wine and sat back and observed Ryan. He was a good guy. And when he looked at Adriana, when he touched her hand or brushed a curl from her face, he did so with such tenderness, it was impossible to not see how much he cared for her.

Although I also told myself I was at exactly the right height to make sure he never had kids if he hurt her.

Then, while Adriana whipped cream for the chocolate mousse, Pender came over to me and placed both paws on my rims, whining. "Down, boy," I told him.

He went to Addy and leaned on her leg, whining, then yelping like he was hurt. "Luke, there's something wrong with him."

"There's nothing wrong," I said, and went to pick him up, giving him a once over. But he didn't want anything to do with my messing, and just buried his head in my armpit. A minute later, the wind picked up.

"Guess that storm rolled in," Ryan said, going to look out on the patio. "We might want to bring in those chairs."

Adriana put the bowl of whipped cream on the table next to the mousse and met my eyes. "What storm?"

"The weatherman on channel 11 said we'll probably get a few inches of rain and up to thirty, forty mile-an-hour gusts of wind," he said. "Where do you store those?"

"The chairs? I guess we could put them in the storage unit out there," I said, getting my keys out of the bowl by the front door.

We went outside, where the pressure had dropped. It felt oppressive, and a moment later a flash of lightning lit the sky, far enough away that the rumble that followed was faint enough to be almost nonexistent, but it was coming.

"Adriana doesn't like storms?" he asked, the wind picking up his words and blowing them around.

For a moment I felt her in my arms, trembling as lightning lit up the Roswell sky. "No, she really doesn't," I told him, unwilling to say more. If she wanted him to know why, she'd tell him.

Chapter 22

Inside, Gina stood at the coffee pot, carefully measuring out scoops of Folger's and rapidly talking about nothing, but Addy wasn't listening, not going by the expression on her face. She was sitting on the countertop over the dishwasher, fixated on her friend and breathing shallowly, on the knife's edge of hyperventilating. But the moment Ryan stepped back inside, she hopped off the counter and went to him, burying her face in his chest and gathering the back of his shirt in her hands, hanging on so tightly, she might never let go.

Gina started the coffee and silently went to the table to gather the mousse and whipped cream, and after putting them in the fridge, whispered to me to grab Pender. "Y'all come over to my place, let's leave them alone," she said. When I didn't move, she added, "Ryan's got this."

I didn't like leaving, but I also knew Gina was right. I needed to let him handle it.

I concentrated on pushing through the wind and ignoring the rumble of thunder, portending the oncoming onslaught of lightning. Pender sniffed the grass and watered it along the way, dressed in a blue Thundershirt Will gave him to supposedly reduce anxiety. Although I figured it was total hokum, right then I could've used one myself.

Gina opened her front door and turned on the living room lights. "Will's at Bradley's, probably will be all night," she said, her tone light. "He's got a toothbrush and a drawer over there, but if you ask him, he's playing it cool."

I tried to laugh, but it came out rough and dry, giving away my nervousness.

She studied me for a minute, then licked her lips. "You wanna come back to my room? We can turn on some music, close the blackout curtains, and pretend it's a perfect moonlit night."

I nodded and followed her to her room, suddenly aware that in all the times I'd been to their apartment, I'd never seen her room. And yet, it was exactly how I imagined it—warm and intimate, sensual and exotic. With the heady, earthy scent of incense mixed with her perfume, and dominated by a white four-poster bed, covered in purple, orange, and blue sari fabric, it was something straight out of a Bollywood set. She turned on her stereo, closed the curtains, and went to the dozens of lanterns hanging around the room and lit the candles, before finally turning on white twinkling lights lost in pink sheer fabric that formed a canopy over the bed.

"I'm gonna change out of these clothes," she said and went to her dresser to pull something out. Taking them to the adjoined bathroom, she told me to make myself comfortable.

Pender took her at her word and pushed the door open to go see her. I turned to call him back, but caught a glimpse of Gina in the mirror. She'd taken off her blouse and stood there in a black bra, unzipping her skirt. I turned away as she slid it past her hips, pulling bucketfuls of cleansing air into my lungs.

"You want a beer?" she asked a moment later, coming out of the bathroom in pink flannel boxers and a white tee. Through it I saw the outlines of her bra.

"No," I said, shaking my head. I'd already had three at home, plus the cup of wine, and I felt the need to stay sober. Then I looked at her again. "Yes. Please."

She padded barefoot down the hall and came back a moment later with two open bottles in her hands. After handing me one, she sat on her bed, tucking her legs under her. Taking a sip of her beer, she looked around at the candles hanging in the lanterns.

"Insomnia," she said. "I don't even have a real light bulb in here because the artificial light messes with my sleep cycle. I'll meditate before bed, maybe do a little yoga… it helps center me so I can sleep. "

"Oh…" I didn't know what else to say.

She stretched out on the bed. "So, what do you want to do?"

I took a long pull of the beer and shrugged, wondering what was wrong with me. It had to be more than the coming storm, more than my roommate's reaction to the coming storm, but with Gina laying on her bed, glowing and tantalizing before me, I was tongue-tied and lost.

She sat up and placed the beer on the bedside table, pulling out the drawer. "I think I've got a deck of cards in here," she said. "We could play rummy. Or war. Or go fish, if that's more you're speed."

The teasing smile on her lips pulled at something inside me, something that released the knots I'd tied inside my stomach. And returning her smile, I pushed closer to the bed, placing my beer next to hers, and told her rummy would be just fine. As we played, I remembered how to be with her and relaxed. In her candlelit bedroom, I forgot about the outside world and began to believe that this, here, now was all that existed. Her and me in this cocoon of exotic intimacy with a funny looking little dog snoring contentedly in the corner.

"Have you seen the trailer for that new Jennifer Lawrence movie?" she asked, shuffling the cards for another hand. "It's coming out next weekend, and I thought we could go see it. If you're interested."

"Yeah, sure," I said, then looked at her. "Gina, can I ask you something?

Aren't there any guys on campus you'd rather go see it with? You know, on a *real* date?"

Her hands stopped mid-shuffle, her eyes on mine for what seemed an eternity before putting the cards together again and starting over. "No."

"But aren't you... Don't you..."

"You're the only one I want to see it with," she said so seriously, I almost let it drop. I wasn't even sure why I'd brought it up in the first place.

I shifted in my chair and made myself say exactly what I didn't want to. "You should be going out with a guy who makes you nervous and excited and... You should be kissed well and thoroughly at the end of the night."

She put the cards aside, a slight smile playing around her lips. "Then kiss me. Well and thoroughly."

"That's not what I meant," I said around the lump in my throat.

Scooting toward me, she placed her bare feet on my rims and pulled me closer to her. "I have been going out with the only guy I want to be with. And as far as getting nervous and excited, I can't even tell you how hard my heart beats when I'm around him. Or how my palms get so sweaty sometimes, I think I ought to take out stock in baby powder. Or how when he touches me, it's like the whole world stops."

Breathless, I focused on the purple flickering lantern just over her left shoulder, trying desperately to get a grip on the whirl of thoughts inside me. "Gina, you can't," I ground out, but that's as far as I got before my voice broke.

"Why not?" she asked so softly I almost couldn't hear her over the pounding in my chest. "Because you don't feel the same way?"

"No, because I can't—"

But her mouth swallowed the rest of my words. Covered them with her lips in a soft dance of tenderness, real and tangible. Kissing her was so easy, so right, it almost felt as if I was coming home. Her tongue slowly tangled with mine, her fingers wove themselves into my hair, and her perfume filled my brain, effectively shorting it out. And then she moaned, a sound so sensual and raw, I wanted to toss her back on the bed, and...

"Stop it, Gina," I said, shoving away from her, making her lose her balance and slide to the floor. "I'm sorry, but I just can't do this."

She looked up at me, more stunned than hurt and slowly stood up. "Can't, or won't? Because I know you felt that just as much as I did, so the only question is whether or not you want to."

Running my hands through my hair, I searched for some answer to that. "I care about you too much to—"

"Bullshit," she said calmly.

"Excuse me?"

"That's bullshit, and you know it."

"No. It's not. I want you to have everything, you deserve everything, and I can't..." I let my eyes turn downward, unable to actually say the words.

"So you're definition of 'everything' is getting fucked by a porn star?"

"No."

"Pretty narrow definition."

"I just mean—"

"You mean athletic, pussy-pounding fucking. But has it occurred to you that all I want is for you to touch me, to hold and kiss me, and make love to me?"

"I..."

"And has it occurred to you, that maybe I just want to hold you and kiss you and find out how we work together?"

I took a couple of long, slow breaths. I knew what it meant to screw some girl, what I didn't know was to how to let Gina see all my vulnerabilities. What I didn't know was how to let myself fall in love with her, because I knew without a shadow of a doubt that all it would take to fall was a whisper, a feather-light touch, a breath, and I'd shatter in her hands. I opened my eyes and looked at her, the most amazing, fascinating, beautiful woman I'd ever met.

If I was honest with myself, I was scared out of mind.

"Gina," I whispered and stopped, unsure what to say next.

She took a step toward me, then another, and wove her fingers in my hair, letting her nails gently graze my scalp, sending a shiver through me. "Can you feel this?" she asked.

I nodded.

"Does it feel good?"

I nodded again, letting my eyes close. And then I felt her warm breath at my neck just before she kissed me below my left ear, so softly, so gently, it pulled on something inside me and lit up a fire I once prayed would die.

"Can you feel this?" she whispered, her lips tickling my ear.

When I groaned in response, she knelt in front of me, and with agonizingly slow movements, unbuttoned my shirt, letting her fingers caress my skin. Letting each light sensation register and build as I focused only on where her butterfly touch landed. Just fingers and the occasional light nail graze against my skin, but it was so intense, I couldn't breathe. And when her lips touched my collarbone, I forgot my own name.

"Can you feel this, Luke?" she asked, reminding me, and I slid my hands around her waist, the warm solidity of her body, so tangible and real, I wondered why I fought so hard against what now seemed inevitable.

Each gesture so slow it lasted into infinity until I couldn't imagine any reality than this one, here, beside her, next to her, touching her, kissing her.

Oh God, did I want to kiss her again. The last time was eons ago. Before light and time. Before life. I tugged on her shirt, and a beatific smile lit her face as she let me pull it over her head.

But before she could lean forward again, I traced the line where black lace met creamy skin with a trembling finger. "Wait," I whispered, surprised at how hoarse my voice was. "I want... I need to..."

I blinked and tried to catch my breath as a parade of nameless faces and wholly unremarkable moments marched swiftly through my brain, where fluids were traded like cheap currency, buying nothing but a single, fleeting instant of satisfaction. I focused on her, kneeling before me, on the rise and fall of her breasts, the gentle slope of her graceful neck, her parted lips, pliant and supple.

"It's different," I heard myself say, unsure what I meant.

"Different how?"

Fighting through fog, I murmured the only word that came to mind. "Real. When you touch me? It's... *real.*"

She laughed, a sound so low and husky, it made me want to swim in it. Instead, I pulled her to me, and when she straddled me, I lost my hands in her hair and my thoughts in her lips.

Somehow we ended up on her bed. Somehow I ended up naked beside her, exploring every part of her smooth skin in slow discovery, just as she discovered every part of mine.

I found she loved it when I kissed the back of her neck, softly, slowly, and she found that along my ribs, just above my injury was so responsive, the first time her warm, silky tongue found it, I nearly came out of my skin, as if all the nerve endings below had gathered and concentrated themselves there.

She looked up at me, nestled between my legs, a wicked grin on her face. "Liked that, huh?"

"Good Christ," I moaned, and closed my eyes, drowning in a drug so potent, I didn't even have it in me to fight its effect as she went back to playing.

And then, somewhere in the dark hours of the night, as Gina came and came, her body pulsing and writhing, her hands buried in my hair as her hips rose up to meet my mouth and tongue, I realized something so profound it seemed utterly simple: *this was it.* This was what I'd been searching for, what I needed my entire life. And this, this perfect give and take was everything I never knew I always wanted.

When the roiling waves finally came to an end, I placed my head on the pillow beside her, and wrapping her in my arms, marveled at the deep, unbelievable satisfaction coursing through my body.

~~~~~

Branded.

That's the word that went through my mind while she caught her breath, and I traced slow circles along her arm, drinking her in. I was branded. My eyelids where she placed gentle twin kisses; my emaciated thighs where she raked her fingernails, almost aggressively, accepting how shrunken they'd become; even my dick she played with, smiling when it awoke in her hands, and kissing it lovingly when it later went back to sleep.

And in a strange way, I almost didn't mind that it had, not in the way that I thought I would. I figured it would bother me immensely, inasmuch as I allowed myself to consider actually *being* in bed with a woman. I figured it would be the single most humiliating moment of my life. But instead, because Gina didn't make a big deal out of it and simply moved on, accepting my body exactly as it was without question and without ridicule, somehow that made it possible for me to accept it and be okay with it, too.

Did she have any idea just how beautiful she was at that moment? Her cheeks flushed, her eyes feverishly brilliant, her lips red and swollen, her body so achingly exquisite in the flickering candlelight, I couldn't imagine anything more magnificent. I pulled her closer, memorizing her body with my fingertips, every freckle, every downy hair, with the concentration of learning Braille.

But even as I pulled her closer, her body stiffened, and in degrees her eyes turned from bright to sober.

Behind me, one of the candles flickered in its lantern and went out, and somehow it felt like the end of something. Like maybe she, too, saw in me whatever it was that made Adriana hold me at arms length, afraid of being hurt.

To clinch it, she raised up on her elbow to look at the dog in the corner. "Does Pender need to go out?"

Swallowing the sharp pain in my chest, I tried to remember how I used to do this. Leave. "What time is it?"

She rolled over and glanced at the clock. "Almost two."

I whistled low under my breath. "Probably. I should get going, anyway," I said as nonchalantly as I could manage.

Nodding, she got up and went around the room blowing out the candles that hadn't gone out of their own volition. When she got to the window, she pushed aside an edge of the curtain. "It's still raining, but it's more of a drizzle now. And foggy as hell out there."

"Oh…" I said, sitting up, unable to take my eyes off her. God, she really was beautiful, standing there glowing in the pink-tinged Christmas lights.

She didn't move but stood there with her back to me, staring out the window. "I'll, um, I'll find out when that movie's showing and let you know, okay?"

"Movie?"

She let the curtain fall back in place and wrapped her arms around her breasts, turning to look at me. "Next weekend. If you still want to go."

It took me a second to get what she was saying, that after what just happened, she wanted to go back to before. Our "dates" that were nothing more than a way for two lonely people to pass a Saturday night when our friends had their own *real* dates.

And I had a choice, I could either play along and pretend it was fine, or I could… I could… *what?*

After a minute, she went to her closet, took a black silk robe from a hook, and slid into it, belting it around her waist with a resolve in her eyes that ran through me like a knife.

"I wouldn't hurt you," I said softly, staring at my feet.

"I know you wouldn't," she said just as softly. "But I don't know if I can do this again."

"Oh." For all her talk about porn stars and definitions, she *did* need a functional dick. Like trying to gather water in a sieve, I picked up my pride as best I could, and looked around for my boxers—they had gotten tossed across the room. And my jeans were in a pile on the opposite side of the bed. One sock was on her bedside table, the other in my chair.

"You mind tossing me those?" I asked pointing at my boxers, leaning off the bed to retrieve my jeans from the floor to cover my embarrassment.

She watched me pull on the boxers, a complicated routine of physically putting one foot in, pulling them halfway up my leg, putting the other foot in, then wiggling and rocking and wiggling some more until the things finally slid over my ass. "I know this is fascinating and all, but could you not watch?" I asked, grabbing my jeans to repeat the procedure.

"Sorry," she whispered and went to the end of the bed, tucking her feet under her as she sat down. "I thought you'd be safe for some reason. I don't know why."

"Harmless Wheelchair Guy," I grunted, wiggling.

"That has nothing to do with it," she said, turning to look at me, before dropping her eyes and going back to staring at the carpet. "I didn't think you'd…"

"What?" I finally asked, buttoning my pants.

She sighed. "Well, Will's gay. And I'm cool with that. I am. I just wish he hadn't slept with me first to figure it out. But I guess if I can be okay with that, I can figure out how to forget this, too."

"Gina, what *are* you talking about?"

Slowly, she turned toward me, but focused on some place on the wall behind me. "He was my best friend. He *is* my best friend, and when I slept with him, it seemed like the next logical step. It seemed like… like a promise. Or inevitable. Or… something. But I was younger and stupider, and I don't know… I thought I would've learned my lesson."

"What lesson?" I asked, beginning to feel dense.

Her eyes met mine briefly before going back to the wall. "To not sleep with someone just because it seems like a good idea at the time. But I thought…" She pushed out a long, slow breath and shrugged. "Can we just chalk it up to a moment of insanity?"

I ran my hands through my hair. *This* part I remembered. That instant of clarity when the pheromones cleared out of your system, the blood was back in your brain where it belonged, and you were left with some girl that all of a sudden you knew for sure you'd just made a mistake with. Maybe you didn't even like her very much, but then sometimes that was kind of a no-brainer when you weren't sure if she'd said her name was Karen or Karla or Michelle. And all that was left was getting out of there as quickly as possible before she turned it into something you had no intention of indulging. Oh yes, I remembered it all too well.

But I made myself look at Gina and feel her in my arms again. Feel her lips on mine. Feel that other moment of clarity, when all of a sudden I knew who I was and what I wanted.

"No," I told her. "I'm not going to chalk it up to anything just so I can go home and forget how it felt to be with you. You want to forget it, you go right ahead, but before I go through that door, you need to know I would never hurt you, I would never leave you, and I would never, ever let you go."

She stood up, and blinking rapidly, went back to the window and pushed aside a larger swath of fabric now that she had a robe on. For the longest time she just stood there, staring out on the wet, foggy parking lot. Out there the cars were lost in thick haze, lit orange-pink by the street lamp. Out there it was cold and empty, foreign and unwelcoming. And watching the rain fall, I realized that whatever she said next meant everything.

I was either going out into that, alone, turning my back on the only woman I would ever love, or I would stay, warm in this perfect cocoon.

Looking at her I knew it was true. How I couldn't see it before now, I didn't know, but on the verge of losing it, I didn't have a doubt in my mind. If she asked me to, I would leave, but it would kill me to do it.

"Luke," she finally whispered to the window, her voice breaking, "I'm afraid of getting hurt again. I loved Will once, too."

Her words floated in the air, and as I let them sink in, she turned away from the window and sat on the end of the bed, asking me with her eyes to stay, to love her, and to keep the promise I made.

"You love me?" I asked, although I wasn't sure if it was a question or a need to believe the unbelievable.

Covering her face with her hands, she nodded.

"You love me," I laughed, reaching for her, wrapping my hands around her silk-clad waist and pulling her to me. "She loves me!" I crowed at the top of my lungs.

And from the other side of the wall a guy shouted, "Great, dude! Now shut the fuck up!"

~~~~~

"How did I not know?" I murmured into her breast before taking her nipple in my mouth again.

She moaned before clearing her throat. "Know what?"

I raised up on an elbow. "You. Me. This. It's been right in front of me this whole time, how could I've not seen it?" After a moment, I rested my head in the valley between her breasts and sighed when she buried her hands in my hair. "I was so afraid," I admitted in a whisper. "I didn't think I was good enough for you, because I…"

"What?" she finally asked, her voice full of love that I suddenly realized had been there all along, I was just too blind to see it.

Breathing her scent deep in my lungs, I shook my head trying to find my words. "I'm glad you didn't know me before. I was such an asshole, and Adriana was smart to stay away from me. I would've hurt her, because I only thought about what I wanted. " I laughed harshly. "I suppose there's some kind of poetic justice in this."

"Hey. No, that's not how this works," she said so sharply, I raised my head to look at her. "Yeah, you made your mistakes, but so did I. This isn't some kind of divine retribution for screwing some chicks you didn't care about."

"Maybe," I conceded, "but I feel like I've failed you somehow—"

"Listen to me," she said, sliding away to sit up. "I freaked out earlier because the last time, the only time I slept with someone I loved, it ruined everything. Right after that, before my heart had even had time to stop pounding, Will told me he was gay. It *shattered* me, and I couldn't even look at him for a very long time."

Her voice cracked and as she wiped away tears from her eyes, I sat up and pulled her to me, letting her wrap her legs around my torso and rest her head on my shoulder.

After a moment, she raised her head again. "I slept with a lot of guys, trying to forget how broken I felt. How angry and betrayed and *hurt* I was. I knew it wasn't Will's fault, but I didn't know how to get past it. I didn't care about any of those guys, either. I couldn't *let* myself care. And then Will came over one day about a year later, and Luke, I almost didn't recognize him. He'd changed completely. He dressed differently, carried himself differently, he even had a different smile. He was happy, finally, and I was miserable."

She shuddered in my arms, and I pulled her even closer, my heart breaking for her.

"We got this place not long after that, and I went through what I jokingly called my 'nun' phase. I couldn't do it anymore, sleep with men I didn't care about, because I realized that somewhere along the way, I lost me." She looked at me for a long minute, and then a sad smile slid across her face. "Does that mean I deserve divine retribution, too?"

I shook my head, then smiling, I tucked a strand of hair behind her ear, loving that I could do that. Loving how she fit against me, in my arms. "Uncle Wally once said the guy I was is still inside, I just had to let him out. Thing is, I don't know how you knew how to find him. I don't know how you helped me figure out how to reach him, but no matter how many times I pushed back, you kept reaching for me."

Tears glittering in her eyes as she touched her lips to mine.

Kissing her, I remembered another night, her hand covering my hand and my unbuttoned fly, wishing I could fall for a girl like her. Knowing all I'd have to do is reach for her, pull her into my arms, and fall. Telling her, foolishly, I didn't need her to save me. And maybe I didn't, but I did need her.

And maybe she saved me anyway.

Epilogue

The scent of chlorine filled my nose and ignited my blood, just as it always did, and I reveled in the intensely powerful rush of adrenaline heightening every sense. The crowd sounded louder. The colors were brighter—the water blue and shimmering, the flags brilliant red and snowy white. Even the dank humidity pushed back against me as I maneuvered my chair over the tile to the starting blocks. Over the blur of sound I heard the announcer say my name, and I waved to the crowd, searching for my friends, my family, screaming loudly for me. They were all here: Uncle Wally and Tricia, Randi, Seamus, and Jeffrey, who waved a giant yellow and blue foam finger from his perch on Uncle Wally's shoulders; Donna and Peter, Maria and Trent, Eric and Alison; Kenny and Alex and Gina's mom, Louise.

But my eyes lingered on my parents, who actually looked happy. Rather than taking out that second mortgage, they decided to sell the house, put everything of value in storage, and took off to travel around the country together, hauling auto parts or furniture or shoes along interstates and living out of the sleeper cab.

"You were right," Mom said when she told me their plans a few months ago, sounding strong and self-assured for the first time in I didn't even know how long. "I can't keep visiting Bethany and wishing for her to come back. And I can't stay here alone. Maybe this'll be the honeymoon your dad and I never had."

When they came by for dinner last night to meet Gina's family, I watched Mom laughing like she used to and looking up at Dad in a way she never had. It occurred to me maybe this was who she would've been if she'd gotten the life she wanted. Happy, secure, alive. Even Dad was different; although I realized I didn't know him well enough to say exactly how, other than he had that same genuine smile usually reserved for Saturday afternoons, building birdhouses. And when he kissed Mom, dancing unabashedly with her in the middle of the Howard's kitchen, I found myself raise a prayer of thanks to God.

"How you doin'?" Frank shouted over the roar of the crowd and refocusing my thoughts. He'd volunteered to be my swim coach after a rehab session about six months ago, and figuring I had nothing to lose, I agreed.

"Fine," I told him, swinging my arms to keep the muscles loose.

"Watch out for Donovan in lane six to your right. He's gonna be your biggest threat, but Estavez in lane two is a strong competitor, too. I wouldn't be surprised if y'all were one, two, and three."

I smiled at him. "Which of those do you see me coming in?"

He laughed. "You just finish the race."

It was funny, the guy was a good foot shorter than Rob, ghostly pale, had wild ginger curls and an uneven beard, but something about him reminded me of Roberto Sanchez. There were even times I expected him to flash me a blinding white smile and attach *papi* to what he said. Course when I mentioned that to Adriana once, she looked at me as if I might be dehydrated from my latest workout.

I glanced up at her in the stands. Leaning affectionately on Ryan, and when I caught her eye, she grinned and waved. Smiling back, I returned her wave. It was good seeing her happy, no matter how much I once fought letting go enough to see she *was* happy. And Ryan was a good guy. Different than Rob— quieter, more reserved, shier around people he didn't know, which is why it took me so long to get to know him—but he loved her deeply. Just as Rob had.

But she was taking her time. One night while we were waiting for the curtain to open on *The Nutcracker,* she asked me if I thought it was okay she was just stringing him along. I shifted in my chair to look at her. "Why do you think you are?"

She shrugged, her cheeks turning pink. "I know how he feels, but I'm not ready to make any kind of commitment. I can't even call him my boyfriend. It's just…"

"Too soon," I supplied, linking my fingers with hers. "He'll wait for you."

Turning toward the deep red velvet curtain as if she could see Ryan through it, she sighed. "I fell so hard, so fast the first time, I can't risk that again."

Squeezing her hand, I settled back in my chair as the first chords swelled out of the orchestra, trying to think of some response to that. I knew how she felt. I knew as well as anyone how it felt to fight gravity and refuse the inevitable, but I also knew if she was ready, when she was ready, she'd realize it wasn't the risk she thought it was.

In the meantime, he continued to pick her up for dancing or miniature golf; in the meantime, he went out with her, Gina and me, Will and Bradley, quietly putting up with the whirlwind of energy with a serene smile on his face; in the meantime, I'd occasionally run into him making coffee in the early hours of morning in our kitchen, having spent the night again.

Watching her go up on her toes to kiss him in the stands, I wondered how long it would take her to recognize what was so obvious to the rest of the world, but Ryan was patient. He would wait.

"All right, buddy," Frank said, holding my goggles in his hand and waiting a moment while I pulled off my old Artesia bulldogs sweatshirt. We'd discussed my start endlessly, debating the merits of sitting on the starting block to dive in versus starting in the water and pushing off the wall. We tried it both ways a hundred times, each time Frank working the stopwatch and taking copious notes. In the end we decided diving gave me a slight advantage, especially against some of these guys who *could* actually dive in.

Transferring to the starting block, I shook my arms again before letting my hand rest on the *Bethany* tattoo above my left nipple—a birthday present to myself and my good luck charm. I looked up at Gina, standing between Will and Bradley and holding both of their hands. She as much as anyone encouraged me to get back into swimming, and even as late as last night I wasn't sure I wanted to compete again. Swim, sure, but compete?

"What are you afraid of?" she asked, raising up on an elbow to look at me.

I pretended to adjust the sleeping bag covering us, between it and her body keeping me warm on an empty country road, I was perfectly toasty, but I wasn't sure how to answer that. "I'm not afraid," I said finally, "it's just that everyone will be there, and that feels like so much pressure, I don't want to let anyone down."

"Let them down by not winning?"

I shrugged, noncommittal, but yeah, that was exactly what I meant.

"We aren't going to watch you win, we're going to watch you swim. And if you win, we'll celebrate your victory. But Luke? If you come in dead last, we'll still celebrate your victory."

Last night, after I took Kenny aside and asked for his daughter's hand, after a dinner that went so well, I knew somehow marrying Gina was exactly the right thing to do, and after she reminded me once again who I am, I made love to her under the stars and asked her to be my wife.

The buzzer sounded loud, and I launched myself into the water, letting it accept me as it always had—the same innocuous force that once invited me in and awoke a part of me that could never truly go back to sleep again. The same crystal solution that, when I was five, seized my soul and never let go.

And as I pushed myself, faster, harder, more powerfully than I ever had, I heard Bethany screaming for me, the sound filling the stadium from the farthest reaches of heaven.

Collaborating with Project Walk

What do we do when our concept of Who We Are explodes? How do we find our way back? How can it be a catalyst for change?

I discovered Project Walk when my sister suggested I look into it, and I can't tell you how grateful I am that she did. I am fortunate enough to live a couple hours from the Project Walk Boston facility, and after years of researching SCIs and the subsequent treatment and rehabilitation, after hundreds of hours of watching videos of men and women pushing their bodies to the absolute breaking point at times, after witnessing the recorded miracles via YouTube, seeing it all in person at the Boston facility confirmed for me why I wrote *Into the Deep End*.

Project Walk is a place of supporting the physical needs of the client, while discovering what the body is capable of—which is often far more than what even the clients' doctors predicted.

The focus is of course on the client, but during my time there, I met husbands, parents, wives, and brothers who were willing to do anything for the people they loved. I also heard stories of men and women who wanted more than anything to get back to where they were. You know, *before*. And it wasn't the clients working out telling me these stories, it was the loved ones, in hushed tones and with their heads held high and brave.

Is it possible to get back to before? Or perhaps the better question is: what is the new after? And can that be good, too, even if it is different? Tough questions, but ones that I believe can be healing.

Stories have the power to change the world. Humans have always gathered to tell stories—they entertain, teach, and open up new worlds to us. Stories start conversations by allowing us to relate to a character's experiences and say *Yes! That's how I feel, too!*

These moments are often healing, especially if family and loved ones don't know *how* to talk to the person living through the aftermath of a life-altering event. Or perhaps it is the person who is dealing with the accident or illness who has no idea how to handle one more thing—like care-taking the care-taker.

That's why I am so excited to collaborate with Project Walk through this new endeavor, Project Talk.

My hope is that through Project Talk, *Into the Deep End* can open the door to these healing conversations if it wasn't open before. Or perhaps open it further. People engage on a deeper level when they are allowed to safely tap into their deeper fears, and my greatest wish is for Luke's story to be some small catalyst for change—perhaps for you, perhaps for someone you love. Or if this book simply gives you a greater appreciation for those within the SCI or traumatic injury community, and inspires you to be a donor, an advocate, a volunteer, then I thank you. From the bottom of my heart.

1. After the accident, Luke is furious and resentful of those around him, and Adriana is best described as a zombie. Do their reactions seem real and believable? Can you relate to their predicaments? To what extent do they remind you of yourself or someone you know?

2. Throughout the book, Luke encounters a host of events and characters who challenge what he thinks it means to be "crippled." How does his thinking change or evolve throughout the course of the story? What events trigger such changes?

3. Luke thought once he was in love with Adriana and made himself keep her at arms' length. Later, he wanted to protect her—perhaps as he would have Bethany? What did you think of his actions? How would you have chosen? Do you agree with his choices?

4. Gina encourages Luke to "change his definition of sex." Before this book, did you agree with Gina that sex is finding out how two people find pleasure together, or with Luke that there's one definition of sex? Has this book changed your thinking? If so, how?

5. What passage(s) from the book stood out to you? Are there situations and/or characters you can identify with? How so?

6. From his own impotence to finding love for the first time after his accident and redefining his conception of himself, Luke struggles with Who He Is, and it sometimes isn't pretty. Did certain parts of the book make you uncomfortable? If so, why did you feel that way? Did this lead to a new understanding or awareness of some aspect of your life you might not have thought about before?

7. What specific themes did the author emphasize throughout the novel? What do you think she is trying to get across to the reader?

8. Do you feel as if your views about disabilities have changed by reading this book? Did you learn something you didn't know before?

Science and Methodology

Traditionally, paralysis rehabilitation and more specifically spinal cord injury rehabilitation has focused on compensation. The thought was that the human nervous system could not reorganize and improve function below the level of injury. Recent research in such areas of stroke and Project Walk's documented success with paralysis over the last two decades, has proven this to be false. At Project Walk we cannot guarantee who will regain function, however, we understand and recognize symptoms that present the potential to improve function below the level of injury for those with a spinal cord injury and improve overall functional recovery for other ailments. We tap into this potential through our world-renowned activity-based recovery program. Our program focuses on using specific exercises that are related to the same movement patterns that occur during human development. Through these movements we are attempting to reestablish patterned neural activity within the central nervous system. These movement patterns are replicated by our clients with the assistance of our highly trained Specialists. Our highly-trained Certified Recovery Specialists have been taught to respond to the unique cues that each client's nervous system gives them, and by providing the proper stimulus, help it to reorganize.

In addition to the customized exercises and highly trained staff, Project Walk also believes that the use of antispasmodic medication and other medications associated with traditional paralysis and spinal cord injury treatment hinder the chance of recovery. Many of our clients have found the elimination of such medications improves their quality of life and helps them to progress in their recovery. As a result of increased activity and less medication, our clients improve their overall health and quality of life.

The Project Walk Method

The Project Walk Method is a proven method based upon nearly two decades of experience working with paralysis as well as current scientific research. Research on activity and how it relates to paralysis has progressed rapidly in the last few years. Especially after a spinal cord injury, the body begins to breakdown physiologically. This is partially caused by reducing the effect of gravity on the body. The negative effects of the wheelchair can be reversed through exercise. The effects of exercise on someone with a spinal cord injury are similar to that of able bodied individuals[1]. Passive exercise alone has been shown to decrease physiological breakdown after a spinal cord injury[2], but we believe weight bearing exercise may have an even greater effect. This type of exercise is what the human body was designed to do, standing, walking, lifting, and ultimately being in an upright position.

Many of the exercises we use are based on patterned neural activity. This is the process through which it is thought the central nervous system develops its structure and function in the growing human being. The continuous repetition of movement may help to create this neural pattern in the brain and spinal cord[3]. Also, relearning a specific motor task may be highly dependent on the repetitive stimuli provided when input from the brain is limited[4]. This is where our highly trained Specialists play a critical role in recovery. They are the best in the world at creating the proper stimulation to not just increase a client's health, but help them regain function below their level of injury.

Project Walk also recognizes the importance of Brain Derived Neurotrophic Factor (BDNF) and exercise. Research suggests that through intense bouts of exercise that BDNF is increased and could result in a stimulation of stepping and an increase in axonal sprouting[5-7]. In short, the increase in BDNF through exercise can assist in reorganization of the nervous system. Additional information on the research behind Project Walk's program or the current studies that Project Walk is conducting can be found in the research section of our website.

Why Project Walk is Unique

Improved Level of Function

The majority of our clients improve their function below their level of injury! We also have the research to prove that approximately 70% of our clients achieve this type of functional return[8]. This is a major difference between Project Walk and other activity-based programs.

Research

Over the past several years, Project Walk has embarked on an ambitious research agenda. Through collaborating with universities and hospitals we have been able to design and implement various projects that have led to publications in multiple peer-reviewed journals and presentations at scientific conferences. This research allows us to refine and evolve our program in ways that other programs cannot.

Wheelchair Free

All of the exercises at Project Walk are completed with the client out of his or her wheelchair. The emphasis is on load bearing activities that may help increase function, bone density, muscle mass, sensation, and circulation[8,9].

Social and Psychological Support

At Project Walk, there are clients who have been in the program for years or just started. Thus, clients can council each other and help to understand the recovery process. Clients are not alone during the recovery process as we have peer support groups and our Specialists who work with spinal cord injuries, ALS, cerebral palsy, multiple sclerosis, traumatic brain injuries, stroke on other mobility related disorders on a daily basis. Project Walk has its own social network dedicated to individuals living with paralysis. This community, Project Walk Connect, allows stories to be shared and connections to happen.

No Medications

Many of our clients find that after starting our program they are able to decrease or completely eliminate their medication programs.

Improved Quality of Life

The combination of exercise and decrease in medication ultimately may result in an increase in health and an improved quality of life. Through an intense exercise program, your body may become more resilient to common spinal cord injury ailments such as pressure sores, urinary tract infections, blood pressure problems and poor circulation. In addition to various complications presented by different forms of paralysis.

Hope

Everyone needs hope. Without hope, recovery is nearly impossible. Clients find that our facility encourages the possibility of recovery. Hope is not discouraged but found within our staff and most importantly our clients.

1. Bickel CS, Slade JM, Haddad F, et al. Acute molecular responses of skeletal muscle to resistance exercise in able-bodied and spinal cord-injured subjects. J Appl Physiol. 2003; 94(6):2255-62
2. Dupont-Versteegden EE, Houle JD, Gurley CM, et al. Early changes in muscle fiber size and gene expression in respose to spinal cord transaction and exercise. Am J Physiol Cell Physiol. 1998; 275(4):1124-33
3. McDonald J, Becker D, Sadowsky C, et al. Late recovery following spinal cord injury. JNeurosurg Spine. 2002; 97(2)
4. Ferreira CK, Beres-Jones JA, Behrman A, et al. Neural reorganization of the functionally isolated human spinal cord occurs after stand training. Program No. 824.19. 2003 Abstract Viewer/Itinerary Planner. Washington DC: Society for Neuroscience, 2003. Online.
5. Jakeman LB, Wei P, Guan Z, et al. Brain-derived neurotrophic factor stimulates hindlimb stepping and sprouting of cholinergic fibers after spinal cord injury. Exp Neurol. 1998; 154(1):170-84
6. Zhou L, Shine HD. Neurotrophic factors expressed in both cortex and spinal cord induce axonal plasticity after spinal cord injury. J Neurosci Res. 2003; 74(2):221-6
7. Vega, SR, T Abel, R Lindschulten et al. Impact of exercise on neuroplasticity-related proteins in spinal cord injured humans. Neuroscience 2008; 153: 1064-1070
8. 1 Harness ET, Yozbatiran N, Cramer SC. Effects of Intense Exercise in Chronic Spinal Cord Injury. Spinal Cord. 2008 46, 733–737
9. 2 Astorino TA, Witzke KA, Harness ET. Efficacy of Multimodal Training to Alter Bone Mineral Density and Body Composition in Persons with Spinal Cord Injury: A Case Study. Poster session presented at: 29th Annual Meeting of the Southwest Chapter of the American College of Sports Medicine; 2009 Oct 23-24; San Diego, CA.

ACKNOWLEDGEMENTS

I'd like to thank my parents, Gordon and Sarah, for giving me the love of reading when I was small, and later, for encouraging me to follow my heart wherever it led.

To my sisters, Leslie and Libby, who put up with my reading when they wanted to play when we were little, and later for becoming my cheerleaders.

To my husband, Jason, and our daughters, Meagan and Claire, thank you for giving me time to write and follow my passion.

To Shannon, Tim, and Brad, thank you for your thought-provoking insights and unwavering support. You have no idea how much that means.

To all those who read early drafts and gave me their (sometimes brutal) feedback—Catherine, Chelsea, Lauren, Beth, and the rest of my writer's group, this book is *so* much better because of you. And to Kelli and Sarah for editing all my typos and wayward commas.

And to all those I have met through writing, because of writing, and out of writing, thank you. You have enriched my life in ways you may never understand, but for which I will always be grateful.

An Excerpt From
The Wisdom To Know The Difference

Chapter 1

The coffee had, as always, one thing going for it: it was hot. Depending on who made it that week, it was either strong enough to remove paint or so weak it tasted like flavored water. Tonight I wondered if tossing it in the dying ficus in the corner would give the thing a stay of execution or unnecessary hope.

In a plastic chair to my left, fellow addict Karen was talking about how she'd started snorting coke with her stepfather because sometimes he'd get so high he couldn't get it up long enough to molest her, and when he could, she'd be so high she didn't care. She'd been thirteen years old, and watching tears roll down her flushed cheeks, I was deeply sad for the little girl she'd been and the wounded woman she'd become. Whatever her life was like outside this room, I didn't know, but in her tailored suits and heels, her hair always pulled back in a sleek bun, she had a sexy aura that she wore like a cloak, hiding her self inside, invisible, protected.

In my mind she was an investment banker or lawyer, but who knew? That was kinda the point of these meetings: for the couple hours we spent together once a week, we were the survivors of a terrible plane crash, and the outside world didn't matter. Granted, all of us had been at the controls and flown the plane directly into the ground, some of us laughing maniacally while doing so, but somehow we had miraculously stepped out of the burning wreckage.

But it also sucked.

It sucked to sit here and listen to Karen describe the shitty things her stepfather had made her do to him, and while it was cathartic for her, I hated knowing that the woman next to me had to get high to suck the man's dick. Or worse.

The deep, urgent need to find and beat the living shit out of her stepfather also sucked because in reality there was nothing I or anyone else could do for her but sit and listen and hope that it was enough to keep her clean for another week.

When she ran out of words, I became aware of the dozens of eyes on me, waiting expectantly for me to say something. But after Karen, the whole what-to-say thing was rough because my biggest pet peeve was the one-upmanship some of these yahoos got off on. As if they were saying, "You think your life's bad; check out how pathetic *I* am!"

On the other hand, there were those who acted like life was hunky-dory. No problems, no worries. That was equally annoying because then my question was, "If life is all rainbows-and-unicorns perfect, why are you here?"

But in the end, it didn't matter. They *were* here, just like I was. The *why* of it wasn't important, because if I let myself get dragged into the reason, somehow that made it all worse. Was Karen's reason somehow more legitimate than mine?

I took a deep breath. "Hi, I'm Todd and I'm an addict..."

I stared into the watery black coffee in my cup, searching for answers that weren't there. Two months ago, my Uncle Nick found a '69 Stingray and hauled it to the body shop where I work. In rough shape, it needed a new chassis, new engine, new seats... new *everything*. The one thing it had was potential, and the minute I saw it, it spoke to me. Not in some freaky Stephen King *Christine* way, but in a "finally, something to *do!*" way.

"Life has fallen into a holding pattern and I'm simply existing," I said. "I want more, but I... God, I end up spending my nights alone because I'm not safe for human consumption."

As with any fall from Grace, I had chosen mine willingly, and as a result, it had blackened my soul. I couldn't *feel* anymore, not really. Hate, anger, and emptiness ate me alive, but what was I going to do about it? Not a damn thing. I had chosen shit, and shit was the payment exacted in return.

Half an hour later, the meeting broke up, and I was drained. It was something I expected, and my only explanation was that absorbing all this negative energy was exhausting. Beside me, Karen turned, her brown eyes roaming the length of me. "I don't think you're unsafe for human consumption."

I smiled, aware of the desire her eyes held. "Then I'm guessing you don't work for the Board of Health."

"Would you like to get some coffee?"

"Coffee?"

"Or... whatever."

I knew what I should have said, after listening to her cry, describing in disgusting detail what she did to her stepfather. I should have said no, gone home, and slept like I was planning to. But looking at her, suddenly I didn't want to be alone. I was tired of being lonely, tired of wanting someone to hold, tired of being the only one who dared touch me...

I grinned. "Whatever sounds great."

Her place wasn't what I expected. Every time I saw her she was so polished she practically shined, and somehow I figured her home would be the same way, but there were shoes and skirts and push-up bras covering every surface.

"I wasn't expecting company," she said by way of apology, moving hose and a robe off the futon for me to sit down and exposing an orange cat. "Oh, hey, Scoundrel." She gave the animal a quick pat and gently shuttled the thing out of the way.

"So, uh, what do you do?" I asked, the thought rolling around in my mind that I wasn't sure I was supposed to know, along with a twin thought that I ought to call a taxi and go home.

"I'm a firefighter," she said flippantly, pulling up her tight skirt to straddle me. "You?"

"Ballerina," I said in the same tone. "How long have you—"

"You really wanna talk?"

She raised up on her knees, her lovely cleavage at eye level while she removed the clip from her brown hair, letting it fall around her face, then settled back down, silk panties moving against my jeans. Her coffee-scented mouth lingered above mine, and any remaining questions about whether I should be here doing this evaporated. I closed my eyes, shutting out the world, and found her mouth, felt her full lips on mine, her tongue moving in unison with her body, stroking and teasing, anxious to get from me what she needed.

It was over quickly; it always is when foreplay and cuddling are forgotten in favor of a full-on, no-holds-barred, exploding orgasm.

In the taxi, I put my head back on the seat, wondering if I should find a new meeting, afraid I was losing my mind, certain I was a complete dick for what I'd just done.

Michael, my sponsor, wasn't very forgiving either when I called him the next morning. "You *know* her history," he shouted. "No doubt you've seen the scars on her arms... cutting herself, cigarette burns..."

I could've told him of the one shaped like the flat of a spoon near her left nipple, but that wouldn't have helped my case. "Yeah, I've seen them," I said tightly, running a hand through my hair.

"Meetings are safe places. To heal, to find someone who understands where you are, not a place to hook-up and fuck with someone's recovery. That's exactly what you did last night."

I imagined him holding the phone to his ear, seething. He was a pretty cool guy, but I longed to drag him into the twenty-first century, kicking and screaming if I had to—his Ron Jeremy look had to go. Shoot, that look didn't even work on Ron Jeremy, and on Michael it was outright disturbing. But he knew his stuff and I loved the guy, usually.

"She asked *me* over. No one made her do that."

"Except her disease," he said so seriously it cut off further argument.

There's a reason addicts are almost forbidden from getting involved in a relationship during their first year of sobriety—we're a damn mess! Our emotions all over the place, mainly because we'd become dependent on a substance that allowed us to avoid emotion altogether.

Don't like your job? Get high. Don't like your life? Get high. Don't like yourself? Get fucking *high*!

But with that escape gone, emotions come flooding in like a tsunami, threatening to drown and destroy. The hardest, healthiest thing to do was let them come. Stand on the beach alone and let them come.

"Todd, what's going on? This isn't you."

Except it was. Once. There was a time when I only had two rules: wear a condom and make sure it's consensual. Beyond that, there were no rules. I made no promises, and if she got hurt, well, I'd never told her I wanted anything from her, and I never offered anything of mine.

"I don't know what to say," I admitted. "It was wrong. I knew it, and I did it anyway. I'm sorry."

He was quiet for a moment. "Next time you even think about screwing with yours or someone else's recovery, you've got to talk to me. Are we clear?"

"Yeah...yeah, we are."

After we hung up, I took a long, hot shower, letting the water hit me at full force. He was right. He usually was, but right now I despised him for it. Almost as much as I despised myself. I wanted to think last night was simply about sex, two bodies using each other for release. But for Karen, it wasn't, and I knew it.

I'd heard the stories of the men she'd used, the ones who had used her. I'd seen the scars. Intimately. She picked me simply because I wasn't the stepfather she needed to forget, and the proof was in the fact that she refused to look at me the whole time. Once that condom was on, she turned away, wanting me to take her from behind, refusing to kiss me, refusing to let me get close. And at the time, it seemed... not okay, but no big deal.

In retrospect it made me sad.

"That Michael?" Brandon asked while I dressed for class, putting on his trademark grey plaid fedora.

"Yeah..."

"Everything okay?"

I didn't even know how to answer that.

Brandon Masters had been my roommate since freshman year. He was also my closest friend. Big and intimidating as hell when he needed to be, which was what made him such a great defensive tackle, he'd plow down anyone in his way without thinking twice, but basically he had the disposition of a chocolate lab. Kinda looked like one too, come to think of it, with those brown eyes and dark brown hair. We'd been friends since junior high, were on the high school football team together, and after I landed in rehab thanks to an ACL tear, he's the one who pulled me out of the tailspin I'd worked myself into.

It happened one warm September Friday night, like any other. I was sixteen, and Carrollton's enormous Standridge Stadium was packed—the high school band playing, the cheerleaders in those hot little skirts. Half-way through the third quarter, I got hit from the side, shredding my anterior cruciate ligament.

As bad as that sucked, the rehab was worse. I was a freaking invalid, hobbling around on crutches and determined to get back out on the field. I'd been playing football since seven years old, and August meant two things: the start of school, and strapping on pads and a helmet to run my ass off on the football field.

So when the doctor told me it'd take a good six months before my knee was healthy enough to do what I was doing before the injury, my only thought was *fuck that!* Three games into the season and I was gonna get benched? Absolutely not!

By late October, I had the coaches, the trainers, and my parents convinced that I was well enough to play, more or less against their better judgment. They all had a stake in my getting better, just like I did, and it was easy to fool people wearing blinders. The doctor, who had no idea what I was doing, prescribed OxyContin for the inevitable pain from playing on a knee that was nowhere near healed. But I told myself it was only until we won the playoffs, and then I'd relax and heal.

Ox had other ideas, and by the time the season ended, I was hooked. I told myself I *needed* it. A *doctor* told me I did. That I'd crush and snort the pills for a more immediate high probably wasn't what the doc had in mind, nor did he expect me to inhale enough of it that I'd feel… God, it was ecstasy! Peaceful and euphoric, dreamy and utterly blissful.

Chasing that high became an obsession, and I'm not sure how long I could've gone on using the stuff, lying to my doctor and parents, but fate stepped in. My senior year, the University of Texas was courting me, wanting me to play football for them. As far as I was concerned, I was on the verge of getting everything I'd ever wanted. With a scholarship to UT, the chance to play ball while going to school seemed like winning the lottery. It would have been, too, except for one little hitch—I was high when I took a mandated drug test. *Really* high.

I lost my scholarship, the blinders fell off everyone's eyes, and I landed in rehab of a completely new variety. Twenty-eight days in a facility for alcoholics, crack addicts, and seventeen-year-old OxyContin users. *Fan-fucking-tastic!*

When I got out, I was so far behind in school I figured I'd never catch up. Granted, before the whole mess I'd been a pretty solid B student, but the pity party I threw myself had me convinced I'd never finish. I dropped out and went to work at my Uncle Nick's auto body shop.

I wasn't very good company, to put it lightly, yet Brandon would hang out with me and put up with my piss-poor mood. Eventually he talked me into getting my GED and applying to the University of North Dallas with him. It was either that or continue to live at my parent's house, repair dented cars, and keep being a miserable SOB. By then, even I had started to get sick of my own attitude.

As Brandon and I headed to the Student Center, my knee was practically cursing in the early January weather. Two weeks ago it was so warm, I'd spent Christmas day in the driveway playing basketball with my brothers and sweating temps that reached the high-seventies. Now, though, winter had reclaimed its territory, and the cold, wet weather caused my knee to complain like an old man.

"I'm gonna run in and grab some breakfast. You wanna come?" he asked.

"Nah, I need to get to class. Thanks, though."

"See ya later, man."

"Yep," I said over my shoulder.

On the wall to my right, the Student Center had a long bulletin board that displayed posters and advertisements for all kinds of things from upcoming drama shows to students looking for roommates. Stuff I usually had no interest in, yet one blue poster caught my eye. It had a grainy image of Michelangelo's *David* and simply said that the School of Art was looking for figure models. At the bottom were fringed tear-offs with a name and campus extension.

I have no idea why I took one and shoved it in my wallet. I mean, figure modeling? It seemed kind of... I don't know, *bizarre*? And the *David* image more or less implied that they were looking for people who were willing to get naked, and I wasn't. Not that I had any problem with that if other people wanted to do it... who was I to judge?

But yeah... *no*.

Totally not for me.

By the middle of the next week, though, the whole idea of it was driving me nuts. Like a song I couldn't get out of my head, it kept coming back at the weirdest moments. At dinner in the cafeteria, priming a car for painting, or sitting in class, that little voice would sneak in and remind me I really ought to call Garrett Brady.

Finally, I pulled that blue slip of paper from my wallet and dialed the campus number on it. Garrett played it cool when he answered, like students were lining up around the corner, begging to bare it all, but when he offered me basically my choice of dates and times, I knew he was desperate.

"Could I just try it once and see how that goes?" I asked not entirely certain this was the best idea I'd ever had, despite the twenty dollars an hour he was offering.

"Sure," I could hear him smiling into the phone. "If you like, you could come by Friday and see. If it works for you, we'll get a schedule set up. If not, no problem. Okay?"

"Yeah... that sounds good."

"Oh, and if you have a robe you want to bring, please do. I've got clean ones, but some people prefer to use their own."

Maybe this really was a dumb idea. "Good to know."

~~~~~

Hanging my jeans on a hook, my heart pounded in my ears, my brain screamed at me to put my pants back on and go home. The cool air hitting my bare skin did nothing to calm my nerves as goose bumps broke out over my body. Wrapping my blue terry cloth robe around me, I tried to ignore the sound of art students filing in and setting up their work areas, chatting about their plans for the night. I tried to ignore the sound of my mother's voice in my head telling me this was really wrong. Of course, the good thing about that voice was it was like ice-water coursing through my veins, and the one thing I really worried about seemed impossible: everything was completely flaccid.

I heard Garrett walk into the room and give a blanket 'good morning' to his students, and I took a deep breath and rounded the corner of the screen. Much to my amazement, no one seemed to pay a whole lot of attention to me, and as I walked to the platform in the center of the room, I realized I had no idea what to do. Garrett had said I'd do a couple poses, but he didn't say of what, and I suddenly had that odd feeling when someone says to sing something.

"What do you want me to sing?"

"I don't care. Just start singing."

Garrett crossed the room, buff and Irish with his ginger hair, blue eyes, and light complexion. I grinned to myself wondering how many girls had signed up for his class just to be in the same room with him. "Do whatever you like; we'll use what you give us."

Okay…

Spotting one of the clean robes, I spread it out on the pedestal, then slipped out of my robe and sat down, pulling my knees into my chest, and wrapping my arms around my legs. Around me I heard the students position themselves for the best viewpoint and begin sketching. Garrett turned on his radio to a country station, and I sat there.

If my dad's older brother Nick spent too much time smoking cigarettes and telling dirty stories to the men he worked with, his wife Mary spent too much time in ashrams finding her "center." Aunt Mary used to babysit me and my two older brothers when we were little and had taught us meditation and yoga, starting around the time I was three and barely potty trained. We never could understand why she wanted three boys to learn "downward-facing dog" except that it kept us quiet and still for longer than five minutes, and that right there was probably the payoff. In any case, I found myself slipping into a meditative state, just breathing as I sat on the robe.

Suddenly, I heard Garrett's voice and opened my eyes. He was holding my robe, telling me I had ten minutes to stand up, stretch, get a drink. As I put my robe back on, I noticed Justin from my biology class, Sarah from English lit, and George from the dorm. But they didn't seem to care that for the last twenty minutes they had been staring at my bare backside—or whatever vantage point they had in the three-sixty around the room—to them it was no big deal.

About halfway through the second round, and in a new position, my body began to feel the affects of sitting in one place for so long. My left arm ached, my right foot had gone to sleep, and I couldn't feel my ass. I tried slipping back into that meditative state, thinking of Tibetan monks who could sit for hours in one position, never moving, but it wasn't working.

I tried taking long, slow, deep breaths, concentrating on the air moving in and out of my lungs. Tried concentrating on the mental image of a Jamaican beach we visited on a family vacation when I was twelve, but my body was too insistent with its demands to walk around, and the cramp I was getting in my right calf was complete agony. Just when I thought I couldn't take another second, Garrett told everyone to pack up their things and handed me my robe.

Past caring about propriety anymore, I laid the robe across my junk and collapsed backwards on the platform, groaning as blood refilled my extremities, causing that funny needle sensation to move throughout most of my body. Without thinking, I raised my arms above my head, arched my back, and went into a full body stretch, flexing every muscle and moaning in relief.

"Excellent job," Garrett said, smiling down at me. "A lot of people don't have the stamina to last that long."

I slipped back into the bathrobe and looked around the room, impressed by the drawings on the tables in various stages of completion. They were astonishingly realistic: sketches of the human form, right down to the bunching muscles of my back, legs, and arms. It was both flattering and humbling.

Dressed once again, I rounded the corner, surprised to see Carrie from my biology class standing by a table. She was beautiful—sapphire eyes, long brown hair, and an engagement ring the size of my knuckle on her left hand. I'd considered asking her out before that ring showed up, sparkling under the florescent lights. She might have been off-limits but that didn't stop me from occasionally fantasizing about her, vividly.

"I thought maybe you'd like to see what I've been working on for the last hour. You make a beautiful drawing," she murmured, handing me her notebook, then laughed. "I probably shouldn't say that though, makes you sound... well, you know what I mean. You're gonna come back, right?"

I focused on the drawings she'd done. She'd used nothing more than a charcoal pencil on cream-colored paper, but the lines and shading... I didn't even have the words to describe what she'd done. Every muscle, every contour, every detail so realistic the image looked as if it was moving. It was breathtaking.

"Well, I can't very well let your education as an artist go unfinished, can I? The masterpieces you are going to create..." If I could have even a small part in that, it seemed an honor and privilege. And I kinda liked the way she, Garrett, and the other students looked at me with respect. I couldn't remember the last time I'd seen that in someone's eyes.

Maybe standing around stark-naked for a bunch of strangers wasn't something I'd feel comfortable talking about over Thanksgiving dinner, but there was a whole list of naked activities I wouldn't talk about at the dining table. At least this one was respectable and educational.

Carrie laughed. "I don't know about masterpieces, but you do make for a great composition."

I smiled, hitching the backpack up higher on my shoulder. "I'll let Garrett know he can count on me for the rest of the semester."

CHAPTER 2

It was early in February, a Monday like any other, and I was in Garrett's class lying on my back, my left arm extended out to the side, my right resting across my forehead as I looked off to my left. My right leg straight out, my left bent with my foot flat on the floor, totally relaxed and languid, I considered going to sleep as I lazed on the platform.

Suddenly the door opened, and the most incredible woman stormed into the room, carrying with her the scent of some warm, exotic perfume. "Garrett, explain to me why Dean Warren is thinking of cutting the art budget!"

"Y'all take a break," Garrett said, then took the woman by the arm. "Shawna, can we talk about this when my class is over?"

As she pulled him to a quiet corner, I put on my robe, sat on a stool, *the better to see you with, my dear,* and observed this magnificent woman. Gorgeous, sexy beyond all reason, and currently, angry as hell—which was actually kind of amusing—her blonde hair was pulled into a messy knot at the base of her neck, her luscious breasts filled her white sweater, a tweed mini-skirt gently cupped her perfectly rounded ass, and long legs plunged in to knee-high leather boots. I wanted to unzip them with my teeth.

And with that, I stared at Harrison's mole until every lascivious thought drained out of my mind. Harrison Maxwell was an interesting guy, late-forties probably, portly, a Baptist preacher in his former life before he decided life was too short to continue living in the closet. He constantly wore a black beret over his floppy mouse-brown hair as if it was a requirement of his new chosen lifestyle, sported a handlebar mustache that made him look both slightly crazy and bizarrely tough, and an inch from his left ear was an ginormous hairy brown mole that kinda freaked me out. He was my anti-Viagra!

Garrett raised his voice slightly. "I have a class here. You can either stay and observe, or go, but either way I'm not discussing this until we are in my office."

She took her full bottom lip between dazzlingly white teeth. "Fine, I'll stay.

But give me something to do. I need to occupy my mind." He went to a container and cut off a block of gray, wet clay, got a handful of tools, and pointed at a nearby empty table.

Going back into my now seemingly poorly chosen position, I watched her roll up the sleeves of her snow-white sweater then begin to pound on the clay with every bit of anger and frustration she was feeling. She was fascinating to watch, and the passion she let loose on that innocent block of clay made me wonder if she was that passionate in everything she did.

I knew I needed to focus on Harrison, but she was simply too enthralling. She was breathing harder now, her hair coming loose from the knot, and as if that wasn't torture enough, her perfect breasts jiggled each time her hand slammed down on the clay.

Seriously, do you really want the entire room to know exactly what you're thinking? Big brown mole, big brown mole, big brown mole...

That helped. A little. But not as much as Garrett calling time, and I hopped up quickly and headed to my little cone of privacy to dress. The moment the last student filed out, she started in on Garrett again, and from the wet slapping sound, she was still pounding on the clay.

"Explain to me..." *Slap!* "how he can do this..." *Slap!* "to the department! I realize we don't bring in..." *Slap!* "as much as the athletic department—"

"By a long shot—"

"But to cut our budget..." *Slap!* "is insane..." *Slap!* "asinine..." *Slap!* "and further proof that the man has no business in that position!" *Slap!*

When I cleared my throat and rounded the corner, Garrett went pink like I just caught him copping a feel—not that I would've blamed him. In truth, he was on the other side of the room, giving each table a swipe with a green sponge. His features rearranged themselves into something close to annoyance, and it hit me: he *liked* her, and I was interrupting. "Oh, Todd, I forgot you were still here."

"Yeah, sorry," I shrugged. "Had to get my clothes back on..."

"*You're* Todd Randall?" Shawna said, and I turned to look at her. She had a strand of hair across her flushed cheek, and I fought the urge to tuck it behind her ear.

"Uh-huh... why?"

"Garrett said you were very good."

Good? I lied on the floor for an hour. How hard was that?

Her unusual silver eyes narrowed on me, and I got the sense she was evaluating something. "I'm going to watch you for a little while, if that's okay with you."

My throat was suddenly dry. I couldn't even remember the last time that happened, if it ever had at all, and nodded.

"Todd, I'll see you Wednesday," Garrett said firmly, my cue to get out of his classroom.

"See you then."

Apparently *watch me* meant dropping by class at random moments to stand in the corner: sometimes staying a couple minutes, sometimes for half the class, sometimes she wouldn't come at all. Each time I got that feeling of being evaluated, tested.

I had no idea what to make of it, but each time that door opened, every sense came alive. Every bit of awareness centered on her standing in the corner near the door, her arms crossed at her chest, her eyes narrowed slightly, searching for whatever she was looking for. More than once I fought the inclination to demand she tell me what she wanted, but two things kept me from doing that—the thirty witnesses of such a display, and the instinct that told me if I did, I would absolutely fail whatever test this was. But I was willing to fail if she'd just tell me what the hell she was looking for.

After nearly three weeks of this, I'd had it. When class was over, I slipped into my robe and walked to her. "I think we need to talk."

Her slow smile made me acutely conscious of the fact that under the robe, I was completely naked. "Get dressed, I'll be in my office."

Ten minutes later I was sitting in a room that, architecturally speaking, was like any other I'd seen at UND: nondescript, industrial, and rather dull. But she had made it warm and cozy with an area rug covering the crappy linoleum, absorbing sound and offering color, and a desk with a beat-to-hell look that seemed to be made of old railroad trestles, which I'm sure the moving guys had loved her for. The whole room smelled like her—warm, sensuous, complex, and vaguely earthy, like the ocean or the desert.

Like sex, some Neanderthal part of my brain whispered. I immediately told it to shut the hell up.

I was having a difficult time looking at her in her tight jeans and even tighter light pink tee that set off the unusual shade of her eyes. When she took off the gray blazer she was wearing, I nearly asked her to put it back on, but since that would have been awkward I focused on the photographs on the walls. The photos were fascinating anyway, and I kinda liked seeing what had moved her, spoken to her at the time each of them were taken.

"Todd," she began, lifting a can of Dr. Pepper to her raspberry lips, "I want to introduce you to a friend of mine. Do you know Scott Mitchell's work?"

I shook my head.

"See that book on the third shelf?" she asked, pointing. "The large one on the left with the white spine and red lettering?"

I walked over to the shelf and pulled it down. On the cover was a black and white photograph of a woman reclining on an old couch. She wasn't wearing much more than a come-hither look, and as erotic as it was, it was artful. *Scott Mitchell – Inner Self,* it said in a fancy red font.

"Look through that, get acquainted with it," she suggested, raising the can to her lips.

Speechless, I brought the book back to my seat. Some of the images were like the ones on the cover, artistic displays of the human body, beautifully capturing the contours and shapes of the subject. In other photographs the subject was fully clothed, sometimes almost ridiculously so, and as I looked through the book, I began to understand what the photographer was trying to say: just because the subject was covered, didn't make them any less nude.

I cleared my throat when I got to the end of the book. "Ms. Clifton—"

"Shawna."

"Shawna… I'm not sure I understand. Clearly he's a brilliant photographer, but what does that have to do with why I'm here?"

She smiled. "Tell me what you saw when you looked through that book."

I frowned, certain if I told her the conclusion I had drawn, she'd laugh at me.

"There's no wrong answer here, just tell me your impression."

I drew idle circles on the cover of the book until I realized I was circling the girl's dark gray areola. Annoyed with myself, I put the book on the oval coffee table. "It's a commentary on society, how people cover up to make themselves feel better, but really it's a false sense of security because what they are hiding is the most beautiful parts of themselves."

"And why did he choose to use nudes?"

"How else was he going to depict their souls?"

Her laugh was musical and wrapped around me like an embrace. Strangely, it pissed me off. "Do you know why I've been watching you?"

"Not a clue," I responded, harsher than I meant to and thoroughly confused by my own reaction.

"It takes more than holding a position to be a good model. It takes more than being gorgeous or having a fantastic body, although you certainly possess those qualities. A good model knows what the artist is looking for and gives it to them. A great model commits to that. He plays the role and gives it everything in his soul. Every gesture, every expression, every *breath* is part of anticipating the artist's wishes and giving over to that completely. The models in that book were chosen because they understood that implicitly. And Todd, you are great enough that you could be in that book, too."

I stood up, needing to move. "So, you've been coming in at random moments and intimidating me because…"

"I wanted to see how you'd react. I wanted to see how committed you are to the process. I wanted to see if—"

"I'd break."

"Exactly."

I pushed a hand through my hair, feeling like I was on the express train to Crazytown, but it wasn't just what she was saying, not solely. It was that... since I walked in here, I felt... *hope*. I felt lighter, as if just being near her could unlock something inside me, something that had once been a vital part of me, but had died. I wasn't sure if I should stay or go, if I should run from the foreign sensation of tranquility or embrace it, call it forth, and claim it as mine. Utterly frightened I collapsed in the chair, the air swollen with possibility and my own panic at what exactly that meant.

I felt her eyes on me, examining me carefully, questioning what was going on as I fought for breath. She reached for the book and opened it to the third or fourth page in. "Read this," she said pointing with her finger, and I forced myself to focus on the words. Under the acknowledgements, it read, *To my dear Shawna, for putting up with my tantrums, for knowing when to talk me down and when to leave me alone, for taking everything I've thrown at you, and going so much farther than the call of duty, thank you.*

"He taught me everything I know about photography," she said proudly, lovingly. "I was his student, his assistant, his talent scout... He used to joke that I did everything but cut his meat and wash his socks, but that's what his wife was for. He was on his third one at the time, wonder why *that* didn't work out..." The playful smile that lit up her face made my heart swell, and I couldn't look away if I had to. She cleared her throat like she realized she wasn't being very professional. I wanted the smile back, though. "I found all the models for that book, and when I tell you Scott will love you, know that I'm not being flippant or exaggerating. You meet him, and he will hire you on the spot and throw more work your way than you'll know what to do with." That smile was back. "He's very loyal that way."

Looking at it, I would have done anything to keep it there. "When can I meet him?"

~~~~~

Saturday morning I stood in my closet wondering which would be the most appropriate for meeting a famous photographer: suit and tie or jeans and button-down? And Brandon was no help. He couldn't stop talking about the fact that Shawna was picking me up in half an hour, and it was kinda freaking me out.

"I don't get it; I'm as hot as you are. Hell, I'm hotter, so why didn't she ask me to meet this photographer?"

"I don't know, man." I reached for a pair of jeans. "Maybe she thought I look better naked."

"Maybe he's a perv and wants to take lewd pictures of you."

"You are so funny."

"Could be a whole black market thing, and he's makin' a fortune in the skin trade."

I was annoyed with him now. "The one Saturday you get up before two in the afternoon and you pick *this* morning?"

"Yeah," he grinned, "cause I had to have a front row seat to this spectacle. Say, you don't think Shawna would let me come with y'all?"

"*I* won't let you come with me."

"Cause you don't want me watchin' you posing for nudie pictures?" he laughed, lying back on his bed. "Yeah, that's probably just as well."

With that I put my blazer on and walked to the door, totally pissed.

"Hey, Todd?"

"What," I growled.

"Good luck today. I hope you get this gig, or whatever." His tone had taken a complete one-eighty, and he actually sounded sincere. "Seriously man, I want this to work out for you. It's kinda awesome."

I sat outside, waiting for Shawna and enjoying the sunshine that promised a warm day. At a little before nine, the only people out were a couple guys across the street mowing the grass. In a few hours, that acre would be packed with college students, playing volleyball in the sand pits or pretending to study under the trees. Odds were pretty good that at least a half-dozen girls would be lying out there topless on their stomachs, working on their tans, and pretending to not notice the guys noticing them. And I'd probably be one of those guys, playing volleyball, and trying to ignore them after Shawna dropped me off. It was still such a stupid game—the whole pretending thing.

Her red cabriolet rounded the corner, top down and Journey blasting out of the speakers, and I smiled bounding down the steps, feeling my heart pound as I approached her car. As I approached her. "Mornin'!" she drawled happily as I got in the car.

"If I tell you I'm kinda nervous will you think any less of me?"

She touched my hand, sending a sudden electrical shock up my arm and through my body. "If meeting Scott Mitchell didn't make you nervous, I'd have to worry about you." With a quick smile, she threw the car into first and tore out of the parking lot, changing gears expertly.

"Where are we meeting Mr. Mitchell?" I asked, missing the brief graze of her hand.

"Call him Scott," she grinned. "He says Mr. Mitchell is his father. We're gonna pick up some coffee, but his studio is in Las Colinas."

Carrying a tray of Starbucks, I followed her into an ancient three-story converted warehouse and an old industrial elevator where she pulled the metal gate closed and pushed the button for the second floor. It gave a rather asthmatic wheeze and lurched to a start, moving so slowly I wondered why we didn't just take the stairs. "Scott keeps saying he's gonna get this thing updated, but he hasn't gotten around to it yet."

"Clearly," I muttered, holding my breath. I'd never been claustrophobic or afraid of plunging to my death before, but it seemed a very strong possibility.

Finally the elevator lurched to a stop, almost gratefully, and she led us through a light-filled space, across gleaming hardwood floors to a wood-and-windowed door. Inside a man was yelling, loudly. "Charles, you deaf son-of-a-bitch, I already told you. I have no interest in buying into that damn magazine!"

Shawna looked up at me and grinned. "Charles DeWalt, editor of *Vintage* magazine."

"Of course it's losing money. You've only been publishing for, what, six months? Why don't you call Anna and ask her to buy in? Lord knows you have your head shoved so far up her ass, you can probably tell me what she had for dinner last night!"

"Anna Wintour, editor of *Vogue*," she whispered, reaching for the doorknob to let us in.

With the sunlight streaming in from the window behind, Scott kinda reminded me of a clean-shaven Jesus. The words coming out of his mouth, however, reminded me nothing of Sunday mornings. He shot us a jubilant smile, as if he was playing with this DeWalt guy and loving it. "I've got people here, Charles... I tell you what, for six months I'll cut you a break. You pay me half my usual rate and don't ever ask me to buy into this venture of yours again... No, I'll pay the models the difference out of my own pocket—no reason they should starve just because you're losing your Valentino shirt... Yeah, I'm just a big softie, the Pope even called the other day and said he wanted to canonize me, but I left the church after my second divorce." He laughed at something Charles said on the other end. "Yeah, Henry the Eighth and I have tons in common, only difference between us is I never actually beheaded anyone." He hung up and rounded his desk, grinning. "Shawna, how are you, sweetheart?"

She went into his arms. "Scott, I want you to meet Todd Randall, the model I was telling you about."

As he turned, his entire demeanor changed, and he gave me a long look, analyzing me with a gaze I'd seen many times in the last month or so. On Shawna's face. "Put the coffees down."

She stepped forward and took the tray from me.

"Turn around."

I did, slowly.

"Huh... Let's get some test shots, see what the camera thinks." I thought Shawna said he was gonna *love* me. So far I felt like a side of beef at the meat-packing plant and about as attractive. "Come on," he called over his shoulder, his boots stomping off at a fast clip.

I let out a breath and followed Shawna across the enormous gleaming studio to Scott, who was standing before a large roll of heavy white paper that hung about eight feet in the air and spilled down to the ground. All around were those lights with the silver umbrellas and a camera on a tripod.

Scott took his place behind the camera. "All right, let's get started."

I had no idea what to do next. Did he want me to pose like one of those cheesy guys in magazines, jacket tossed over one shoulder, checking his watch?

Sing something.

What do you want me to sing?

I don't care. Just start singing...

"Shawna..." he muttered impatiently.

She glided toward me. "Take off your jacket." I did. "This is just like in the art studio. You're going to pose, and Scott's going to take a picture of it. No big deal, okay?"

I nodded. "Yeah, sure, it's nothing."

She smiled. "You're gonna do great!"

Soft as a whisper she went up on her toes and kissed my cheek so quick, I thought I had imagined it, except the lingering warmth sure wasn't a dream. In a blink, she turned and hurried over to where Scott stood, carrying my jacket like it was somehow precious.

In a way, it was just like the art studio, only faster. I'd pose; he'd take a picture. I'd pose again; he'd take another one. And just like in the art studio, I stayed away from the cheesy poses. If he wanted some dork looking like he was late for a bus, then he totally had the wrong dork... uh, *guy*. That didn't seem to be the case though, and after, I don't know, a dozen poses he nodded at Shawna.

"No tats, no piercings, one scar on his right knee. ACL tear from the looks of it," she recounted. For a second I wondered how she knew all that, but then, *duh!* she probably could have recited to him where every single mole and freckle was on my body. It could be rather erotic, except that in that grocery-list voice, it seemed about as sexy as having an intimate connection to all the holes in a block of Swiss cheese.

"Take your shirt off," he said briskly.

Again with the "you're-wasting-my-time attitude." It was really starting to annoy me. They'd set this meeting up, and he was acting like *I* was a pain in *his* ass? Shoot, I could still be sleeping! But again, Shawna stepped forward to take my button-down, then motioned for the white tee, smiling as if she was telling me this was part of the game.

"Okay, a couple more and then we're done," Scott grumbled. *Done.* That was a beautiful word.

After a few more he stopped, turned, and went to his office. I frowned at Shawna, completely perplexed. I dressed as quickly as I could, wanting to get out of there. Clearly it hadn't gone well. Clearly he hadn't *loved* me. Not that I needed this gig, but it was a little insulting.

This whole thing had been from start to finish, beginning with Shawna staring at me for weeks on end, doing her mind-fuck on me, and now getting dressed in some asshole's studio who treated me with about the same amount of respect as a damn dog. No, worse. At least a dog gets a biscuit after performing.

I didn't care how beautiful she was or how hot she got me—and good god she did—I was done with this bullshit.

"Scott's a hard man to get to know," she said as if that excused his behavior.

"You seem to know him just fine!"

"I've also known him a really long time." She put her hand on my arm. "I'm telling you, he likes you. Come back to his office with me and see." I stared at her. She wanted me to put up with *more* of his bull? "Please," she nearly whispered, those ethereal silver eyes held me. "I don't want you walking out of here thinking I played you. I can see in your eyes how angry you are, and I… please, just a few more minutes?"

I don't know why I agreed, but something about her made me feel like I'd walk across hot coals barefoot if she asked. And as she slipped her hand into mine, I fatally hoped Scott didn't have a bed of burning embers in his office, cause my shoes would be coming off.

Scott was sitting at his desk, reviewing the pictures he'd taken of me on his Mac and grinning like an idiot. "The camera *adores* you," he said, focusing on me. "Nearly every image is flawless. Look at how your blue eyes practically glow in this one… And here, your smile is electrifying! Your poses, your body, your entire damn look… Todd, I can't wait to get these out to those crones up in New York, they're gonna cream all over themselves!"

What was this guy, bi-polar? Two minutes ago, I was a wad of grape bubble-yum stuck to his Timberlands, now I'm… cream-worthy? Shawna shot me another *go with it* look, and I took a breath and sat in one of the chairs opposite his desk where I could see the pictures, too.

He sighed and took me in, this time with a look similar to the ones Shawna got treated to. "Please forgive the Mr. Hyde routine. I get a lot of guys coming in here thinking they're hot shit, and most of them are just as good-looking as you are. And probably ninety percent of them have ridiculously over-inflated egos, used to everyone kissing their ass because they are pretty. Or so stupid, they're lucky they got their shoes tied that morning and found their way here at all. Most of the time they have nothing to back up that ego, or they have no business walking around without a helmet, much less posing for some of the top designers in the world."

I shifted uncomfortably in my chair, still miffed, but trying to chill out if not for him, then for Shawna. "What happens next?"

"Shawna's going to walk you through a lot of it at first. She'll help you with the legal crap and teach you how to pose with other models, et cetera. Trust her implicitly. She knows her stuff, and she's very good. And here's my card. My private number is on there, so feel free to call me with any questions or concerns. Okay?"

"Wait, I haven't actually agreed to anything yet," I reminded him, looking at the card. Heavy-weight paper, embossed, impressive if you got off on that kind of thing. I didn't. "How do I know I even want to do this?"

He laughed. "I offer you the world on a platter and you say, 'Let me think about it?' Okay, talk it over with Shawna, your parents, whoever, and give me a call when you are ready. No pressure, no deadline. Sound good?"

"Uh-huh." I stood, shoving that business card in my wallet.

"Give me a call, Todd," he said, shaking my hand. "We'll do incredible things together."

For ordering information or to find more about
The Wisdom to Know the Difference, visit www.leesafreeman.com.

CPSIA information can be obtained
at www.ICGtesting.com
Printed in the USA
BVOW11s1009120318
510355BV00031B/1311/P